THE RIDDLE OF RAGNAROK by Theodore Sturgeon—Balder was dead, and evidence pointed to a Giant as murderer, but would even an enemy of the gods kill the most beloved being in the universe . . . ?

SMALL LORDS by Frederik Pohl—How long could men survive as slaves to a tiny, warlike race of Midges . . . ?

THE LAW-TWISTER SHORTY by Gordon R. Dickson—How could one small human argue any case and win in a court composed of ten-foot-tall bearlike beings . . . ?

STRAGGLER FROM ATLANTIS by Manly Wade Wellman—Cast up among warlike giants in a distant threatening land, he was the last survivor of Atlantis. . . .

On earth and in distant realms, in the remote past and the barely imaginable future, creatures and behemoths, leviathans and terrifying man-sized insects, all these and more await you in—

GIANTS

Isaac Asimov's
Magical Worlds of Fantasy #5

GIANTS

Isaac Asimov's Magical Worlds of Fantasy #5

—— EDITED BY ——

Isaac Asimov,
Martin H. Greenberg,
and Charles G. Waugh

A SIGNET BOOK

NEW AMERICAN LIBRARY

CONTENTS

INTRODUCTION
GIANTS IN THE EARTH
by Isaac Asimov

Giants are such a common element in fantasies, myths, and legends of all societies that one must wonder where the notion comes from. Even the Bible adds its voice to the subject: "There were giants in the earth in those days" (Genesis 6:4).

To be sure, there are giants in the earth *these* days. The blue whale of Antarctic waters is not only the largest animal alive today but is probably the largest animal that ever lived. The sequoias and redwoods of the Pacific Coast are not only the largest and tallest plants alive today but probably the largest plants that ever lived.

People lived parochial lives in ancient times, rarely traveling more than a few miles from home, and tales of large animals in foreign climes must have lost nothing in the telling. As the tales passed from mouth to mouth, they undoubtedly grew ever more dramatic. Thus, whales became Biblical "leviathans" and hippopotamuses became Biblical "behemoths," and in the tales of the medieval rabbis, both leviathans and behemoths became monsters of truly mountainous size.

But giants need not merely be the magnifications of distant truths. They can be the outcome of reason. In myth-making days, it was natural to suppose that the forces of nature were expressions of life. The wind was the breath of gods; storms were the result of their anger; the lightning was their hurled

7

artillery. Volcanoes arose from the overflowing forges of underground gods, and earthquakes from their uneasy shifting when asleep, or in chains. Naturally, for living things (presumably humanoid in shape) to produce these effects, gods must be colossal in strength and size. It makes sense, doesn't it?

Then, too, in ancient times, it sometimes happened that a settled civilization decayed, stumbled, and was overrun by a more primitive, but more vigorous, band of warriors. We can picture the warriors wondering at the works of the civilization they have conquered—the massive walls surrounding the cities, the large temples or other structures, and so on.

Being innocent of the advanced technology developed by the civilization they have conquered, they cannot imagine how those structures were made. They themselves could not have done it, and it would therefore be ridiculous to suppose that the inferior people they had conquered could have done it. The logical assumption was that a race of giants did it.

The Dorian barbarians who overthrew the Mycenaean kingdoms of Greece noted the thick, large-stoned walls of Mycenae and assumed they were built by those giants called Cyclopes. We still speak of large walls built of unpolished stones held in place by their own weight rather than by mortar as "cyclopean."

And it's not only naive ancients who believed this. Some people today, surveying the pyramids of Egypt and convinced that the ancient Egyptians could not have built them, fantasize their own version of giants and demigods as having built them. They naively suggest that astronauts from other worlds did the job. (Why astronauts, with technologies capable of interstellar flight, should have constructed huge piles of stone rather than have built something of steel and concrete beats me.)

We have the advantage today of knowing that there were indeed giants in the past—in the long, long past. For a period of a hundred million years, the land thundered under the legs of giant reptiles. The brachiosaur was the bulkiest and most massive land animal that ever lived, the tyrannosaur the most dreadful carnivore. There were pteranodons, which were flying reptiles that, in some cases, were as large as a large airplane.

Could some "racial memory" have implanted in the human mind giants and monsters derived from these reptiles, all of whom died out some sixty million years before the first primitive hominids made their appearance? As an example, could the dragons of so many myths be the pteranodons in reality? Not likely. It is much more reasonable to suppose that dragons were originally an expression of the giant pythons and anacondas that do exist. They were trimmed out with wings merely because that was commonly done as an expression of speed (think of winged horses such as Pegasus), and their fire-breathing is an expression of the poison venom of some snakes.

Of course, if an extinct creature is only recently extinct, it might serve. The elephant bird, or aepyornis, of Madagascar still survived in medieval times. It weighed half a ton and was the largest bird that ever existed. It must surely have been the inspiration for the flying bird-monster, the "roc," that we find in the Sinbad tales of the *Arabian Nights*.

Of course, even creatures never encountered in life by any human beings leave their bones behind, bones that are fossilized to a greater or lesser extent. It was only in the nineteenth century that these fossil remnants were correctly interpreted, but that doesn't mean they weren't found, and misinterpreted, in earlier centuries.

In prehistoric times, for instance, there were pygmy elephants and hippopotamuses on the Mediterranean islands. Even a pygmy elephant has a large skull, and some of these were dug up in historic times on the island of Sicily. It was natural to assume them to be remnants of humanoid giants. The nasal cavity in the skull looked as though it might represent a large centrally located single eye. That could be the origin of the giant one-eyed Cyclops (Greek for "circular eye") in the *Odyssey*.

Did humanoid giants ever exist? The closest example, as far as we know, is a giant primate that lived until a few million years ago.

Human beings are themselves giant primates, for we are

among the largest of the entire group. The only primate that is clearly larger and more massive than we are is the male gorilla, but there was once a super-gorilla we call *Gigantopithecus* (Greek for "giant ape"). He could stand up to nine feet tall and must have weighed something like eight hundred pounds.

The diet of *Gigantopithecus* was apparently very much like that of human beings, and it had teeth that were very human in shape but were, of course, much larger. In fact, when modern paleontologists first came across such teeth, it seemed possible that they might be those of outsize human beings. It took a while before other bones were discovered that made the apishness of *Gigantopithecus* abundantly clear.

It might well be that such teeth, showing up here and there, seemed evidence of the onetime existence of fearsome humanoid giants.

There remains one other point to make. We have all— every one of us—at one time lived in a world of giants. When we were infants and small children, we were surrounded by giants. These were, for the most part, benevolent giants, but not in every case. And even when benevolent, the giants often denied us what we wanted and it was clear that we could not fight their power. So it was a frightening and frustrating world, and we may all be permanently scarred with the fear of the large in consequence.

In any case, here are stories, not only of giant human beings, but of giant sharks, giant insects, and so on. The giants are not always villains, but whatever they are, they always pluck at some primal uneasiness within us, so we are bound to be fascinated with the tales.

THE RIDDLE OF RAGNAROK

by Theodore Sturgeon

Winner of the Nebula, Hugo, and International Fantasy awards, Theodore Sturgeon (1918–1985) has written nearly as much fantasy as science fiction. Classic examples include "It" (a spontaneously generated monster terrorizes a farm family), "The Graveyard Reader" (a man deciphers the language of graves), and "Shadow, Shadow, on the Wall" (an abused child seeks sanctuary in shadows).

The following ingenious story first summarizes Norse mythology, then offers a codicil about the final war between the giants and the gods.

Joy was not joy in Asgard, for all the ale and the heady mead, the singing and the wild hard laughter. Clink and clatter and clash rang the arms; whip and whicker and thud the arrows. Sinews were tuned and toned and honed and hardened, and speech was mighty, and much of the measureless night belonged to the unearthly yielding of the Aesir goddesses, whose limbs were magic.

Here were the heroes of Earth, here the dazzle-winged Valkyrs; here in the halls of not-quite-forever they feasted and fought and found that which mortality is too brief and too fragile to grant.

The Aesir were made for joy, and the heroes had earned it, and their joys were builded of battle, and to battle they built.

The battle they faced was the battle of Ragnarok; they would fight the Giants at Ragnarok; they would dare death at Ragnarok, and there they would die.

There was woe in the winds about Asgard. It was there like a bitterness in the drinking horns and it cut like cold. Hope lay frozen in the iron ground, moon-silver mantled the battlements like a winding sheet, and against the stars the eagles floated, crying a harsh despair.

Heroes new-come to Valhalla heard of it, after their feast of honor, after they settled into the halls of the brave and looked about them and called this cold and mighty land their own. Sooner or later they asked and were told:

In the spring of the world when the mountains were new and the sea not salt, and Yggdrasil, tree of trees, but a blooming shrub, good Odin the sky-father, seeker of wisdom, descended a Well where dwelt Mimir the Wise. For a terrible price, the least part of which was one of his eyes, he was given knowledge unthinkable.

Odin learned the Runes, and the way to take from the Giants the skaldic mead which makes him who tastes it a poet. He learned the ways of wild things and the tricks of the halflings issuing from unspeakable unions between the Giants and the elf folk. But of all he learned, the greatest and most terrible was the doom of Asgard: the certain victory of the Giants at Ragnarok.

Ever after, Odin was dedicated to forestalling that Day. Never again did he laugh, and only his silent wife Frigga knew completely his torment, and would silently brood over it and weep as she spun threads of gold. At the feasts, Odin presided but would not eat; two great wolves who lay at his feet had his share. He seemed never to join altogether in the company, though he always attended.

He would sit at the board in his golden palace Gladsheim with his wolves and his two ravens—Hugin, who was Thought, and Munin, who was Memory—who used to fly the world and return to him with news of all that happened in it; and he would ponder. And sometimes in his kirtle of gray and his dazzling blue hood he would walk the battlements or stand searching the sky.

Then he might call Tyr, war's god, or Thor, mightiest of them all, and give them tasks and duties, the purpose of which only he could know; these were the means of strengthening Asgard and delaying Ragnarok; but for what? for what? Asgard was doomed.

So it was that all colors in Asgard bore a tint of sadness, and a piece of every voice was mourning.

A sadness such as this was a wonder, but it was not the only wonder of Asgard. There was once a greater wonder than the wisdom of Odin or the strength of Thor: it was a thing more beautiful even than the one part of Asgard visible to mortal eyes, the rainbow bridge of Heimdall. The god Freyr, of the fruits of Earth, never served the world so well, the songs of Freyr herself lent less glory to the world than did the young god Balder.

In this atmosphere of awe and strangeness, of power and of powers, Balder moved with the confidence of a child in a loving home. His quality was a brightness—not like that of gold, or steel, but that of summer mornings, clean hair, first love, or high new notes from some seasoned lute. He was goodness and all kindness, and he was loved as no man nor no thing was ever loved before or since.

Balder was loved by god and hero alike, by Giant and elf and halfling, by the beasts, by the rocks and the very sky. It was said, in Balder's time, that only he could keep life in doomed Asgard; only such light as his could cancel the dark shadow of Ragnarok.

He shed his light wherever he went, and he went everywhere. There lay in him no evil. He was welcomed, not only in Asgard, but in Jotunheim where the Giants dwelt. Hela, who ruled over the dead, found a smile—even she—for Balder, and in the blackest heart of the wilderness the bears sat like kittens and watched him pass.

As all things must somehow be matched and balanced, and since one of the Aesir could move freely in all realms, so there was the son of a Giant who drank and sang in Valhalla and Gladsheim when he willed; he was the laughing devil Loki. His eyes saw more than did the ravens of Odin, and his heart was a catacomb in which his loyalties and his loves could be led and lost.

Yet so quick was his wit and so hilarious his mischief that he might have been tolerated in doomed Asgard for these alone. But least of all things did he need to earn a place at the feasts of Gladsheim; he was sworn blood-brother to Odin in payment of an old partnership in the dawn of the world, and he could not be challenged.

So he went his way, careless; and about him was no fidelity nor anything which could be predicted, save his love for Balder: this, in the world, was as inescapable as sun, as frost, or any other pervading natural force.

Now on a terrible morning bright Balder woke wondering; he felt something which was, for him, most strange. He went to Frigga, his mother, and told her of it, and she listened and questioned him, and listened again, until she could tell him that what he felt was fear.

"Fear, Mother?" he said.

"Aye," she said; "a kind of warning, a foreboding of danger."

"I like it not, Mother."

"Nor do I; I shall take it from thee."

And take it she did.

What has never been done before or since, Frigga did; and if it were not that time is counted differently in Asgard than elsewhere, she would never have had time enough. All about Asgard she went, and among the Vanir, their neighbors; even through Jotunheim she walked, her mission opening gates before her like a magic key. She went also to the world of men, where, they say, she walked in the season between flower and frost, so that to this day Earth turns glorious for a time in memory of her, and then the leaves fall and the trees feign death in memory of what followed.

And she went to places where dwelt neither gods nor men, nor Giants: places with names better not recalled.

And to everyone and every thing she met—to stones and sky and all who lived between them; to roots however deep and to high air-sucking blossoms; to the blood-bearers, warm and cold; to all with fangs, feathers or fins, hands or hooves;

and to the wind, and to ice, and the sea; to all these she spoke saying, "I bring tidings of evil: the unthinkable has happened, and Balder is touched by fear. Give me thy promise that, from thee, harm shall never come to him! That is all I ask of thee."

Gladly then, gladly the high and the tall, the ancient, the once-living and the never-alive—all gave their bond; and not from them could harm come to Balder.

Back then to Asgard went Frigga, wearily. She noticed as she entered that high by the gate grew a tumble of glossy leaves and waxen white berries. She smiled then at the mistletoe, a green given to small and happy magics, and let it be, asking nothing of it. She sought out Balder and told him of what she had done, kissed his bright face and fell in a swoon.

She slept then, for a time long even in Asgard.

II

The news blew through stark Asgard like a warm wind, and the Aesir rejoiced. It was almost as if Ragnarok itself was removed from their thoughts—indeed, might not this be an inroad on their doom? For was not Balder of the Aesir? And were not the Aesir to die at Ragnarok? Yet now it was also true that no harm could come to Balder. . . .

Ragnarok receded, and even Odin nearly smiled. He had, however, the habit of pondering, and it was a trouble to him that Ragnarok could be, or that Balder might live through it, but not both. He buried this problem in a silent place within him and there worked on it mightily.

Balder was given a feast at Gladshiem, with such singing, such tries of arms, such mountains of succulent food and oceans of mead as were memorable even in Asgard.

And it came about that Balder found himself standing in the courtyard, laughing, while all about him the warriors of Gladshiem and of Valhalla rushed at him with sword and mace, nocked and aimed their arrows, plunged and lunged at him with sword and lance.

The lances bent away from his shining body and the swords

met a stony nothingness about him and bounced away ringing. The arrows rose to pass him, or slipped aside.

Above on her throne, Frigga sat watching. She was pale still from her ordeal and perhaps overwrought because of it. She kept touching her lips as if to stop their trembling, or perhaps to check some warning she knew was unneeded. This was Balder's pleasure and that of the gods and heroes about him; should she then call caution as if he were still her golden babe?

At length her eye fell upon Loki, who stood to the side, where Balder's blind brother Hodar sat, stony eyes wide and an eager smile on his mouth, trying with all his heart to know the details of Balder's joy. Summoning Loki, the god-queen waved her ladies back, and met the mischief-maker's bold gaze with a great pleading.

"I say this to thee myself, good Loki," she said quietly, "rather than send the message, that you may know it pains me. But I fear a mischief, and to think of mischief is to think of thee. No one loves Balder better than thee, and I believe it—yet I were happier with you gone from this hall. Indulge me, then. . . ."

Something indescribable and ugly moved in Loki's bright eyes, yet he smiled. "Since you ask, lady," he said and turned away, adding arrogantly over his shoulder, "but do not command me, I shall go."

He sprang down the steps and out into the night.

Frigga drew her shawl of tiny feathers close about her and shivered. Her ladies, cooing like a cote, closed about her. For long moments they whispered to her and to each other, until her great kindness asserted itself and she began, in turn, to soothe them in their concern.

"I am weary and foolish," she said; "none knows better than I how safe he is. Yet . . ." She paused while the laughing god turned his back to a black-armored hero swinging a knobbed mace, and paled until the weapon slipped from the mailed hand in midstroke and crashed into the wall. "Yet will I be happier when this noisy childishness is done."

"But Lady Frigga—you missed nothing. Did not all the world promise not to harm him?"

"Whatever I missed matters not," Frigga said.

"Was there something, then?" asked a soft voice.

Frigga widened her eyes and turned to the woman, a stranger to her—but the halls were populous and this a great festival; folk had come from afar.

"Only the mistletoe," said Frigga comfortingly, and the other ladies laughed at the idea of the gentle mistletoe as a danger.

Later, the woman was gone from her side, and was seen kneeling by blind Hoder, to help him, with her words, see the action, it seemed. And Frigga was pleased, for she saw the blind god's head come up, and heard him laugh and cry out, "Balder! May I cast at thee?"

"Ay; I am fair game tonight!" cried Balder, and went to stand before his brother. "Here I am before thee; may fortune favor thy aim!" he said mockingly.

Then Hoder rose, and raised his arm. The woman was seen to turn him a little, better to face Balder squarely. Then Hoder hurled the sprig of mistletoe that he held, and it pierced Balder's heart. Balder uttered one great cry, all astonishment and no fear, and he fell, and he died.

Dark Hela, ruler of the underworld Niflheim, took the murdered god hungrily, as one who had waited long aeons; and indeed she had. And when Balder's second brother Hermod came there at Frigga's bidding, to ransom Balder back, Hela yielded to this degree: that if every living thing would weep for him, she would surrender him, but if a single one would not mourn, then forever he would be Hela's.

Back Hermod came with the word, and indeed it seemed a simple matter, for already all creation wept, the midges keened, and great splashes of color dripped from the rainbow bridge.

Yet in Jotunheim dwelt a Giantess, a strange, ageless creature steeped in sorcery and locked away from the world. All around her was weeping, even the Giants finding the death of this one enemy more than they could bear. Yet she would not weep for him nor anyone.

"Balder? Balder? Let the dead stay dead. Only dry tears will ye get from me. I had no good from this Balder, nor will

I give him good." And no other word would she say; and so was Balder's death sealed.

And who killed him? Who killed the bright one who had no enemies, who had done no ill? Who was capable of an act so monstrous, so useless and cruel?

The heartsick Hoder testified that the mistletoe, which he examined afterward, smelt of Giant.

Who, being part Giant, had access to Gladshiem?

The woman who had given the mistletoe to Hoder and urged him to throw it had disappeared. Who was she? Or— was it a woman? Who was the greatest of all adepts at disguise; who had once fought a battle with the god Herindal in the shape of a seal?

The answer to all these questions was the same: *Loki, Loki, Loki*.

And Loki was found outside, not impossibly far from the gate whence the mysterious womanthing had fled, still sparkling with anger at having been asked to leave the hall. No one had seen him nor knew what he had done since he left.

So he was brought in, and chained. He said he was innocent and no more than that. Since the blood-brother of Odin could not be slain, he was lowered into a foul pit; and above him was suspended a frightful serpent in such wise that its venom dripped on him. And he was doomed to hang there until Ragnarok.

Then a pall settled over Asgard. Frigga, when she could, spun her golden threads and was silent. Great Odin brooded, Tyr and Thor, without guidance or orders, cast war and thunder about the earth as the casual spirit moved them.

Odin's twin ravens, Hugin, who was Thought, and Munin, who was Memory, quarreled bitterly over the fact that Munin had taken unto himself the duty of reporting to Odin the events of that evil night, while Hugin felt it was his privilege.

They went their separate ways, and though they might have been recalled by a word from Odin, he had not the word, for he cared no longer what happened in the world of men, or indeed in his own house.

So indeed it seemed true that Balder was needed in Asgard,

lest the mere shadow of Ragnarok settle over the Aesir and crush them before there could be a battle at all.

This is the story which was told and retold for more than seven thousand years, as men count time. This, for all that while, was the complexion of Asgard. There, for a million moments measured by drops of scalding venom, hung Loki. And this is the prelude to the prelude of Ragnarok.

III

Munin flew high, and higher, turning one bright eye and then the other to the frozen land below. He flew because he must seek, he sought because he could not forget: his name was Memory.

He remembered the days when he perched on Odin's shoulder, waiting to be sent to the world of men, waiting for the long, companionable flight back during which he reported to his fellow all he had observed. He remembered the pleasant homecomings, the rasp of Hugin's voice as the other raven told Odin of what they had seen.

And he remembered the night of Balder's death, and Hugin's infuriating silence, and his own croakings and bleatings as he reported what had happened in and around the fateful hall.

He remembered Hugin's brilliant black stare as he spoke on and on, and the total anger of that insulted bird. He remembered the countless years of loneliness and idleness since, and he had had enough.

Between two crags he saw a dark fir, and in its lower branches he discerned a swaying lump just different enough in shape from a pinecone to be what he was looking for.

He folded his wings and dropped closer. Ay: no pinecone had moldy feathers acquiver in the wind, an ivory beak pressed to a molted breast too sparse to hide it.

He fluttered to the branch, worked his claws about amongst the close-set needles until he found comfort, and settled.

"Hugin," he said. "Hugin."

Slowly the scaly eyelid on his side opened, just far enough to identify the speaker. It closed immediately.

"Parrot!" spat Hugin; it was his first word in seven thousand years, as men count time.

"Hugin, old comrade . . ." Munin paused to collect himself, to remind himself that he had come here to renew his partnership with Hugin, and that he must under no circumstance let Hugin make him angry. "What has thee been doing?"

"What thee sees," said Hugin shortly, still not deigning to open his eyes.

"Ah, Hugin. Remember the times we've had, the—"

Hugin raised a warning claw.

"I remember nothing. I am not a foolscap, a storage shelf, a . . . a macaw like thee. I am Hugin and my name is Thought."

"Ahh. And what has thee been thinking for seven thousand years, as men count time?"

"Of thine inexcusable perfidy, lovebird. What else?"

"But surely . . . thought thee not of the old days, of the great flights we—"

"I've no truck with memories, as thee should know. There were more important things with which to concern myself."

"The death of Balder."

"I told thee," said Hugin in some irritation, and at last opening his eyes, "what it was I thought about."

"About *me?* About what I did that night, when thee closed thine eyes and had naught to say, with the very world cracking about our heads?"

"I had to *think!*"

Munin recognized, slowly, that Thought without Memory had indeed done nothing but turn over and over that last insult. For the first time he felt a great welling pity for his comrade.

"All those years . . . thinking about me," he said. "Ah, Hugin!"

"It was a great evil thee did me, Munin," said the other plaintively.

"Ay, it was," said Munin with some hypocrisy, which he immediately compounded with "I am a simple soul, friend

Hugin, and do not understand exactly what the evil was, though I grant thee it was enormous."

"Thee conveyed those events . . . whatever they were . . . out of memory, without Thought! This was never our way, Munin!"

"Ah, that I know. That I knew then, but never understood. Before that night, we had long hours of flight for your thinking. In the press of circumstance, when Balder died, there was time to speak only as things occurred. Tell me, Hugin, is not the relation of things exactly as seen—is that not speaking the truth? That is all I did."

"Ay, it is the truth, just as a mound of bricks is a mansion. Truths must be arranged, Munin."

"And arranged, they are a different thing?"

"They can be used for a different purpose."

"I am a simple soul," Munin said again. "Could thee demonstrate the point for me, in such a way that I will understand and not insult thee again?—for I miss thee sore, Hugin," he added with a rush.

He saw Hugin softening visibly, and pressed his advantage. "I'll tell thee exactly what I reported to Odin that night. If thought can make of these events a total different from what memory itself yields, I shall believe thee truly, and never insult thee again."

"Agreed. And will thee then fly back with me to Odin and behave thyself properly, henceforth leaving the final reports to me?"

"Gladly."

"Then tell me these events from the beginning. You understand that I have been without memory for some while now."

"But never again!" said Munin heartily, and launched into an account of the events surrounding the death of Balder, from the god's awakening with the strange fear, to the imprisonment of Loki. "Thus are the guilty found and justly punished!" he finished triumphantly. "What has Thought to say on this?"

"Only that Loki is not guilty."

Munin stared at him in amazement. "I don't see that!"

"Don't see! Don't see!" jeered Hugin. "Know, parakeet,

that thy two eyes are petty instruments which, at their best, are purblind. I have in here,'' he croaked loudly, overcoming Munin's approaching interruption, ''a third eye which sees what you do not. *That* is what thought is for!''

''It cannot make me see what it sees,'' said Munin ruefully.

''It can in time,'' said Hugin. He sounded alive and in inexplicably high humor. ''Come!'' And before the puzzled Munin knew what was happening, he flapped skyward.

''Where are we going?''

''To Jotunheim.''

''But Loki's in Gladshiem—or under it.''

''Ay, But if he's innocent, some Giant is guilty, and Jotunheim's the place for Giants.''

''But-but-but . . . thee don't *know* Loki's not guilty!''

''The ways of thought,'' said Hugin didactically, ''are not those of observation and reporting. Thought is not limited to facts; facts are, thee will remember, but the bricks used to fill in a thinker's design.''

And until they reached Jotunheim, he would say no more.

IV

As they sailed over the low, wide, forbidding city, Hugin asked, ''The Giantess—she who refused to weep for Balder. Does thee know her name, and where she dwells?''

''Of course. She is Borga, a recluse and a small sorceress, and she dwells in yonder spire. But there is no connection, Hugin, between her and Balder or even Loki. I think—''

''*I* think,'' said Hugin loftily, and led the way to the spire. They alighted on the roof, and Hugin said, ''Ravens are great mimics, and among ravens, thee has special talent, no? Can thee imitate the voice of Loki?''

''That I can, to frighten Loki himself if I choose,'' said Munin, most startlingly in Loki's exact tone.

Hugin cocked his weather-beaten head to one side and said, also in Loki's voice, ''This is but a poor imitation of thy talent, friend, but would it serve to baffle a Giant?''

''It baffles me,'' said Munin, awed.

''I thank thee for the lesson, then,'' said Hugin. His eyes

sparkled in a way new to his fellow. "Now lead the way in some secret fashion which you, oh, Mimir among birds, surely know in this place, so that we may come upon the lady in her chamber unobserved."

Speechless with astounded pleasure, Munin crept to the crooked eave and along it to an odorous smokehole. Cautiously he put his head inside, and finding the firebed cold, gestured to Hugin.

Hugin passed him, whispering *"Silence!"* and inched into the room.

It was an almost circular turret room, fitted out as a combination bedroom and alchemical laboratory. Around it ran shelves filled with an inconceivable clutter of bins, bottles and bags, boxes, books and basins.

On the bed lay Borga, and Hugin croaked—but silently—in surprise. For by human standards she was exquisite; even among the Aesir she would have passed as attractive. Nay, as wondrously fair.

She was hardly the withered crone Hugin had expected. Turning from her, he edged along the shelf to which he had hopped. Coming to a large, long-necked flask which lay on its side, empty, he considered it critically, shifted it slightly so that its open mouth and neck almost paralleled the smooth wall. Then he thrust his beak into the flask, finding that there was just room for his jaws to open comfortably.

To do this, he had to lie almost on his side. He gestured with one claw for Munin to do likewise. Then, with an effect that made Munin's feathers all stand on end, he uttered a protracted and horrible groan, in an exact mimicry of Loki's voice. The sound of it as it emerged from the flask was most extraordinary. The wall's curvature made it seem to come from everywhere at once.

Borga left her bed in a way which challenged description. Levitation, the power of which she certainly possessed, seemed to play no part in it, but she came straight upward while still flat on her back. She rose in the air, fell back, bounced once, and landed cowering at the far side of the chamber. Her head whipped from side to side, as if she were afraid to leave it facing in one direction for more than the smallest part of a second.

"Wh-who . . . wh-what's that?" she quavered.

Hugin moaned again, and the Giantess seemed to shrink into herself.

Again she cast about wildly. "Where— Art here?"

"Nay; in Gladshiem," Hugin intoned. He then made a spattering-hissing sound, which was like hot fat dropping into a fire followed by an agonized gasp. "Ai-ee, it burns . . . *it burns . . .*"

"By what magic—"

"How do I speak to thee? Largely through the holes in thy conscience, little sorceress. *Very* little sorceress," Hugin added scornfully. "I cannot come to thee; would that I could."

From that she seemed to take great courage. She rose and composed herself, and said in a voice more clear, "I have heard of thy torment, Loki, and I am sorry it is so extensive. But thee cannot deny that thee led thyself into it."

"But I am innocent!"

"To a degree," said Borga, and Munin, his awe renewed nodded at Hugin. "But considering thy mainfold sins, and the many that went unpunished, thee cannot claim complete injustice. And no one will believe thee! Tell me, whose fault is that, friend liar?" Her tone became increasingly confident and mocking. "Thee has interrupted my rest, good Loki. Why?"

"To . . . to tell thee . . ." Again that shocking hiss, and the gasp. "Did thee never love me, Borga?"

Now she laughed. It was not pleasant. "Well thee knows! I spurned thee always! Thee wanted not me. Thee wanted an amusement, something different—a sorceress who was a daughter of the Giant vizier."

Loki's voice said, slyly, *"Always?"*

She began to speak, then stopped, pale. "What do thee mean?"

Hugin laughed. It was chilling. "Did thee enjoy Balder?"

"How dare . . ." And then she was overcome by what seemed to be curiosity. "How did you know?"

"What let thee think Balder would notice such as thee?"

Hugin jeered harshly. "Stupid! to lull thyself into believing Balder would court and cozen and bargain for such coarse flesh as thine! The veriest sparrow could have told thee about guileless Balder, were it not for thy blinding conceit!"

"But he did! He did!" she wailed. "And he made my head swim so . . . and he came so close, and then put me by and asked that of me that no Giant must ever share with the Aesir . . . and I refused, and closer again he came . . . and he said he loved . . . and I, I was lost, and I told him the Great Secret of Mimir, and then he took me, laughing . . ."

She burst into a wild weeping, which was drowned out by a cascade of coarse laughter, echoing round and round the room.

While it still echoed, Hugin snatched out his beak and whispered to Munin, "Can thee mimic Balder?"

"Ay," said Munin, "but 'twould be a desecration!"

"Desecrate away, friend parrot. We have this pullet's neck on the block."

"What must I say?"

"Some Aesir lovemaking nonsense."

Munin put his beak into the jar, and Balder's voice, hollowed by the resonant glass, rang out: "Beloved, thy limbs glow, nay, they dazzle me. Hide thyself in mine arms quickly. I die, I wither away standing so near the sun . . ."

"Balder!" she shrieked.

On the second syllable Hugin had pulled Munin's beak out and thrust in his own, and was again making that jarring, jeering laughter. "Na, na, not Balder; Loki, who swore to have thee whether thee'd have him or not. Loki, who fought Herindal in the shape of a seal. Loki, who can take any shape he chooses—ay, and any sorceress! It was I, I, Loki ye bedded with; thinking it was Balder—ay, and ye enjoyed it, crone!

"It was I who stole thy Secret of Secrets, not Balder. And when next thee saw Balder, thee went to him mouthing and simpering, and thee took his honest innocence as a spurning. And for that thee killed him, that and for fear that he'd tell your Secret! Do you see what thee've done, thou thick-witted slut? Thee killed bright Balder for bedding thee when he did not; for spurning thee which he did not; and for possessing a Secret which thee never told him!''

She stumbled across to the bed and crouched on the edge of it, gasping as if she had been whipped. Slowly, then, she looked up, and she had a crooked smile on her face. She forced words out between her teeth:

"Then, Loki, for the crime I have done, I am free, and thee hang in the pit. For what thee led me to do, all the world accuses thee. Hang there, then; thy punishment is just!"

Hugin pulled out his beak and almost comically scratched his head with his claw.

Munin whispered, "What is this Secret?"

"I don't know. I don't know. I must think." He closed his eyes tight.

Munin was painfully reminded of the night Balder was killed, when Hugin went into this kind of trance and would say nothing until he had thought it all out. He glanced down. Borga the sorceress was waiting, breathing heavily. Abruptly Hugin slid his beak into the jar again, and Loki's ghostly tones emerged. "The Secret . . ."

For a moment Borga was absolutely still. Then she flung her head up. "What of the Secret?"

Hugin said nothing.

Borga whimpered, "Thee . . . thee haven't told the Aesir?"

Hugin intoned, "Think thee I have?"

"No," she whispered, "no, we . . . we would know. This is very . . . brave," she said with difficulty. "If thee told, they'd free thee."

"And come for thee," Hugin hazarded.

"Ay." She shivered. "If the Giants leave anything of me."

"So which is it to be, Borga?"

"I don't . . . understand."

Munin saw Hugin's eyes squeeze tight shut for a moment. Then he said, "I'll draw thee a problem, and thee may tell me if it is correctly stated. Stay in thy chamber for as long as thy safety lasts, and I shall assuredly tell the Aesir all I know. When the Giants hear of it they will kill thee. Or—".

"No!" she cried.

"Or," he went on relentlessly, "come to Gladsheim and confess to Odin that thee murdered Balder. I shall be freed and banished and thee will die."

"Either way, I die!"

"Ay. But there is this difference. Free me, and the Aesir never know the Secret. They will be content with their murderer. At least thee can make amends for thy stupidity without damage to the Giants."

She was silent a long time. Then she said, "Devil!" in a way which must have hurt her throat. After that, "When . . . when must I—"

"It will take thee three days to reach Gladsheim. On the fourth dawn from tomorrow's, I shall tell Odin the Secret or I shall greet thee. Choose."

She clutched her hands tight against her face for a moment, and then lowered them. She said calmly, "I will go, then."

She is brave, thought Munin. She is foolish and in some ways stupid, but she is brave.

But the Secret—the Secret; what of that? Munin looked anxiously at Hugin.

Hugin's eyes were screwed shut again. At length he said, in Loki's voice, "And when I am free, how can thee be sure I will not tell the Aesir our little Secret after all?"

"Thee wouldn't! Thy fealty's with us! Thee's a Giant!"

"Only half, Borga. Thee'll just have to trust me."

"Ay," she said, her expression cloaked, but her eyes hot, "we'll trust thee."

"Then farewell, Borga." And suddenly, in a strained tone, "*I have suffered enough!*"

Ay, thought Munin, that would be Loki's way. Always a flash of drama. He drew Hugin close. "What of the Secret? Can we learn it?"

In answer, Hugin pointed. Borga had moved to a table; she was drawing out a sheet of foolscap, a quill, ink. She sat down to write.

"To Omir, her father the Giant vizier," Munin whispered. With a bird's eye and more memories than the human race, he could read it easily. " *'This is goodbye, father, and a wish that I could be mourned, but I cannot. Know then that I was tricked by Loki in ways I am too ashamed to write here; that that through this I, yes, I, father, killed Balder; and that I have done the greatest evil of all in revealing to Loki the Secret of Mimir. I go now to Gladsheim to die for the useless murder, and Loki will be freed. See that he dies, for he cannot be trusted. Do not pursue me nor change this plan in any particular, lest the Giants lose the field at Ragnarok.' "*

"Shall we take the paper?" whispered Munin when she had done.

"We need it not. Come." Hugin seemed about to burst with joy.

V

Silently they crept along the shelf to the fire hole and squirmed through it to the brooding night of Jotunheim. Together they took wing.

Ah, like the old days; to Odin, together! thought Munin joyfully.

"Thee have made thy point, good Hugin," he said, when they were over halfling country. "The facts I had never added up to the yield of your thought. How? How could you do it?"

"By flights above fact," said Hugin, "and the gathering of the facts below. . . . Now, when first thee told me the story of Balder's death, thought took me to a path wherein Loki, though an instrument, was not actually guilty. Following this, I could assume that if Loki were innocent, the strange woman at the feast was not Loki disguised, but a stranger.

"What kind of stranger? A Giant, bearing some small charm to keep us from detecting her. You will, friend Munin, of course remember that she did not appear at the feast until Loki was cast out. He would have detected her, spell or no spell, half-Giant that he is. She stayed hidden, probably in the crowd.

"And we know, too, that she arrived to find Balder apparently invulnerable, and that she skilfully pressed Frigga to reveal her oversight with the mistletoe. The rest of this woman's work was seen by all."

"But," Munin objected, "how did thee conclude it was truly a woman?"

"Because at the outset it seemed a woman's crime. If a man is killed and has no known enemies, and especially if there is no obvious gain from his death, then the heart is involved somewhere.

"Balder, however, was not as other men, other gods. If he spurned anyone, it was in innocence and without intent, and the whole world knew that. Hence his death had to be for two reasons—because of a woman's scorn, and because of something else. It is easy to visualize a smitten lady killing herself over Balder; it is inconceivable that she would kill Balder unless something else were involved."

"What led thee to Borga?"

"The noisiest clue of all, Munin. It was she alone who would not weep for him. This is one thing all Asgard overlooked because suspicion of Loki was so strong—just as all Asgard has forgotten that Loki wept.

"So once we were led to Borga, we had merely to let her conscience work in our favor. The voice of Loki in her room spoke never from knowledge, save what she supplied. And so we forced her to confess, and further, to give herself up."

"Thee, not we," said Munin reverently. "And what of the Secret?"

"We do not know it completely, but we know enough. Borga wrote, . . . *lest the Giants lose at Ragnarok.* And that is sufficient, from what thee've told me—it is word straight from the heart of the Giant domain that such a thing is possible, the first such since Odin entered the Well of Mimir the Wise, in the dawn of time."

"Mimir . . . he is a Giant!" cried Munin, fluttering excitedly. "And it must be one false seed he slipped amongst the treasures he gave Odin! And Odin—good Odin—never doubted it!"

"As was said by our false Loki," chuckled Hugin, " '*I have suffered enough!*' We shall take a weight from the sky-father, friend Munin. Perhaps he will wish to confront Mimir with the lie—that great tragic lie that the Giants must win the field at Ragnarok. But thought tells me he need not: Fate never dictated the doom of Asgard.''

''Will Asgard be victorious then?''

''The Aesir will win if they fight best, and that is all they would ever wish.''

Before them spread the frontiers of Asgard. Happily they flew—Munin, who bore seven thousand years of doom and mourning, seeing now a return to the great days, and Hugin, who bothered himself not with memories, content that hereafter he would be the one to speak to the sky-father.

Joy is now joy in Asgard, with its ale and its heady mead, the singing and the wild hard laughter. Clink and clatter and clash ring the arms; whip and whicker and thud, the arrows. Sinews are tuned and toned and honed and hardened, and speech is mighty, and much of the measureless night belongs to the unearthly yielding of the Aesir goddesses, whose limbs are magic.

Here are the heroes of Earth, here the dazzle-winged Valkyrs; here in the halls of forever they feast and fight and find that which mortality is too brief and too fragile to grant.

The Aesir are made for joy and the heroes have earned it, and their joys are builded of battle, and to battle they build. The battle they face is the battle of Ragnarok. They will fight the Giants at Ragarok. They will dare death at Ragarok . . .

. . . and there *they need not die!*

STRAGGLER FROM ATLANTIS
by Manly Wade Wellman

A prolific, and award-winning, short story writer, Manly Wade Wellman (1903—   ) has worked primarily in the fields of fantasy, horror, and science fiction. Many of his stories, such as those in Who Fears the Devil *(1963), have a strong regional and poetic flavor reminiscent of Jesse Stuart and Robert Penn Warren.*

What follows is the first of a series of yarns about the last survivor of Atlantis—whom we met before in Wizards. *Now he's attacking a problem too big for giants.*

Then he knew, or maybe he dreamed he knew, that he wasn't sea-driven, wind-driven, any more. Those hours or eternities that had thrown him high like a stone from a sling, plunged him into strangling abysses of ocean, hurtled him in a drench and rattle of rain with the wreckage to which he clung, they were past. He was alive and out of the sea, lying peacefully face down on sand and pebbles. The waves only murmured, as though to comfort him.

He could feel the sun's warm caress on his naked back, after the wind and storm and dark clouds like smothering robes. He had not died and gone wherever one goes when one dies. He was alive and ashore somewhere. He might even be safe.

Rolling over, he opened his eyes to see where he had been flung by the tempest that couldn't kill him. He sprawled on a white beach. Inland showed clumps of rich-leaved trees; in the sky overhead were scattered soft clouds, green and rose and pearl, like the feathers of softly tinted birds. Almost within reach of his hand lodged the splintered wooden gate that had served him in some measure as a raft, the great gate that had earlier stood in the garden wall of Theona, queen of Atlantis.

Of Atlantis. He, too, was of Atlantis—wait; of Atlantis no more. For Atlantis was lost Atlantis now, sunk to ocean's deep bottom, with Queen Theona and all her people. How he had survived he could not imagine, nor where, nor on what unknown shore.

Shakily, creakily he stood up, feeling the soreness in his battered muscles. He wore only sandals and a drenched rag of blue loincloth. His tanned flesh was soaked into ridges on his lean legs, his broad, panting chest, the bunchy brawn of his arms. He put up a hand to shove back his mane of dark, drenched hair. That hand shook, like an old man's. He sensed hunger within him. How long since he had eaten the delicately roasted bird and white bread and drunk the perfumed wine in Queen Theona's garden? Days ago, a lifetime ago?

Among a scatter of shoreside rocks, limpets clung. Stooping, he managed to pry loose two of them. With a big stone he broke their shells and ate them. Almost at once, they seemed to give him back a trifle of strength. He knelt to tug more strongly at a third limpet—and a shadow slid across him.

He started up. A foot was planted beside him, a vast, flat foot clad in laced leather. Its leg was like a tree trunk, meaty of calf, knuckle-kneed. Over him leaned a huge face, set on shoulders twice the height of his. Its bearded lips drew back from square cobbles of teeth. It leaned almost down on him.

"Where did you come from?" asked a thundering voice, in a language he knew.

A mighty hand fell upon his arm.

Gathering the strength from somewhere, he whirled free of it. The great head still hung close to him, and he threw a fist, with all the boxer's skill that was his. It slammed home on the bearded jaw and he heard the giant howl out in surprised pain. But then his quivering legs gave under him and he fell down, not even feeling the sand as it came up to meet him. Something like sleep flowed over him.

Again he roused, to a tingling taste of wine in his mouth. He made himself sit up, rubbing his eyes. The giant was there; no, half a dozen were there, looming around him like crags. They were all twice as broad as he and, sitting, were as tall as he would be standing. They were leather-clad, shaggy, staring. One of them propped him against a monstrous upflung knee and proffered a big stone bottle. He drank again, deeply. His head cleared.

"Thank you," he said huskily. "What people are you?"

A giant leaned forward. His shield-wide face was tufted with coarse black hair. His lower lip looked puffy, as though bruised.

"We ask you the same, little one," he rumbled. "What people are you, and what are you doing in our country where little ones dare not come for fear of us?"

"My name is Kardios."

"Karidos," repeated the one who held him against that big knee. A free hand, big as a basket, clamped a ruddy-bearded chin. "What sort of name is that?"

Kardios grinned. "I was brought up to think it was a good one. It means the heart."

The bruise-lipped giant grunted, and Kardios looked at him. "When it comes to that, what about your name?"

"I am Yod," boomed the other. "Kardios—the heart, eh? A heart can be wounded."

"I've the head and the hand to protect my heart," said Kardios, feeling better with every moment.

"Ha!" Yod roared his gigantic scorn. "A head no bigger than a fist, a hand like a forked twig."

Kardios shoved aside the bottle and made himself stand up quickly. He glared into Yod's big, bulging eyes.

"Get a weapon to fit your hand and give me one to fit mine," he said evenly. "You're a giant, but you're clumsy to the look. I'll wager that before you raised your arm to strike, I'd have you cut open and your tripes shed out on the ground.''

Silence all around at that. The giants squatted and gazed at him. He made a show of ignoring them, glancing this way and that beyond the circle to see where they had brought him. He must have been carried well inland, for the sea was not visible at all. Grass grew richly underfoot, with here and there a tuft of trees, palms and what seemed to be orchard growth. At some distance loomed a row of tawny bluffs, in which he thought he saw flecks of darkness like caves. Then he gazed all around at the giants, and grinned, showing his teeth to the gum.

"Bold words, dwarf," said another of the group at last. This one sat on a lump of rock, as though he presided. His great face was deeply folded in wrinkles, but there was no weakness of age in it. His white beard flowed like a blizzard. Over his shoulders hung a cloak of shaggy black skin, perhaps from an immense wild bull. On the knuckly hand that stroked his beard shone a gold ring set with jewels—this people knew metals and the fashioning of them. He gazed at Kardios from under white-tufted brows.

"Bold words," he said again, "from a man all alone among many bigger than he."

"I've spoken bolder than that, against dangers more worth fearing," replied Kardios. "What will you do to punish my boldness? Kill me and eat me, or just kill me? There are enough of you to try."

A grumble went up from several, but the whitebearded one lifted a spadelike hand.

"Be patient; you know we may need him," he quieted his companions. Then, not unkindly: "Think, Kardios, if you know how. My name is Enek, and these people of mine, the Nephol, look to me for command and judgment. Why should we give you wine to strengthen you if we meant to kill you?"

"Wine," Kardios said after him. "Let me help my wits with more of it."

The bottle was given him. He took a long pull and wiped his mouth.

"You've said that people my size are afraid to come here," he reminded them. "I didn't come here, I was washed here by the sea. Now you say that there's a reason to keep me alive. That sounds as if my size will be of help, though you're all about eight times bigger than I am, and think bigness is a good thing."

"Not always good," said Enek gravely. "You've guessed wisely, Kardios. There's a place the smallest of us can't go, and we want you to go there."

Kardios sat down again in the midst of them. Yod still scowled, and Kardios cocked his head and grinned.

"Yod doesn't seem anxious for anything I can do," he suggested.

"Leave Yod alone," Enek bade him. "It was Yod who found you fainting, and brought you here to us after you'd hit him when he tried to help."

"Then stop trying to frighten me, Yod," said Kardios. "I didn't live through the swallowing of Atlantis by the sea to be frightened by anything."

"We've heard speak of Atlantis," said the redbearded giant who had given Kardios wine. "Some sort of strange, shining island kingdom, they say."

"It was," amended Kardios. "You Nephol are looking at a rare specimen. Maybe a few of our ships were out in safe waters, but I doubt if anyone other than myself got away from the end of Atlantis itself."

They all goggled again, and Kardios laughed. He was feeling better all the time.

"What are you trying to tell us?" asked Enek. "What happened?"

"Well," said Kardios, "I suppose I was more or less responsible."

At that, they stared at him the more fixedly, and he laughed again.

"I wasn't a citizen of the capital at the shore," he said. "I lived back in the hills, cutting wood and growing grapes, and I was young enough to want to better myself. So I strapped on my sword and slung my harp on my shoulder. I took the trail right down to the gold and jasper palace of Queen

Theona, where she'd ruled longer than anybody ever could accurately tell. I thought she might want me for her palace guard, or to make music for her, or perhaps both."

"So you're a harper, too," grumbled Yod. "You seem to value yourself for that as well as for being a fighter."

"I've always done what I could to harp and fight well. I had surpassed all the country harpers and fighters I knew, and in my part of Atlantis there are—there were good harpers and fighters. But at the palace, and it was big enough to be a palace even for people your size, the guards at the gate laughed at me. After I'd stopped them from laughing—"

"How did you stop them?" broke in one of the listeners.

"The only way. Queen Theona came out on a balcony and watched me stop the laughter of the second one. Then she ordered the bodies carried away and the widows comforted. And she said for me to come into her garden and show if I was equally good with my harp."

"Perhaps Kardios should have a harp," said Enek. "His story sounds as if it should be sung, here and there."

A harp appeared from somewhere and was thrust into Kardios's hand. It was a big one, of course, made from the horned skull of an antelope, with strings of silver wire. Kardios tuned it expertly and struck a chord. It sounded well.

"In her garden, her women and her advisers listened while I played and sang," he said. "After a while, Theona told them they could go and leave me alone with her. She poured wine—good wine, though I'm not disparaging the wine you've given me—and offered me some food."

"This queen, older than anyone could remember," put in Enek. "What was she like?"

"I can say only that she was more beautiful than the stars or the moon," said Kardios. "Than the sun at morning or evening. Than the jewels and gold she wore. She looked at me and told me she would like me to make a a song about her."

"Did you?" prompted Enek. "What was the song?"

"I'll try to remember."

Kardios plucked the strings until he found his tune. He cleared his throat and sang:

"Atlantis, Atlantis has flowered forever,
For Theona has reigned as her queen,
Worshipped and honored and loved,
   but kissed never—
So is Theona, and always has been.

"Fairer Theona than moon or than sun,
Fairer than stars in the vault of the skies;
No man can say when her reign was begun,
Lovely and queenly and regal and wise.

"So it was told by the gods in high heaven,
Atlantis shall live and forever prevail
Until her sweet lips in a love-kiss are given;
So runs the prophecy, so says the tale.

"Forever Atlantis has flowered, but this
Is told of Theona—the moment that she
Grants to a lover the boon of a kiss,
Atlantis, Theona, will drown in the sea."

He muted the strings. "I'm afraid I'm not in my best voice," he apologized.

"That was a good song, and well sung," Enek praised him. "What then, Kardios? What when you'd finished?"

"Theona sat beside me and said, 'Kiss me.' "

All their great lungs breathed deeply, drawing air like bellows.

"I told her to remember the prophecy. She laughed, more sweetly than music, and again she said, 'Kiss me.' So I kissed her."

"Huh?" grunted Yod. "You kissed her."

"And Atlantis sank," said Kardios.

"If that's true, how did you live?" Enek demanded.

"Ask the gods," replied Kardios. "Ask the sea and the storm. But don't ask me. If some god was making a joke on me, it was a rough one. I got hold of the garden gate somehow, and I don't know how long I spun and churned over the sea, in rain, in hail. Days? It must have been days. I don't know. But here I am.''

"Do you believe him, Enek?" asked Yod.

"I believe him," Enek made answer, so quietly that he sounded almost casual. "It's a strange story, but it sounds true. It was no joke of a god, Kardios. You lived and came here because there's something here for you to do."

"You've already said that," Kardios reminded him. "What is it, and why should I do it?"

"Because we helped you back to life," Enek answered at once. "We came out today, to see in what state the storm had left our shore. It was Yod who was going ahead, found you half fainting, and got his lip bruised for his pains. Now, if you're not grateful enough to help us in return for helping you, be practical enough to think how we'd act if we were ungrateful for anything."

Kardios laughed, and this time several of the giants laughed with him. It was like rolling thunder.

"What is it I am to do?" he asked again.

"You'll need strength to hear about it," said Enek. "It's nearly sundown, and night hasn't been a happy time hereabouts in recent months. Come home with us and eat and sleep."

"I'll be grateful for those chances, at least."

They all got up and walked ponderously toward the distant bluffs.

Kardios walked among them. His first impression had been a correct one. These giants were powerful creatures, but they moved slowly. Even in his weaknened condition he could have run from them easily, but he did not. As they tramped along together, Enek told Kardios what troubled them.

Moons ago, there had been a great bolt of fire from heaven, and the Nephol were sure the gods spoke to them. Some of them saw the bolt strike, not far from where they lived in caves. These reported that it seemed to burst into a great shattered spray of blazing embers, which flew in all directions. But from its very midst, a living, moving thing came away safe.

"We call him Fith," said Enek.

"Why?" asked Kardios.

"It is like the noise he makes," said the ruddy-bearded giant who had given Kardios wine, and whose name was Jipi.

Enek continued the story. Fith had seemed to be daunted, or at least uncomfortable in the light of day, and had scrambled shapelessly away to where an ancient dry well opened. He slid himself into it, out of sight. That well, said Enek, had been thought enchanted, once the home of spirits. The Nephol had come at twilight to sing and burn sweet herbs at the well's opening, to honor what surely must be something sent from the gods.

"Then Fith came out," said Enek. "He flowed out—I saw him flow out like a torrent of foam. He pulled one of us down and . . . *flowed* over him. We ran, we were sick with fear. We did not come back until the next sunrise. There were only bones there, as clean and dry as though they had lain beside the well for a year."

"Now you're telling a story as strange to me as my story of the drowning of Atlantis seemed to you," said Kardios. "You thought this Fith was heaven-sent—"

"Did he not come from the sky?" Enek pointed out. "Isn't that the home of gods?"

"I've heard our priests say there isn't any particular home of gods," Karidos remembered. "Anyway, Fith went into a well that you thought of as a sort of home of underground spirits."

"And he makes his home there."

"Where is that well?"

"There," said Enek, pointing with a finger like a bludgeon.

They were approaching a stream, with the cave-pocked bluffs on its far side. A grassless level lay before them, extending to the near bank. Upon this lay what appeared to be a tumble of pale rocks, around a dark blotch of emptiness. Two spotted goats were tethered to pegs nearby.

"You will understand," said Enek, "that, however Fith's flying chariot was destroyed, he managed to land safely at a convenient place for him. That well was very close to where he came free of the wreck."

"Do you think he knew it would be there?" suggested Kardios.

"Possibly, even though he came here from the stars. It didn't seem haphazard."

The giants sidled away from the place as they walked, and Kardios suddenly broke from among them and trotted toward the dark spot. As he came close, he saw that the strew of pale objects was made up of bones—animal bones, great and small. The goats bleated plaintively, and Kardios smiled at them, for he liked animals. At the very brink of the hole he knelt. Enek was right, it was a smallish round opening. Kardios might slide his own sinewy body into it, but it was too narrow for any of the giants. He peered down. Far below, like a distant coin of silver, showed a disk of pallid light. It reminded Kardios of the phosphorescent glow of certain kinds of fungus.

He rose and came quickly back to the giants as they approached the stream. "What are those goats doing there?" he asked.

"They are for Fith," replied Enek. "Living things are what he wants. Offerings keep him from hunting us. But dead meat he will not touch."

"At least you haven't made a god of him as yet, with these sacrifices," said Kardios.

Enek sighed unhappily, and Jipi and Yod sighed with him.

"For all practical purposes, he might as well be a god, and a downright evil one at that," said Jipi. "He's here. He takes prey. But let's get on to the caves. The sun has almost set."

So it had, somewhere to seaward behind them. The giants speeded their heavy feet to the margin of the stream and crossed, one by one, on an arrangement of rough rocks. On the other side stretched a level open space, tramped hard by big feet, below the bluffs and their tiers of caves. Kardios saw fires at the mouths of those caves above and below, and giant heads peered out, like dwellers at the windows of a great tenement building such as Atlantis had known.

His escorting party split up, heading for caves here and there. Enek and Jipi guided Kardios to a ladder. Its sides were great treetrunks with the bark long worn away. Up went Enek, then Kardios, and Jipi last of all.

They reached a shelf of rock. Enek led the way along it, to a tall, broad cave opening. Inside glowed a fire. The cave was a tall roomy one and appeared to have beeen enlarged by powerful chippings into the rock. A giant woman leaned above the fire, clad in loose garment of rough weave that fell to her feet. She had gray hair, in two cable-like braids, and Kardios thought her seamed face was a kindly one. She looked up from her cooking.

"Enek," she cried. "I'm glad you've come back safe." Then she stared down at Kardios. "Who's this small one?"

"He's Kardios, a friend and a helper," said Enek. "Kardios. my wife's name is Lotay. She's going to give us some supper. You eat with us, Jipi."

Lotay brought out wide clay platters. From the fire she lifted a spit with savory-smelling collops of roast meat strung on it, and poked in the ashes for roots backed in wrappings of charred leaves. Enek drew a bronze knife as long as a sword and sliced meat into a dish for Kardios. Lotay filled pottery cups with wine from a leather bag. But before they sat down to eat, Enek and Jipi went to the door of the cave. Kardios watched as they carefully lifted into place a sort of barrier, of thorny branches and tendrils woven into a close network. It filled the opening from side to side and from top to bottom. They pegged it stoutly, making sure that no gaps were left anywhere. Then, at last, all four sat down at the fireside and took up their well-filled plates.

"This meat is excellent," said Kardios. "What is it, Enek?"

"The hind foot of an elephant, if you know what elephants are."

"We had them in Atlantis, for parades and for hauling stones and timbers, but I never ate elephant before." Kardios took another mouthful. "It's as tender and juicy as fine pork."

The baked root, when broken open, presented a tasty accompaniment. The wine was better than what Kardios had awakened to among the giants. As they ate, Enek told Kardios more things. The Nephol were an ancient people but not a numerous one; those in this cave community numbered perhaps fifty. But other human races, peoples of Kardios's size, feared them and left them alone. Only on certain days were there meetings at the boundaries of the Nephol territory, where the giants traded tanned hides and uncut gems for woven fabrics and tools of bronze and polished stone.

"You see, those other peoples know that we are heaven-born," put in Jipi. "We are descended from the sons of the gods, who mated with the strongest and most beautiful daughters of men."

After the meal was finished, Lotay shyly asked Kardios to take off his salt-encrusted sandals. She sat beside the fire with them, rubbing them with pieces of fat and working them back to suppleness. Enek and Jipi and Kardios found seats on blocks of stone near a rear wall. A great store of various weapons was kept there. They were stacked against the rock or hung from pegs driven into cracks. Enek found a beautifully tanned leopard skin.

"Perhaps this can replace that poor rag of a loincloth," he said.

"Thank you." Kardios put it on, admiring the spots on the fur. "Now, suppose you tell me more about how I am supposed to deal with Fith."

"Which means your mind is made up to do it," said Jipi, smiling.

"I made it up almost at once. You've said that Fith eats the living sacrifices you put out there."

"He would rather catch us to eat, but he takes the beasts we give him every night," said Enek. "We've given him very many of those. Goats, hogs, cows—he takes them, even bears and tigers we have trapped and tied up at the doorway of his hole. Once even an elephant, though he spent a while sucking the flesh from that."

"I've been wondering why you never just stopped up that hole, by daytime, with him inside it," said Kardios.

"We've done that. With earth and rocks. He throws them out, or somehow burrows through them. When he wants to come out and eat, he comes out."

"I see. All right, when you've given him all your beasts, what's going to happen then?"

"How often we've taken council about that," said Enek sadly. "Fith will come for us then. I've said that when that happens, I must be the first to be given him." He stroked his white beard. "I'll go out to him. Jipi will be chief after me."

"As the chief, I'd have to be the prey for him on the next night," declared Jipi.

The two boulderlike heads nodded at each other. It had been agreed upon, then, long ago.

"And you've never been able to fight him," said Kardios.

"Oh, we've tried fighting," said Enek. "Our bravest have tried. But he moves too quickly for any of the Nephol. And he—he's of no shape, and of all shapes. He changes like a cloud, like a bad dream."

"That's a new sort of creature to me," confessed Kardios. "Indeed, he must be from the stars. We had monsters on Atlantis, but they kept honestly to one shape. You Nephol have had advantages we haven't. But you say he can devour big beasts, big men. What teeth he must have."

"No teeth," declared Jipi. "We told you that he flows away on the other side, leaving the bones."

Kardios grinned drily. "Are you sure you're not offering me as a sacrifice?"

Enek shook his great head. "If we began to give him men, even men of your size, then I'm afraid he'd truly become a god. And what benefit would that sacrifice be to us? He'd only come back the next night, seeing his way by the light he himself sheds."

"Can he climb as high as this cave?"

Enek nodded. Lotay, working on the sandals, seemed to shudder.

"We can't have Fith for a god," said Jipi stubbornly. "The sun has been our god, and Fith stays out of the sun's light. The sun is kind. Kindness is stronger than fear."

"Not always," Kardios told him. "Fear doesn't have pity. I feel like saying you're lucky I'm here to dispose of Fith for you."

"How will you do that?" wondered Jipi. "You've said you'd go down into his hole to him, but what then?"

"Leave that to me," said Kardios, wondering in his own heart how he would manage. "I'll need a good weapon, of course. The best."

"Ah," and Enek actually smiled with his great teeth, "now you bargain."

"I'm in a position where I must bargain. Look at me; I wasn't left more than a rag or two by that ride through the stormy ocean."

"Clothes, too?" asked Enek. "All right, Kardios, our women will make clothes for you. And take any weapon you want." He pointed to the arsenal stacked against the wall. "Just what sort of a weapon would hurt Fith?"

"He knows what pain is," said Kardios, gazing toward the front of the cave. "Your fabric of thorns yonder seems to keep him out. In other words, thorns pain him. And if he has a sense of pain, it's there to warn him away from injury."

"That's true," said Jipi. "You're wise, Kardios."

"I'm practical," amended Kardios.

Enek tramped over to the weapons and fumbled among them. "Here, Kardios," he said. "If you think thorns may be bad for him, how about this?"

He held it out. A great, stout pole of dark wood, and from the end hung, on a length of plaited leather cord, a ball as big as Kardios's two fists. This was cased in rawhide, and all over it projected ugly bronze spikes. Enek wagged it in his hand. The spiked ball swung like the end of a flail.

"Could you strike him with that?" he asked. "And another stroke, and more strokes until—"

But Kardios was not watching the play with the flail-weapon. He had come quickly to Enek's side. Stooping, he picked up something else from the display.

"This sword," he said.

Its icy-blue blade was as long as his leg, and three fingers broad at the point where it was set in a handle of leather lashings. He inspected it carefully. It was not of bronze, not of silver. Its two edges, his practiced eye told him, were keen enough to shave with. Its point tapered leanly as a needle.

"That's a curiosity," said Jipi, joining them. "It came out of the fire when Fith's chariot smashed and flamed up on the ground."

"And the heat blistered all the ground there," added Enek. "We scouted later, and there lay that blade you're holding. At first we thought it was a snake. But Jipi picked it up and brought it here to work on and sharpen. But it's not big enough for a grown man's weapon, and we don't let children play with it; they can easily cut themselves."

"It's big enough for me," said Kardios, poising it.

The balance was excellent. He took the point in his other hand. The blade bent springily, like a tough withe.

"And the temper of the metal," he said. "This wouldn't break like a bronze sword. It's harder than silver." He held it to his nose and sniffed. "It has a smell like brine. What is it?"

"We never saw any other like it," replied Jipi. "It came out of the earth under that heat. The earth was a red, crumbly sort. Sometimes we use that earth for paint."

Kardios whipped the sword through the air. It sang musically. He whirled it around his head, listening.

"Let me have this to fight Fith," he said.

"Not these thorns?" said Enek, holding out the flail.

"This is a thorn that might spike down your terrible Fith like a beetle on a pin." Kardios tested the point with his thumb. "I like it."

"Remember, Fith is quick," warned Jipi. "We've tried to throw spears at him. He only dodges away."

"Perhaps you don't throw quickly enough. Let him dodge with me. I can dodge, too."

He swept the sword above his head in a twinkle of light from the fire, then slashed it down at his ankles. He leaped over the blade as it slashed, spun it in the air to slash again while he jumped again. Enek grunted. Kardios paced lightly across the rocky floor.

"You," he said suddenly to Jipi, "take a spear and throw it at me."

"What are you asking?" cried Enek, and Lotay, too, looked up in amazement.

"If Jipi can strike me with a thrown spear, I'd be too slow for Fith," said Kardios. He walked out into the center of the floor and stood with bare feet apart, springy-legged, the sword half lifted in his hand. "Throw, Jipi."

Jipi grimaced. From the stand of weapons he selected a spear. It was as long as he, with a shaft made of a tall hardwood sapling, bound with rings of copper wire. The head was of beautifully polished blue flint, as long as Kardios's forearm, bound into the cleft end of the wood with lashings of sinew. Jipi balanced it on his palm and nodded above it as one who knows his weapon.

"You're sure you want this?" he asked Kardios.

"I'm sure, Jipi. Try me, I say."

Jipi's tall body flexed itself smoothly. The spear drove through the firelight.

Karidos writhed to his left. The spear hurtled past. He made a lightning slash with the sword. It bit the shaft in two, and the pieces clattered on the rock. Kardios laughed as he came to salute with his blade.

Enek drew a long amazed breath. "You'll do, Kardios. If you were twice as tall—"

"If I were twice as tall, I'd be about ten times slower. I couldn't go down and fight Fith tomorrow."

He carefully leaned the sword back in its place against the wall and sat down by the fire. He yawned.

"Yes, let's sleep," said Enek. "It will do all of us good to sleep."

"It will do me a good in particular," said Kardios.

Lotay brought him his sandals and spread the spotted hide of a cow for him, then offered him a woolen coverlet. He stretched out gratefully. Enek and Lotay lighted a big candle in a sconce of baked clay and plodded to where a dark opening led to an inner cave, their sleeping quarters. Jipi found bedding and relaxed near where the weapons were gathered. Almost at once, Kardios heard Jipi's deep, regular breathing as he drifted into slumber.

Kardios did not close his own eyes. Stealthily he put on his sandals and stole to where the screen of thorns blocked the mouth of the outer cave. Crouching there, he listened. At last, with the utmost care, he twitched back a corner of the screen and slipped through. A thorn scraped his side, but he did not care. He tucked the screen in place and tiptoed along the ledge to the ladder, swung quickly down, and stood up in the open space before the caves.

Half a moon hovered above the eastern horizon. That was light enough. Kardios stole across the hard earth to the stream. He could make out the rocks at the crossing, and he stepped carefully from each to the next until he had gained the far bank. He stood and looked toward the place where bones littered the ground at the mouth of the well, and where the two goats had been tethered.

But he could not see the goats. They seemed to be cloaked in a softly glowing mist. It lay over them, a sort of half-defined clump of it. As Kardios watched, the mist stirred and churned. It seemed to thicken, to become more solid there. Then it rolled across the earth; it stole as though with a rhythmic motion. It came clear of where the goats had been. And where the goats had been there showed only another scatter of bones in the moonlight.

That had been Fith, in the act of feeding.

Even as Kardios told himself these things, Fith also seemed to come to a conclusion. Fith's substance stirred and humped itself. A point rose in the midst of that substance, grew taller and made a lumpy ball at the top. The lump swung around toward Kardios, like a head looking at him. In that lump glowed a rosy light, stronger than the blur of Fith's radiance.

"Here I am, Fith!" cried Kardios.

Instantly the luminous mass rushed at him, ponderously swift.

Kardios whirled and ran. If he had brought a weapon—but he had not. Ahead of him showed a dark, brushy clump, and into it he dived like a rabbit, exulting as he felt the rake of brambles. Fith was there close behind him, but stopped as Kardios wallowed out on the other side of the brush.

Goats eaten or not, Fith wanted Kardios. Kardios ran again, to the streamside this time, straddling quickly from rock to rock. He had barely gained the far bank before Fith was catching up. Fith had changed shape, as Enek said that shapeless shape could be changed. Kardios heard a panting behind him. The pallid mass had lengthened itself, to come writhing along like a snake after a lizard.

Like a lizard Kardios ran, as fast as he had ever run. None of the big Nephol could outrun Fith, but Kardios could. He reached the bluffs, the big ladder, and lizardlike he swarmed up. Fith was at the bottom. Kardios dashed along the ledge, slid in past the thorny screen, feeling the rake of more sharp points. He worked the screen back into place. Outside, Fith slithered along the ledge and scraped and panted, but could not come in.

"Your dark world must be a sad world," Kardios addressed Fith. "You must go out at night and hunt for food. I'm glad I'm not you."

Fith subsided. Maybe Fith went away. Kardios paid no more attention. Again he sought his cowskin pallet and pulled the coverlet over himself. Jipi, sound asleep, did not stir. Kardios stretched at full length and crossed his arms behind his head.

He had seen Fith, he had tested Fith's speed and, to some extent, Fith's pursuit methods. He wondered again if he could have made a stand in the night if he had brought along that sword Enek had granted him. Maybe. He drew deep breaths, and went sound asleep.

Sleeping, he dreamed. He was back in the palace garden on Atlantis. Theona sat on the bench with him. Her beauty was music, there so close and so sweet. Her mouth closed on his, a yearning, seeking mouth, as though she found in him the perfect triumph of her timeless existence. Then came the abrupt rush and churning of water all around, and the water fell away and became Fith, a flow and wriggle of pursuing movement. After that came wakening, to the sound of heavy feet. Enek was awake in the cave and so was Lotay, who stooped by the fire to brown flat cakes on a tilted stone.

"Good morning," said Kardios, coming to his feet. "When do we go after Fith?"

"Eat first," said Enek, beckoning also to the wakened Jipi.

"A little," agreed Kardios. "I eat lightly before a fight, and perhaps I have reason to feast later."

He washed his face in a clay pot of water.

Breakfast was grilled fish and those cakes. They were of barley meal, coarse but palatable. Lotay gave him a dish of honey to trickle upon them. Kardios was hungry but he took only a few mouthfuls, and a sip or two of wine.

"If you are ready now—" said Enek.

"I'm ready." Kardios took the sword from its place. "Let me have cord, to swing this to my wrist so I won't lose it."

The cord was given him.

"And what kind of light for the bottom of that well? I don't mean to trust Fith's light, it might go out."

Enek brought a chunk of green cane, as long as Kardios's arm. Within it were nested live coals, closely swaddled in dry moss. The open end was plugged with clay, and holes had been bored through the tough outer substance of the cane. Kardios took it, examined it, then swung it through the air. Tiny flames burst out through the holes, then died down as he held it still.

"That will be splendid," Kardios approved.

Outside the cave, the bright morning was around them. Enek and Jipi went down the ladder with Kardios. Lofty shapes of the Nephol were abroad and came after them—men only, perhaps all the men of the community. Kardios estimated about twenty. They followed Kardios and his companions across the stepping stones. Their journey was watched by women, and by children small only by comparison with their mothers.

They reached the mouth of the well, strewn around with polished bones. Kardios peered down again, and again he saw the coinlike spot of soft light far below. He made fast the lanyard from the sword hilt to his right wrist, took the torch in his left, and sat down. "Now," he told them, "I want to go down head first. Tie a cord to my left ankle."

A coil of line, braided of tanned leather thongs, was produced by Jipi. "We'd better tie both ankles," he said. "This cord will cut deep into one ankle."

"No, only my left," demurred Kardios. "I don't want to

land down there with my feet tied together, and Fith coming. Do as I say, Jipi."

Jipi shrugged. He tore a furred strip from the edge of his mantle and wound it around Kardios's left ankle. Around this padding he drew a loop of the cord and knotted it. Kardios stood up. Enek touched his shoulder, with fingers like great ridged roots.

"Luck go with you, Kardios," he said solemnly. "You're small enough to go into the well, but your heart is as great as any of ours." He considered the praise he had spoken. "Greater," he amended.

"Thank you," said Kardios. "Hold fast to the cord and let me go down fairly fast."

He rose to his knees and yet again he looked into the deep shaft. Once more he saw, seeping from far below, the ghost of light.

"Here I go," he said.

He thrust in both torch and sword and slid after them head first, like a fox gliding into its burrow.

The noose clutched bitingly at his ankle. They were lowering him like a bucket. He twiddled the torch into a rosy glow. The shaft, he saw, was like a chimney, a straight, perpendicular tube into which his body could slide, easily but not roomily. The sides of it were almost glossily smooth. The rock looked volcanic, but its smoothness must be something that Fith had done. He had had months in which to accomplish it, for his own sliding ease.

Down. Down. Kardios wondered how many lengths of his own body he had descended. Blood beat in his ears, but he felt no fuzziness of the wits. He was healthy, thank whatever gods must be thanked. He remembered men he had seen, men called wise in Atlantis back when anybody called things anything in Atlantis. They stood on their heads for long spaces, bringing the blood there to spur their minds. Then they sat up and prophesied or gave advice. Kardios could not remember anything that any of them said that was worth remembering.

The pale patch of light grew wider below him. He must be approaching it. Where that light would be, Fith would be.

Kardios let the sword dangle from the lanyard and put out his right hand to touch the smooth wall of the tubelike shaft. The touch slowed his descent a trifle, so that the drag of the cord on his ankle slackened. Now, there, down there, he caught a glimpse of salty rock flooring. That was where he was coming to, where he was to meet Fith and make a battle.

"I'll do it," he promised himself, half aloud.

And then he was coming into open space at the bottom of the well. As his head cleared the bottom of the shaft, he saw that here was a considerable grotto of some sort. He came to the bottom, landing on one hand and the free foot. Writhing around, he caught the hilt of the sword again and with a flick of it severed the rope that was tied to his left ankle. He stood up quickly in the middle of the floor, and whirled the torch for light to see better where he was.

There was already light to show him that, without the torch. It was a place of rough rock, plenty of level expanse underfoot, as much as a fair-sized hall. All around were jagged, dull walls, slanting inward to where, overhead, they came into a curved roof like the inside of a slipshod dome. As much room here, Kardios thought, as had been in the garden of Theona, now sunk to where it was sunken. Looking swiftly this way and that, he judged that this place had been fashioned somehow, though he could not guess just now what that somehow was. The hazy light showed him a darker blotch to the side, where a corridor seemed to lead away. Opposite this, in a jagged corner, lay the light's source.

It looked like a bank of soft sand heaped in among the rocks, palely glowing, as an unpolished jewel might glow under a directed radiance. That softness spread widely, farther across than the tallest of the Nephol people. He thought the glow pulsated, then wondered if this was not a sort of motion, a stir in that substance. There was sound, too, like breathing: *fith, fith.* Then it was Fith, plainer to see here than last night by the glow of half a moon. As Kardios looked, Fith paid attention to him in turn.

For the mass moved, it defined itself. It was not slackness, giving off that blur of light. It began to move itself out from among the rocks where it nested, and it seemed to take on form. It spread like a great, flattened ray, such as once he had seen swimming underwater, when he had looked over the side of a fishing boat off his home shore that was shore no longer. Fith crept on outflung projections like flukes that reached right and left: At the center, the expanse rose into a crest. Deep within that center shone the stronger light Kardios had seen the night before, rosy-tinged with a thought of green. Even as Kardios stared, the central light moved within the inner mass, moved forward in it as though to face him.

"Here I am again, Fith," Kardios addressed it. "They sent me down here to fight you. Let's make it a good one."

It seemed able to hear him. It crept toward him across the floor. Its inner bulk humped forward. Its flukes moved gropingly ahead, its substance flowed into them. It took a new position and headed toward him from that one, coming, coming.

Kardios poised, fencer-fashion, on light feet. He brought his sword to center guard position, point to the fore, ready for thrust or cut. Fith approached faster, rising and swelling and breathing, *fith, fith*. Out came a flaplike projection, like a questing tentacle.

Kardios slid his right foot forward and swiftly stooped his long body into a smooth, skilful lunge. The swordpoint licked out, and at the very wink of the right time he brought the blade down for a sweeping, slicing cut. That extension of pale substance parted before the razory edge like a strand of wool. The severed piece went squirming away. The pale hummock of substance recoiled upon itself, almost as swiftly as Kardios recovered from his lunge, drawing his extended foot backward and falling on guard again.

"Did you taste it, Fith?" he cried. "Can you taste as well as hear? Come on, try me again."

Fith knew what he said. For Fith came on to try him again. This time the pale bulk flowed out like foamy water, seemed to blanket the floor. It stole suddenly into action. As it did so, it bunched again, and now it seemed to be moving on bumpy protuberances beneath, moved on them as on legs. The rosy light within glowed stronger. It pulsed. Other parts of the body extended, questing like feelers, like arms. Kardios nipped one of them off with a quick, slicing cut, ducked low to escape another. Fith came charging.

So fast did Fith squatter forward that for a moment Kardios was backed almost against a jagged wall. He couldn't let himself be trapped there. Again he struck at a questing length of Fith's substance. It barely flicked him as he severed it, and its touch was like a tongue of flame upon his his forearm. Desperately he crouched, then hurled himself in a great, flying leap above the oncoming bulk of Fith. He landed on his feet just beyond, ran half a dozen steps and faced around.

"I'm not one of those clumsy giants, Fith," he cried. "You didn't catch me. Here I am. You must keep me amused."

Fith was drawing into a new shape. This shape rose up. It grew to the height of one of the Nephol, higher than that. It was giving itself legs, two clumsy bolsters on which it stood. It put forth arms. It was imitating the form of man. At the top, in the blob that might simulate a head, the rosy glow throbbed at him. *Fith, fith,* the creature panted.

"You've been observing things," said Kardios. "But you're clumsy at sculpture. Well, why do we wait?"

The giant shape came at him in a squattering run.

Kardios thrust, backed away, thrust again, and then Fith was all over him. Fith had shot out in all directions and had fallen upon him like a blanket.

The sword drove into Fith's midmost part and Kardios drew it up, with a strong, full-armed rake of a sweep. The edge divided the enveloping tissue like canvas. Next instant, Kardios scrambled and floundered through that great gash, won clear like a netted bird slipping out at a gap in the mesh. He danced away, tingling as though hot water had been thrown upon him. The mass he had escaped tried to draw itself together again, there almost at his knee. He looked down to where the red light flickered, close within reach.

At once he sped his blade in a mighty drawing cut. The edge sank deep into the soft pallor, seemed to grate as it struck something more solid inside. He drew it to him with all his strength, cutting the redness in two.

The close air hummed, shrieked all around them. The red glow of awareness in Fith's tissue blinked out.

Kardios backed clear, his sword ready. But Fith was dying. The panting breath labored, then stopped. The great sprawl of substance seemed to slacken, to shrivel, before Kardios's very eyes. The pale light dimmed, grew faint.

Kardios whirled his torch. The flames jumped out to show that Fith sprawled motionless and shrunken there. The grotto was silent.

Stepping close, Kardios prodded with his sword point, poked again. There was no responding movement.

He had done it.

Moving the torch to keep its flame bright, he looked around him. There hung the cut end of the rope that had let him down. He went to it and drew it into a loop under his arms and knotted it securely. Then he took hold of the slack and tugged on it strongly. After a moment, he pulled again. The rope tightened. High above, at the surface of the ground, they were pulling to lift him.

He hung limp in the noose, barely clutching the torch in his left hand and dangling the sword from his right wrist. He was more weary than he had had time to realize, and he felt blistered and singed from where Fith had touched him. It seemed to take far longer to be drawn up than it had taken to be let down.

They were all there at the top, the Nephol. Enek put out a hand to Kardios, then drew it back. "Fith burned you," he said.

"He scorched me here and there, but I killed him," announced Kardios, and mustered his grin with it. "He was all you said he was, and more. Killing him, I felt sorry for him a little—that foreign thing, alone and hungry and hunting. But fighting men should be careful about being sorry. Anyway, he's dead, fading into nothing down there. Close up that hole again. This time it will stay closed."

"How did you fight him?" asked Yod.

"As I've fought you, getting out of his way and countering. That's how I'd beat you."

"Of course you could beat me," Yod grated, as though the words were dragged out of him. "How could I raise a hand to you now?"

"How, indeed?" wondered Kardios. "You and I are friends."

They wanted to carry Kardios in triumph back to the caves, but he would not let them. In the space before the bluff, the giant women gathered to anoint his scald-like wounds with pleasant balms. Jipi brought him another stone bottle of what was the best wine Kardios had tasted among the Nephol. When the night came down, all sat fearlessly in the open. They sang, like gigantic birds.

"You may live among us as long as you like, Kardios," said Enek, presiding over a supper cooked on a dozen fires. "Since Atlantis is gone, let this be your home. You will be chief, as I am. All of us will bow to you."

"That's why I'd better be going somewhere else," said Kardios. "You and I talked about religion yesterday evening, discussed how sometimes ordinary things get to be gods. I don't feel ambitions to be bowed to. Bowing to someone grows into stranger notions about holiness and supreme powers and so on."

"But where will you go?" asked Yod, gnawing the thigh bone of a boar. "We can't tell you much of the countries to inland, except that there are small peoples, like you."

"I'll have to find out for you."

"The sword is yours, as we agreed," said Enek.

That night Kardios slept the sleep of exhaustion and triumph. In the morning the women brought the garments they had made. There was a short tunic of blue with white points, that fitted him as though made to his measure, and a cape of soft black wool worked with gold. He put these things on and Enek offered him the sword, for which overnight had been made a bronze-studded leather scabbard and a belt just right for Kardios's lean waist.

"You'll need provisions," said Jipi, fetching a pouch with a band to sling it to the shoulders. "Here are bread and roast meat and dried fruit. And this flask, you liked our wine. Drink on your journey, and remember us as friends."

There was no visible trail inland. Kardios said his farewells and struck out across a field shagged with coarse grass. On the far side, under the shade of a belt of trees, he stopped and turned.

The Nephol stood back there, a throng of huge men and women, with big children among them. Enek towered to the front of them. When he saw that Kardios was looking, he raised his mighty hand as though in blessing. The other Nephol flung up their hands, too, a forest of hands.

Kardios waved back to them, full-armed. His heart felt all the warmer as he plunged in among the unknown trees.

The sword he had won jogged against his thigh as he strode. He dropped his hand to the hilt. That hilt fitted his hand as though made for it. And who could say? Perhaps it had been made for his hand, in readiness for what it had done for him and the Nephol against Fith, in readiness for what it would do in future. No man was alone and friendless if he had a proper sword.

Walking past the trunks. Kardios felt a happy surge of expectation within him, a sense of adventure perhaps waiting in the next clearing. He began to hum a tune. He hummed it again, until he had the melody and the tempo to suit the words he was putting together in his mind. At last he began to sing:

"My sword, what wonders shall we twain not do?
The world is ours, to roam and render clean.
Against whatever peril comes in view
My arm is strong, your point and edge are keen.

"For storming citadels, for holding clear
From soil and sloth, for glory in the sun,
For showing enemies the face of fear,
My good companion, you and I are one."

HE WHO SHRANK

by Henry Hasse

During a career which spanned more than a third of a century, Henry Hasse produced three SF novels and more than thirty shorter stories, with the bulk of his work appearing in the 1940s and 1950s.

Today, he is remembered for two things: for this wondrous novelette of a man shrinking into infinitely smaller universes (based on the fallacious ninteenth-century ideas of Nicholas Odger) and for having coauthored Ray Bradbury's first short story ("Pendulum," 1941).

Years, centuries, aeons, have fled past me in endless parade, leaving me unscathed: for I am deathless, and in all the universe alone of my kind. Universe? Strange how that convenient word leaps instantly to my mind from force of old habit. Universe? The merest expression of a puny idea in the minds of those who cannot possibly conceive whereof they speak. The word is a mockery. Yet how glibly men utter it! How little do they realize the artificiality of the word!

That night when the Professor called me to him he was standing close to the curved transparent wall of the astrono-laboratory looking out into the blackness. He heard me enter, but did not look around as he spoke. I do not know whether he was addressing me or not.

"They called me the greatest scientist the world has had in all time."

I had been his only assistant for years, and was accustomed to his moods, so I did not speak. Neither did he for several moments and then he continued:

"Only a half year ago I discovered a principle that will be the means of utterly annihilating every kind of disease germ. And only recently I turned over to others the principles of a new toxin which stimulates the worn-out protoplasmic life-cells, causing almost complete rejuvenation. The combined results should nearly double the ordinary life span. Yet these two things are only incidental in the long list of discoveries I have made to the great benefit of the race."

He turned then and faced me, and I was surprised at a new peculiar glow that lurked deep in his eyes.

"And for these things they call me great! For these puny discoveries they heap honors on me and call me the benefactor of the race. They disgust me, the fools! Do they think I did it for them? Do they think I care about the race, what it does or what happens to it or how long it lives? They do not suspect that all the things I have given them were but accidental discoveries on my part—to which I gave hardly a thought. Oh, you seem amazed. Yet not even you, who have assisted me here for ten years, ever suspected that all my labors and experiments were pointed toward one end, and one end alone."

He went over to a locked compartment which in earlier years I had wondered about and then ceased to wonder about, as I became engrossed in my work. The professor opened it now, and I glimpsed but the usual array of bottles and test-tubes and vials. One of these vials he lifted gingerly from the rack.

"And at last I have attained the end," he almost whispered, holding the tube aloft. A pale liquid scintillated eerily against the artificial light in the ceiling. "Thirty years, long years, of ceaseless experimenting, and now, here in my hand—success!"

The Professor's manner, the glow deep in his dark eyes, the submerged enthusiasm that seemed at every instant about to leap out, all served to impress me deeply. It must indeed be an immense thing he had done, and I ventured to say as much.

"Immense!" he exclaimed. "Immense! Why—why it's so immense that—. But wait. Wait. You shall see for yourself."

At that time how little did I suspect the significance of his words. I was indeed to see for myself.

Carefully he replaced the vial, then walked over to the transparent wall again.

"Look!" He gestured toward the night sky. "The unknown! Does it not fascinate you? The other fools dream of some day traveling out there among the stars. They think they will go out there and learn the secret of the universe. But as yet they have been baffled by the problem of a sufficiently powerful fuel or force for their ships. And they are blind. Within a month *I* could solve the puny difficulty that confronts them; could, but I won't. Let them search, let them experiment, let them waste their lives away, what do I care about them?"

I wondered what he was driving at, but realized that he would come to the point in his own way. He went on:

"And suppose they do solve the problem, suppose they do leave the planet, go to other worlds in their hollow ships, what will it profit them? Suppose that they travel with the speed of light for their own lifetime, and then land on a star at that point, the farthest point away from here that is possible for them? They would no doubt say: 'We can now realize as never before the truly staggering expanse of the universe. It is indeed a great structure, the universe. We have traveled a far distance; we must be on the fringe of it.'

"Thus they would believe. Only I would know how wrong they were, for I can sit here and look through this telescope and see stars that are fifty and sixty times as distant as that upon which they landed. Comparatively, their star would be infinitely close to us. The poor deluded fools and their dreams of space travel!"

"But, Professor," I interposed, "just think—"

"Wait! Now listen. I, too, have long desired to fathom the

universe, to determine what it is, the manner and the purpose
and the secret of its creation. Have you ever stopped to
wonder *what* the universe is? For thirty years I have worked
for the answer to those questions. Unknowing, you helped me
with your efficiency on the strange experiments I assigned to
you at various times. Now I have the answer in that vial, and
you shall be the only one to share the secret with me."

Incredulous, I again tried to interrupt.

"Wait!" he said. "Let me finish. There was the time when
I also looked to the stars for the answer. I built my telescope,
on a new principle of my own. I searched the depths of the
void. I made vast calculations. And I proved conclusively to
my own mind what had theretofore been only a theory. I
know now without doubt that this our planet and other planets
revolving about the sun, are but electons of an atom, of
which the sun is the nucleus. And our sun is but one of
millions of others, each with its alotted number of planets,
each system being an atom just as our own is in reality.

"And all these millions of solar systems, or atoms, taken
together in one group, form a galaxy. As you know, there are
countless numbers of these galaxies throughout space, with
tremendous stretches of space between them. And what are
these galaxies? Molecules! They extend through space even
beyond the farthest range of my telescope! But having penetrated that far, it is not difficult to make the final step.

"All of these far-flung galaxies, or molecules, taken together as a whole, form—what? Some indeterminable element or substance on a great, ultramacrocosmic world! Perhaps
a minute drop of water, or a grain of sand, or wisp of smoke,
or—good God!—an eyelash of some creature living on that
world!"

I could not speak. I felt myself grow faint at the thought he
had propounded. I tried to think it could not be—yet what did
I or anyone know about the infinite stretches of space that
must exist beyond the ranges of our most powerful telescope?

"It can't be!" I burst out. "It's incredible, it's—monstrous!"

"Monstrous? Carry it a step further. May not that ultra-
world *also* be an electron whirling around the nucleus of an

atom? And that atom only one of millions forming a molecule? And that molecule only one of millions forming—"

"For God's sake, stop!" I cried. "I refuse to believe that such a thing can be! Where would it all lead? Where would it end? It might go on—forever! And besides," I added lamely, "what has all this to do with—your discovery, the fluid you showed me?"

"Just this. I soon learned that it was useless to look to the infinitely large; so I turned to the infinitely small. For does it not follow that if such a state of creation exists in the stars above us, it must exist identically in the atoms below us?"

I saw his line of reasoning, but still did not understand. His next words fully enlightened me, but made me suspect that I was facing one who had gone insane from his theorizing. He went on eagerly, his voice the voice of a fanatic:

"If I could not pierce the stars above, that were so far, then I would pierce the atoms below, that were so near. They are everywhere. In every object I touch and in the very air I breathe. But they are minute, and to reach them I must find a way to make myself as minute as they are, and more so! This I have done. The solution I showed you will cause every individual atom in my body to *contract*, but each electron and proton will also decrease in size, or diameter, in direct proportion to my own shrinkage! Thus will I not only be able to become the size of an atom, but can go down, down into infinite smallness!"

II

When he had stopped speaking I said calmly: "You are mad."

He was imperturbed. "I expected you to say that," he answered. "It is only natural that that should be your reaction to all that I have said. But no, I am not mad, it is merely that you are unacquainted with the marvelous propensities of 'Shrinx.' But I promised that you should see for yourself, and that you shall. You shall be the first to go down into the atomic universe."

My original opinion in regard to his state of mind remained unshaken.

"I am sure you mean well, Professor," I said, "but I must decline your offer."

He went on as though I hadn't spoken:

"There are several reasons why I want to send you before I myself make the trip. In the first place, once you make the trip there can be no returning, and there are a number of points I want to be quite clear on. You will serve as my advance guard, so to speak."

"Professor, listen. I do not doubt that the stuff you call 'Shrinx' has very remarkable properties. I will even admit that it will do all you say it will do. But for the past month you have worked day and night, with scarcely enough time out for food and hardly any sleep at all. You should take a rest, get away from the laboratory for a while."

"I shall keep in contact with your consciousness," he said, "through a very ingenious device I have perfected. I will explain it to you later. The "Shrinx' is introduced directly into the bloodstream. Shortly thereafter your shrinkage should begin, and continue at moderate speed, never diminishing in the least degree so long as the blood continues to flow in your body. At least, I hope it never diminishes. Should it, I shall have to make the necessary alterations in the formula. All this is theoretical of course, but I am sure it will all work according to schedule, and quite without harm."

I had now lost all patience. "See here, Professor," I said crossly, "I refuse to be the object of any of your wild-sounding experiments. You should realize that what you propose to do is scientifically impossible. Go home and rest—or go away for a while—"

Without the slightest warning he leaped at me, snatching an object from the table. Before I could take a backward step I felt a needle plunge deep into my arm, and cried out with the pain of it. Things became hazy, distorted. A wave of vertigo swept over me. Then it passed, and my vision cleared. The Professor stood leering before me.

"Yes, I've worked hard and I'm tired. I've worked thirty years, but I'm not tired enough nor fool enough to quit this thing now, right on the verge of the climax!"

His leer of triumph gave way to an expression almost of sympathy.

"I am sorry it had to come about this way," he said, "but I saw that you would never submit otherwise. I really am ashamed of you. I didn't think you would doubt the truth of my statements to the extent of really believing me insane. But to be safe I prepared your allotment of the 'Shrinx' in advance, and had it ready; it is now coursing through your veins, and it should be but a short time before we observe the effects. What you saw in the vial is for myself when I am ready to make the trip. Forgive me for having to administer yours in such an undignified manner."

So angered was I at the utter disregard he had shown for my personal feelings, that I hardly heard his words. My arm throbbed fiercely where the needle had plunged in. I tried to take a step toward him, but not a muscle would move. I struggled hard to break the paralysis that was upon me, but could not move a fraction of an inch from where I stood.

The Professor seemed surprised too, and alarmed.

"What, paralysis? That is an unforeseen circumstance! You see, it is even as I said: the properties of 'Shrinx' are marvelous and many."

He came close and peered intently into my eyes, and seemed relieved.

"However, the effect is only temporary," he assured me. Then added: "But you will likely be a bit smaller when the use of your muscles returns, for your shrinkage should begin very shortly now. I must hurry to prepare for the final step."

He walked past me, and I heard him open his private cupboard again. I could not speak, much less move, and I was indeed in a most uncomfortable, not to mention undignified, position. All I could do was to glare at him when he came around in front of me again. He carried a curious kind of helmet with ear-pieces and goggles attached, and a number of wires running from it. This he placed upon the table and connected the wires to a small flat box there.

All the while I watched him closely. I hadn't the least idea what he was going to do with me, but never for a moment did

I believe that I would shrink into an atomic universe; that was altogether too fantastic for my conception.

As though reading my thought the Professor turned and faced me. He looked me over casually for a moment and then said:

"I believe it has begun already. Yes, I am sure of it. Tell me, do you not feel it? Do not things appear a trifle larger to you, a trifle taller? Ah, I forgot that the paralyzing effect does not permit you to answer. But look at me—do I not seem taller?"

I looked at him. Was it my imagination, or some kind of hypnosis he was asserting on me, that made me think he was growing slightly, ever so slightly, upward even as I looked?

"Ah!" he said triumphantly. "You have noticed. I can tell it by your eyes. However, it is not I who am growing taller, but you who are shrinking."

He grasped me by the arms and turned me about to face the wall. "I can see that you doubt," he said, "so look! The border on the wall. If you remember, it used to be about even with your eyes. Now it is fully three inches higher."

It was true! And I could now feel a tingling in my veins, and a slight dizziness.

"Your shrinkage has not quite reached the maximum speed," he went on. "When it does, it will remain constant. I could not stop it now even if I wanted to, for I have nothing to counteract it. Listen closely now, for I have several things to tell you.

"When you have become small enough I am going to lift you up and place you on this block of Rehyllium-X here on the table. You will become smaller and smaller, and eventually should enter an alien universe consisting of billions and billions of star groups, or galaxies, which are only the molecules in this Rehyllium-X. When you burst through, your size in comparison with this new universe should be gigantic. However, you will constantly diminish, and will be enabled to alight on any one of the spheres of your own choosing. And—after alighting—you will continue—always down!"

At the concept I thought I would go mad. Already I had

become fully a foot shorter, and still the paralysis gripped me. Could I have moved I would have torn the Professor limb from limb in my impotent rage—though if what he said was true, I was already doomed.

Again it seemed as though he read my mind.

"Do not think too harshly of me," he said. "You should be very grateful for this opportunity, for you are going on a marvelous venture, into a marvelous realm. Indeed, I am almost jealous that you should be the first. But with this," he indicated the helmet and box on the table, "I shall keep contact with you no matter how far you go. Ah, I see by your eyes that you wonder how such a thing could be possible. Well, the principle of this device is really very simple. Just as light is a form of energy, so is thought. And just as light travels through an 'ether' in the form of waves, so does thought. But the thought waves are much more intangible—in fact, invisible. Nevertheless the waves are there, and the coils in this box are so sensitized as to receive and amplify them a million times, much as sound waves might be amplified. Through this helmet I will receive but two of your six sensations: those of sound and sight. They are the two major ones, and will be sufficient for my purpose. Every sight and sound that you encounter, no matter how minute, reaches your brain and displaces tiny molecules there that go out in the form of thought waves and finally reach here and are amplified. Thus my brain receives every impression of sight and sound that your brain sends out."

I did not doubt now that his marvelous "Shrinx" would do everything he said it would do. Already I was but one-third of my original size. Still the paralysis showed no sign of releasing me, and I hoped that the Professor knew whereof he spoke when he said the effect would be but temporary. My anger had subsided somewhat, and I think I began to wonder what I would find in that other universe.

Then a terrifying thought assailed me—a thought that left me cold with apprehension. If, as the Professor had said, the atomic universe was but a tiny replica of the universe we knew, would I not find myself in the vast empty spaces between the galaxies *with no air to breathe?* In all the vast calculations the Professor had made, could he have overlooked such an obvious point?

Now I was very close to the floor, scarcely a foot high. Everything about me—the Professor, the tables, the walls—were gigantically out of proportion to myself.

The Professor reached down then, and swung me up on the table top amidst the litter of wires and apparatus. He began speaking again, and to my tiny ears his voice sounded a deeper note.

"Here is the block of Rehyllium-X containing the universe you soon will fathom," he said, placing on the table beside me the square piece of metal, which was nearly half as tall as I was. "As you know, Rehyllium-X is the densest of all known metals, so the universe awaiting you should be a comparatively dense one—though you will not think so, with the thousands of light-years of space between stars. Of course I know no more about this universe than you do, but I would advise you to avoid the very bright stars and approach only the dimmer ones. Well, this is good-by, then. We shall never see each other again. Even should I follow you—as I certainly shall as soon as I have learned through you what alterations I should make in the formula—it is impossible that I could exactly trace your course down through all the spheres that you will have traversed. One thing already I have learned: the rate of shrinkage is too rapid; you will be able to stay on a world for only a few hours. But perhaps that is best, after all. This is good-by for all time."

He picked me up and placed me upon the smooth surface of the Rehyllium-X. I judged that I must be about four inches tall then. It was with immeasurable relief that I finally felt the paralysis going away. The power of my voice returned first, and expanding my lungs I shouted with all my might.

"Professor!" I shouted. "Professor!"

He bent down over me. To him my voice must have sounded ridiculously high pitched.

"What about the empty regions of space I will find myself in?" I asked a bit tremulously, my mouth close to his ear. "I would last but a few minutes. My life will surely be snuffed out.''

"No, that will not happen," he answered. His voice beat upon my eardrums like thunder, and I placed my hands over my ears.

He understood, and spoke more softly. "You will be quite safe in airless space," he went on. "In the thirty years I have worked on the problem, I would not be likely to overlook that point—though I will admit it gave me much trouble. But as I said, 'Shrinx' is all the more marvelous in the fact that its qualities are many. After many difficulties and failures, I managed to instill in it a certain potency by which it supplies sufficient oxygen for your need, distributed through the bloodstream. It also irradiates a certain amount of heat; and, inasmuch as I consider the supposed subzero temperature of space as being somewhat exaggerated, I don't think you need worry about any discomfort in open space.''

III

I was scarcely over an inch in height now. I could walk about, though my limbs tingled fiercely as the paralysis left. I beat my arms against my sides and swung them about to speed the circulation. The Professor must have thought I was waving good-by. His hand reached out and he lifted me up. Though he tried to handle me gently, the pressure of his fingers bruised. He held me in his open hand and raised me up to the level of his eyes. He looked at me for a long moment and then I saw his lips form the words "good-by." I was terribly afraid he would drop me to the floor a dizzy distance below, and I was relieved when he lowered me again and I slid off his hand to the block of Rehyllium-X.

The Professor now appeared as a giant towering hundreds of feet into the air, and beyond him, seemingly miles away, the walls of the room extended to unimaginable heights. The ceiling above seemed as far away and expansive as the dome of the sky I had formerly known. I ran to the edge of the block and peered down. It was as though I stood at the top of a high cliff. The face of it was black and smooth, absolutely perpendicular. I stepped back apace lest I lose my footing and fall to my death. Far below extended the vast smooth plain of the table top.

I walked back to the center of the block, for I was afraid of the edge; I might be easily shaken off if the Professor were to accidentally jar the table. I had no idea of my size now, for there was nothing with which I could compare it. For all I knew I might be entirely invisible to the Professor. He was now but an indistinguishable blur, like a far-off mountain seen through a haze.

I now began to notice that the surface of the Rehyllium-X block was not as smooth as it had been. As far as I could see were shallow ravines, extending in every direction. I realized that these must be tiny surface scratches that had been invisible before.

I was standing on the edge of one of these ravines, and I clambered down the side and began to walk along it. It was as straight as though laid by a ruler. Occasionally I came to intersecting ravines, and turned to the left or right. Before long, due to my continued shrinkage, the walls of these ravines towered higher than my head, and it was as though I walked along a narrow path between two cliffs.

Then I received the shock of my life, and my adventure came near to ending right there. I approached one of the intersections. I turned the sharp corner to the right. I came face to face with the How-Shall-I-Describe-It.

It was a sickly bluish white in color. Its body was disc-shaped, with a long double row of appendages—legs—on the underside. Hundreds of ugly-looking spikes rimmed the disk body on the outer and upper edges. There was no head and apparently no organ of sight, but dozens of snakelike protuberances waved in my face as I nearly crashed into it. One of them touched me and the creature backed swiftly away, the spikes springing stiffly erect in formidable array.

This impression of the creature flashed upon my mind in the merest fraction of time, for you may be sure that I didn't linger there to take stock of its pedigree. No indeed. My heart choked me in my fright; I whirled and sped down the opposite ravine. The sound of the thing's pursuit lent wings to my feet, and I ran as I had never run before. Up one ravine and down another I sped, doubling to right and left in my effort to lose my pursuer. The irony of being pursued by a germ occurred to me, but the matter was too serious to be funny. I ran until I was out of breath, but no matter which way I turned and doubled the germ was always a hundred paces behind me. Its organ of sound must have been highly sensitive. At last I could run no more, and I darted around the next corner and stopped, gasping for breath.

The germ rushed a short distance past me and stopped, having lost the sound of my running. Its dozens of tentacular sound organs waved in all directions. Then it came unhesitatingly toward me, and again I ran. Apparently it had caught the sound of my heavy breathing. Again I dashed around the next corner, and as I heard the germ approach I held my breath until I thought my lungs would burst. It stopped again, waved its tentacles in the air and then ambled on down the ravine. Silently I sneaked a hasty retreat.

Now the walls of these ravines (invisible scratches on a piece of metal!) towered very high above me as I continued to shrink. Now too I noticed narrow chasms and pits all around me, in both the walls at the sides and the surface on which I walked. All of these seemed very deep, and some were so wide that I had to leap across them.

At first I was unable to account for these spaces that were opening all about me, and then I realized with a sort of shock that the Rehyllium-X was becoming *porous*, so small was I in size! Although it was the densest of all known metals, no substance whatsoever could be so dense as to be an absolute solid.

I began to find it increasingly difficult to progress; I had to get back and make running jumps across the spaces. Finally I sat down and laughed as I realized the futility and stupidity of this. Why was I risking my life by jumping across these spaces that were becoming wider as I became smaller, when I had no particular destination anyway—except down. So I may as well stay in one spot.

No sooner had I made this decision, however, than something changed my mind.

It was the germ again.

I saw it far down the ravine, heading straight for me. It might have been the same one I had encountered before, or its twin brother. But now I had become so small that it was fully fifteen times my own size, and very sight of the huge beast ambling toward me inspired terror into my heart. Once more I ran, praying that it wouldn't hear the sound of my flight because of my small size.

Before I had gone a hundred yards I stopped in dismay. Before me yawned a space so wide that I couldn't have leaped half the distance. There was escape on neither side, for the chasm extended up both the walls. I looked back. The germ had stopped. Its mass of tentacles was waving close to the ground.

Then it came on, not at an amble now but at a much faster rate. Whether it had heard me or had sensed my presence in some other manner, I did not know. Only one thing was apparent: I had but a few split seconds in which to act. I threw myself down flat, slid backward into the chasm, and hung there by my hands.

And I was just in time. A huge shape rushed overhead as I looked up. So big was the germ that the chasm which had appeared so wide to me, was inconsequential to it; it ran over the space as though it weren't there. I saw the double row of the creature's limbs as they flashed overhead. Each one was twice the size of my body.

Then happened what I had feared. One of the huge claw-like limbs came down hard on my hand, and a sharp spur raked across it. I could feel the pain all through my arm. The anguish was insufferable. I tried to get a better grip but couldn't. My hold loosened. I dropped down—down—

IV

"This is the end."

Such was my thought in that last awful moment as I slipped away into space. Involuntarily I shut my eyes, and I expected at any moment to crash into oblivion.

But nothing happened.

There was not even the usual sickening sensation that accompanies acceleration. I opened my eyes to a Stygian darkness, and put out an exploring hand. It encountered a rough wall which was flashing upward past my face. I was falling, then; but at no such speed as would have been the case under ordinary circumstances. This was rather as if I were floating downward. Or was it downward? I had lost all sense of up or down or sideways. I doubled my limbs under me and kicked out hard against the wall, shoving myself far away from it.

How long I remained falling—or drifting—there in that darkness I have no way of knowing. But it must have been minutes, and every minute I was necessarily growing smaller.

For some time I had been aware of immense masses all around me. They pressed upon me from every side, and from them came a very faint radiance. They were of all sizes, some no larger than myself and some looming up large as mountains. I tried to steer clear of the large ones, for I had no desire to be crushed between two of them. But there was little chance of that. Although we all drifted slowly along through space together, I soon observed that none of these masses ever approached each other or deviated the least bit from their paths.

As I continued to shrink, these masses seemed to spread out, away from me; and as they spread, the light which they exuded became brighter. They ceased to be masses, and became swirling, expanding, individual stretches of mist, milky white.

They were nebulae! Millions of miles of space must stretch between each of them! The gigantic mass I had clung to, drawn there by its gravity, also underwent this nebulosity, and now I was floating in the midst of an individual nebula. It spread out as I became smaller, and as it thinned and expanded, what had seemed mist now appeared as trillions and trillions of tiny spheres in intricate patterns.

I was in the very midst of these spheres! They were all around my feet, my arms, my head! They extended farther than I could reach, farther than I could see. I could have reached out and gathered thousands of them in my hand. I could have stirred and kicked my feet and scattered them in chaotic confusion about me. But I did not indulge in such reckless and unnecessary destruction of worlds. Doubtless my presence here had already done damage enough, displacing millions of them.

I scarcely dared to move a muscle for fear of disrupting the orbits of some of the spheres or wreaking havoc among some solar systems or star groups. I seemed to be hanging motionless among them, or if I were moving in any direction, the motion was too slight to be noticeable. I didn't even know if I were horizontal or vertical, as those two terms had lost all meaning.

As I became smaller, of course the spheres became larger and the space between them expanded, so that the bewildering maze thinned somewhat and gave me more freedom of movement.

I took more cognizance now of the beauty around me. I remembered what the Professor had said about receiving my thought waves, and I hoped he was tuned in now, for I wouldn't have had him miss it for anything.

Every hue I had ever known was represented there among the suns and encircling planets: dazzling whites, reds, yellows, blues, greens, violets, and every intermediate shade. I glimpsed also the barren blackness of suns that had burnt out; but these were infrequent, as this seemed to be a very young universe.

There were single suns with the orbital planets varying in number from two to twenty. There were double suns that revolved slowly about each other as an invisible axis. There were triple suns that revolved slowly about one another—strange as it may seem—in perfect trihedral symmetry. I saw one quadruple sun: a dazzling white, a blue, a green, and a deep orange. The white and the blue circled each other on the horizontal plane while the green and the orange circled on the vertical plane, thus forming a perfect interlocking system. Around these four suns, in circular orbits, sped sixteen planets of varying size, the smallest on the inner orbits and the largest on the outer. The effect was a spinning, concave disc with the white-blue-green-orange rotating hub in the center. The rays from these four suns, as they bathed the rolling planets and were reflected back into space in many-hued magnificence, presented a sight both beautiful and weird.

I, determined to alight on one of the planets of this quadruple sun as soon as my size permitted, did not find it hard to maneuver to a certain extent; and eventually, when I had become much smaller, I stretched alongside this solar system, my length being as great as the diameter of the orbit of the outermost planet! Still I dared not come too close, for fear the gravity of my bulk would cause some tension in the orbital field.

I caught glimpses of the surface of the outer, or sixteenth planet, as it swung past me. Through rifts in the great billowing clouds I saw vast expanses of water, but no land; and then the planet was moving away from me, on its long journey around to the other side of the suns. I did not doubt that by the time it returned to my side I would be very much smaller, so I decided to move in a little closer and try to get a look at the fifteenth planet which was then on the opposite side but swinging around in my direction.

I had discovered that if I doubled up my limbs and thrust out violently in a direction opposite that in which I wished to move, I could make fairly good progress, though the effort was somewhat strenuous. In this manner I moved inward toward the sun-cluster, and by the time I had reached the approximate orbit of the fifteenth planet I had become much smaller—was scarcely one-third as long as the diameter of its orbit! The distance between the orbits of the sixteenth and fifteenth planets must have been about 2,500,000,000 miles, according to the old standards I had known; but to me the distance had seemed but a few hundred yards.

I waited there, and finally the planet hove into view from out of the glorious aurora of the suns. Nearer and nearer it swung in its circle, and as it approached I saw that its atmosphere was very clear, a deep saffron color. It passed me a scant few yards away, turning lazily on its axis opposite the direction of flight. Here, too, as on planet sixteen, I saw a vast world of water. There was only one fairly large island and many scattered small ones, but I judged that fully nine-tenths of the surface area was ocean.

I moved on in to planet fourteen, which I had noticed was a beautiful golden-green color.

By the time I had maneuvered to the approximate four-teenth orbit I had become so small that the light of the central suns pained my eyes. When the planet came in sight I could easily see several large continents on the lighted side; and as the dark side turned to the suns, several more continents became visible. As it swung past me I made comparisons and observed that I was now about five times as large as the planet. When it came around again I would try to effect a landing. To attempt a contact with it now would likely prove disastrous to both it and myself.

As I waited there and became smaller my thoughts turned to the Professor. If his amazing theory of an infinite number of sub-universes was true, then my adventure had hardly begun; wouldn't begin until I alighted on the planet. What would I find there? I did not doubt that the Professor, receiving my thought waves, was just as curious as I. Suppose there was life on this world—hostile life? I would face the dangers while the Professor sat in his laboratory far away. This was the first time that aspect of it occurred to me; it had probably never occurred to the Professor. Strange, too, how I thought of him as "far away." Why, he could merely have reached out his hand and moved me, universe and all, on his labora-tory table!

Another curious thought struck me: here I was waiting for a planet to complete its circle around the suns. To any beings who might exist on it, the elapsed time would represent a year; but to me it would only be a number of minutes.

At that, it returned sooner than I expected it, curving around to meet me. Its orbit, of course, was much smaller than those of the two outer planets. More minutes passed as it came closer and larger. As nearly as I could judge I was about one-fifth its size now. It skimmed past me, so closely that I could have reached out and brushed its atmosphere.

And as it moved away I could feel its steady tugging, much as if I were a piece of metal being attracted to a magnet. Its speed did not decelerate in the least, but now I was moving along close behind it. It had "captured" me, just as I had hoped it would. I shoved in closer, and the gravity became a steady and stronger pull. I was "falling" toward it. I swung around so that my feet were closest to it, and they entered the atmosphere, where the golden-green touched the blackness of space. They swung down in a long arc and touched something solid. My "fall" toward the planet ceased. I was standing on one of the continents of this world.

V

So tall was I that the greatest part of my body still extended out into the blackness of space. In spite of the fact that the four suns were the distance of thirteen orbits away, they were of such intense brilliance now that to look directly at them would surely have blinded me. I looked far down my tapering length at the continent on which I stood. Even the multicolored light reflected from the surface was dazzling to the eye. Too late I remembered the Professor's warning to avoid the brighter suns. Close to the surface a few fleeting wisps of cloud drifted about my limbs.

As the planet turned slowly on its axis I of course moved with it, and shortly I found myself on the side away from the suns, in the planet's shadow. I was thankful for this relief—but it was only temporary. Soon I swung around into the blinding light again. Then into the shadow, and again into the light. How many times this happened I do not know, but at last I was entirely within the planet's atmosphere; here the rays of the sun were diffused, and the light less intense.

Miles below I could see but a vast expanse of yellow surface, stretching unbroken in every direction. As I looked far behind the curving horizon it seemed that I caught a momentary glimpse of tall, silvery towers of some far-off city; but I could not be sure, and when I looked again it had vanished.

I kept my eyes on that horizon, however, and soon two tiny red specks became visible against the yellow of the plain.

Evidently they were moving toward me very rapidly, for even as I looked they became larger, and soon took shape as two blood-red spheres. Immediately I visioned them as some terrible weapons of warfare or destruction.

But as they came close to me and swerved up to where I towered high in the thin atmosphere, I could see that they were not solid at all, as I had supposed, but were gaseous, and translucent to a certain extent. Furthermore, they behaved in a manner that hinted strongly of intelligence. Without visible means of propulsion they swooped and circled about my head, to my utter discomfiture. When they came dangerously close to my eyes I raised my hand to sweep them away, but they darted quickly out of reach.

They did not approach me again, but remained there close together, pulsating in midair. This queer pulsating of their tenuous substance gave me the impression that they were conferring together; and of course I was the object of their conference. Then they darted away in the direction whence they had come.

My curiosity was as great as theirs had seemed to be, and without hesitation I set out in the same direction. I must have covered nearly a mile at each step, but even so, these gaseous entities easily outdistanced me and were soon out of sight. I had no doubt that their destination was the city—if indeed it were a city I had glimpsed. The horizon was closer now and less curved, due to my decrease in height; I judged that I was barely five or six hundred feet tall now.

I had taken but a few hundred steps in the direction the two spheres had gone, when to my great surprise I saw them coming toward me again, this time accompanied by a score of—companions. I stopped in my tracks, and soon they came close and circled about my head. They were all about five feet in diameter, and of the same dark red color. For a minute they darted about as though studying me from every angle; then they systematically arranged themselves in a perfect circle around me. Thin streamers emanated from them, and merged, linking them together and closing the circle. Then other streamers reached slowly out toward me, wavering, cautious.

This, their manner of investigation, did not appeal to me in the least, and I swept my arms around furiously. Instantly all was wild confusion. The circle broke and scattered, the streamers snapped back and they were spheres again. They gathered in a group a short distance away and seemed to consider.

One, whose color had changed to a bright orange, darted apart from them and pulsated rapidly. As clearly as though words had been spoken, I comprehended. The bright orange color signified anger, and he was rebuking the others for their cowardice.

Led by the orange sphere they again moved closer to me; this time they had a surprise for me. A score of streamers flashed out quick as lightning, and cold blue flames spluttered where they touched me. Electric shocks ran through my arms, rendering them numb and helpless. Again they formed their circle around me, again the streamers emerged and completed the circle, and other streamers reached out caressingly. For a moment they flickered about my head, then merged, enveloping it in a cold red radiance. I felt no sensation at all at the touch, except that of cold.

The spheres began to pulsate again in the manner I had observed before, and immediately this pulsating began I felt tiny needlepoints of ice pierce my brain. A question became impinged upon my consciousness more clearly than would have been possible by spoken word:

"Where do you come from?"

I was familiar with thought transference, had even practiced it to a certain extent, very often with astonishing success. When I heard—or received—that question, I tried hard to bring every atom of my consciousness to bear upon the circumstances that were the cause of my being there. When I had finished my mental narration and my mind relaxed from the tension I had put upon it, I received the following impressions:

"We receive no answer; your mind remains blank. You are alien, we have never encountered another of your oganism here. A most peculiar organism indeed is one that becomes steadily smaller without apparent reason. Why are you here, and where do you come from?'' The icy fingers probed deeper and deeper into my brain, seeming to tear it tissue from tissue.

Again I tried, my mind focusing with the utmost clearness upon every detail, picturing my course from the very minute I entered the Professor's laboratory to the present time. When I finished I was exhausted from the effort.

Again I received the impression: ''You cannot bring your mind sufficiently into focus; we receive only fleeting shadows.''

One of the spheres again changed to a bright color, and broke from the circle. I could almost imagine an angry shrug. The streamers relaxed their hold on my brain and began to withdraw—but not before I caught the fleeting impression from the orange one, who was apparently addressing the others: ''—very low mentality.''

''You're not so much yourself!'' I said aloud. But of course such a crude method of speech did not register upon them. I wondered at my inability to establish thought communication with these beings. Either my brain was of such a size as to prevent them from receiving the impression (remember I was still a four or five-hundred-foot giant on this world), or their state of mentality was indeed so much higher than mine, that I was, to them, lower than the lowest savage. Possibly both, more probably the latter.

But they were determined to solve the mystery of my presence before I passed from their world, as I would surely do in a few hours at my rate of shrinkage. Their next move was to place themselves on each side of me in vertical rows extending from far down near the ground up to my shoulders. Again the luminous ribbons reached out and touched me at the various points. Then as at a given signal they rose high into the air, lifting me lightly as a feather! In perfect unison they sped toward their city beyond the horizon, carrying me perpendicularly with them! I marveled at the manner in which such gaseous entities as these could lift and propel such a material giant as myself. Their speed must have exceeded by far that of sound—though on all this planet there was no sound except the sound of my body swishing through the air.

In a very few minutes I sighted the city, which must have covered an area of a hundred miles square near the edge of a rolling green ocean. I was placed lightly on my feet at the very edge of the city, and once more the circle of spheres formed around my head and once more the cold tendrils of light probed my brain.

"You may walk at will about the city," came the thought, "accompanied by a few of us. You are to touch nothing whatever, or the penalty will be extreme; your tremendous size makes your presence here among us somewhat hazardous. When you have become much smaller we shall again explore your mind, with somewhat different method, and learn your origin and purpose. We realize that the great size of your brain was somewhat of a handicap to us in our first attempt. We go now to prepare. We have awaited your coming for years."

Leaving only a few there as my escort—or guard—the rest of the spheres sped toward a great domed building that rose from a vast plaza in the center of the city.

I was very much puzzled as to their last statement. For a moment I stood there wondering what they could have meant—"we have awaited your coming for years." Then trusting that this and other things would be answered in the due course of their investigation, I entered the city.

It was not a strange city insofar as architecture was concerned, but it was a beautiful one. I marveled that it could have been conceived and constructed by these confluent globules of gas who at first glance seemed anything but intelligent, reasoning beings. Tall as I was, the buildings towered up to four and five times my height, invariably ending in doomed roofs. There was no sign of a spire or angle as far as my eye could see; apparently they grated harshly on the senses of these beings. The entire plan of the city was of vast sweeping curves and circular patterns, and the effect was striking. There were no preconceived streets or highways, nor connecting spans between buildings, for there was no need for them. The air was the natural habitable element of this race, and I did not see a one of them ever touch and ground or any surface.

They even came to rest in midair, with a slow spinning motion. Everywhere I passed among them they paused, spinning, to observe me in apparent curiosity, then went on about their business, whatever it was. None ever approached me except my guards.

For several hours I wandered about in this manner, and finally when I was much smaller I was bade to walk toward the central plaza.

In the circular domed building the others awaited my coming, gathered about a dais surmounted by a huge oval transparent screen of glass or some similar substance. This time only one of the spheres made contact with my brain, and I received the following thought: "Watch."

The screen became opaque, and a vast field of white came into view.

"The great nebula in which this planet is but an infinitesimal speck," came the thought.

The mass drifted almost imperceptibly across the screen, and the thought continued:

"As you see it now, so it appeared to us through our telescopes centuries ago. Of course the drifting motion of the nebula as a whole was not perceptible, and what you see is a chemically recorded reproduction of the view, which has been speeded up to make the motion visible on the screen. Watch closely now."

The great mass of the nebula had been quiescent, but as I watched, it began to stir and swirl in a huge spiral motion, and a vast dark shadow was thrown across the whole scene. The shadow seemed to recede—no, grew smaller—and I could see that it was not a shadow but a huge bulk. This bulk was entering the nebula, causing it to swirl and expand as millions of stars were displaced and shoved outward.

The thought came again: "The scene has been speeded up a millionfold. The things you see taking place actually transpired over a great number of years; our scientists watched the phenomenon in great wonder, and many were the theories as to the cause of it. You are viewing yourself as you entered our nebula."

I watched in a few minutes the scene before me, as these sphere creatures had watched it over a period of years; saw myself grow smaller, gradually approach the system of the four suns and finally the gold-green planet itself. Abruptly the screen cleared.

"So we watched and waited your coming for years, not knowing what you were or whence you came. We are still very much puzzled. You become steadily smaller, and that we cannot understand. We must hurry. Relax. Do not interfere with our process by trying to think back to the beginning, as you did before; it is all laid bare to us in the recesses of your brain. Simply relax, think of nothing at all, watch the screen."

I tried to do as he said, again I felt the cold probing tendrils in my brain, and a lethargy came over my mind. Shadows flashed across the screen, then suddenly a familiar scene leaped into view: the Professor's laboratory as I had last seen it, on the night of my departure. No sooner had this scene cleared than I entered the room, exactly as I had on that night. I saw myself approach the table close behind the Professor, saw him standing as he had stood, staring out at the night sky; saw his lips move.

The spheres about me crowded close to the screen, seemed to hang intent on every motion that passed upon it, and I sensed great excitement among them. I judged that the one who was exploring my mind, if not all of them, were somehow cognizant not only of the words the Professor and I spoke in those scenes, but of their meaning as well.

I could almost read the Professor's lips as he spoke. I saw the utter amazement, then incredulity, then disbelief, on my features as he propounded his theory of macrocosmic worlds and still greater macrocosmic worlds. I saw our parley of words, and finally his lunge toward me and felt again the plunge of the needle into my arm.

As this happened the spheres around me stirred excitedly.

I saw myself become smaller, smaller, to be finally lifted onto the block of Rehyllium—X where I became still smaller and disappeared. I saw my meeting with the germ, and my wild flight; my plunge into the abyss, and my flight down through the darkness, during which time the entire screen before me became black. The screen was slightly illuminated again as I traveled along with the great masses all around me, and then gradually across the screen spread the huge nebula, the same one these sphere creatures had seen through their telescopes centuries ago. Again the screen cleared abruptly, became transparent.

"The rest we know," came the thought of the one who had searched my brain. "The rest the screen has already shown. He—the one who invented the—what he called "Shrinx'—he is a very great man. Yours has indeed been a marvelous experience, and one which has hardly begun. We envy you, lucky being; and at the same time we are sorry for you. Anyway, it is fortunate for us that you chose our planet on which to alight, but soon you will pass away even as you came, and that we cannot, and would not, prevent. In a very few minutes you will once more become of infinitesimal size and pass into a still smaller universe. We have microscopes powerful enough to permit us to barely glimpse this smaller atomic universe, and we shall watch your further progress into the unknown until you are gone from our sight forever."

I had been so interested in the familiar scenes on the screen that I had lost all conception of my steady shrinkage. I was now very much smaller than those spheres around me.

I was as interested in them as they were in me, and I tried to flash the following thought:

"You say that you envy me, and are sorry for me. Why should that be?"

The thought came back immediately: "We cannot answer that. But it is true; wonderful as are the things you will see in realms yet to come, nevertheless you are to be pitied. You cannot understand at present, but someday you will."

I flashed another thought: "Your organism, which is known to me as gaseous, seems as strange to me as mine, a solid, must seem to you. You have mentioned both telescopes and microscopes, and I cannot conceive how beings such as yourselves, without organs of sight, can number astronomy and microscopy among the sciences."

"Your own organs of sight," came back the answer, "which you call 'eyes,' are not only superfluous, but are very crude sources of perception. I think you will grant that loss of them would be a terrible and permanent handicap. Our own source of perception is not confined to any such conspicuous organs, but envelops the entire outer surface of our bodies. We have never had organs and appendages such as those with which you are endowed so profusely, for we are of different substance; we merely extend any part of our bodies in any direction at will. But from close study of your structure, we conclude that your various organs and appendages are very crude. I predict that by slow evolution of your own race, such frailties will disappear entirely."

"Tell me more about your own race," I went on eagerly.

"To tell everything there is to tell," came the answer, "would take much time; and there is little time left. We have a very high sociological system, but one which is not without its faults, of course. We have delved deep into the sciences and gone far along the lines of fine arts—but all of our accomplishments along these lines would no doubt appear very strange to you. You have seen our city. It is by no means the largest, nor the most important, on the planet. When you alighted comparatively near, reports were sent out and all of our important scientists hurried here. We were not afraid because of your presence, but rather, were cautious, for we did not know what manner of being you were. The two whom you first saw were sent to observe you. They had both been guilty of a crime against the community, and were given the choice of the punishment they deserved, or of going out to investigate the huge creature that had dropped from the sky. They accepted the latter course, and for their bravery— for it was bravery—they have been exonerated."

VI

I would have liked greatly to ask more questions, for there were many phases that puzzled me; but I was becoming so very small that further communication was impossible. I was

taken to a laboratory and placed upon the slide of a micro-
scope of strange and intricate construction and my progress
continued unabated down into a still smaller atomic universe.

The method was the same as before. The substance became
open and porous, spread out into open space dotted with the
huge masses which in turn became porous and resolved into
far-flung nebulae.

I entered one of the nebulae and once more star-systems
swung all around me. This time I approached a single sun of
bright yellow hue, around which swung eight planets. I maneuvered to the outermost one, and when my size permitted,
made contact with it.

I was now standing on an electron, one of billions forming
a microscopic slide that existed in a world which was in turn
only an electron in a block of metal on a laboratory table!

Soon I reached the atmosphere, and miles below me I
could see only wide patches of yellow and green. But as I
came nearer to the surface more of the details became discernible. Almost at my feet a wide yellow river wound
sluggishly over a vast plateau which fell suddenly away into a
long line of steep precipices. At the foot of these precipices
stretched a great green expanse of steaming jungle, and farther beyond a great ocean, smooth as green glass, curved to
the horizon. A prehistoric world of jungles and great fern-like
growths and sweltering swamps and cliffs. Not a breeze
stirred and nowhere was there sight of any living thing.

I was standing in the jungle close to the towering cliffs,
and for a half mile in every direction the trees and vegetation
were trampled into the soil where my feet had swung down
and contacted.

Now I could see a long row of caves just above a ledge
halfway up the side of the cliff. And I did not doubt that in
each cave some being was peering furtively out at me. Even
as I watched I saw a tiny figure emerge and walk out on the
ledge. He was very cautious, ready to dash back into the cave
at any sign of hostility on my part, and his eyes never left
me. Seeing that nothing happened, others took heart and
came out, and soon the ledge was lined with tiny figures who
talked excitedly among themselves and gesticulated wildly in

my direction. My coming must surely have aroused all their superstitious fears—a giant descending out of the skies to land at their very feet.

I must have been nearly a mile from the cliff, but even at that distance I could see that the figures were barbarians, squat and thick-muscled, and covered with hair; they were four-limbed and stood erect, and all carried crude weapons.

One of them raised a bow as tall as himself and let fly a shaft at me evidently as an expression of contempt or bravado, for he must have known that the shaft wouldn't reach half the distance. Immediately one who seemed a leader among them felled the miscreant with a single blow. This amused me. Evidently their creed was to leave well enough alone.

Experimentally I took a step toward them, and immediately a long line of bows sprang erect and scores of tiny shafts arched high in my direction to fall into the jungle far in front of me. A warning to keep my distance.

I could have strode forward and swept the lot of them from the ledge; but wishing to show them that my intentions were quite peaceful, I raised my hands and took several backward steps. Another futile volley of arrows. I was puzzled, and stood still; and as long as I did not move neither did they.

The one who had seemed the leader threw himself down flat and, shielding his eyes from the sun, scanned the expanse of jungle below. Then they seemed to talk among themselves again, and gestured not at me, but at the jungle. Then I comprehended. Evidently a hunting party was somewhere in that jungle which spread out around my feet—probably returning to the caves, for already it was nearing dusk, the sun casting weird conflicting streaks across the horizon. These people of the caves were in fear that I would move around too freely and perhaps trample the returning party underfoot.

So thinking, I stood quietly in the great barren patch I had leveled, and sought to peer into the dank growth below me. This was nearly impossible, however, for clouds of steam hung low over the tops of the trees.

But presently my ears caught a faint sound, as of shouting,

far below me, and then I glimpsed a long single file of the barbarian hunters running at full speed along a well-beaten game path. They burst into the very clearing in which I stood, and stopped short in surprise, evidently aware for the first time of my gigantic presence on their world. They let fall the poles upon which were strung the carcasses of the day's hunt, cast but one fearful look up to where I towered, then as one man fell flat upon the ground in abject terror.

All except one. I doubt if the one, who burst from the tangle of trees last of all, even saw me, so intent was he in glancing back into the darkness from which he fled. At any rate he aroused his companions with a few angry, guttural syllables, and pointed back along the path.

At that moment there floated up to me a roar that lingered loud and shuddering in my ears. At quick instructions from their leader the hunters picked up their weapons and formed a wide semicircle before the path where they had emerged. The limb of a large tree overhung the path at this point, and the leader clambered up some overhanging vines and was soon crouched upon it. One of the warriors fastened a vine to a large clumsy-looking weapon, and the one in the tree drew it up to him. The weapon consisted merely of a large pointed stake some eight feet long, with two heavy stones fastened securely to it at the halfway point. The one in the tree carefully balanced this weapon on the limb, directly over the path, point downward. The semicircle of hunters crouched behind stout lances set at an angle in the ground.

Another shuddering roar floated up to me, and then the beast appeared. As I caught sight of it I marveled all the more at the courage of these puny barbarians. From ground to shoulder the beast must have measured seven feet tall, and was fully twenty feet long. Each of its six legs ended in a wide, horny claw that could have ripped any of the hunters from top to bottom. Its long tapering tail was horny too, giving me the impression that the thing was at least partly reptilian; curved fangs fully two feet long, in a decidedly animal head, offset that impression, however.

For a long moment the monstrosity stood there, tail switching ceaslessly, glaring in puzzlement out upon the circle of puny beings who dared to confront it. Then, as its tail ceased switching and it tensed for the spring, the warrior on the limb above launched his weapon—launched it and came hurtling down with it, feet pressed hard against the heavy stone balance!

Whether the beast below heard some sound or whether a sixth sense warned it, I do not know; but just in time it leaped to one side with an agility belied by its great bulk, and the pointed stake drove deep into the ground, leaving the one who had ridden it lying there stunned.

The beast uttered a snarl of rage; its six legs sprawled outward, its great belly touched the ground. Then it sprang out upon the circle of crouching hunters. Lances snapped at the impact, and the circle broke and fled for the trees. But two of them never rose from the ground, and the lashing horned tail flattened another before he had taken four steps.

The scene took place in a matter of seconds as I towered there looking down upon it, fascinated. The beast whirled toward the fleeing ones and in another moment the destruction would have been terrible, for they could not possibly have reached safety.

Breaking the spell that was on me I swung my hand down in a huge arc even as the beast sprang for a second time. I slapped it in midair, flattening it against the ground as I would have flattened a bothersome insect. It did not twitch a muscle, and a dark red stain seeped outward from where it lay.

The natives stopped in their flight, for the sound of my hand when I slapped the huge animal had been loud. They jabbered noisily among themselves, but fearfully kept their distance, when they saw me crouched there over the flattened enemy who had been about to wreak destruction among them.

Only one had seen the entire happening. He who had plunged downward from the tree was only momentarily stunned: he had risen dizzily to his feet as the animal charged out among his companions, and had been witness to the whole thing.

Glancing half contemptuously at the others, he now approached me. It must have taken a great deal of courage on his part, for, crouched down as I was, I still towered above the tallest trees. He looked for a moment at the dead beast, then gazed up at me in reverent awe. Falling prone, he beat his head upon the ground several times, and the others followed his example.

Then they all came forward to look at the huge animal.

From their talk and gestures, I gathered that they wanted to take it to the caves; but it would take ten of the strongest of them even to lift it, and there was still a mile stretch of jungle between them and the cliffs.

I decided that I would take it there for them if that was their want. Reaching out, I picked up the leader, the brave one, very gently. Placing him in the cupped hollow of my hand, I swung him far up to the level of my eyes. I pointed at the animal I had slain, then pointed toward the cliffs. But his eyes were closed tightly as if his last moment had come, and he trembled in every limb. He was a brave hunter, but this experience was too much. I lowered him to the ground unharmed, and the others crowded around him excitedly. He would soon recover from his fright, and no doubt some night around the campfires he would relate this wonderful experience to a bunch of skeptical grandchildren.

Picking the animal up by its tapering tail I strode through the jungle with it, flattening trees at every step and leaving a wide path behind me. I neared the cliffs in a few steps, and those upon the ledge fled into the caves. I placed the huge carcass on the ledge, which was scarcely as high as my shoulders, then turned and strode away to the right, intending to explore the terrain beyond.

For an hour, I walked, passing other tribes of cliff dwellers who fled at my approach. Then the jungle ended in a point by the sea and the line of cliffs melted down into a rocky coast.

It had become quite dark now, there were no moons and the stars seemed dim and far away. Strange night cries came from the jungle, and to my left stretched wide, tangled marshes through which floated vague phosphorescent shapes. Behind me tiny fires sprang up on the face of the cliffs, a welcome sight, and I turned back toward them. I was now so much smaller that I felt extremely uneasy of being alone and un-armed at night on a strange planet abounding in monstrosities.

I had taken only a few steps when I felt, rather than heard, a rush of wings above and behind me. I threw myself flat upon the ground, and just in time, for the great shadowy shape of some huge night-creature swept down and sharp talons raked my back. I arose with apprehension after a few moments, and saw the creature winging its way back low over the marshes. Its wingspread must have been forty feet. I reached the shelter of the cliffs and stayed close to them thereafter.

I came to the first of the shelving ledges where the fires burned, but it was far above me now. I was a tiny being crouched at the base of the cliffs. I, an alien on this world, yet a million years ahead of these barbarians in evolution, peered furtively out into the darkness where glowing eyes and half-seen shapes moved on the edge of the encroaching jungle; and safe in their caves high above me were those so low in the state of evolution that had only the rudiments of a spoken language and were only beginning to learn the value of fire. In another million years perhaps a great civilization would cover this entire globe: a civilization rising by slow degrees from the mire and the mistakes and the myths of the dawn of time. And doubtlessly one of the myths would concern a great godlike figure that descended from the skies, leveled great trees in its stride, saved a famous tribe from destruction by slaying huge enemy beasts, and then disap-peared forever during the night. And great men, great think-ers, of that future civilization would say: "Fie! Perposterous! A stupid myth."

But at the present time the godlike figure which slew enemy beasts by a slap of the hand was scarcely a foot high, and sought a place where he might be safe from a possible attack by those same beasts. At last I found a small crevice, which I squeezed into and felt much safer than I had out in the open.

And very soon I was so small that I would have been unnoticed by any of the huge animals that might venture my way.

VII

At last I stood on a single grain of sand, and other grains towered up like smooth mountains all around me. And in the next few minutes I experienced the change for the third time—the change from microscopic being on a gigantic world to a gigantic being floating amid an endless universe of galaxies. I became smaller, the distance between galaxies widened, solar systems approached and neared the orbit of the outermost planet. I received a very unexpected, but very pleasant, surprise. Instead of myself landing upon one of the planets—and while I was yet far too large to do so—the inhabitants of this system were coming out to land on me!

There was no doubt about it. From the direction of the inner planets a tapering silvery projectile moved toward me with the speed of light. This was indeed interesting, and I halted my inward progress to await developments.

In a few minutes the space rocket ship was very close. It circled about me once, then with a great rush of flame and gases from the prow to break the fall, it swooped in a long curve and landed gracefully on my chest! I felt no more jar than if a fly had alighted on me. As I watched it, a square section swung outward from the hull and a number of things emerged. I say "things" because they were in no manner human, although they were so tiny that I could barely distinguish them as minute dots of gold. A dozen of them gathered in a group a short distance away from the space ship.

After a few moments, to my surprise, they spread huge golden wings, and I gasped at the glistening beauty of them. They scattered in various directions, flying low over the surface of my body. From this I reasoned that I must be enveloped in a thin layer of atmosphere, as were the planets. These bird creatures were an exploring party sent out from one of the inner planets to investigate the new large world which had entered their system and was approaching dangerously close to their own planet.

But, on second thought, they must have been aware—or soon would be—that I was not a world at all, but a living, sentient being. My longitudinal shape should make that apparent, besides the movements of my limbs. At any rate they displayed unprecedented daring by coming out to land on me. I could have crushed their frail ship at the slightest touch or flung it far out into the void beyond their reach.

I wished I could see one of the winged creatures at closer range, but none landed on me again; having traversed and circled me in every direction they returned to the space ship and entered it. The section swung closed, gases roared from the stern tubes and the ship swooped out into space again and back toward the sun.

What tiding would they bear to their planet? Doubtless they would describe me as an inconceivably huge monstrosity of outer space. Their scientists would wonder whence I came; might even guess at the truth. They would observe me anxiously through their telescopes. Very likely they would be in fear that I would invade or wreck their world, and would make preparations to repulse me if I came too near.

In spite of these probabilities I continued my slow progress toward the inner planets, determined to see and if possible land upon the planet of the bird creatures. A civilization that had achieved space travel must be a marvelous civilization indeed.

As I made my way through space between the planets by means of my grotesque exertions, I reflected upon another phase. By the time I reached the inner planets I would be so much smaller that I could not determine which of the planets was the one I sought, unless I saw more of the space ships and could follow their direction. Another interesting thought was that the inner planets would have sped around the green sun innumerable times, and years would have passed before I reached there. They would have ample time to prepare for my coming, and might give me fierce reception if they had many more of the space ships such as the one I had seen.

And they did indeed have many more of them, as I discovered after an interminable length of time during which I had moved ever closer to the sun. A red-tinged planet swung in a wide curve from behind the blazing green of the sun, and I awaited its approach. After a few minutes it was so close that

I could see a moon encircling the planet, and as it came still nearer I saw the rocket ships.

This, then, was the planet I sought. But I was puzzled. They surely could not have failed to notice my approach, and I had expected to see a host of ships lined up in formidable array. I saw a host of them all right, hundreds of them, but they were not pointed in my direction at all; indeed, they seemed not to heed me in the least, although I must have loomed large as their planet came nearer. Perhaps they had decided, after all, that I was harmless.

But what seemed more likely to me was that they were confronted with an issue of vastly more importance than my close proximity. For as I viewed the space ships they were leaving the atmosphere of their planet, and were pointing toward the single satellite. Row upon row, mass upon endless mass they moved outward, hundreds, thousands of them. It seemed as though the entire population was moving *en masse* to the satellite!

My curiosity was immediately aroused. What circumstances or condition could cause a highly civilized race to abandon their planet and flee to the satellite? Perhaps, if I learned, I would not want to alight on that planet. . . .

Impatiently I awaited its return as it moved away from me on its circuit around the sun. The minutes seemed long, but at last it approached again from the opposite direction, and I marveled at the relativity of size and space and time. A year had passed on that planet and satellite, and many things might have transpired since I had last seen them.

The satellite swung between the planet and myself, and even from my point of disadvantage I could see that many things had indeed transpired. The bird people were building a protective shell around the satellite! Protection—from what? The shell seemed to be of dull gray metal, and already covered half the globe. On the uncovered side I saw land and rolling oceans. Surely, I thought, they must have the means of producing artificial light; but somehow it seemed blasphemous to forever bar the surface from the fresh pure light of the green sun. In a manner I felt sorry for them in their circumstances. But they had their space ships, and in time could move to the vast unexplored fields that the heavens offered.

More than ever I was consumed with curiosity, but was still too large to attempt a contact with the planet, and I let it pass me for a second time. I judged that when it came around again I would be sufficiently small for its gravity to "capture" me and sufficiently large that the "fall" to the surface would in no means be dangerous; and I was determined to alight.

Another wait of minutes, more minutes this time because I was smaller and time for me was correspondingly longer. When the two spheres hove into view again I saw that the smaller one was now entirely clad in its metal jacket, and the smooth unbroken surface shimmered boldly in the green glare of the sun. Beneath that barren metal shell were the bird people with their glorious golden wings, their space ships, their artificial light, and atmosphere, and civilization. I had but a glance for the satellite, however; my attention was for the planet rushing ever closer to me.

Everything passed smoothly and without mishap. I was becoming an experienced "planet hopper." Its gravity caught me in an unrelenting grip, and I let my limbs rush downward first in their long curve, to land with a slight jar on solid earth far below.

Bending low, I sought to peer into the murky atmosphere and see something of the nature of this world. For a minute my sight could not pierce the half gloom, but gradually the surface became visible. First, I followed my tapering limbs to where they had contacted. As nearly as I could ascertain from my height, I was standing in the midst of what seemed to be a huge mass of crushed and twisted metal!

Now, I thought to myself, I have done it. I have let myself in for it now. I have wrecked something, some great piece of machinery it seems, and the inhabitants will not take the matter lightly. Then I thought: the inhabitants? Who? Not the bird people, for they have fled, have barricaded themselves on the satellite

Again I sought to pierce the gloom of the atmosphere, and

by slow degrees more details became visible. At first my gaze only encompassed a few miles, then more, and more, until at last the view extended from horizon to horizon and included nearly an entire hemisphere.

Slowly the view cleared and slowly comprehension came; and as full realization dawned upon me, I became momentarily panic-stricken. I thought insanely of leaping outward into space again, away from the planet, breaking the gravity that held me; but the opposite force of my spring could likely send the planet careening out of its orbit and it and all the other planets and myself might go plunging toward the sun. No, I had put my feet on this planet and I was here to stay.

But I did not feel like staying, for what a sight I had glimpsed! As far as I could see in every direction were huge, grotesque metal structures and strange mechanical contrivances. The thing that terrified me was that these machines were scurrying about the surface all in a apparent confusion, seemed to cover the entire globe, seemed to have a complete civilization of their own, and nowhere was there the slightest evidence of any human occupancy, no controlling force, no intelligence, nothing save the machines. And I could not bring myself to believe that they were possessed of intelligence!

Yet as I descended ever closer to the surface I could see that there was no confusion at all as it had seemed at first glance, but rather was there a simple, efficient, systematic order of things. Even as I watched, two strange mechanisms strode toward me on great jointed tripods, and stopped at my very feet. Long, jointed metal arms, with clawlike fixtures at the ends, reached out with uncanny accuracy and precision and began to clear away the twisted debris around my feet. As I watched them I admired the efficiency of their construction. No needless intricacies, no superfluous parts, only the tripods for movement and the arms for clearing. When they had finished they went away, and other machines came on wheels, the debris was lifted by means of cranes and hauled away.

I watched in stupefaction the uncanny activities below and around me. There was no hurry, no rush, but every machine from the tiniest to the largest, from the simplest to the most complicated, had a certain task to perform, and performed it directly and completely, accurately and precisely. There were machines on wheels, on treads, on tracks, on huge multijointed tripods, winged machines that flew clumsily through the air, and machines of a thousand other kinds and variations.

Endless chains of machines delved deep into the earth, to emerge with loads of ore which they deposited, to descend again.

Huge hauling machines came and transported the ore to roaring mills.

Inside the mills machines melted the ore, rolled and cut and fashioned the steel.

Other machines builded and assembled and adjusted intricate parts, and when the long process was completed the result was—more machines! They rolled or ambled or flew or walked or rattled away under their own power, as the case might be.

Some went to assist in the building of huge bridges across rivers and ravines.

Diggers went to level down forests and obstructing hills, or went away to the mines.

Others built adjoining mills and factories.

Still others erected strange, complicated towers thousands of feet high, and the purpose of these skeleton skyscrapers I could not determine. Even as I watched, the supporting base of one of them weakened and buckled, and the entire huge edifice careened at a perilous angle. Immediately a host of tiny machines rushed to the scene. Sharp white flames cut through the metal in a few seconds, and the tower toppled with a thunderous crash to the ground. Again the white-flame machines went to work and cut the metal into removable sections, and hoisters and haulers came and removed them. Within fifteen minutes another building was being erected on the exact spot.

Occasionally something would go wrong—some worn-out part ceased to function and a machine would stop in the middle of its task. Then it would be hauled away to repair shops, where it would eventually emerge good as new.

I saw two of the winged machines collide in midair, and

metal rained from the sky. A half-dozen of the tripod clearing machines came from a half-dozen directions and the metal was raked into huge piles: then came the cranes and hauling machines.

A great vertical wheel with slanting blades on the rim spun swiftly on a shaft that was borne forward on treads. The blades cut through trees and soil and stone as it bore onward toward the near-by mountains. It slowed down, but did not stop, and at length a straight wide path connected the opposite valley. Behind the wheel came the tripods, clearing the way of all debris, and behind them came machines that laid down long strips of metal, completing the perfect road.

Everywhere small lubricating machines moved about, periodically supplying the others with the necessary oil that insured smooth movement.

Gradually the region surrounding me was being leveled and cleared, and a vast city was rising—a city of meaningless, towering, ugly metal—a city covering hundreds of miles between the mountains and sea—a city of machines—ungainly, lifeless—yet purposeful—for what? What?

In the bay, a line of towers rose from the water like fingers pointing at the sky. Beyond the bay and into the open sea they extended. Now the machines were connecting the towers with wide network and spans. A bridge! They were spanning the ocean, connecting the continents—a prodigious engineering feat. If there were not already machines on the other side, there soon would be. No, not soon. The task was gigantic, fraught with failures, almost impossible. *Almost?* A world of machines could know no almost. Perhaps other machines did occupy the other side, had started the bridge from there, and they would meet in the middle. And for what purpose?

A great wide river came out of the mountains and went winding toward the sea. For some reason a wall was being constructed diagonally across the river and beyond, to change its course. From some reason—or unreason.

Unreason! That was it! Why, why, why, I cried aloud in an anguish that was real; why all of this? What purpose, what meaning, what benefit? A city, a continent, a world, a civilization of machines! Somewhere on this world there must be the one who caused all this, the one intelligence, human or unhuman, who controls it. My time here is limited, but I have time to seek him out, and if I find him I shall drag him out and feed him to his own machines and put a stop to this diabolism for all time!

I strode along the edge of the sea for five hundred miles, and rounding a sharp point of land, stopped abruptly. There before me stretched a city, a towering city of smooth white stone and architectural beauty. Spacious parks were dotted with winged colonnades and statues, and the buildings were so designed that everything pointed upward, seemed poised for flight.

That was one half of the city.

The other half was a ruinous heap of shattered white stone, of buildings leveled to the ground by the machines, which were even then intent on reducing the entire city to a like state.

As I watched I saw scores of the flame-machines cutting deep into the stone and steel supporting base of one of the tallest buildings. Two of the ponderous air machines, trailing a wide mesh-metal network between them, rose clumsily from the ground on the outskirts of the city. Straight at the building they flew, and passed one on each side of it. The metal netting struck, jerked the machines backward, and the tangled mass of them plunged to the ground far below. But the building, already weakened at the base, swayed far forward, then back, hung poised for a long shuddering moment and then toppled to the ground with a thunderous crash amid a cloud of dust and debris and tangled framework.

The flame-machines moved on to another building, and on a slope near the outskirts two more of the air machines waited. . . .

Sickened at the purposeless vandalism of it all, I turned inland; and everywhere I strode were the machines, destroying and building, leveling to the ground the deserted cities of the bird people and building up their own meaningless civilization of metal.

At last I came to a long range of mountains which towered up past the level of my eyes as I stood before them. In two steps I stood on the top of these mountains and looked out upon a vast plain dotted everywhere with the grotesque machine-made cities. The machines had made good progress. About two hundred miles to the left a great metal dome rose from the level of the plain, and I made my way toward it, striding unconcerned and recklessly amidst the machines that moved everywhere around my feet.

As I neared the domed structure a row of formidable-looking mechanisms, armed with long spikes, rose up to bar my path. I kicked out viciously at them and in a few minutes they were reduced to tangled scrap, though I received a number of minor scratches in the skirmish. Others of the spiked machines rose up to confront me with each step I took, but I strode through them, kicking them to one side, and at last I stood before an entranceway in the side of the huge dome. Stooping, I entered, and once inside my head almost touched the roof.

I had hoped to find here what I sought, and I was not disappointed. There in the center of the single spacious room was The Machine of all Machines; the Cause of it All; the Central Force, the Ruler, the Controlling Power of all the diabolism running riot over the face of the planet. It was roughly circular, large and ponderous. It was bewilderingly complicated, a maze of gears, wheels, switchboards, lights, levers, buttons, tubing, and intricacies beyond my comprehension. There were circular tiers, and on each tier smaller separate units moved, performing various tasks, attending switchboards, pressing buttons, pulling levers. The result was a throbbing, rhythmic, purposeful unit. I could imagine invisible waves going out in every direction.

I wondered what part of this great machine was vulnerable. Silly thought. No part. Only it—itself. It was The Brain.

The Brain. The Intelligence. I had searched for it, and I had found it. There it was before me. Well, I was going to smash it. I looked around for some kind of weapon, but finding none, I strode forward bare-handed.

Immediately a square panel lighted up with a green glow,

and I knew that The Brain was aware of my intent. I stopped. An odd sensation swept over me, a feeling of *hate*, of *menace*. It came from the machine, pervaded the air in invisible waves.

"Nonsense," I thought: "it is but a machine after all. A very complicated one, yes, perhaps even possessed of intelligence; but it only has control over other machines, it cannot harm me." Again I took a resolute step forward.

The feeling of menace became stronger, but I fought back my apprehension and advanced recklessly. I had almost reached the machine when a wall of crackling blue flame leaped from floor to roof. If I had taken one more step I would have been caught in it.

The menace, and hate, and imagined rage at my escape, rolled out from the machine in ponderous, almost tangible waves, engulfing me, and I retreated hastily.

I walked back toward the mountains. After all, this was not *my* world—not my universe. I would soon be so small that my presence amid the machines would be extremely dangerous, and the tops of the mountains was the only safe place. I would have liked to smash The Brain and put an end to it all, but anyway, I thought, the bird people were now safe on the satellite, so why not leave this lifeless world to the machines?

It was twilight when I reached the mountains, and from a high grassy slope—the only peaceful place on the entire planet, I imagined—I looked out upon the plain. Tiny lights appeared as the machines moved about, carrying on their work, never resting. The clattering and clanking of them floated faintly up to me and made me glad that I was a safe distance from it all.

As I stood out toward the dome that housed The Brain, I saw what I had failed to see before. A large globe rested there on a framework, and there seemed to be unusual activity around it.

A vague apprehension tightened around my brain as I saw machines enter this globe, and I was half prepared for what happened next. The globe rose lightly as a feather, sped upward with increasing speed, out of the atmosphere and into space, where, as a tiny speck, it darted and maneuvered with perfect ease. Soon it reappeared, floated gracefully down upon the framework again, and the machines that had mechanically directed its flight disembarked from it.

The machines had achieved space travel! My heart sickened with sudden realization of what that meant. They would build others—were already building them. They would go to other worlds, and the nearest one was the satellite. . . . encased in its protective metal shell. . . .

But then I thought of the white-flame machines that I had seen cut through stone and metal in a few seconds. . . .

The bird people would no doubt put up a valiant fight. But as I compared their rocket projectiles against the efficiency of the globe I had just seen, I had little doubt as to the outcome. They would eventually be driven out into space again to seek a new world, and the machines would take over the satellite, running riot as they had done here. They would remain there just as long as The Brain so desired, or until there was no more land for conquest. Already this planet was overrun, so they were preparing to leave.

The Brain. An intricate, intelligent mechanical brain, glorying in its power, drunk with conquest. Where had it originated? The bird people must have been the indirect cause, and no doubt they were beginning to realize the terrible menace they had loosed on the universe.

I tried to picture their civilization as it had been long ago before this thing had come about. I pictured a civilization in which machinery played a very important part. I pictured the development of this machinery until the time when it relieved them of many tasks. I imagined how they must have designed their machines with more and more intracacy, more and more finesse, until only a few persons were needed in control. And then the great day would come, the supreme day, when mechanical parts would take the place of those few.

That must have indeed been a day of triumph. Machines supplying their every necessity, attending to their every want, obeying their every whim at the touch of a button. That must have been Utopia achieved!

But it had proven to be a bitter Utopia. They had gone forward blindly and recklessly to achieve it, and unknowingly they had gone a step too far. Somewhere, amid the machines they supposed they had under their control, they were imbued with a spark of intelligence. One of the machines added unto itself—perhaps secretly; built and evolved itself into a terribly efficient unit of inspired intelligence. And guided by that intelligence, other machines were built and came under its control. The rest must have been a matter of course. Revolt and easy victory.

So I pictured the evolution of the mechanical brain that even now was directing activities from down there under its metal dome.

And the metal shell around the satellite—did not that mean that the bird people were expecting an invasion? Perhaps, after all, this was not the original planet of the bird people; perhaps space travel was not an innovation among the machines. Perhaps it was on one of the far inner planets near the sun that the bird people had achieved the Utopia that proved to be such a terrible nemesis; perhaps they had moved to the next planet, never dreaming that the machines could follow; but the machines had followed after a number of years, the bird people being always driven outward, the machines always following at leisure in search of new spheres of conquest. And finally the bird people had fled to this planet, and from it to the satellite; and realizing that in a few years the machines would come again in all their invincibility, they had then ensconced themselves beneath the shell of metal.

At any rate: they did not flee to a faraway safe spot in the universe as they could have very easily done. Instead, they stayed; always one sphere ahead of the marauding machines, they must always be planning a means of wiping out the spreading evil they had loosed.

It might be that the shell around the satellite was in some way a clever trap! But so thinking, I remembered again the white-flame machines and the deadly efficiency of the globe I had seen, and then my hopes faded away.

Perhaps someday they would eventually find a way to check the spreading menace. But on the other extreme, the machines might spread out to other solar systems, other galaxies, until some day, a billion years hence, they would occupy every sphere in this universe. . . .

Such were my thoughts as I lay prone there upon the grassy slope and looked down into the plain, down upon the ceaseless clatter and the ceaseless moving of lights in the dark. I was very small now; soon, very soon, I would leave this world.

My last impression was of a number of the space globes, barely discernible in the dusk below: and among them towering up high and round, was one much larger than the others, and I could guess which machine would occupy that globe.

And my last thought was a regret that I hadn't made a more determined effort to destroy that malicious mechanism, The Brain.

So I passed from this world of machines—the world that was an electron on a grain of sand that existed on a prehistoric world that was but an electron on a microscopeslide that existed on a world that was but an electron in a piece of Rehyllium-X on the Professor's laboratory table.

VIII

It is useless to go on. I have neither the time nor the desire to relate in detail all the adventures that have fallen me, the universes I have passed into, the things I have seen and experienced and learned on all the worlds since I left the planet of the machines.

Ever-smaller cycles . . . infinite universes . . . never-ending . . . each presenting something new . . . some queer variation of life or intelligence. . . . Life? Intelligence? Terms I once associated with things animate, things protoplasmic and understandable. I find it hard to apply them to all the divergencies of shape and form and construction I have encountered. . . .

Worlds young . . . warm . . . volcanic and steaming . . . the single cell emerging from the slime of warm oceans to propagate on primordial continents . . . other worlds, innumerable . . . life divergent in all branches from the single cell

. . . amorphous globules . . . amphibian . . . crustacean . . . reptilian . . . plant . . . insect . . . bird . . . mammal . . . all possible variations of combinations . . . biological monstrosities indescribable . . .

Other forms beyond any attempt at classification . . . beyond all reason or comprehension of my puny mind . . . essences of pure flame . . . others gaseous, incandescent and quiescent alike . . . plant forms encompassing an entire globe . . . crystalline beings sentient and reasoning . . . great shimmering columnar forms, seemingly liquid, defying gravity by some strange power of cohesion . . . a world of sound-vibrations, throbbing, expanding, reverberating in unbroken echoes that nearly drove me crazy. . . globular brainlike masses utterly dissociated from any material substance . . . intra-dimensional beings, all shapes and shapeless . . . entities utterly incapable of registration upon any of my senses except the sixth, that of instinct . . .

Suns dying . . . planets cold and dark and airless . . . last vestiges of once proud races struggling for a few more meager years of sustenance . . . great cavities . . . beds of evaporated seas . . . small furry animals scurrying to cover at my approach . . . desolation . . . ruins crumbling surely into the sands of barren deserts, the last mute evidence of vanished civilizations . . .

Other worlds . . . a-flourished with life . . . blessed with light and heat . . . staggering cities . . . vast populations . . . ships plying the surface of oceans, and others in the air . . . huge observatories . . . tremendous strides in the sciences . . .

Space flight . . . battles for the supremacy of worlds . . . blasting rays of super-destruction . . . collision of planets . . . disruption of solar systems . . . cosmic annihilation . . .

Light space . . . a universe with a tenuous, filmy something around it, which I burst through . . . .all around me not the customary blackness of outer space I had known, but light . . . filled with tiny dots that were globes of darkness . . . that were burnt-out suns and lifeless planets . . . nowhere a shimmering planet, nowhere a flaming sun . . . only remote specks of black amid the high-satiated emptiness . . .

*   *   *

How many of the infinitely smaller atomic cycles I have passed into, I do not know. I tried to keep count of them at first, but somewhere between twenty and thirty I gave it up; and that was long ago.

Each time I would think: "This cannot go on forever—it *cannot;* surely this next time I must reach the end."

But I have not reached the end.

Good God—how can there be an end? Worlds composed of atoms . . . each atom similarly composed. . . . The end would have to be an indestructible solid, and that cannot be; all matter divisible into smaller matter. . . .

What keeps me from going insane? I want to go insane!

I am tired . . . a strange tiredness neither of mind nor body. Death would be a welcome release from the endless fate that is mine.

But even death is denied me. I have sought it . . . I have prayed for it and begged for it. . . . But it is not to be.

On all the countless worlds I have contacted, the inhabitants were of two distinctions: they were either so low in the state of intelligence that they fled and barricaded themselves against me in superstitious terror—or were so highly intellectual that they recognized me for what I was and welcomed me among them. On all but a few worlds the latter was the case, and it is on these types that I will dwell briefly.

These beings—or shapes or monstrosities or essences—were in every case mentally and scientifically far above me. In most cases they had observed me for years as a dark shadow looming beyond the farthest stars, blotting out certain starfields and nebulae . . . and always when I came to their world they welcomed me with scientific enthusiasm.

Always they were puzzled as to my steady shrinking, and always when they learned of my origin and the manner of my being there, they were surprised and excited.

In most cases gratification was apparent when they learned definitely that there were indeed great ultramacrocosmic universes. It seemed that all of them had long held the theory that such was the case.

On most of the worlds, too, the beings—or entities—or whatever the case might be—were surprised that the Professor, one of my fellow creatures, had invented such a marvelous vitalized element as "Shrinx."

"Almost unbelievable," was the general consensus of opinion; "scientifically he must be centuries ahead of the time on his own planet, if we are to judge the majority of the race by this creature here"— meaning me.

In spite of the fact that on nearly every world I was looked upon as mentally inferior, they conversed with me and I with them, by various of their methods, in most cases different variations of telepathy. They learned in minute detail and with much interest all of my past experiences in other universes. They answered all of my questions and explained many things besides, about their own universe and world and civilization and scientific achievements, most of which were completely beyond my comprehension, so alien were they in nature.

And of all the intra-universal beings I have had converse with, the strangest were those essences who dwelt in outer space as well as on various planets; identifiable to me only as vague blots of emptiness, total absences of light or color or substance; who impressed upon me the fact that they were Pure Intelligences, far above and superior to any material plane; but who professed an interest in me, bearing me with them to various planets, revealing many things and treating me very kindly. During my sojourn with them, I learned from experience the total subservience of matter to influences of mind. On a giant mountainous world I stepped out upon a thin beam of light stretched between two crags, and willed with all my consciousness that I would not fall. And I did not.

I have learned many things. I know that my mind is much sharper, more penetrative, more grasping, than ever before. And vast fields of wonder and knowledge lie before me in other universes yet to come.

But in spite of this, I am ready for it all to end. This strange tiredness that is upon me—I cannot understand it. Perhaps some invisible radiation in empty space is satiating me with this tiredness.

Perhaps it is only that I am very lonely. How very far away

I am from my own tiny sphere! Millions upon millions . . .
trillions upon trillions . . . of light-years. . . . Light years!
Light cannot measure the distance. And yet it is no distance: I
am in a block of metal on the Professor's laboratory table. . . .

Yet how far away into space and time I have gone! Years
have passed, years far beyond my normal span of life. I am
eternal.

Yes, eternal life . . . that men have dreamed of . . . prayed
for . . . sought after . . . is mine—and I dream and pray and
seek for death!

Death. All the strange beings I have seen and conversed
with, have denied it. I have implored many of them to release
me painlessly and for all time—but to no avail. Many of them
were possessed of the scientific means to stop my steady
shrinkage—but they would not stop it. None of them would
hinder me, none of them would tamper with the things that
were. Why? Always I asked them why, and they would not
answer.

But I need no answer. I think I understand. These beings of
science realized that such an entity as myself should never be
. . . that I am a blasphemy upon all creation and beyond all
reason . . . they realized that eternal life is a terrible thing
. . . a thing not to be desired . . . and as punishment for
delving into secrets never meant to be revealed, none of them
will release me from my fate. . . .

Perhaps they are right, but oh, it is cruel! Cruel! The fault
is not mine, I am here against my own will.

And so I continue ever down, alone and lonely, yearning
for others of my kind. Always hopeful—and always disappointed.

So it was that I departed from a certain world of highly
intelligent gaseous beings; a world that was in itself composed of a highly rarefied substance bordering on nebulosity.
So it was that I became even smaller, was lifted up in a
whirling, expanding vortex of the dense atmosphere, and
entered the universe which it composed.

Why I was attracted by that tiny, far-away speck of yellow,
I do not know. It was near the center of the nebula I had

entered. There were other suns far brighter, far more attractive, very much nearer. This minute yellow sun was dwarfed by other suns and sun-clusters around it—seemed insignificant and lost among them. And why I was drawn to *it,* so far away, I cannot explain.

But mere distance, even space distance, was nothing to me now. I had long since learned from the Pure Intelligence the secret of propulsion by mind influence, and by this means I propelled myself through space at any desired speed not exceeding that of light; as my mind was incapable of imagining speed faster than light, I of course could not cause my material body to exceed it.

So I neared the yellow sun in a few minutes, and observed that it had twelve planets. And as I was far too large to yet land on any sphere, I wandered far among other suns, observing the haphazard construction of this universe, but never losing sight of the small yellow sun that had so intrigued me. And at last, much smaller, I returned to it.

And of all the twelve planets, one was particularly attractive to me. It was a tiny blue one. It made not much difference where I landed, so why should I have picked it from among the others? Perhaps only a whim—but I think the true reason was because of its constant pale blue twinkling, as though it were beckoning to me, inviting me to come to it. It was an unexplainable phenomenon; none of the others did that. So I moved closer to the orbit of the blue planet, and landed upon it.

As usual I didn't move from where I stood for a time, until I could view the surrounding terrain; and then I observed that I had landed in a great lake—a chain of lakes. A short distance to my left was a city miles wide, a great part of which was inundated by the flood I had caused.

Very carefully, so as not to cause further tidal waves, I stepped from the lake to solid ground, and the waters receded somewhat.

Soon I saw a group of five machines flying toward me; each of them had two wings held stiffly at right angles to the body. Looking around me I saw others of these machines winging toward me from every direction, always in groups of five, in V formation. When they had come very close they began to dart and swoop in a most peculiar manner, from them came sharp staccato sounds, and I felt the impact of many tiny pellets upon my skin! These beings were very warlike, I thought, or else very excitable.

Their bombardment continued for some time, and I began to find it most irritating; these tiny pellets could not harm me seriously, could not even pierce my skin, but the impact of them stung. I could not account for their attack upon me, unless it be that they were angry at the flood I had caused by my landing. If that were the case they were very unreasonable, I thought; any damage I had done was purely unintentional, and they should realize that.

But I was soon to learn that these creatures were very foolish in many of their actions and manners; they were to prove puzzling to me in more ways than one.

I waved my arms around, and presently they ceased their futile bombardment, but continued to fly around me.

I wished I could see what manner of beings flew these machines. They were continually landing and rising again from a wide level field below.

For several hours they buzzed all around while I became steadily smaller. Below me I could now see long ribbons of white that I guessed were roads. Along these roads crawled tiny vehicles, which soon became so numerous that all movement came to a standstill, so congested were they. In the fields a large part of the populace had gathered, and was being constantly augmented by others.

At last I was sufficiently small so that I could make out closer details, and I looked more intently at the beings who inhabited this world. My heart gave a quick leap then, for they somewhat resembled myself in structure. They were four-limbed and stood erect, their method of locomotion consisting of short jerky hops, very different from the smooth gliding movement of my own race. Their general features were somewhat different too—seemed grotesque to me—but the only main difference between them and myself was that their bodies were somewhat more columnar, roughly oval in shape and very thin, I would say almost frail.

Among the thousands gathered there were perhaps a score who seemed in authority. They rode upon the backs of clumsy-looking, four-footed animals, and seemed to have difficulty in keeping the excited crowd under control. I, of course, was the center of their excitement; my presence seemed to have caused more consternation here than upon any other world.

Eventually a way was made through the crowd and one of the ponderous four wheeled vehicles was brought along the road opposite to where I stood. I supposed they wanted me to enter the rough boxlike affair, so I did so, and was hauled with many bumps and jolts over the rough road toward the city I had seen to the left. I could have rebelled at this barbarous treatment, but I reflected that I was still very large and this was probably the only way they had of transporting me to wherever I was going.

It had become quite dark, and the city was aglow with thousands of lights. I was taken into a certain building, and at once many important-looking persons came to observe me

I have stated that my mind had become much more penetrative than ever before, so I was not surprised to learn that I could read many of the thoughts of these persons without much difficulty. I learned that these were scientists who had come here from other immediate cities as quickly as possible—most of them in the winged machines, which they called "planes"—when they had learned of my landing here. For many months they had been certain that I would land. They had observed me through their telescopes, and their period of waiting had been a speculative one. And I could now see that they were greatly puzzled, filled with much wonderment, and no more enlightenment about me than they had been possessed of before.

Though still very large, I was becoming surely smaller, and it was this aspect that puzzled them most, just as it had on all the other worlds. Secondly in their speculations was the matter of *where* I had come from.

Many were the theories that passed among them. Certain they were that I had come a far distance. Uranus? Neptune?

Pluto? I learned that these were the names of the outmost planets of this system. No, they decided; I must have come a much farther distance than that. Perhaps from another far-away galaxy of this universe! Their minds were staggered at that thought. Yet how very far away they were from the truth.

They addressed me in their own language, and seemed to realize that it was futile. Although I understood everything they said and everything that was in their minds, they could not know that I did, for I could not answer them. Their minds seemed utterly closed to all my attempts at thought communication, so I gave it up.

They conversed then among themselves, and I could read the hopelessness in their minds. I could see, too, as they discussed me, that they looked upon me as being abhorrent, a monstrosity. And as I searched the recesses of their minds, I found many things.

I found that it was the inherent instinct of this race to look upon all unnatural occurrences and phenomena with suspicion and disbelief and prejudiced mind.

I found that they had great pride for their accomplishments in the way of scientific and inventive progress. Their astronomers had delved a short distance into outer space, but considered it a very great distance; and having failed to find signs of intelligent life upon any immediate sphere, they leaped blindly and fondly to the conclusion that their own species of life was the dominant one in this solar system and perhaps—it was a reluctant perhaps—in the entire universe.

Their conception of a universe was a puny one. True, at the present time there was extant a theory of an expanding universe, and in that theory at least they were correct, I knew, remembering the former world I had left—the swirling, expanding wisp of gaseous atmosphere of which this tiny blue sphere was an electron. Yes, their "expanding universe" theory was indeed correct. But very few of their thinkers went beyond their own immediate universe—went deeply enough to even remotely glimpse the vast truth.

They had vast cities, yes. I had seen many of them from my height as I towered above their world. A great civilization, I had thought then. But now I know that great cities do not make great civilizations. I am disappointed at what I have found here, and cannot even understand why I should be disappointed, for this blue sphere is nothing to me and soon I will be gone on my eternal journey downward. . . .

Many things I read in these scientists' minds—things clear and concise, things dim and remote; but they would never know.

And then in the mind of one of the persons, I read an idea. He went away, and returned shortly with an apparatus consisting of wires, a headphone, and a flat revolving disc. He spoke into an instrument, a sort of amplifier. Then a few minutes later he touched a sharp pointed instrument to the rotating disc, and I heard the identical sounds reproduced which he had spoken. A very crude method, but effective in a certain way. They wanted to register my speech so that they would have at least something to work on when I had gone.

I tried to speak some of my old language into the instrument. I had thought I was beyond all surprises, but I was surprised at what happened. For nothing happened. I could not speak. Neither in the old familiar language I had known so long ago, nor in any kind of sound. I had communicated so entirely by thought transference on so many of the other worlds, that now my power of vocal utterance was gone.

They were disappointed. I was not sorry, for they could not have deciphered any language so utterly alien as mine was.

Then they resorted to the mathematics by which this universe and all universes are controlled; into which mathematical mold the eternal All was cast at the beginning and has moved errorlessly since. They produced a great chart which showed the conglomerated masses of this and other galaxies. Then upon a black panel set in the wall, was drawn a circle—understandable in any universe—and around it ten smaller circles. This was evidently their solar system, though I could not understand why they drew but ten circles when I had seen twelve planets from outer space. Then a tiny spot was designated on the chart, the position of this system in its particular galaxy. Then they handed the chart to me.

It was useless. Utterly impossible. How could I ever indicate my own universe, much less my galaxy and solar system, by such puny methods as these? How could I make them know that my own universe and planet were so infinitely large in the scheme of things that *theirs* were practically nonexistent? How could I make them know that their universe was not *outside* my own, but *on my planet?*—superimposed in a block of metal on a laboratory table, in a grain of sand, in the atoms of glass in a microscopic slide, in a drop of water, in a blade of grass, in a bit of cold flame, in a thousand other variations of elements and substances all of which I had passed down into and beyond, and finally in a wisp of gas that was the cause of their "expanding universe." Even could I have conversed with them in their own language I could not have made them grasp the vastness of all those substances existing on worlds each of which was but an electron of an atom in one of trillions upon trillions of molecules of an infinitely larger world! Such a conception would have shattered their minds.

It was very evident that they would never be able to establish communication with me even remotely, nor I with them; and I was becoming very impatient. I wanted to be out of the stifling building, out under the night sky, free and unhampered in the vast space which was my abode.

Upon seeing that I made no move to indicate on the chart which part of their puny universe I came from, the scientists around me again conversed among themselves; and this time I was amazed at the trend of their thoughts.

For the conclusion which they had reached was that I was some freak of outer space which had somehow wandered here, and that my place in the scale of evolution was too far below their own for them to establish ideas with me either by spoken language (of which they concluded I had none) or by signs (which I was apparently too barbaric to understand)!! This—this was their unanimous conclusion! This, because I had not uttered any language for them to record, and because the chart of their universe was utterly insigificant to me! Never did it occur to them that the opposite might be true— that I might converse with them but for the fact that their minds were too weak to register my thoughts!

Disgust was my reaction to these short-sighted conclusions

of their unimaginable minds—disgust which gave way to an old emotion, that of anger.

And as that one impulsive, rising burst of anger flooded my mind, a strange thing happened:

Every one of the scientists before me dropped to the floor in a state of unconsciousness.

My mind had, indeed, become much more penetrative than ever before. No doubt my surge of anger had sent out intangible waves which had struck upon their centers of consciousness with sufficient force to render them insensible.

I was glad to be done with them. I left the four walls of the building, emerged into the glorious expansive night under the stars and set out along the street in a direction that I believed would lead me away from the city. I wanted to get away from it, away from this world and the people who inhabited it.

As I advanced along the streets all who saw me recognized me at once and most of them fled unreasonably for safety. A group of persons in one of the vehicles tried to bar my progress, but I exercised my power of anger upon them; they drooped senselessly and their vehicle crashed into a building and was demolished.

In a few minutes the city was behind me and I was striding down one of the roads, destination unknown; nor did it matter, except that now I was free and alone as it should be. I had but a few more hours on this world.

And then it was that the *feeling* came upon me again, the strange feeling that I had experienced twice before: once when I had selected the tiny orange sun from among the millions of others, and again when I had chosen this tiny blue planet. Now I felt it for a third time, more strongly than ever, and now I knew that this feeling had some very definite purpose for being. It was as though something, some power beyond question, drew me irresistibly to it; I could not resist, nor did I want to. This time it was very strong and very near.

Peering into the darkness along the road, I saw a light some distance ahead and to the left, and I knew that I must go to that light.

When I had come nearer I could see that it emanated from

a house set far back in a grove of trees, and I approached it without hesitation. The night was warm, and a pair of double windows opened upon a well-lighted room. In this room was a man.

I stepped inside and stood motionless, not yet knowing why I should have been drawn there.

The man's back was toward me. He was seated before a square dialed instrument, and seemed to be listening intently to some report coming from it. The sounds from the box were unintelligible to me, so I turned my attention to reading the man's mind as he listened, and was not surprised to learn that the reports concerned myself.

"—casualities somewhat exaggerated, though the property damage has reached millions of dollars," came the news from the box. "Cleveland was of course hardest hit, though not unexpectedly, astronomical computators having estimated with fair accuracy the radius of danger. The creature landed in Lake Erie only a few miles east of the city. At the contact the waters rose over the breakwater with a rush and inundated nearly one-third of the city before receding, and it was well that the greater part of the populace had heeded the advance warnings and fled. . . . All lake towns in the vicinity have reported heavy property damage, and cities as far east as Erie, and as far west as Toledo, have reported high flood waters. . . . All available Government combat planes were rushed to the scene in case the creature should show signs of hostility. . . . Scientific men who have awaited the thing's landing for months immediately chartered planes for Cleveland . . . Despite the elaborate cordons of police and militiamen, the crowds broke through and entered the area, and within an hour after the landing roads in every direction were congested with traffic. . . . For several hours scientists circled and examined the creature in planes, while its unbelievable shrinkage continued. . . . The only report we have from them is that, aside from the contour of its great bell-shaped torso, the creature is quite amazingly correct anatomically. . . . An unofficial statement from Dr. Hilton U. Cogsworthy of the Alleghany Biological Society, is to the effect that such a creature *isn't*. That it cannot possibly exist. That the whole thing is the result of some kind of mass hypnotism on a gigantic scale. This, of course, in lieu of some reasonable explanation. . . . Many persons would like to believe the 'mass hypnotism' theory, and many always will; but those who have seen it and taken photographs of it from every angle know that it does exist and that its steady shrinking goes on. . . . Professor James L. Harvey of Miami University has suffered a stroke of temporary insanity and is under the care of physicians. The habitual curiosity seekers who flocked to the scene are apparently more hardened. . . . The latest report is that the creature, still very large, has been transported under heavy guard to the Cleveland Institute of Scientific Research, where is gathered every scientist of note east of the Mississippi. . . . Stand by for further news flashes. . . ."

The voice from the box ceased, and as I continued to read the mind of the man whose back was toward me, I saw that he was deeply absorbed in the news he had heard. And the mind of this person was something of a puzzle to me. He was above the average intelligence of those on this world, and was possessed of a certain amount of fundamental scientific knowledge; but I could see immediately that he was not a scienitifically trained mind. By profession he was a writer— one who recorded fictious "happenings" in the written language, so that others might absorb and enjoy them.

And as I probed into his mind I was amazed at the depth of imagination there, a trait almost wholly lacking in those others I had encountered, the scientists. And I knew that at last here was one with whose mind I might contact . . . here was one who was different from the others . . . who went deeper . . . who seemed on the very edge of the truth. Here was one who thought: "—this strange creature, which has landed here . . . alien to anything we have ever known . . . might it not be alien even to our universe? . . . The strange shrinking . . . from that phenomenon alone we might conclude that it has come an inconceivable distance . . . its shrinking may have begun hundreds, thousands of years ago . . . and if we could but communicate with it, before it passes from Earth forever, what strange things might it not tell us!"

The voice came from the box again, interrupting these thoughts in his mind.

"Attention! Flash! The report comes that the alien space-creature, which was taken to the Scientific Research Institute for observation by scientists, has escaped, after projecting a kind of invisible mind force which rendered unconscious all those within reach. The creature was reported seen by a number of persons after it left the building. A police squad car was wrecked as a direct result of the creature's "mind force," and three policemen were injured, none seriously. It was last seen leaving the city by the northeast, and all persons are ordered to be on the lookout and to report immediately if it is sighted."

Again the report from the box ceased, and again I probed into the man's mind, this time deeper, hoping to establish a contact with it which would allow for thought-communication.

I must have at least aroused some hidden mind-instinct, for he whirled to face me, overturning his chair. Surprise was on his face, and something in his eyes that must have been fear.

"Do not be alarmed," I flashed. "Be seated again."

I could see that his mind had not received my thought. But he must have known from my manner that I meant no harm, for he resumed his seat. I advanced further into the room, standing before him. The fear had gone out of his eyes and he only sat tensely staring at me, his hands gripping the arms of the chair.

"I know that you would like to learn things about myself," I telepathed; "things which those others—your scientists—would have liked to know."

Reading his mind I could see that he had not received the thought, so I probed even deeper and again flashed the same thought. This time he did receive it, and there was an answering light in his eyes.

He said "Yes," aloud.

"Those others, your scientists," I went on, "would never have believed nor even understood my story, even if their minds were of the type to receive my thoughts, which they are not."

He received and comprehended that thought, too, but I could see that this was a great strain on his mind and could not go on for long.

"Yours is the only mind I have encountered here with which I could establish thought," I continued, "but even now it is becoming weakened under the unaccustomed strain. I wish to leave my record and story with you, but it cannot be by this means. I can put your mind under a hypnotic influence and impress my thoughts upon your subconscious mind, if you have some means of recording them. But you must hurry; I have only a few more hours here at the most, and in your entire lifetime it would be impossible for you to record all that I could tell."

I could read doubt in his mind. But only for one instant did he hesitate. Then he rose and went to a table where there was a pile of smooth white paper and a sharp pointed instrument—pen—for recording my thoughts in words of his own language.

"I am ready," was the thought in his mind.

So I have told my story. Why? I do not know, except that I wanted to. Of all the universes I have passed into, only on this blue sphere have I found creatures even remotely resembling myself. And they are a disappointment; and now I know that I shall never find others of my kind. Never, unless—

I have a theory. Where is the beginning or the end of the eternal All I have been traversing? Suppose there is none? Suppose that, after traversing a few more atomic cycles, I should enter a universe which seemed somehow familiar to me; and that I should enter a certain familiar galaxy, and approach a certain sun, a certain planet—and find that I was back where I started from so long ago: back on my own planet, where I should find the Professor in the laboratory still receiving my sound and sight impressions!! An insane theory; an impossible one. It shall never be.

Well, then, suppose that after leaving this sphere—after descending into another atomic universe—I should choose *not to alight on any planet?* Suppose I should remain in empty space, my size constantly diminishing? That would be one way of ending it all, I suppose. Or would it? Is not my body matter, and is matter infinite, limitless eternal? How then could I ever reach a "nothingness"? It is hopeless. I am eternal. My mind too must be eternal or it would surely have snapped long ago at such concepts.

I am so very small that my mind is losing contact with the mind of him who sits here before me writing these thoughts in words of his own language, though his mind is under the hypnotic spell of my own and he is oblivious to the words he writes. I have clambered upon the top of the table beside the pile of pages he has written, to bring my mind closer to his. But why should I want to continue the thought-contact for another instant? My story is finished, there is nothing more to tell.

I shall never find others of my kind. . . . I am alone. . . . I think that soon, in some manner, I shall try to put an end to it. . . .

I am very small now . . . the hypnosis is passing from his mind . . . I can no longer control it . . . the thought-contact is slipping. . . .

EPILOGUE

National Press-Radio Service, Sept. 29, 1937 (through Cleveland *Daily Clarion*):—Exactly one year ago today was a day never to be forgotten in the history of this planet. On that day a strange visitor arrived—and departed.

On September 29, 1936, at 3:31 P.M., that thing from outer space known henceforth only as "The Alien" landed in Lake Erie near Cleveland, causing not so much destruction and terror as great bewilderment and awe, scientists being baffled in their attempts to determine whence it came and the secret of its strange steady shrinking.

Now, on the anniversary of that memorable day, we are presenting to the public a most unusual and interesting document purported to be a true account and history of that strange being, The Alien. This document was presented to us only a few days ago by Stanton Cobb Lentz, renowned author of "The Answer to the Ages" and other serious books, as well as of scores of short stories and books of the widely popular type of literature known as science-fiction.

You have read the above document. While our opinion as to its authenticity is frankly skeptical, we shall print Mr. Lentz's comment and let you, the reader, judge for yourself whether the story was related to Mr. Lentz by The Alien in the manner described, or whether it is only a product of Mr. Lentz's most fertile imagination.

"On the afternoon of September 29, a year ago," states Mr. Lentz, "I fled the city as did many others, heeding the warning of a possible tidal wave, should The Alien land in the lake. Thousands of persons had gathered five or six miles to the south, and from there we watched the huge shape overhead, so expansive that it blotted out the sunlight and plunged that section of the country into a partial eclipse. It seemed to draw nearer by slow degrees until, about 3:30 o'clock, it began its downward rush. The sound of contact as it struck the lake was audible for miles, but it was not until later that we learned the extent of the flood. After the landing all was confusion and excitement as combat planes arrived and very foolishly began to bombard the creature and crowds began to advance upon the scene. The entire countryside being in such crowded turmoil, it took me several difficult hours to return to my home. There I listened to the varied reports of the happenings of the past several hours.

"When I had that strange feeling that someone was behind me, and when I whirled to see The Alien standing there in the room, I do not presume to say that I was not scared. I was. I was very much scared. I had seen The Alien when it was five or six hundred feet tall—but that had been from afar. Now it was only ten or eleven feet tall, but was standing right before me. But my scaredness was only momentary, for something seemed to enter and calm my mind.

"Then, although there was no audible sound, I became aware of the thought: 'I know that you would like to learn things about myself, things which those others—your scientists—would have liked to know.'

"This was mental telepathy! I had often used the theory in my stories, but never had I dreamed that I would experience such a medium of thought in real fact. But here it was.

" 'Those others, your scientists,' came the next thought,

'would never have believed nor even understood my story, even if their minds were of the type to receive my thoughts, which they are not.' And then I began to feel a strain upon my mind, and knew that I could not stand much more of it.

"Then came the thought that he would relate his story through my subconscious mind if I had some means of recording it in my own language. For an instant I hesitated; and then I realized that time was fleeing and never again would I have such an opportunity as this. I went to my desk, where only that morning I had been working on a manuscript. There was paper and ink in plenty.

"My last impression was of some force seeming to spread over my mind; then a terrific dizziness, and the ceiling seemed to crash upon me.

"No time at all had seemed to elapse, when my mind regained its normal faculties; but before me on the desk was a pile of manuscript paper closely written in my own longhand. And—what many persons will find it hard to believe—standing upon that pile of written paper upon my desk top was The Alien—now scarcely two inches in height—and steadily and surely diminishing! In utter fascination I watched the transformation that was taking place before my eyes—watched until The Alien had become entirely invisible. Had descended down into the topmost sheet of paper there on my desk. . . .

"Now I realize that the foregoing document and my explanation of it will be received in many ways. I have waited a full year before making it public. Accept it now as fiction if you wish. There may be some few who will see the truth of it, or at least the possibility; but the vast majority will leap at once to the conclusion that the whole thing is a concoction of my own imagination; that, taking advantage of The Alien's landing on this planet, I wrote the story to fit the occasion, very appropriately using The Alien as the main theme. To many this will seem all the more to be true, in face of the fact that in most of my science-fiction stories I have poked ridicule and derision and satire at mankind and all its high vaunted science and civilization and achievements—always more or less with my tongue in my cheek however, as the expression has it. And then along comes this Alien, takes a look at us and concludes that he is very disappointed, not to mention disgusted.

"However, I wish to represent a few facts to help substantiate the authenticity of the script. Firstly: for some time after awakening from my hypnosis I was beset by a curious dizziness, though my mind was quite clear. Shortly after The Alien had disappeared I called my physician, Dr. C. M. Rollins. After an examination and a few mental tests he was greatly puzzled. He could not diagnose my case; my dizziness was the aftereffect of a hypnosis of a type he had never before encountered. I offered no explanation except to say that I had not been feeling well for the past several days.

"Secondly: the muscles of my right hand were so cramped from the long period of steady writing that I could not open my fingers. As an explanation I said that I had been writing for hours on the final chapters of my latest book, and Dr. Rollins said: 'Man, you must be crazy.' The process of relaxing the muscles was painful.

"Upon my request Dr. Rollins will vouch for the truth of the above statements.

"Thirdly: when I read the manuscript the writing was easily recognizable as my own free, swinging longhand up to the last few paragraphs, when the writing became shaky, the last few words terminating in an almost undecipherable scrawl as The Alien's contact with my mind slipped away.

"Fourthly: I presented the manuscript to Mr. Howard A. Byerson, fiction editor of the National Newspaper Syndicate Service, and at once he misunderstood the entire idea. 'I have read your story, Mr. Lentz,' he said a few days later, 'and it certainly comes at an appropriate time, right the anniversary of The Alien's landing. A neat idea about the origin of The Alien, but a bit farfetched. Now, let's see, about the price; of course we shall syndicate your story through our National Newspaper chain, and—'

" 'You have the wrong idea,' I said. 'It is not a story, but a true history of The Alien as related to me by The Alien, and I wish that fact emphasized: if necessary I will write a letter of explanation to be published with the manuscript. And I am not selling you the publication rights, I am merely giving you the document as the quickest and surest way of presenting it to the public.'

" 'But surely you are not serious? An appropriate story by Stanton Cobb Lentz, on the eve of the anniversary of The Alien's landing, is a scoop; and you—'

" 'I do not ask and will not take a cent for the document,' I said; 'you have it now, it is yours, so do with it as you see fit.'

"A memory that will live with me always is the sight of The Alien as last seen by me—as last seen on this earth—as it disappeared into infinite smallness there upon my desk—waving two arms upward as if in farewell. . . .

"And whether the above true account and history of The Alien be received as such, or as fiction, there can be no doubt that on a not far-off September, a thing from some infinite sphere above landed on this earth—and departed.''

FROM THE DARK WATERS
by David A. Drake

*An emerging superstar of horror and action science
fiction, David Drake (1945–   ) lives in North
Carolina, fairly close to fellow writer Manly Wade
Wellman. Hammer's Slammers (1979) and Time Safari
(1982) are two of Drake's most important books so
far.*

*Here, Vettius, a pragmatic Roman Legate, who
has experienced a remarkable number of occult adventures, must face the giant Moby Dick of killer
sharks in a story predating Jaws.*

The brassy sea rocked as a small shark felt the bite of hooks
deep in its belly and tried to tear loose. Hlovida was crouched
low over her tile oven in the shelter forward, scrunching
something in her teeth. "Careful, careful," she cackled in a
voice still burred with the German of her early childhood.
"One'll fill his belly with you, Dercetus, I can see it."

The Libyan mate, braced ready with a boat pike for the
captive his crewmates were hauling aboard, ignored the wizened cook. Sweat beads jeweled his scarred black skin but
could not cool him in the breathless air.

"Shut up, old fool," Vettius muttered. With his merchant
friend he lay under the awning that stretched from the deckhouse to the broken stump of the mast. The light canvas hung
as limp as the jib sail, seeming to trap more heat than it

turned. Dama only shrugged moodily and leaned his sight form sideways out of the shadow. The sternpost of their ship, the *Purple Ibis*, curled over the deckhouse in a gentle sweep. It had been too many years since the encaustic paint had been renewed on its bird's-head finial, but it was still a graceful piece of carving. A handsome enough ship, in fact, before the storm. Eighty feet long, it had a three-sided deckhouse aft and a low, roofed shelter in the bow for the cook and her traps. Between mast and bow, a single open hatch gave access to the hold. Forward from the deckhouse ran a low rail, polished by decades of calloused hands. The smooth line broke amidships on the starboard side where raw splinters still gaped. . . .

After the first thrashing, the little shark drove straight away from the merchantman. The line and wire leader were heavy but the full shock of the fish would have snapped either. There was no need to wear the shark down, though. A brown-mottled tiger shark struck its lesser kinsman, scalloping out a huge mouthful that cut the hooked beast nearly in half. Its tail lashed briefly in the instant before a dozen other sharks ripped it apart in savage hunger. In the bloody explosion of teeth and fragments, the fishline parted and the sailor holding it stumbled backward.

Dama's face was impassive. His eyes were turned toward the sea, but in his mind it was the dark, pitching surface of the night before.

They were scudding in the bright moonlight, the breeze off the Mauretanian coast nudging them gently towards Massilia and only the helmsman awake. The first gust came as lightning from a clear sky. It heeled the vessel on to her beamends. Dama's right hand locked on a stanchion in a reflex developed during years of shepherding cargoes through foul weather. Vettius' massive body hit the slatted wall of the deckhouse, but his long cavalry sword was clear in his hand. The wind slackened momentarily.

The high, wet clouds, that piled up over the vineyards of the shore began to flow across the moon. Catfooted crewmen scurried to reef the sail. The ship rocked back sluggishly, logy with the weight of bolted silk in her hold. Then, in the dread silence punctuated only by the captain's frantic orders, the second gust struck. The half-furled sail, a new panel of stout Egyptian linen, blasted out of the hands of the seamen. The full force of the wind snapped at the mast that was as old as the hull, dried and weathered by the sucking heat of forty years. It parted with a crash, taking the captain and three sailors over the side with it.

The merchantman wallowed in the swells like a drunken whore. There was a single chance of saving the seamen clinging to the mast and air-bulged sail. Vettius sheathed his sword as naturally as he had drawn it and wrapped his powerful legs around the deck rail. The rising wind muffled the swish of the lead rope as he spun the loaded end twice around his head. Ignoring storm and the ship's pitching, he arced the rope over the drifting mass of top hamper.

The captain dropped the sheet he held and tugged at the lead. Already the vessel had drifted fifty yards. The floating man's triumphant cry crescendoed horribly as foam and a colored shadow bloomed in the water around him. The moon glared through the clouds for one last time as the dark sea filled with fins roiling in ghastly delight. The mast trembled among them. Crippled, the Purple Ibis *continued drifting. Rain began to slash down, but the survivors could still hear the screams from the darkness.*

"Another hook," Derecetus ordered in a husky voice. He breathed with his whole body, slowly but in deep, sudden intakes.

The seaman who held the line picked himself up from the deck. He did not look at the mate. For an instant his eyes caught those of the remaining common sailor, a Syrian like himself, before replying in the bad Greek of the sea lanes, "There's no wire for leaders. It's no use."

The mate's left hand, dark and as broad as a wine bowl, took the seaman gently behind the jaw and brought his face around. The pike Dercetus still held added no more to the threat than did the spiked plate on a war elephant's forehead.

"There's wire," the mate said. "There's wire enough to string every shark in this sea—and by Moloch! I will."

Vettius chuckled deep in his throat as he watched the seaman slink towards the companionway. "Afraid," he explained conversationally to Dama. "Mithra, I know them. Like the centurion who told me an outpost had already been overrun when I ordered him to relieve it. When he learned he could lead out his section or have me flay him alive"—the big soldier grinned as his finger traced down the scabbard of the cavalry sword—"he led it out. Which was just as well for him."

Dama indicated the mate's broad back with a not-quite-casual thumb. "I know how he feels, with him and the captain as close as they were . . ."

Vettius gestured obscenely with both hands, his smile tolerant but amused.

". . . but this won't bring anybody back. And feeding the sharks around us doesn't make me feel easier, at any rate."

Hlovida shuffled towards the mate from the cooking shelter, hunched as if her bones were on the verge of shattering. Twenty years before, she had been beautiful; time had been cruel. At forty her fine blond hair had become white and dull, so brittle that the left side of her skull was half-naked like an ill-thatched roof. Gray-brown discolorations marked her wrinkled skin and both cheeks bore flat sores. Her clothes were shapeless and filthy, so old that she might have been wearing them when the slavers bought her from a garrison on the Rhastian frontier.

"No, don't do that," she said, her voice breaking in the middle of an attempt to caress. She reached a crooked hand towards the mate's bare shoulder. "I told you, you'll be in a shark's belly soon if you try to hook another. I can see things, now that I've got my beauty back; yes I can."

Dercetus turned suddenly from the pattern of fins and gray shadows streaking the sea. His look of rapt loathing twisted into nausea as he took in the clawed fingers on his arm. Grunting an oath, he jerked away and lurched down the ladder in search of the seaman.

Hlovida's glance brushed the remaining sailor regretfully,

then locked onto the passengers. The Cappadocian merchant's blond hair reminded her of her youth, but his stubby body was beneath her addled fancy. Instead, she curtsied under the awning and seated herself at Vettius' side. "Yes, I can see everything," she said, stroking her own cheek. Her voice had an odd rhythm, not wholly distasteful. "The king's coming for poor Dercetus, and he'll take the rest of us too."

Vettius turned his back ostentatiously.

"Ooh!" the woman shrilled, "he's so strong and wise—what do I need with you men?"

"What indeed?" Dama agreed under his breath as the cook rose and flounced to the rail, but her voice jagged on saying, "He's wise, you know? Not like a fish, not even like a man. Down in the deep he lives, and he eats the men the wrecks send to him. Down in the deep, where the seas are as black as he is white . . . but once in a lifetime, in lifetimes, he comes up to take his feed live. He's the king, the king of all the seas."

Dama scowled. "She's mad for men, Dercetus mad for sharks . . . why don't you and I try to pilot this hulk to Circe's island or the Styx, Lucius? Then we could all be mad together."

The ship trembled as something rough-scaled brushed the keel. The merchant broke off his fantasy to call, "Get away from the rail, old woman; there's fish out there that wouldn't make three gulps of you."

Hlovida tittered, irrationally gay again. "Hoo! Not yet. But wait till the king comes. He's bigger than this whole ship, and he'll eat us all, one and one and one and one and one. See how fast he's coming? He's still deep now but rising, rising . . ."

Vettius shook his head. "A shark eighty feet long?" he said with a grimace. "She *is* mad."

"Maybe she means a physeter," Dama suggested idly. "I saw a herd spouting once near Taprobane."

"She's mad," Vettius repeated.

Calloused feet scuffled on the companionway. First the Syrian appeared on deck, then the heavily muscled mate with a dozen bronze leaders coiled over his arm. "String it,"

Dercetus ordered the seaman, tossing the wire at his feet; and to the cook, "Give him some pork."

"There's not much . . ." Hlovida suggested doubtfully.

"There'll be enough," Dercetus stated with a short, barking laugh. "As far north as the storm blew us, we'll fetch up on the coast of Spain any day. And maybe I'll boat one of these before he's eaten by his friends—then we'll have meat!"

The cook rummaged barehanded in the deck well where several amphoras were buried to their necks in sand. The gobbet she finally flipped to the sailor was so ripe and blackened that Dama was as glad as not to see it go over the side. Two thick-shanked hooks hid in its heart. A fifteen-foot hammerhead, mishapen and savage even among its present company, slammed the bait and took it straight down. The line hummed.

Dama shook his head and walked to the other rail, divorcing himself from the useless struggle.

"They're as bad as men," Vettius said, amused to watch other killers at work. "As soon as they see one of their own hurt, they're on him. This one doesn't feel the hooks yet. Wait till he does and tries to throw them out—Dercetus won't need the pike to finish any of this pack."

The seaman bracing against the line had fashioned mittens from a hide in the cargo. As the leather dragged on it, the hard linen cord purred and stank. Unexpectedly, the other sharks avoided the hooked hammerhead although their movements changed. Instead of slipping lazily around the becalmed vessel, each began circling its own wake. One leaped, a grisly sight with its jaws spread and a glazed yellow eye glaring at the ship. Something had gone wrong. Even Dercetus, poised at the rail as blank-eyed as the shark, felt that.

The sea was a sheet of hammered bronze. Dama could see deep down below its foamless surface. Miles, it seemed, but that was the distortion. He had never known air to be so still.

"She's rising!" someone called, and the merchant could hear the sailor's quick steps as the man tried to coil the line. It slackened faster than he could pull it in. And something was rising in the liquid depths of Dama's vision, too, a colorless dot quivering in the amber water. It grew, took an indeterminate shape. It was speeding straight up at the ship with the speed of a falling star. An outline formed and flowed with colour: the dirty white of an old shroud.

"Shark!" Dama bawled. He leaped back from the port rail.

Alone of the men on deck, Vettius glanced at the puzzled Cappadocian. The hammerhead was alongside now, strangely quiescent as the Syrian jerked its head out of the water and bent over the rail for another handful of line. "Hold him!" Dercetus ordered sharply. His right arm poised to slam the heavy pike through the shark's braincase.

The sea fountained an enormous cone of pallid white. Jaws crunched together, their sound muted by the roar of falling water and a glancing impact that rocked the vessel. Ignored in the brittle chaos, the hammerhead arrowed off with the severed leader still trailing from its mouth. The Syrian had locked his calves around the rail. They remained there. Six-inch teeth had sheared off the man's body above his loincloth while his blood sprayed a semicircle of deck behind him.

The huge shark, white except where blood had spattered it, shot out of the sea like a cork bobber released on the bottom. With its dorsal fin still under water, the pointed snout already towered twenty feet above the surface. Dercetus screamed in indecision. He tripped away in fear; then, with the shark still rising, hatred carried him back in a great lunge, jabbing his pike into the great side.

The iron head threw sparks as it scrunched harmlessly across the scales; it was as if the mate had speared a thrusting block of coral. Instead of sliding back into the sea, the shark twisted its body stiffly towards the ship. The rail shattered. Dama dived over the hatch coaming, head first. Derecetus was left nakedly alone amidships when Vettius leaped for his bundled gear in the deckhouse. Letting his useless spear clatter over the side, the big Libyan tried to follow the merchant. His feet skidded on blood and shot him outward towards the rail.

The shark's jaw thudded harmlessly above him but the deck's pitch tipped Dercetus into something worse. Caught between the shark and the planking, he screamed. As the huge beast continued to grind back into the sea, its belly scales rasped the mate to bloody ruin. Face and chest, touched by the serrated hide, were flayed to the bones. Nothing but a carmine track remained of the right leg below the knee, and the full length of the left fibula was exposed. The sea slapped thunderously, rolling the ship again.

Vettius stripped layers of oil-rich wool from his bow case, ignoring the remaining Syrian frozen open-mouthed beside him. Dercetus made enough noise for two, the soldier thought with detachment. Or a dozen. Well, he couldn't howl for long.

Dama's head, haloed by the sunlight, poked above the deck. "Clear," the bigger man said. "It went back over the side." Dama hopped the rest of the way out of the hatch. His tunic was torn, and in his right hand he clasped a hatchet snatched up in the hold.

"Ah," Hlovida crooned softly. She darted to Dercetus' side and began binding tourniquets above the blood spurting from his maimed limbs. Neither Vettius nor the little merchant considered helping her. Each had seen dying men before; also men better off dead. The cook's German-thickened voice buzzed as she worked, saying, "Oh, poor darling. How could you be so reckless when your Hlovida warned you?"

"By the Blood, do fish get that big?" Vettuis marveled to his friend. His hornbow was strung in his hands now. Its fat cord stretched over a yard between ivory tips. Again the sea wove with sharks, their dark sinuosities grimly overshadowed by the pale monster now leading them.

"Isn't he strong, dear one?" Hlovida chortled as she sponged the weakly protesting Dercetus. "And wise, too. He never comes to the surface when anyone might escape."

The dorsal fin of the white shark was a dozen feet high and all of it was out of the water. Unlike any other shark Vettius had seen, this one was from belly to fins a uniform moldly hue that made the big soldier think of graveworms. No albino, though, not with its cruel yellow eyes. More like something which had spent centuries in the depths, which was absurd. It swam stiffly, as if an obelisk with fins.

"It's not for him to be killed by men," the old Marcomann

woman concluded cheerfully, "so he'll kill us all soon." Dercetus shrieked as the sponge touched a rib gnawed to the marrow by adamantine scales.

Vettius drew his bow and shot without pausing for conscious aim. The bowstring slapped the inside of his left wrist, leaving a welt because he had not taken time to strap on his bracer. He cursed, less at the pain than the ineffectiveness of his shot. The arrow struck as intended at the root of the high dorsal fin; the narrow iron point may have penetrated, but the transmitted impact shattered the shaft. Vettius nocked another arrow but did not draw the bow. "Now what?" he snarled.

"Now we wait for a breeze to bring us to land," Dama answered, wiping his palms on his tunic before regripping the hatchet.

"Oh, there won't be any wind while he's here," Hlovida said, nodding archly towards the great shark. "*He* rules the sea." She tittered as she dragged the mate towards her shelter.

At midnight the air was silent. Vettius stirred, spat. He and Dama could follow the ripples in the moonlight, spreading faintly until they shivered apart in the track of the circling sharks. The remaining seaman was huddled in the deckhouse. From forward came a faint scraping noise that Dama tried to ignore.

"We have to kill that fish," Vettius said flatly, his back to the mast and his stubbled jaw cradled between his knees.

The merchant grinned and spread his hands, palms down. "Sure, and I'd like a chance to study the carcass. Don't know how we'll get it aboard, but if you can kill something that big, you can figure that out too. . . ."

"Well, we can't just wait here and watch it," the soldier growled irritably. "You saw what it did to him and the other." Vettius' spade-aboard hand gestured forward.

"I didn't say we should get too near the rail," protested Dama more seriously, "but we're sure to strike land soon."

"How do we know?" Vettius demanded. He slapped his bow against his thigh for emphasis, setting the waxed cord singing. "What if that bitch is right again and we'll never see land so long as that thing dogs us?

Dama let out a skeptical hiss.

"Anyway, I want to kill it," the bigger man admitted sheepishly. "It's out there laughing at us and . . . I want to end it."

Dama laughed out loud. "Well, there's a fine reason to risk our lives. But if neither spears nor arrows do the job, what do we do?"

"Um," the soldier grunted. "Well, I've got a notion about arrows, enough of them in the right places. Now if you're willing . . ."

The sun had merged sea and sky so that the *Purple Ibis* seemed to float within a bronze drum. The perpendicular rays exposed every dreadful line of the white shark. It cruised just as it had all the morning and the previous day. More sharks followed it than before. As far down as Dama's eyes could peer into the clear, golden water, nothing swam but sharks. He tossed the pork-baited line over the side. The fat meat floated a dozen feet from the ship, rocking slightly from the unbalanced weight of the leader. None of the smaller sharks left their grim formation.

The great white shark sank smoothly, the tip of its dorsal fin leaving a narrow track of foam before it, too, dipped below the surface. The shrinking torpedo shape continued to circle down into the lucid depths for as long as it was visible.

"He's gone," the soldier announced tensely, peering over the port rail. Dama licked his lips. He leaned over the rail, but his weight was balanced on the balls of his feet.

Vettius half-drew his bow. Three more arrows poked out of his left hand, each point gripped between a pir of fingers. He remembered how his friend had described the first appearance of the shark, a growing dot far down in the water. Now he saw it himself—

"Ready!" Vettius called. He drew the arrow to the head but still looked over his shoulder back into the sea. "Ready, ready—NOW!"

Dama porpoised, flinging himself down the companion-way. He was still in the air when the white shark burst upward, a corpse-colored volcano. Its gullet was pale pink, a cathedral of flesh arched darkly on either side by five gill slits. Washed clean by the sea, its saw-edged teeth winked in the sun.

Vettius slapped his first arrow into the centre of the rising belly. If the great fish noticed, its actions gave no sign. Curving its body like a fifty-ton boar tusk, the shark arced over the high stern of the *Ibis*. Deck stringers cracked under the awesome impact. Vettius dropped his weapons and thrust himself backward reflexively as the white bulk hurtled towards him. He had expected to fire three, perhaps all four of his readied arrows, but it had not occurred to him that the fish might throw itself aboard. Ferocity had guided it, that or something else not to be considered at the instant.

Two-thirds of the shark's length lay on the deck, the snout a pace short of Hlovida's shelter. The enormous tail threshed out of the water and slashed across the deckhouse from starboard to port. Light wood exploded into splinters that fanned the sea. With them pitched the screaming sailor bloodied by the tearing impact but all too conscious of the shapes arrowing towards where he must land. Water choked his cry; then a column of bloody froth spurted high into the air.

The ship wallowed. Forward of the mast stump, where the deck sloped nearest the sea, there was almost no freeboard left. The shark's body loomed over Vettius, a scaly, deadly surge that reached the port rail just as he cleared it. The soldier's biceps knotted hugely as they took the shock of his full weight on the rail. He hung there, his hobnailed boots skittering in the water as the ship rolled. A corner of his mind doubted any of the other sharks would leave the water to strike, but the overburdened vessel was perilously near foundering.

There was a mighty splash to starboard and the ship yawed violently to port as the shark dropped back into the sea. Vettius went under to the throat. As the ship righted itself, he used his momentum to spring out of the sea and back onto the deck. Behind him, teeth clashed.

The fish had left only shambles behind it. The mast stump was gone, broken off flush with the planking. The beast's flailing body had sheared away almost everything from the stern forward: bitts, deckhouse, railings, and the steering oar. At least the jib sail had survived, though it hung limp as Tiberius' prick. Mithra, unless there came a breeze . . .

Dama climbed on deck with a questioning eyebrow cocked. "I hit him," Vettius said morosely. He glanced around for his bow. For all the good it did. Look at him there."

The sharks were all circling again. There was nothing else on the sea or in it.

"I told you you'd never kill him," the blurred voice said. The soldier's face went gray beneath his wiry black hair and eyebrows. He turned to the cook.

Dama touched the big man's arm. "We're not sharks," he said quietly.

Blissfully ignorant of how close she had come to death, Hlovida prattled on, "You'll starve, you know. There's nothing left but a little grain and enough oil to coat the jar." She giggled. "All the meat's gone, over the side, lost—and you'll not be fishing more, will you?"

In three jumps, both men were under the shelter and jerking the stoppers from amphoras. Dercetus' left leg was stuck to the neck of one jar. The black ichor oozing through the bandage cracked as Dama eased the mate aside, and he screamed himself awake. The amphora held less than a peck of wheat. The meat containers sloshed with stinking brine, nothing else.

"Did they hurt you, dearest?" Hlovida cooed as she ran her speckled hands down Dercetus' face. She had wrapped the mate mummy-fashion in what had been one or more layers of her own garments. It would not have helped for them to start clean, Dama thought grimly, considering the way Dercetus leaked where his skin was gone.

"The bitch hid the rest of the grain on her," Vettius suggested huskily. His great hands closed on the cook's shoulders and threw her back on the deck. Insanely, the woman began to scream, "Oh! Oh! You'll rape me for my beauty!"

Dama jerked loose her sash. A paper-wrapped packet hidden somewhere within the Marcomann's clothing thumped the deck and skittered down a broken plank. The Cappadocian's hand speared it before it could slip into the hold. "Castor and Pollux, she *has* got something!" he cried.

Through a chorus of sobs, Hlovida shrieked, "No, you won't take my beauty?"

Vettius backhanded her into silence.

The blond merchant peeled away two layers of scrap papyrus while his friend watched anxiously. Inside lay a large, flat crystal. It was clear in the centre, translucently white around the chipped edges. Part of one side had been scraped concave by a sharp instrument. "Rock salt?" Vettius queried. He ignored the cook groaning softly behind him.

"I don't . . ." Dama muttered. He touched a loose granule to his tongue. It tasted faintly metallic and had a gritty, insoluble texture. The merchant spat it out, spat again to clear the saliva from his mouth. "Poison!" he said. "There's enough arsenic here to wipe out a city."

His tongue touched his lips as another thought occurred to him. "What does a cook do with poison, old woman?"

Hlovida was on her knees and snuffling. "He wouldn't look at me because I wasn't pretty any more," she mumbled. "I saved some of the money each time I bought supplies—"

"Stole it, she means," Vettius interjected sardonically, but the merchant hushed him swiftly.

"My sisters, they used to use it to make men look at them. So white, such white skins they had. Oh!" she concluded with a wail. "Nobody would look at me any more!"

"Dis," the Cappadocian whispered, "no wonder her mind's gone."

"Don't take it, will you?" Hlovida begged. A gnarled, poison-blotched hand crept towards the crystal.

Vettius' great paw caught it first, tossed it in the air. "We've got a better use for it," he stated flatly.

"Umm," Dama agreed, "but he may not take it. He's . . . that is, it isn't . . . well, it doesn't act like a shark."

"It'll take the bait we offer it," Vettius promised with a stark grin. "And that's all we have, isn't it?"

Dama followed the big soldier's eyes forward. "Yes," he admitted, "I guess it is." He checked the edge of his hatchet.

*   *   *

Knocking Hlovida down wasn't enough. Vettius finally tied the screaming woman to the rail before he could return to Dama in the forward shelter. For a man as near death as he was, Dercetus fought like a demon. It took all the soldier's strength to hold him down while Dama smashed through the bone at mid-thigh, just beneath the new tourniquet. The merchant drained his grisly trophy over the side, watching the blood dilute outward in semicircles.

A brown-mottled tiger shark broke momentarily from the pack, then rejoined it without noticeable interchange with any of the other sharks. The white shark rolled so that its left eye glared at the ship through the air; then it dived away more swiftly than before. The others—the sea was rotten with sharks—went wild in leaping and corkscrews but did not approach the *Purple Ibis*.

"Quick," the merchant requested. Vettius' dagger ripped a deep channel into the thigh muscle and he inserted the crystal. Two quick twists of rag and a knot closed the flesh back over the poison. Dama grunted and threw the leg overboard.

"Should have the pike ready," he said.

"What for?" the soldier queried with a chuckle. "Think he'll fool with us any more if this doesn't work?"

The great shark shot skyward with all its rigid power. The mate's leg was there and then gone, and spray fountained as the fish bellied back into the sea. The white shadow slipped beneath the ship. Wood rasped, then splintered tremulously as the keel tore away. The whole leaping, gasping pack of killers was approaching the vessel from all sides. Perhaps they sensed as both men did that the ship could break up at any moment.

Dama swore. "Even that wasn't enough poison," he said. "Look—it knows something's wrong but it's not about to roll belly up."

The white shark paused in its assault on the hull and shook itself side to side. It did not appear seriously disordered and the trembling slackened to an end. "You'll never kill him!" Hlovida shrieked from where she was bound. She lashed her head so violently that some of the brittle hair snapped and floated into the sea. "Men can't kill him!"

Vettius grimaced and started for the cook. Dama again caught his arm. "Let her rave, Lucius."

"Raving or not, she's been right too often," the soldier growled. "I don't want her finding more of that to say. It comes true."

Before he could act, the shark slid back towards the ship through foam-muddled water. "Watch it!" Dama called, but Vettius had already seen the danger. One tail flick, a second, and the shark was on them. But instead of another graceful leap to bring its body down shatteringly on weakened timbers, the sleek movements dissolved into a spasm working forward from the tail. The shark's nose bumped the ship almost gently and the beast backed off. It vomited hugely into the sea: Dercetus' leg already bleached white by stomach acid, and a less identifiable lump that must have been the sailor.

"He'll come out of it now," Dama said bleakly. He had seen enough men poisoned to know that the survivors were the ones who turned their stomachs out quickly. A glance overboard gave him the dizzy feeling that he could step off the rail and run across the backs of the sharks. A big hammerhead, the bronze glint of a leader trailing back from its mouth, nuzzled the ejecta avidly. Seared again by the poison, the white shark lurched forward uncontrolled and snouted its T-headed relative. The lesser shark turned lazily. Its jaws opened incredibly wide, so wide they appeared to dislocate in the instant before they slammed closed on the white shark's belly.

"God of Calvary," Dama breathed, his lips forming words unspoken since his childhood. His fingers gouged bruises in Vettius' rigid arm. "Lord of the meek, be with us now!"

The huge fish arched into a flat bow, ripping loose the slaty hammerhead. A bloody gobbet of flesh had torn away. Scales proof against Man's weapons crunched apart under jaw muscles with thirty tons of rending power.

The rest of the pack went mad.

The sea blasted apart in a fury of blood and froth. The other sharks ringed the great white like doles about a wounded tiger. Twisting mightily, the white shark broke away in a dive. Already a score of platter-sized gaps in its hide streamed red into the sea. But there was time in the depths for wounds to scar; for reflection, perhaps, if a shark's mind could reflect. . . .

Poison-riddled muscles spasmed again, shattering the smooth thrust for sanctuary. The rest was carnage. When the enormous tail flipped a small blue through the air broken-backed, the nearest of the pack bolted the new victim. The others continued to squirm toward the wounded white with deadly intent. The great fish did not die easily, but nothing could have survived that thrashing chaos. Logy with arsenic, ever more tattered by its maddened kin, the shark hurled itself from the carmine water in a convulsive arc. As it fell back, Dama caught its eye. It was glazed and empty.

"There's a cloud south of us," Dama said at last. "Maybe we're due for some wind."

Vettius continued to scan the bloody water about the ship. It had suddenly been drained of life. Dercetus moaned, out of sight forward.

"Rest easy, darling," Hlovida cackled grossly. "I'll never leave you."

SMALL LORDS

by Frederik Pohl

Since the late 1930s, Frederik Pohl (1919–)
has been involved in literary endeavors as agent,
editor, or writer and he certainly has to be considered
one of the giants of American science fiction. Some
of his works we consider personal favorites are
The Space Merchants (with C. M. Kornbluth), 1953;
The Age of the Pussyfoot, 1966; and The Best of
Frederik Pohl, 1975.

In the following story, visiting earthmen cause big
problems for Lilliputian starmen.

1

Cliteman picked his way mincingly along the greenish sands
of the beach. It was nearly dark, and that made it bad,
because he had to watch where he was stepping. The crazy
young ones were just as likely as not to run across his path
for a thrill. And if he missed seeing one in the dusk, and
stepped on it . . .

He swallowed and moved closer to the water's edge. It
might be best, everything considered, to swim back; but he
didn't like the thought of that brackish water in the sores on
his back. The foreman had given him an unusually hard time
that day—well, maybe the foreman's wife had given *him* a
hard time that morning and he was just taking it out on
Cliteman. If the foreman had a wife.

Cliteman stopped at the outskirts of the little village he called Salt Lake City and whistled, as he had learned it was best to do. The greenish, jewellike lights in the windows of the tiny houses were all on; and the larger, bluer lights in the streets gave Cliteman a pretty good view, even though the light from setting Canopus was rapidly dwindling.

Cliteman saw that one of the midges was waving at him, and he squatted down. The midge was big for its race, very nearly half an inch tall. It stood on two legs like a man; it had two arms like a man, and a head like a man's head. The glossy eyes that covered nearly the whole head were not a man's, of course, and the shrill, piping voice was closer to the stridulations of an insect.

It was waving him away from the village off the beach. Cliteman saw why; there was some sort of gathering on the sands, several hundred of the midges. Without resentment, he waded into the shallows and around the town, though the sting of the water on his scarred legs was extremely painful.

But that wasn't important to Cliteman at the moment. What was important was that he was almost unbearably hungry. If only Morris had found something decent to eat for a change! A couple dozen of the big pink shellfish perhaps, or one of those big, six-legged swimming things that tasted faintly of peach-pits . . .

Splat. Cliteman yelled involuntarily as the biting greenish spark charred a tiny crater in his shoulder. One of the midges was standing threateningly on a rock in his path aiming at him with the glistening small hand weapons that they used for disciplining the earthmen—or for killing each other as the occasion arose.

Splat. Another spark flared close by, this one only a warning. Cliteman clutched his shoulder and, ever so gently, moved farther out into the water. It was important not to move quickly; the spray a fast-moving foot might kick up was enough to drown a midge.

And that was about all he needed. If he killed one of them, that would be the end of everything. Cliteman vividly remembered what had happened to Fuller when he had crushed one of the little aliens. Quite by accident; but the aliens either didn't know that, or didn't care.

It wasn't that they were deliberately cruel in the way they destroyed Fuller; or at least, Cliteman thought it wasn't. But these beings were tiny and humans huge; they had only tiny weapons against the gross flesh monoliths from the exploring ship. Death at the hands of the midges was like death from an army of raging termites. It came with a hundred, a thousand, ten thousand little, painful, finally fatal wounds. Perhaps there weren't any good ways to die, Cliteman thought, but certainly there were few that were worse.

As quickly as he could, Cliteman hurried down the brackish sea's shore, each step a carefully planned, meticulously executed problem in engineering. He tried to stay ankle-deep in the water, away from possible wandering midges on the beach, but not so deep that his steps would splash any who might come by. The foot carefully lifted and carefully brought forward; the toe pointed out just so, slipped into the water ahead as delicately as the top liqueur in a pousse-café.

Just ahead was the little cape the aliens had indicated the human giants might use for their own, free and clear. "Morris!" cried Cliteman. "Hello there!"

No answer; not even the gleam of firelight, where Morris should already have had the fire going, cooking whatever he had been able to turn up in the way of food. Morris was the official provider for the humans, permitted by the tiny aliens to labor only half a day on the crude projects they had assigned the others, so that he might have time to find and prepare the enormous masses of food the giants required. "Morris! Are you there?"

But he wasn't there. Cliteman was alone.

Canopus was down now, and the only light was from the bluish star they called Neighbor. From Earth, Neighbor was only a tiny spot of light—twelfth-magnitude or thereabouts—smaller than the 200-inch telescope. But it happened to hang close in space to the system of Canopus. Though its absolute magnitude was only four or five times the brightness of the sun, it was close enough so that in the night sky it seemed brighter than Earth's moon, bright enough to see by, uncomfortably bright to look at direct.

There was not, however, light enough to make it easy for Cliteman to tend his nets. After half an hour he hauled in his catch; something throbbed and leaped in the purse. He pulled on the long, precious ropes with his mouth watering, it wasn't until he had the net on the sand, maddeningly empty, that he saw he had neglected to fasten the other end. The prey had escaped; he grimly tied the necessary knots, and cast it out again.

Cliteman lay down on the beach to wait. It was getting chilly—the planet's air was thin. Canopus provided plenty of heat by day, but with the setting of their sun the temperature dropped thirty or forty degrees in as many minutes. The fire was a comfort, but of course it didn't do to make it large—everything on the planet's surface was on a smallish scale; the largest vegetation was not much taller than a man. Already in only a few months, they had nearly denuded the little cape that was set aside for them of burnable brush, and there was no way of knowing if the midges would permit them to extend their foraging inland. The trouble was, they couldn't talk to the midges. It was not merely a matter of language, but the auditory range of the little aliens was pitched bat-high; only the sharpest whistles of the earthmen could be heard by the midges—as bass rumbles, no doubt.

Cliteman stared wearily at Neighbor through half-closed eyes. Somewhere about Neighbor, the interstellar ship would be orbiting now, while its scout rockets surveyed the half-dozen planets they had located from space. The ship had been gone six months; it would be gone six months more, at least.

There was a grave doubt in Cliteman's mind that any of them would survive another six months of this.

There had been ten men in the scout rocket that set down on Canopus's sixth planet. Three were dead—Fuller under the weapons of the midges, Breck and Hogarth when the rocket crashed. Morris was sick—it was no charity that made the midges let him have his half-day off; even the tiny aliens could see that the radioman was in bad shape.

And the rest of them were slaves.

Something whistled through the air high overhead—a hundred yards or more. Cliteman instinctively stood up and raised his hand to identify himself. It was a midge flyer, one of the foot-long jets that he had seen from time to time on mysterious errands, no doubt diverted from whatever course it had been pursuing by the sight of his fire. It circled, with a thin noise like a swinging whip, and Cliteman saw the pattern of colored lights on its dragonfly wings that seemed to be an identification marking. "Take a good look!" he mumbled to himself. He looked more closely himself, and saw that this particular jet was much smaller than others he had seen. It couldn't have been more than three or four inches long, he guessed, as it spiraled down within a few yards of his head. No doubt a one-"man"-ship, to be used for—for . . .

Cliteman lowered his hands sourly, craning his neck to stare down the shore where Morris should have been coming, but wasn't. He didn't *know* what the midges might use a one-man jet for. Did they have wars? Perhaps; and perhaps a small jet might be a fighter. But it was only a guess, and the chances were extremely good that any guess any of the earthmen might make about the midges was quite wrong. There had been no chance to learn; the scout rocket had come in without orbiting—though no amount of orbiting would have done much good, since no conceivable midge installation would have been visible from space. They had observed nothing in the descent, beyond the bare outlines of the planet's geography; they had crashed in landing, and had stumbled out into an aroused hornet's nest of mighty little warriors.

And from then on, nothing.

The tiny jet whipped once more around him and shot out over the water. Cliteman touched his sore shoulder with a gentle hand, starting absently after it.

Then he focused his eyes and his attention. Something was floundering in the net.

Dinner! He jumped for the ropes that he and Morris had so painstakingly pierced together and pulled the purse toward shore. Whatever it was that was in the net, it was of a size that promised a full meal! Be damned to Morris, Cliteman thought rebelliously; let him go hungry then! He carefully jockeyed the net into the shallows, and in Neighbor's blue-white light he saw the thrashing sea-creature's struggles break the surface of the water. He played it as any angler plays a trout, fully concentrated, aware of nothing but his net and his prey . . .

Disastrously aware of nothing; for disaster came.

He heard, a little too late, the deeper, slower whistle of the jet again. He looked up a little too late, and saw it settling down toward the water, close inshore, just beyond his net.

The jet's tiny pilot was landing!

Cliteman pulled frantically at the ropes; then dropped them. Too late! The jet seemed to falter and swerve, as though the pilot had at least seen the treacherous snarl of ropes, and the leaping sea-creature in the water before him. Too late! The tiny aircraft had already touched its narrow keel to the water; it bounced on one cord and spun around another; it plowed into the tangle of the net itself and flipped over.

Cliteman, panicky, leaped knee-deep into the water and clutched at the doll-sized aircraft. He roared and jerked his hands away; stupid of him to have touched the jet exhaust! He grasped it gently around the middle of the fuselage and lifted it, held it in his hand, staring. It was impossible to see the pilot in only the light from Neighbor; in a moment he brought it to the fire and set it down on a little rock, and knelt to peer inside the little transparent hatch.

The pilot was inside, all right; but motionless. Unconscious, perhaps, or dead.

In either case, there was no doubt in Cliteman's mind that he was in trouble.

2

Morris limped slowly toward the reservation.

He was hungry, in spite of the wearing, burning pain in his chest that had been getting worse ever since the rocket crash; and he was bone-tired. His whole back was a pattern of new scars as well; it had taken quite a few applications of the midge's weapons before he understood that this day was not like all the other days, that this day the midges did not intend to permit him to leave his work halfway through the day. The scars were the penalty he had to pay for not understanding; but it didn't make them less painful.

Besides, there would be trouble with Cliteman, Morris knew with resignation. How close to the beast they had all returned! Take the case of Sanford Cliteman, lieutenant in the Space Force, respected citizen, loved husband and father of two. Morris had played many a game of chess with Cliteman on the way out; the lieutenant had been a skilled opponent, generous in victory, good-natured in defeat.

Yet, what about the time three days before when Morris had torn the net and there had been no dinner ready for Cliteman? The man's anger had been animal—and Morris himself had flared into anger in response; the two of them had come close to a fistfight. Animal!

But how could they help it? They were treated as beasts, mindless prime movers suitable for clearing land for the strange midge farms, or for scrabbling at the earth to make culverts and irrigation ditches. If they offended, they were given a beast's punishment, a touch of the whip. If they served well, they got a beast's reward, to be turned loose at sundown—free to feed and sleep. That was the greatest gift the midges ever gave.

"Why?" Morris demanded, puffing and holding his bad leg as he limped along. It seemed impossible that the midges should not realize they were intelligent, highly civilized beings. They had seen the rocket; they could not imagine beasts could create or man such a machine. But there was simply no sign of an attempt at communication.

In the fury of the first fight, the earthmen had been completely off guard. The rocket had crashed; that put an end to the book's rules about first contact on an alien planet. They had stumbled out of the wreck, mostly unharmed, mostly hurt or shaken up. They had been greeted with fire from the midge hand weapons, and even more serious fire from what might have been the equivalent of self-propelled artillery. Well, maybe they should have reacted quicker, Morris thought; they could have stuck together, leaped back into the rocket in spite of the threat of fire and explosion, armed themselves, fought off the aliens. But in the split second when that was still possible they had wavered.

Carrasquel had drawn his gun and begun return fire; but the equation one bullet—one midge did not balance to the advantage of the earthmen. Undoubtedly Carrasquel had killed a few, but what was the use of killing a few—or a hundred—or a thousand? Fuller hadn't had a gun, but he had stamped at them as though they were insects. It was Fuller the midges destroyed, in cold blood, while he lay in helpless anguish under the shock of their concentrated fire. Concentrated, that was it; the midges had leaped into action, each group fixed firmly on a target; the humans in their surprise had blundered and scattered. And they never had really got together again. The midge tactics had evidently been to keep them apart, for the fire was most punishing when any two of the earthmen tried to come together. . . .

And now there were Cliteman and himself, who had been driven miles and miles across country, under the stings of the pursuing midges in their vehicles and their aircraft. He knew where Carrasquel and Boehm were, because he'd chanced to see Boehm and they'd been able to shout to each other for a moment; the others he hadn't even seen in months.

But if only the midges had waited—if only the midges had tried to make contact, come to appreciate that earthmen were their superiors, in any imaginable scale of intellectual values. . .

But come to think of it, Morris told himself dourly, that was no longer so very true.

Morris labored around the little hill that went down to the water and saw Cliteman fiddling with something on the ground. There was no smell of cooking fish; there was something wrong. "Cliteman, what's the matter?"

The lieutenant jumped up, startled, his eyes wild. Then he saw who it was. "Oh, Morris. This damn midge— Where the hell have you been? I've been starving— Never mind that. Look what I've got here!"

Morris looked, and opened his eyes, and looked again. He whispered, "Sweet love of heaven!"

"What am I going to do?" Cliteman demanded. "Look at the damn things, Morris. They're hurt! They might be dying, for all I know."

"They?"

Cliteman said bitterly, "Three of them; three little midges, out for a little excursion. Momma Midge and Poppa Midge and Little Bitty Baby Midge—I guess. And what do you think they'll make of that, Morris? I've been sitting here trying to make up my mind to chuck them back in the drink."

"No, Cliteman!"

Cliteman stared at him woodenly for a second. "Remember Fuller?" he asked after a moment.

"I know, Cliteman, but . . ."

"They'll think *I* killed them! And how do I know? Maybe I did. If I hadn't been pulling in the net just when they landed their stinking plane it would have been all right! But here they are, and do you know what comes next, Morris? Because I don't!"

Morris lowered himself gingerly to the ground—something he was reluctant to do, because it wasn't always easy getting up again. "Shut up a minute," he ordered, and looked closely at the midge plane.

There were three of them in it, all right. Two stirring faintly, one motionless. Dead? Morris had no idea. They all had their eyes open, but as far as Morris or Cliteman knew, midges had nothing to close their eyes with; neither of them had ever seen one blink. The transparent canopy was smashed open. Apparently, Cliteman's first frantic idea was to get the three of them out of the plane, but once he'd opened the canopy he hadn't dared touch them.

Morris stared dazedly at the tiny machine. It was a beautifully made child's toy; any kid on earth would have given his chance of immortality for one like it. Three inches long, five inches from wingtip to where the other wingtip would have been if it hadn't been crumpled flat. It was still in working condition except for the wings and the canopy—at any rate, tiny red and purple lights winked on what might have been the instrument panel, and something that Morris couldn't see was making a faint, high-pitched hum.

Morris propped himself on an elbow and ventured to touch one of the midges with a delicately questing finger. It moved slightly, but whether it was cold to the touch or warm he couldn't have said.

He noticed silvery threads and rods, so small they were almost invisible, tangled in a little heap on a flat rock beside the ship. "What's that?"

Cliteman took a deep breath. He sounded a little more human as he said, "I don't know. I thought they might be—well, radio antennas or something. I broke them off. Didn't want them calling for help."

Morris shook his head. Cliteman cried, "Don't tell me I shouldn't have done that! Maybe I shouldn't have, but—curse it, Morris, I was scared! Don't forget Fuller."

Morris sighed. He said wearily, "I'm hungry," and pushed himself to a sitting position, still looking at the little plane. "They kept me working till dark," he said absently. "I guess they decided I'm well enough to put in a full day's work now. Or maybe that I'm not well enough to be worth pampering—might as well work me to death. I don't suppose you caught anything to eat?"

"Morris, don't you see what trouble we're in?"

Morris looked at Cliteman soberly. "They'll blame us for sure!" Morris noted that it was "us" who had become responsible for what had happened to the midge plane. "Look, Morris, the way I see it there are only two things we can do. One, we can get rid of it—sink it in the ocean, and hope they never find it. Maybe they won't. Maybe they won't connect us with what happened to the plane."

"And maybe they will," said Morris.

"All right, they will," Cliteman agreed. "Sure, why kid ourselves? So that only leaves one thing. It's time for us to make our break, Morris. Like we talked about. We'll cut straight across country till we find that big river and stay right with it. It can't be more than ten miles. We won't miss the rocket, it's too big. What do you say, Morris? We've been planning to do it anyhow as soon as you were feeling better. Well, this just moves the date up. We can't wait. It's too big a risk, Morris; remember Fuller. What about it? If we . . ."

"Shut up." Cliteman blinked and stared. "No, *shut up!*" Morris sat straight, peering at the sky. It wasn't anger that had made him tell the lieutenant to shut up, although he felt something that came close to anger.

He had heard something.

He listened; the two of them listened.

They heard it, and then in a moment they saw: The faint whistle, the patterned lights of a midge jet circling overhead.

3

"Act busy!" cried Cliteman. "Start putting wood on the fire!"

He himself leaped toward the net, where the neglected fish-thing was feebly flapping away what remained of its strength. He drew it in while Morris laboriously got to his feet and fed the fire. Cliteman grasped the slippery creature, reckless of possible teeth or stinging spines. He bashed it expertly against a rock and then took a closer look at it. It was tentacled, not much over a foot long and plump as a frog's belly. Cliteman quickly skewered it on a gnarled stem of green wood and handed it to Morris to broil.

"But you didn't clean it!" Morris protested. "We can't eat this without . . ."

"Cook it! We aren't going to eat it, you idiot. Just look busy until that damn plane goes away."

Cliteman glanced warily up. It was still there, perhaps not as close, but well within the range of the sound its jets made. He swore under his breath, looked around undecidedly, and settled on adding more fuel to the fire. He bent down for branches, and abruptly jumped up as though he had seen an adder. "What's the matter?" Morris demanded, startled.

"That thing!" Cliteman's voice was shaky. He was staring at the wrecked midge flier on the ground before him. He darted a quick look over his shoulder, then jumped toward it, obviously intending to stamp it into the ground.

"Wait!" screamed Morris, blocking Cliteman's path.

"Out of the way!"

"No, Cliteman! You'll kill them!"

"You're damn well told I'll kill them. We're crazy to

leave that thing in plain sight. Those others will come back any minute, and if they see it, wham! We're done for, man!''

"Wait!" ordered Morris in a totally different voice, a voice of command.

Cliteman stopped and stared.

Morris said tightly, "It's murder. I won't let you do it.''

Cliteman stood poised, and his eyes were hard on the limping man. He held the twisted stick of firewood in his hand. For a moment it seemed that the stick would be a club, to strike at Morris; but there was a nearing whistle and a fleck of light that darted about their heads. Both men jumped. They had forgotten the midge jet, but the jet had not forgotten them. It came swooping in on them like an earthly plane circling living pylons; and if there had been a chance before, that chance was gone.

Perhaps it had been only curiosity that made the midge pilot come close to the quarreling Titans; perhaps he had caught a glimpse of the wreck. Whatever, it did him in; for the stick that might have been a club became a flyswatter; Cliteman swung, as quickly, as thoughtlessly as a polar relay, and slapped the prying midge plane out of the air. There was a faint ringing crunch as the tree trunk hit the plane, and a distant hiss and tiny crack as the plane slammed into the water and exploded; and that was the end of that.

"Now we are in for it," said Cliteman after a moment. And, after a moment more, "I'm sorry."

Morris only shook his head. It was late to be sorry. "Clean that fish, will you?" he said.

"Clean— What?"

"That fish," said Morris irritably. "Or whatever it is. We're going to have to eat it, you know. We're going to have a long night ahead of us."

He turned his back on the other man and bent to look at the crashed midge flyer that had started the trouble. They were alive after all, he saw absently; all three of the occupants were moving and one of them was chirping excitedly. Not that it mattered to Morris, not any more. . . .

Picture a pair of horrid monsters, obelisk-tall, deformed beyond human experience, rampaging about Levittown or thundering in the surf at Laguna Beach. Picture them dropped from space in a queer, enormous vessel the like of which no man had ever seen, their voices a quivering diapason that hurts the ear and shakes the spine. Picture them feasting on whale sharks or such enormous offal from the sea, quarreling among themselves, and striking out to clout an airliner in ruins from the sky.

It is no wonder, thought Morris, *that the midges don't want us around.*

But if the positions had been reversed—would we have at least have tried to communicate?

But—if the positions had been reversed—would we have allowed the monsters to live at all?

Morris sighed, and blew on the chunk of greasy flesh he was holding, and forced himself to eat.

The two men ate in silence. Above them, and outward to the sea, there was a clustering swarm of midge aircraft, not approaching, but observing every move. They had begun to arrive within minutes after Cliteman had struck at the midge plane. They were waiting for something.

Whatever it was it couldn't be long in coming.

"Hurry up!" Cliteman grumbled hoarsely. Morris nodded but didn't answer; there wasn't much to say.

They had planned for a month, and the sum of their planning was this: someday they would make a break for the rocket. It would not be impossible, for between them and the spot where the rocket had crashed lay dense brush—towering jungle, by midge standards; it would be hard for the little creatures to bring much force to bear against them. On the other hand, it would not be very fruitful, for the rocket had crashed. As a plan, it had only one real advantage; it was better than nothing.

It would have been better, thought Morris with detachment, *if we could have waited until I was stronger—until the*

*ship returned from Neighbor, and maybe another rocket might
come down—until the chances were somehow better . . .*

But that was exactly what was no longer possible. For
there was no doubt that whatever the earthmen's status with
the midges had been, the destruction of the plane had changed
it for the worse.

"Morris! What the devil's that?"

Cliteman was pointing.

Something bright and fast was gliding toward them in the
water. It was long—six or eight feet, easily—but not very
wide. It looked rather like a mechanized small canoe, with a
row of lights and brighter lights fixed forward.

Hiss, *splat*. A fat blue spark leaped from the prow of the
thing toward them, fell short and sizzled in the water.

"I didn't know the midges had battleships," said Morris in
amazement, and then shook himself. "Come on; let's get out
of here!"

"Hold it!" Cliteman caught him by the shoulder, his eyes
huge and fearful as he stared down the beach. In the pale
light from Neighbor it was hard to see what was going on.
But once again there were lights, hundreds of them it seemed;
they dipped and bobbed and joggled and came on. Morris
saw at last what the lights belonged to. They were wheeled
machines—not earthly wheels, thin in proportion to their
diameter, but constructed like flabby steam rollers, creeping
forward on rubbery cylinders. There were scores and hundreds of them. Tanks? Something very like tanks, at any rate;
in a moment they opened fire, too, and the giants from earth
were caught in a criss-cross of flying sparks. *"We're cut
off!"* cried Cliteman. *"Run!"*

But it was a little late to run.

A fat blue spark caught Cliteman on the shoulder and spun
him around, yelling. Morris dropped to the ground as another
hissed past him, and he could smell the dry, chemical bite of
ozone in his nose, taste the metallic eddy-currents in his
teeth. "They can see us in the firelight!" Cliteman yelled,
and began to kick furiously at the little campfire. Burning
sticks scattered into the brush, sparks flew up from the fire-

redder, milder sparks than those that came from the midge weapons, but sparks that could burn all the same.

The fire from the midge tanks on the beach came in thick volleys now, and it was impossible that all of them should miss. These were no mere bee stings like the hand weapons, Morris discovered; he yelled, holding his arm, as he discovered it. A couple of shots from these heavy weapons could easily kill.

He lifted his head. "We've got to get out of here! Look!" The flying brands from the fire had not conveniently gone out; the brush was beginning to blaze.

"It'll give them something to think about," Cliteman snarled, and plunged toward the mainland, bobbling and weaving and yelling. It was miraculous that he wasn't struck down by the massed fire from the beach—yet perhaps not so miraculous, for what human gunners could have kept their heads in the face of a charging, bellowing monster a tenth of a mile tall? He got free, Morris following, and in a moment they were in the momentary shelter of the deep brush inland. Behind them, yellow flames and floating sparks rose up toward the bright night sky; ahead was only darkness.

Morris leaned against a twelve-foot tree, panting hoarsely. "What—what next?" he gasped, fighting for breath.

Cliteman breathed a long, shuddering sigh. "What do you think? We'll try for the rocket, and then—" He stopped, hesitated, swore and said roughly, "Come on!"

Morris limped painfully after. And then? *Idiot question*, he thought wearily; there isn't any "and then." They might make it to the rocket and they might not; but whatever happened, there was no future for them.

He paused to catch his breath. Apart from the din Cliteman made pounding through the brush ahead, it was quiet in the woods. The blue-white light from Neighbor filtered down through the leaves. There was a sighing, whispering noise behind him that might have been the fire they left, and might have been the wind; he didn't turn his head to look. He didn't even look up at the distant overhead whistling that, beyond doubt, was the sound of midge jets looking for them. They would be hard to spot in the brush—at least until daylight.

Resolutely, he didn't think beyond daylight.

Cliteman was getting pretty far ahead. Morris stood up. He spread his fingers for a moment, and glanced at the little wrecked midge plane. It had been a foolish impulse to pick it up from the sand beside the fire. It might have been safe enough there; the little creatures would have been cooked alive. But were they any safer with him? He glanced at them; they were still moving, at least. Perhaps he should put them on the ground and leave them, he thought. . . .

But he didn't. In a moment he closed his fingers over the tiny ship and limped after Cliteman.

4

Morris was sitting at his instrument board, transmitting the news of their arrival to Earth. He was well fed, well rested, his wounds entirely healed; the Earth signals were coming through, giving landing instructions and congratulations to the whole crew. Things were fine. The only little flaw was that, for some reason, the rocket motors of the ship were coughing explosively, jarring him, making it hard to receive the faint signal from Earth . . .

"Wake up, Morris!"

He sat up with a start and looked around.

No radio instruments, no ship, no signals from Earth.

He was half propped against a tree, in the woods, and a soft rain was filtering down through the leaves overhead. Sharp coughing explosions were coming from somewhere nearby. The rockets? Then he remembered. No, not rockets. It was midge flyers, dropping their little missile-bombs, stabbing into the unseen ground beneath the treetops, trying to connect with Cliteman and himself. None of them were coming very close—but the midges had plenty of bombs.

Morris coughed raspingly and stood up. Cliteman was grumbling, "It's getting light. Do you see the rocket?"

Morris bent and retrieved the little midge ship. The three occupants were still moving—more weakly, he thought.

Something was glittering, out beyond the fringes of the dense wood. Perhaps a quarter of a mile away, catching light from setting Neighbor, washed out by the beginning glow of Canopus itself.

"Is that it?"

"No, you idiot! Can't you see it's moving?" Cliteman muttered to himself, pacing back and forth, staring out. The younger man was pretty near collapse, Morris judged. That made two of them. He squinted at the glittering thing. It was moving, all right—well, that ruled out the possibility of its being the rocket. But what was it? Something low to the ground and metallic, crawling back and forth in an open stretch. Large, as midge standards went—a yard or more long. Perhaps it was some sort of agricultural machinery, gang plows, sowers, whatever the midges used. The small community where Morris had been a forced laborer had had nothing like it; but, of course, he hadn't seen anything like enough of the midge civilization to judge what technological heights it might attain.

He glanced up, and saw the glimmer of midge jets circling about. The distant cough of the little bombs seemed to come mostly toward the west, in the direction of setting Neighbor; and looking at the patterned jets, Morris realized that most of them were over there too. Now, why should they think we're over that way? he wondered.

And then he knew.

"Cliteman! If you were a midge, where would you expect us to head for?"

Cliteman scowled fretfully. "How the devil do I know? Oh—toward the rocket, I guess. Where else is there?"

"Nowhere else, Cliteman! So—they're probably concentrated around the rocket. And if you'll look at those jets . . ."

Cliteman looked surprised, then merely worried again. "You're right, I suppose. Well—let's try that way. God knows we won't be any worse off, even if we don't find it!"

But they did.

They had to pay a price, because the midge jets were thick as wasps about a nest, but in the glimmering, predawn light they saw the looming tail rockets of their scout towering over the trees that lay between.

They paused for just a second to catch their breath, then Cliteman bellowed, "All right, let's get going!" And he lumbered out of the shelter of the woods, Morris limping and scuttling along behind him.

It was a matter of seconds only, and then the midge aircraft had them spotted. *Thank God*, thought Morris with a part of his brain as he ran, *Thank God they don't seem to have guns on the jets!* But the little buzzing craft came racing in at them as though they intended to ram, swerving off at the last moment, dropping little rice-grain objects that spun and crashed like tiny firecrackers—but louder and more dangerously than any firecrackers that Morris had ever seen.

Cliteman was roaring and flailing his arms as he ran; perhaps that helped, for the midge jets could have come closer still, and then they would not have missed. As it was they veered away short, and though the tiny bombs made ant craters fly up all about the running feet of the earthmen, and the pelting sand from the blasts stung their bare flesh, there were no direct hits. The attackers buzzed by in squads and formations and several of them made Morris duck fearfully as, Kamikazelike, they swooped in directly at his head. That would be no mere wound; the things, small as they were, had the speed and impact of a bullet. But if the pilots had intended to ram, they missed, or changed their minds; and the two men were untouched all the way across the wide sandy field with its fuzzy little growth of midge crops . . .

And there was the rocket.

"Hurry, hurry!" cried Cliteman over his shoulder, and Morris tried to respond:

For the midges were waiting:

Ranked about the rocket were little squares of midge troops, or police, or whatever it was in the midge race that fired electric cannon at invading Earthmen. Even a dozen yards away, Morris could hear the thin cheeping as the midges caught sight of them and prepared to open fire. *Splat! Splatsplatsplatsplat!* A burst of the searing little sparks clustered about Cliteman's head and shoulders; he roared, for though most had been near misses, the one that connected had brought agony with it. He stumbled and half fell against the open port of the rocket. *Splat!* Apparently it was hard for the midge gunners to bring their pieces to bear on a moving target, even so huge a one as an Earthman; for the next burst stained the sides of the rocket itself. Cliteman leaped and struggled and made it inside.

Lurching after him, Morris caught confused pictures of the rocket. There had been changes! Up against the hull of the rocket there was a shiny, spiraling ramp—not to the main port, that the humans used, but to a neat, square-cut hole, burned out of the hull by the looks of it. *Of course, of course,* Morris told himself fretfully, running and dodging and panting, *of course the midges wouldn't have left it alone! Would we have left such a thing alone if it had landed in New York?* No doubt the rocket had swarmed with the little things since the first moment after they landed . . .

And what damage they might have done inside Morris didn't bother to speculate. It didn't matter; they couldn't move the rocket, couldn't escape by flying away—and lacking that it didn't matter how terrible a fight they put up, or what weapons they could contrive from the blasters and handguns they might find. One of them was more than a million midges in mass, but they were outnumbered not by millions but by billions . . .

And then there was no more time for thought.

The midge gunners had found the range, and he was stung by a thousand flaming sparks. Only hand weapons so far, but he had already seen that even the hand weapons could kill. They had killed Fuller, months before, and they might kill him now. He screamed and jolted forward, swerving and bobbling, and if anything saved his life it was the appearance of Cliteman at the door of the rocket, drawing part of the fire. For a moment Morris thought dazedly that Cliteman had come to his rescue, but only for a moment. He saw Cliteman's dancing, convulsing body, and knew that—of course, of course!—there had been midges even inside the rocket, waiting!

But even so—it was better inside the rocket than out. For outside it was plain death.

Morris plunged toward the door as Cliteman was plunging out. They collided and fell.

Morris jolted to the ground, and the breath left him. So this was the end, he thought wearily. Well, let it come . . .

But something was nagging at him.

He remembered what he was carrying, what he held in his hand all through the long fight, protecting it, trying to find the right place and the right time to put it down.

The wrecked midge flyer!

The tiny figures inside still moved, he saw, and he was glad. With almost the last of his strength, the maddening blue sparks charring him by inches, he stretched out his hand and opened the fingers, gently—about to set the flyer on the ground.

And then his fingers closed on it again.

Morris sat up, staring at the little machine. Heedless of the scorching fire from the midge weapons, heedless of the doing, singing jets overhead.

The pain no longer mattered. It was a fact of life, and there was nothing he could do about it. He put it out of his mind.

Morris set the midge flyer on the ground. He stood up, raised his huge foot over it, brought it down—fast, hard, brutal . . .

And stopped. The foot, huge as Cheops's tomb above the little flyer, halted and hovered, while the tiny creatures inside stared up with huge eyes.

Morris pulled back his foot. Slowly, solemnly, he shook his head—"*no*" to the left, "*no*" to the right.

He bent, picked up the flyer again, set it carefully away, and slumped to the ground.

Lord help us, he thought, *Lord help us, that's all I can do . . .*

And then he closed his eyes, and waited for the pain to end, with the end of all pain that is dying.

But death didn't come.

There was an agony and a fiery burning, but not death. It was hard to tell if there were new wounds falling on Morris's ravaged back, or only the endured pain of the old ones. There was pain, all right; but bearable pain—not the cruel, killing pain that Fuller must have felt, that Morris had expected.

He opened his eyes.

The massed weapons of the midges were ranged on him; but they weren't firing.

He looked around. Overhead the midge flyers swooped and whistled; but they weren't dropping their destructive small bombs.

Morris raised himself on his arms, fearing to hope, hoping for an end to fear. Beside him, Cliteman's incredulous voice said, "They aren't shooting at us!"

It was true. And there before them both was the answer.

The little flyer that Morris had so carefully carried, so carefully set out of harm's way. There was no one in it now; but one tiny midge sat painfully on the ground beside it, looking up at them.

If the flat, huge-eyed face wore an expression, Morris couldn't read it. But what he could read beyond question was the fact that the other two were gone—to the midges manning the guns, beyond doubt. Gone to tell them that—that . . .

"Why, they must have told the others we meant no harm," whispered Cliteman, and looked wonderingly at Morris.

Morris nodded slowly.

Cliteman pulled himself painfully to his feet. "Morris the Destroyer," he breathed, and there was no irony in his tone. "Morris the Giver of Life. You showed them we didn't want to kill, and they understood."

He helped Morris to his feet, and the two of them stood regarding the slowly advancing midges, now with their weapons turned to the ground.

"I'm glad," said Cliteman; "I'm glad you took such good care of the three in the plane."

5

Executive Officer Yardsley, favoring his bandaged and splinted arm, squinted at his desk calculator and announced, "We're in an orbit that'll hold us for a while, I guess. Any word from the landing party?"

"I'll check with the radio room," said the Officer of the Deck, and dialed its combination on the intercom.

Yardsley leaned back, patting the bandages on his arm. Outside the viewscreen, bright Canopus blazed at them. It had been a rough trip, complicated with hostile inhabitants on the planet of the star called Neighbor. He was entirely ready for the long, peaceful trip back to earth, as soon as they collected the crew of the scout rocket that had gone down to look over the Canopan planet—it couldn't be too long or too peaceful for Executive Officer Yardsley. He had made the mistake of volunteering for the landing party on the planet that circled Neighbor; and when the aborigines turned out to be large green anthropoids with Stone Age culture and surly tempers, he had been one of those who had been on the receiving end of the slung stones that greeted them.

The O.O.D. was listening with considerable interest to whatever it was the radio room had to report, Yardsley noted. At last he said, "Good-oh, thanks," and hung up.

"Well?" demanded Yardsley.

"Oh, they've had a ball," the O.O.D. told him, grinning. "The radio room just established contact, and they haven't got the whole story yet. But enough. They had a little trouble at first, but now they've established contact with the native population. Civilized, Yardsley—and got machines, aircraft, everything. And, oh, yes—they only average about half an inch high!"

"Half an inch high," repeated Yardsley, remembering the green anthropoids. He sighed. "Wouldn't you know it? I had a free choice—I could have gone with them, or I could have landed on Neighbor. Just my luck to pick the one that was *dangerous*."

THE MAD PLANET

by Murray Leinster

Murray Leinster was a pseudonym for Will F. Jenkins (1896–1975), a writer of very entertaining science fiction for fifty years. As samples of his best work we would recommend The Forgotten Planet *(1954),* The Pirates of Zan *(1959), and* The Best of Murray Leinster *(1976).*

Indeed, the following story (1920) plus two sequels became The Forgotten Planet—*adventures set in a far future in which giant insects dwarf dengenerate mankind.*

In all his lifetime of perhaps twenty years, it had never occurred to Burl to wonder what his grandfather had thought about his surroundings. The grandfather had come to an untimely end in a rather unpleasant fashion which Burl remembered vaguely as a succession of screams coming more and more faintly to his ears while he was being carried away at the top speed of which his mother was capable.

Burl had rarely or never thought of the old gentleman since. Surely he had never wondered in the abstract of what his great-grandfather thought, and most surely of all, there never entered his head such a purely hypothetical question as the one of what his man-times-great-grandfather—say of the year 1920—would have thought of the scene in which Burl found himself.

He was treading cautiously over a brownish carpet of fungus growth, creeping furtively toward the stream which he knew by the generic title of "water." It was the only water he knew. Towering far above his head, three man-heights high, great toadstools hid the grayish sky from his sight. Clinging to the foot-thick stalks of the toadstools were still other fungi, parasites upon the growth that had once been parasites themselves.

Burl himself was a slender young man wearing a single garment twisted about his waist, made from the wing-fabric of a great moth the members of his tribe had slain as it emerged from its cocoon. His skin was fair, without a trace of sunburn. In all his lifetime he had never seen the sun, though the sky was rarely hidden from view save by the giant fungi which, with monster cabbages, were the only growing things he knew. Clouds usually spread overhead, and when they did not, the perpetual haze made the sun but an indefinitely brighter part of the sky, never a sharply edged ball of fire. Fantastic mosses, misshapen fungus growths, colossal molds and yeasts, were the essential parts of the landscape through which he moved.

Once as he had dodged through the forest of huge toadstools, his shoulder touched a cream-colored stalk, giving the whole fungus a tiny shock. Instantly, from the umbrellalike mass of pulp overhead, a fine and impalpable powder fell upon him like snow. It was the season when the toadstools sent out their spores, or seeds, and they had been dropped upon him at the first sign of disturbance.

Furtive as he was, he paused to brush them from his head and hair. They were deadly poison, as he knew well.

Burl would have been a curious sight to a man of the twentieth century. His skin was pink, like that of a child, and there was but little hair upon his body. Even that on top of his head was soft and downy. His chest was larger than his forefathers' had been, and his ears seemed almost capable of independent movement, to catch threatening sounds from any direction. His eyes, large and blue, possessed pupils which could dilate to extreme size, allowing him to see in almost complete darkness.

He was the result of the thirty thousand years' attempt of the human race to adapt itself to the change that had begun in the latter half of the twentieth century.

At about that time, civilization had been high, and apparently secure. Mankind had reached a permanent agreement among itself, and all men had equal opportunities to education and leisure. Machinery did most of the labor of the world, and men were only required to supervise its operation. All men were well-fed, all men were well-educated, and it seemed that until the end of time the earth would be the abode of a community of comfortable human beings, pursuing their studies and diversions, their illusions and their truths. Peace, quietness, privacy, freedom were universal.

Then, just when men were congratulating themselves that the Golden Age had come again, it was observed that the planet seemed ill at ease. Fissures opened slowly in the crust, and carbonic acid gas—the carbon dioxide of chemists—began to pour out into the atmosphere. That gas had long been known to be present in the air, and was considered necessary to plant life. Most of the plants of the world took the gas and absorbed its carbon into themselves, releasing the oxygen for use again.

Scientists had calculated that a great deal of the earth's increased fertility was due to the larger quantities of carbon dioxide released by the activities of man in burning his coal and petroleum. Because of those views, for some years no great alarm was caused by the continuous exhalation from the world's interior.

Constantly, however, the volume increased. New fissures constantly opened, each one adding a new source of carbon dioxide, and each one pouring into the already laden atmosphere more of the gas—beneficent in small quantities, but as the world learned, deadly in large ones.

The percentage of the heavy, vaporlike gas increased. The whole body of the air became heavier through its admixture. It absorbed more moisture and became more humid. Rainfall increased. Climates grew warmer. Vegetation became more luxuriant—but the air gradually became less exhilarating.

Soon the health of mankind began to be affected. Accustomed through long ages to breathe air rich in oxygen and poor in carbon dioxide, men suffered. Only those who lived on high plateaus or on tall mountain tops remained unaffected. The plants of the earth, though nourished and increasing in size beyond those ever seen before, were unable to dispose of the continually increasing flood of carbon dioxide.

By the middle of the twenty-first century it was generally recognized that a new carboniferous period was about to take place, when the earth's atmosphere would be thick and humid, unbreathable by man, when giant grasses and ferns would form the only vegetation.

When the twenty-first century drew to a close the whole human race began to revert to conditions closely approximating savagery. The lowlands were unbearable. Thick jungles of rank growth covered the ground. The air was depressing and enervating. Men could live there, but it was a sickly, fever-ridden existence. The whole population of the earth desired the high lands, and as the low country became more unbearable, men forgot their two centuries of peace.

They fought destructively, each for a bit of land where he might live and breathe. Then men began to die, men who had persisted in remaining near sea level. They could not live in the poisonous air. The danger zone crept up as the earth fissures tirelessly poured out their steady streams of foul gas. Soon men could not live within five hundred feet of sea level. The lowlands went uncultivated, and became jungles of a thickness comparable only to those of the first carboniferous period.

Then men died of sheer inanition at a thousand feet. The plateaus and mountaintops were crowded with folk struggling for a foothold and food beyond the invisible menace that crept up, and up—

These things did not take place in one year, or in ten. Not in one generation, but in several. Between the time when the chemists of the International Geophysical Institute announced that the proportion of carbon dioxide in the air had increased from .04 percent to .1 percent and the time when at sea level 6 percent of the atmosphere was the deadly gas, more than two hundred years intervened.

Coming gradually, as it did, the poisonous effects of the deadly stuff increased with insidious slowness. First the lassitude, then the heaviness of brain, then the weakness of body. Mankind ceased to grow in numbers. After a long period, the race had fallen to a fraction of its former size. There was room in plenty on the mountaintops—but the danger level continued to creep up.

There was but one solution. The human body would have to inure itself to the poison, or it was doomed to extinction. It finally developed a toleration for the gas that had wiped out race after race and nation after nation, but at a terrible cost. Lungs increased in size to secure the oxygen on which life depended, but the poison, inhaled at every breath, left the few survivors sickly and filled with a perpetual weariness. Their minds lacked the energy to cope with new problems or transmit the knowledge which in one degree or another, they possessed.

And after thirty thousand years, Burl, a direct descendant of the first president of the Universal Republic, crept through a forest of toadstools and fungus growths. He was ignorant of fire, or metals, of the uses of stone and wood. A single garment covered him. His language was a scanty group of a few hundred labial sounds, conveying no abstractions and few concrete things.

He was ignorant of the uses of wood. There was no wood in the scanty territory furtively inhabited by his tribe. With the increase in heat and humidity the trees had begun to die out. Those of northern climes went first, the oaks, the cedars, the maples. Then the pines—the beeches went early—the cypresses, and finally even the forests of the jungles vanished. Only grasses and reeds, bamboos and their kin, were able to flourish in the new, steaming atmosphere. The thick jungles gave place to dense thickets of grasses and ferns, now become treeferns again.

And then the fungi took their place. Flourishing as never before, flourishing on a planet of torrid heat and perpetual miasma, on whose surface the sun never shone directly because of an ever-thickening bank of clouds that hung sullenly overhead, the fungi sprang up. About the dank pools that festered over the surface of the earth, fungus growths began to cluster. Of every imaginable shade and color, of all monstrous forms and malignant purposes, of huge size and flabby volume, they spread over the land.

The grasses and ferns gave place to them. Squat footstools, flaking molds, evil-smelling yeasts, vast mounds of fungi inextricably mingled as to species, but growing, forever growing and exhaling an odor of dark places.

The strange growths now grouped themselves in forests, horrible travesties on the vegetation they had succeeded. They grew and grew with feverish intensity beneath a clouded or a haze-obscured sky, while above them fluttered gigantic butterflies and huge moths, sipping daintily of their corruption.

The insects alone of all the animal world above water were able to endure the change. They multiplied exceedingly, and enlarged themselves in the thickened air. The solitary vegetation—as distinct from fungus growths—that had survived was now a degenerate form of the cabbages that had once fed peasants. On those rank, colossal masses of foliage, the stolid grubs and caterpillars ate themselves to maturity, then swung below in strong cocoons to sleep the sleep of metamorphosis from which they emerged to spread their wings and fly.

The tiniest butterflies of former days had increased their span until their gaily colored wings should be described in terms of feet, while the larger emperor moths extended their purple sails to a breadth of yards upon yards. Burl himself would have been dwarfed beneath the overshadowing fabric of their wings.

It was fortunate that they, the largest flying creatures, were harmless or nearly so. Burl's fellow tribesmen sometimes came upon a cocoon just about to open, and waited patiently beside it until the beautiful creature within broke through its matted shell and came out into the sunlight.

Then, before it had gathered energy from the air, and before its wings had swelled to strength and firmness, the tribesmen fell upon it, tearing the filmy, delicate wings from its body and the limbs from its carcass. Then, when it lay helpless before them, they carried away the juicy, meat-filled

limbs to be eaten, leaving the still living body to stare helplessly at this strange world through its many faceted eyes, and
become a prey to the voracious ants who would soon clamber
upon it and carry it away in tiny fragments to their underground city.

Not all the insect world was so helpless or so unthreatening.
Burl knew of wasps almost the length of his own body who
possessed stings that were instantly fatal. To every species of
wasp, however, some other insect is predestined prey, and
the furtive members of Burl's tribe feared them but little as
they sought only the prey to which their instinct led them.

Bees were similarly aloof. They were hard put to it for
existence, those bees. Few flowers bloomed, and they were
reduced to expedients once considered signs of degeneracy in
their race. Bubbling yeasts and fouler things, occasionally the
nectarless blooms of the rank, giant cabbages. Burl knew the
bees. They droned overhead, nearly as large as he was himself, their bulging eyes gazing at him with abstracted preoccupation. And crickets, and beetles, and spiders—

Burl knew spiders! His grandfather had been the prey of
one of the hunting tarantulas, which had leaped with incredible ferocity from his excavated tunnel in the earth. A vertical
pit in the ground, two feet in diameter, went down for twenty
feet. At the bottom of that lair the black-bellied monster
waited for the tiny sounds that would warn him of prey
approaching his hiding place *(Lycosa fasciata)*.

Burl's grandfather had been careless, and the terrible shrieks
he uttered as the horrible monster darted from the pit and
seized him had lingered vaguely in Burl's mind ever since.
Burl had seen, too, the monster webs of another species of
spider, and watched from a safe distance as the misshapen
body of the huge creature sucked the juices from a three-foot
cricket that had become entangled in its trap.

Burl had remembered the strange stripes of yellow and
black and silver that crossed upon its abdomen *(Epiera fasciata)*.
He had been fascinated by the struggles of the imprisoned
insect, coiled in a hopeless tangle of sticky, gummy ropes the
thickness of Burl's finger, cast about its body before the
spider made any attempt to approach.

Burl knew these dangers. They were a part of his life. It was his accustomedness to them, and that of his ancestors, that made his existence possible. He was able to evade them; so he survived. A moment of carelessness, an instant's relaxation of his habitual caution, and he would be one with his forebears, forgotten meals of long-dead, inhuman monsters.

Three days before, Burl had crouched behind a bulky, shapeless fungus growth while he watched a furious duel between two huge horned beetles. Their jaws, gaping wide, clicked and clashed upon each other's impenetrable armor. Their legs crashed like so many cymbals as their polished surfaces ground and struck against each other. They were fighting over some particularly attractive bit of carrion.

Burl had watched with all his eyes until a gaping orifice appeared in the armor of the smaller of the two. It uttered a shrill cry, or seemed to cry out. The noise was, actually, the tearing of the horny stuff beneath the victorious jaws of the adversary.

The wounded beetle struggled more and more feebly. At last it collapsed, and the conqueror placidly began to eat the conquered before life was extinct.

Burl waited unto the meal was finished, and then approached the scene with caution. An ant—the forerunner of many—was already inspecting the carcass.

Burl usually ignored the ants. They were stupid, short-sighted insects, and not hunters. Save when attacked, they offered no injury. They were scavengers, on the lookout for the dead and dying, but they would fight viciously if their prey were questioned, and they were dangerous opponents. They were from three inches, for the tiny black ants, to a foot for the large termites.

Burl was hasty when he heard the tiny clickings of their limbs as they approached. He seized the sharp-pointed snout of the victim, detached from the body, and fled from the scene.

Later, he inspected his find with curiosity. The smaller victim had been a minotaur beetle, with a sharp-pointed horn like that of a rhinoceros to reinforce his offensive armament, already dangerous because of his wide jaws. The jaws of a beetle work from side to side, instead of up and down, and this had made the protection complete in no less than three directions.

Burl inspected the sharp, daggerlike intrument in his hand. He felt its point, and it pricked his finger. He flung it aside as he crept to the hiding-place of his tribe. There were only twenty of them, four or five men, six or seven women, and the rest girls and children.

Burl had been wondering at the strange feelings that came over him when he looked at one of the girls. She was younger than Burl—perhaps eighteen—and fleeter of foot than he. They talked together, sometimes, and once or twice Burl shared with her an especially succulent find of foodstuffs.

The next morning he found the horn where he had thrown it, sticking in the flabby side of a toadstool. He pulled it out, and gradually, far back in his mind, an idea began to take shape. He sat for some time with the thing in his hand, considering it with a faraway look in his eyes. From time to time he stabbed at a toadstool, awkwardly, but with gathering skill. His imagination began to work fitfully. He visualized himself stabbing food with it as the larger beetle had stabbed the former owner of the weapon he had in his hand.

Burl could not imagine himself coping with one of the fighting insects. He could only picture himself, dimly, stabbing something that was food with this death-dealing thing. It was no longer than his arm and though clumsy to the hand, an effective and terribly sharp implement.

He thought: Where was there food, food that lived, that would not fight back? Presently he rose and began to make his way toward the tiny river. Yellow-bellied newts swam in its waters. The swimming larvae of a thousand insects floated about its surface or crawled upon its bottom.

There were deadly things there, too. Giant crayfish snapped their horny claws at the unwary. Mosquitoes of four-inch wingspread sometimes made their humming way above the river. The last survivors of their race, they were dying out for lack of the plant juices on which the male of the species lived, but even so they were formidable. Burl had learned to crush them with fragments of fungus.

He crept slowly through the forest of toadstools. Brownish fungus was underfoot. Strange orange, red, and purple molds clustered about the bases of the creamy toadstool stalks. Once Burl paused to run his sharp-pointed weapon through a fleshy stalk and reassure himself that what he planned was practicable.

He made his way furtively through the forest of misshapen growths. Once he heard a tiny clicking, and froze into stillness. It was a troop of four or five ants, each some eight inches long, returning along their habitual pathway to their city. They moved sturdily, heavily laden, along the route marked with the black and odorous formic acid exuded from the bodies of their comrades. Burl waited until they had passed, then went on.

He came to the bank of the river. Green scum covered a great deal of its surface, scum occasionally broken by a slowly enlarging bubble of some gas released from decomposing matter on the bottom. In the center of the placid stream the current ran a little more swiftly, and the water itself was visible.

Over the shining current, water-spiders ran swiftly. They had not shared in the general increase of size that had taken place in the insect world. Depending upon the capillary qualities of the water to support them, an increase in size and weight would have deprived them of the means of locomotion.

From the spot where Burl first peered at the water the green scum spread out for many yards into the stream. He could not see what swam and wriggled and crawled beneath the evil-smelling covering. He peered up and down the banks.

Perhaps a hundred and fifty yards below, the current came near the shore. An outcropping of rock there made a steep descent to the river, from which yellow shelf-fungi stretched out. Dark red and orange above, they were light yellow below, and they formed a series of platforms above the smoothly flowing stream. Burl made his way cautiously toward them.

On his way he saw one of the edible mushrooms that formed so large a part of his diet, and paused to break from the flabby flesh an amount that would feed him for many days. It was too often the custom of his people to find a store of food, carry it to their hiding place, and then gorge themselves for days, eating, sleeping, and waking only to eat again until the food was gone.

Absorbed as he was in his plan of trying his new weapon, Burl was tempted to return with his booty. He would give Saya of this food, and they would eat together. Saya was the maiden who roused unusual emotions in Burl. He felt strange impulses stirring within him when she was near, a desire to touch her, to caress her. He did not understand.

He went on, after hesitating. If he brought her food, Saya would be pleased, but if he brought her of the things that swam in the stream, she would be still more pleased. Degraded as his tribe had become, Burl was yet a little more intelligent than they. He was an atavism, a throwback to ancestors who had cultivated the earth and subjugated its animals. He had a vague idea of pride, unformed but potent.

No man within memory had hunted or slain for food. They knew of meat, yes, but it had been the fragments left by an insect hunter, seized and carried away by the men before the perpetually alert ant colonies had sent their foragers to the scene.

If Burl did what no man before him had done, if he brought a whole carcass to his tribe, they would envy him. They were preoccupied solely with their stomachs, and after that with the preservation of their lives. The perpetuation of the race came third in their consideration.

They were herded together in a leaderless group, coming to the same hiding place that they might share in the finds of the lucky and gather comfort from their numbers. Of weapons, they had none. They sometimes used stones to crack open the limbs of the huge insects they found partly devoured, cracking them open for the sweet meat to be found inside, but they sought safety from their enemies solely in flight and hiding.

Their enemies were not as numerous as might have been imagined. Most of the meat-eating insects have their allotted prey. The sphex—a hunting wasp—feeds solely upon grasshoppers. Other wasps eat flies only. The pirate-bee eats bumblebees only. Spiders were the principal enemies of man, as they devour with a terrifying impartiality all that falls into their clutches.

Burl reached the spot from which he might gaze down into the water. He lay prostrate, staring into the shallow depths. Once a huge crayfish, as long as Burl's body, moved leisurely across his vision. Small fishes and even the huge newts fled before the voracious creature.

After a long time the tide of underwater life resumed its activity. The wriggling grubs of the dragonflies reappeared. Little flecks of silver swam into view—a school of tiny fish. A larger fish appeared, moving slowly through the water.

Burl's eyes glistened and his mouth watered. He reached down with his long weapon. It barely touched the water. Disappointment filled him, yet the nearness and the apparent practicability of his scheme spurred him on.

He considered the situation. There were the shelf-fungi below him. He rose and moved to a point just above them, then thrust his spear down. They resisted its point. Burl felt them tentatively with his foot, then dared to thrust his weight to them. They held him firmly. He clambered down and lay flat upon them, peering over the edge as before.

The large fish, as long as Burl's arm, swam slowly to and fro below him. Burl had seen the former owner of his spear strive to thrust it into his opponents, and knew that a thrust was necessary. He had tried his weapon upon toadstools— had practiced with it. When the fish swam below him, he thrust sharply downward. The spear seemed to bend when it entered the water, and missed its mark by inches, to Burl's astonishment. He tried again and again.

He grew angry with the fish below him for eluding his efforts to kill it. Repeated strokes had left it untouched, and it was unwary, and did not even try to run away.

Burl became furious. The big fish came to rest directly beneath his hand. Burl thrust downward with all his strength. This time the spear, entering vertically, did not seem to bend. It went straight down. Its point penetrated the scales of the swimmer below, transfixing that lazy fish completely.

An uproar began. The fish, struggling to escape, and Burl,

trying to draw it up to his perch, made a huge commotion. In his excitement Burl did not observe a tiny ripple some distance away. The monster crayfish was attracted by the disturbance, and was approaching.

The unequal combat continued. Burl hung on desperately to the end of his spear. Then there was a tremor in Burl's support, it gave way, and fell into the stream with a mighty splash. Burl went under, his eyes open, facing death. And as he sank, his wide-open eyes saw waved before him the gaping claws of the huge crayfish, large enough to sever a limb with a single stroke of their jagged jaws.

He opened his mouth to scream—a replica of the terrible screams of his grandfather, seized by a black-bellied tarantula years before—but no sound came forth. Only bubbles floated to the surface of the water. He beat the unresisting fluid with his hands—he did not know how to swim. The colossal creature approached leisurely, while Burl struggled helplessly.

His arms struck a solid object, and grasped it convulsively. A second later he had swung it between himself and the huge crustacean. He felt a shock as the mighty jaws closed upon the corklike fungus, then felt himself drawn upward as the crayfish released his hold and the shelf-fungus floated to the surface. Having given way beneath him, it had been carried below him in his fall, only to rise within his reach just when most needed.

Burl's head popped above water and he saw a larger bit of the fungus floating near by. Less securely anchored to the rocks of the riverbank than the shelf to which Burl had trusted himself, it had been dislodged when the first shelf gave way. It was larger than the fragment to which Burl clung, and floated higher in the water.

Burl was cool with a terrible self-possession. He seized it and struggled to draw himself on top of it. It tilted as his weight came upon it, and nearly overturned, but he paid no heed. With desperate haste, he clawed with hands and feet until he could draw himself clear of the water, of which he would forever retain a slight fear.

As he pulled himself upon the furry, orange-brown upper

surface, a sharp blow struck his foot. The crayfish, disgusted at finding only what was to it a tasteless morsel in the shelf-fungus, had made a languid stroke at Burl's wriggling foot in the water. Failing to grasp the fleshy member, the crayfish retreated, disgruntled and annoyed.

And Burl floated downstream, perched, weaponless and alone, frightened and in constant danger, upon a flimsy raft composed of a degenerate fungus floating soggily in the water. He floated slowly down the stream of a river in whose waters death lurked unseen, upon whose banks was peril, and above whose reaches danger fluttered on golden wings.

It was a long time before he recovered his self-possession, and when he did he looked first for his spear. It was floating in the water, still transfixing the fish whose capture had endangered Burl's life. The fish now floated with its belly upward, all life gone.

So insistent was Burl's instinct for food that his predicament was forgotten when he saw his prey just out of his reach. He gazed at it, and his mouth watered, while his cranky craft went downstream, spinning slowly in the current. He lay flat on the floating fungoid, and strove to reach out and grasp the end of the spear.

The raft tilted and nearly flung him overboard again. A little later he discovered that it sank more readily on one side than on the other. That was due, of course, to the greater thickness—and consequently greater buoyancy—of the part which had grown next the rocks of the riverbank.

Burl found that if he lay with his head stretching above that side, it did not sink into the water. He wriggled into this new position, then, and waited until the slow revolution of his vessel brought the spear shaft near him. He stretched his fingers and his arm, and touched, then grasped it.

A moment later he was tearing strips of flesh from the side of the fish and cramming the oily mess into his mouth with great enjoyment. He had lost his edible mushroom. That danced upon the waves several yards away, but Burl ate contentedly of what he possessed. He did not worry about what was before him. That lay in the future, but suddenly he realized that he was being carried farther and farther from

Saya, the maiden of his tribe who caused strange bliss to steal over him when he contemplated her.

The thought came to him when he visualized the delight with which she would receive a gift of part of the fish he had caught. He was suddenly stricken with dumb sorrow. He lifted his head and looked longingly at the river banks.

A long, monotonous row of strangely colored fungus growths. No healthy green, but pallid, cream-colored toadstools, some bright orange, lavender, and purple molds, vivid carmine "rusts" and mildews, spreading up the banks from the turgid slime. The sun was not a ball of fire, but merely shone as a bright golden patch in the haze-filled sky, a patch whose limits could not be defined or marked.

In the faintly pinkish light that filtered down through the air, a multitude of flying objects could be seen. Now and then a cricket or a grasshopper made its bulletlike flight from one spot to another. Huge butterflies fluttered gayly above the silent, seemingly lifeless world. Bees lumbered anxiously about, seeking the cross-shaped flowers of the monster cabbages. Now and then a slender-waisted, yellow-stomached wasp flew alertly through the air.

Burl watched them with a strange indifference. The wasps were as long as he himself. The bees, on end, could match his height. The butterflies ranged from tiny creatures barely capable of shading his face to colossal things in the folds of whose wings he could have been lost. And above him fluttered dragonflies, whose long, spindlelike bodies were three times the length of his own.

Burl ignored them all. Sitting there, an incongruous creature of pink skin and soft brown hair upon an orange fungus floating in midstream, he was filled with despondency because the current carried him forever farther and farther from a certain slender-limbed maiden of his tiny tribe, whose glances caused an odd commotion in his breast.

The day went on. Once, Burl saw upon the blue-green mold that spread upward from the river a band of large, red Amazon ants, marching in orderly array, to raid the city of a colony of black ants, and carry away the eggs they would find there. The eggs would be hatched, and the small black creatures made the slaves of the brigands who had stolen them.

The Amazon ants can live only by the labor of their slaves, and for that reason are mighty warriors in their world. Later, etched against the steaming mist that overhung everything as far as the eye could reach, Burl saw strangely shaped, swollen branches rearing themselves from the ground. He knew what they were. A hard-rinded fungus that grew upon itself in peculiar mockery of the vegetation that had vanished from the earth.

And again he saw pear-shaped objects above some of which floated little clouds of smoke. They, too, were fungus growths, puffballs, which when touched emit what seems a puff of vapor. These would have towered above Burl's head, had he stood beside them.

And then, as the day drew to an end, he saw in the distance what seemed a rage of purple hills. They were tall hills to Burl, some sixty or seventy feet high, and they seemed to be the agglomeration of a formless growth, mutiplying its organisms and forms upon itself until the whole formed an irregular, cone-shaped mound. Burl watched them apathetically.

Presently, he ate again of the oily fish. The taste was pleasant to him, accustomed to feed mostly upon insipid mushrooms. He stuffed himself, though the size of his prey left by far the larger part uneaten.

He still held his spear firmly beside him.

It had brought him into trouble, but Burl possessed a fund of obstinacy. Unlike most of his tribe, he associated the spear with the food it had secured, rather than the difficulty into which it had led him. When he had eaten his fill he picked it up and examined it again. The sharpness of its point was unimpaired.

Burl handled it meditatively, debating whether or not to attempt to fish again. The shakiness of his little raft dissuaded him, and he abandoned the idea. Presently he stripped a sinew from the garment about his middle and hung the fish about his neck with it. That would leave him both hands free.

Then he sat cross-legged upon the soggily floating fungus, like a pink-skinned Buddha, and watched the shores go by.

Time had passed, and it was drawing near sunset. Burl, never having seen the sun save as a bright spot in the over-hanging haze, did not think of the coming of night as "sunset." To him it was the letting down of darkness from the sky.

Today happened to be an exceptionally bright day, and the haze was not as thick as usual. Far to the west, the thick mist turned to gold, while the thicker clouds above became blurred masses of dull red. Their shadows seemed like lavender, from the contrast of shades. Upon the still surface of the river, all the myriad tints and shadings were reflected with an incredible faithfulness, and the shining tops of the giant mushrooms by the river brim glowed faintly pink.

Dragonflies buzzed over his head in their swift and angular flight, the metallic luster of their bodies glistening in the rosy light. Great yellow butterflies flew lightly above the stream. Here, there, and everywhere upon the water appeared the shell-formed boats of a thousand caddis flies, floating upon the surface while they might.

Burl could have thrust his hand down into their cavities and seized the white worms that inhabited the strange craft. The huge bulk of a tardy bee droned heavily overhead. Burl glanced upward and saw the long proboscis and the hairy hinder legs with their scanty load of pollen. He saw the great, multiple-lensed eyes with their expression of stupid preoccupation, and even the sting that would mean death alike for him and for the giant insect, should it be used.

The crimson radiance grew dim at the edge of the world. The purple hills had long been left behind. Now the slender stalks of ten thousand round-domed mushrooms lined the river bank and beneath them spread fungi of all colors, from the rawest red to palest blue, but all now fading slowly to a monochromatic background in the growing dusk.

The buzzing, fluttering, and the flapping of the insects of the day died slowly down, while from a million hiding places there crept out into the deep night soft and furry bodies of great moths, who preened themselves and smoothed their feathery antennae before taking to the air. The strong-limbed crickets set up their thunderous noise—grown gravely bass with the increasing size of the organs by which the sound was made—and then there began to gather on the water those slender spirals of tenuous mist that would presently blanket the stream in a mantle of thin fog.

Night fell. The clouds above seemed to lower and grow dark. Gradually, now a drop and then a drop, now a drop and then a drop, the languid fall of large, warm raindrops that would drip from the moisture-laden skies all through the night began. The edge of the stream became a place where great disks of coolly glowing flame appeared.

The mushrooms that bordered on the river were faintly phosphorescent *(Pleurotus phosphoreus)* and shone coldly upon the "rusts" and flake-fungi beneath their feet. Here and there a ball of lambent flame appeared, drifting idly above the steaming, festering earth.

Thirty thousand years before, men had called them "will-o'-the-wisps," but Burl simply stared at them, accepting them as he accepted all that passed. Only a man attempting to advance in the scale of civilization tries to explain everything that he sees. The savage or the child is most often content to observe without comment, unless he repeats the legends told him by wise folk who are possessed by the itch of knowledge.

Burl watched for a long time. Great fireflies whose beacons lighted up their surroundings for many yards—fireflies Burl knew to be as long as his spear—shed their intermittent glows upon the stream. Softly fluttering wings, in great beats that poured torrents of air upon him, passed above Burl.

The air was full of winged creatures. The night was broken by their cries, by the sound of their invisible wings, by their cries of anguish and their mating calls. Above him and on all sides the persistent, intense life of the insect world went on ceaselessly, but Burl rocked back and forth upon his frail mushroom boat and wished to weep because he was being carried from his tribe, and from Saya—Saya of the swift feet and white teeth, of the shy smile.

Burl may have been homesick, but his principal thoughts

were of Saya. He had dared greatly to bring a gift of fresh meat to her, meat captured as meat had never been known to be taken by a member of the tribe. And now he was being carried from her!

He lay, disconsolate, upon his floating atom on the water for a great part of the night. It was long after midnight when the mushroom raft struck gently and remained grounded upon a shallow in the stream.

When the light came in the morning, Burl gazed about him keenly. He was some twenty yards from the shore, and the greenish scum surrounded his now disintegrating vessel. The river had widened out until the other bank was barely to be seen through the haze above the surface of the river, but the nearer shore seemed firm and no more full of dangers than the territory his tribe inhabited. He felt the depth of the water with his spear, then was struck with the multiple usefulness of that weapon. The water would come to but slightly above his ankles.

Shivering a little with fear, Burl stepped down into the water, then made for the bank at the top of his speed. He felt a soft something clinging to one of his bare feet. With an access of terror, he ran faster, and stumbled upon the shore in a panic. He stared down at his foot. A shapeless, flesh-colored pad clung to his heel, and as Burl watched, it began to swell slowly, while the pink of its wrinkled folds deepened.

It was no more than a leech, sharing in the enlargement nearly all the lower world had undergone, but Burl did not know that. He thrust at it with the side of his spear, then scraped frantically at it, and it fell off, leaving a blotch of blood upon the skin where it came away. It lay, writhing and pulsating, upon the ground, and Burl fled from it.

He found himself in one of the toadstool forests with which he was familiar, and finally paused, disconsolately. He knew the nature of the fungus growths about him, and presently fell to eating. In Burl the sight of food always produced hunger—a wise provision of nature to make up for the instinct to store food, which he lacked.

Burl's heart was small within him. He was far from his tribe, and far from Saya. In the parlance of this day, it is

probable that no more than forty miles separated them, but
Burl did not think of distances. He had come down the river.
He was in a land he had never known or seen. And he was
alone.

All about him was food. All the mushrooms that surrounded him were edible, and formed a store of sustenance
Burl's whole tribe could not have eaten in many days, but
that very fact brought Saya to his mind more forcibly. He
squatted on the ground, wolfing down the insipid mushroom
in great gulps, when an idea suddenly came to him with all
the force of inspiration.

He would bring Saya here, where there was food, food in
great quantities, and she would be pleased. Burl had forgotten
the large and oily fish that still hung down his back from the
sinew about his neck, but now he rose, and its flapping
against him reminded him again.

He took it and fingered it all over, getting his hands and
himself thoroughly greasy in the process, but he could eat no
more. The thought of Saya's pleasure at the sight of that, too,
reinforced his determination.

With all the immediacy of a child or a savage he set off at
once. He had come along the bank of the stream. He would
retrace his steps along the bank of the stream.

Through the awkward aisles of the mushroom forest he
made his way, eyes and ears open for possibilities of danger.
Several times he heard the omnipresent clicking of ants on
their multifarious businesses in the wood, but he could afford
to ignore them. They were short-sighted at best, and at worst
they were foragers rather than hunters. He only feared one
kind of ant, the army ant, which sometimes travels in hordes
of millions, eating all that it comes upon. In ages past, when
they were tiny creatures not an inch long, even the largest
animals fled from them. Now that they measured a foot in
length, not even the gorged spiders whose distended bellies
were a yard in thickness dared offer them battle.

The mushroom forest came to an end. A cheerful grasshopper *(Ephigger)* munched delicately at some dainty it had
found. Its hind legs were bunched beneath it in perpetual
readiness for flight. A monster wasp appeared above—as

long as Burl himself—poised an instant, dropped, and seized the luckless feaster.

There was a struggle, then the grasshopper became helpless, and the wasp's flexible abdomen curved delicately. Its sting entered the jointed armor of its prey, just beneath the head. The sting entered with all the deliberate precision of a surgeon's scalpel, and all struggle ceased.

The wasp grasped the paralyzed, not dead, insect and flew away. Burl grunted, and passed on. He had hidden when the wasp darted down from above.

The ground grew rough, and Burl's progress became painful. He clambered arduously up steep slopes and made his way cautiously down their farther sides. Once he had to climb through a tangled mass of mushrooms so closely placed, and so small, that he had to break them apart with blows of his spear before he could pass, when they shed upon him torrents of a fiery red liquid that rolled off his greasy breast and sank into the ground *(Lactarius deliciosus)*.

A strange self-confidence now took possession of Burl. He walked less cautiously and more boldly. The mere fact that he had struck something and destroyed it provided him with a curious fictitious courage.

He had climbed slowly to the top of a red clay cliff, perhaps a hundred feet high, slowly eaten away by the river when it overflowed. Burl could see the river. At some past floodtime it had lapped at the base of the cliff on whose edge he walked, though now it came no nearer than a quarter-mile.

The cliffside was almost covered with shelf-fungi, large and small, white, yellow, orange, and green, in indescribable confusion and luxuriance. From a point halfway up the cliff the inch-thick cable of a spider's web stretched down to an anchorage on the ground, and the strangely geometrical pattern of the web glistened evilly.

Somewhere among the fungi of the cliffside the huge creature waited until some unfortunate prey should struggle helplessly in its monster snare. The spider waited in a motionless, implacable patience, invincibly certain of prey, utterly merciless to its victims.

Burl strutted on the edge of the cliff, a silly little pink-skinned creature with an oily fish slung about his neck and a draggled fragment of a moth's wing about his middle. In his hand he bore the long spear of a minotaur beetle. He strutted, and looked scornfully down upon the whitely shining trap below him. He struck mushrooms, and they had fallen before him. He feared nothing. He strode fearlessly along. He would go to Saya and bring her to this land where food grew in abundance.

Sixty paces before him, a shaft sank vertically in the sandy, clayey soil. It was a carefully rounded shaft, and lined with silk. It went down for perhaps thirty feet or more, and there enlarged itself into a chamber where the owner and digger of the shaft might rest. The top of the hole was closed by a trap door, stained with mud and earth to imitate with precision the surrounding soil. A keen eye would have been needed to perceive the opening. But a keen eye now peered out from a tiny crack, the eye of the engineer of the underground dwelling.

Eight hairy legs surrounded the body of the creature that hung motionless at the top of the silk-lined shaft. A huge misshapen globe formed its body, colored a dirty brown. Two pairs of ferocious mandibles stretched before its fierce mouthparts. Two eyes glittered evilly in the darkness of the burrow. And over the whole body spread a rough, mangy fur.

It was a thing of implacable malignance, of incredible ferocity. It was the brown hunting spider, the American tarantula *(Mygale Hentzii)*. Its body was two feet and more in diameter, and its legs, outstretched, would cover a circle three yards across. It watched Burl, its eyes glistening. Slaver welled up and dropped from its jaws.

And Burl strutted forward on the edge of the cliff, puffed up with a sense of his own importance. The white snare of the spinning spider below him impressed him as amusing. He knew the spider would not leave its web to attack him. He reached down and broke off a bit of fungus growing at his feet. Where he broke it, it was oozing a soupy liquid and was full of tiny maggots in a delirium of feasting. Burl flung it down into the web, and then laughed as the black bulk of the hidden spider swung down from its hiding place to investigate.

*   *   *

The tarantula, peering from its burrow, quivered with impatience. Burl drew near, and nearer. He was using his spear as a lever now, and prying off bits of fungus to fall down the cliffside into the colossal web. The spider, below, went leisurely from one place to another, investigating each new missile with its palpi, then leaving them, as they appeared lifeless and undesirable prey. Burl laughed again as a particularly large lump of shelf-fungus narrowly missed the black-and-silver figure below. Then—

The trap door fell into place with a faint click, and Burl whirled about. His laughter turned to a scream. Moving toward him with incredible rapidity, the monster tarantula opened its dripping jaws. Its mandibles gaped wide. The poison fangs were unsheathed. The creature was thirty paces away, twenty paces—ten. It leaped into the air, eyes glittering, all its eight legs extended to seize, fangs bared—

Burl screamed again, and thrust out his arms to ward off the impact of the leap. In his terror, his grasp upon his spear had become agonized. The spear point shot out, and the tarantula fell upon it. Nearly a quarter of the spear entered the body of the ferocious thing.

It struck upon the spear, writhing horribly, still struggling to reach Burl, who was transfixed with horror. The mandibles clashed, strange sounds came from the beast. Then one of the attenuated, hairy legs rasped across Burl's forearm. He gasped in ultimate fear and stepped backward—and the edge of the cliff gave way beneath him.

He hurtled downward, still clutching the spear which held the writhing creature from him. Down through space, eyes glassy with panic, the two creatures—the man and the giant tarantula—fell together. There was a strangely elastic crash and crackling. They had fallen into the web beneath them.

Burl had reached the end of terror. He could be no more fear-struck. Struggling madly in the gummy coils of an immense web, which ever bound him more tightly, with a wounded creature that still strove to reach him with its poison fangs—Burl had reached the limit of panic.

He fought like a madman to break the coils about him. His

arms and breast were greasy from the oily fish, and the sticky web did not adhere to them, but his legs and body were inextricably fastened by the elastic threads spread for just such prey as he.

He paused a moment, in exhaustion. Then he saw, five yards away, the silvery and black monster waiting patiently for him to weary himself. It judged the moment propitious. The tarantula and the man were one in its eyes, one struggling thing that had fallen opportunely into its snare. They were moving but feebly now. The spider advanced delicately, swinging its huge bulk nimbly along the web, paying out a cable after it, coming inexorably toward him.

Burl's arms were free, because of the greasy coating they had received. He waved them wildly, shrieking at the pitiless monster that approached. The spider paused. Those moving arms suggested mandibles that might wound or slap.

Spiders take few hazards. This spider was no exception to the rule. It drew cautiously near, then stopped. Its spinnerets became busy, and with one of its six legs, used like an arm, it flung a sheet of gummy silk impartially over both the tarantula and the man.

Burl fought against the descending shroud. He strove to thrust it away, but in vain. In a matter of minutes he was completely covered in a silken cloth that hid even the light from his eyes. He and his enemy, the giant tarantula, were beneath the same covering, though the tarantula moved but weakly.

The shower ceased. The web spider had decided that they were helpless. Then Burl felt the cables of the web give slightly, as the spider approached to sting and suck the sweet juices from its prey.

The web yielded gently as the added weight of the black-bellied spider approached. Burl froze into stillness under his enveloping covering. Beneath the same silken shroud the tarantula writhed in agony upon the point of Burl's spear. It clashed its jaws, shuddering upon the horny barb.

Burl was quiet in an ecstasy of terror. He waited for the poison fangs to be thrust into him. He knew the process. He had seen the leisurely fashion in which the giant spiders delicately stung their prey, then withdrew to wait without impatience for the poison to do its work.

When their victim had ceased to struggle, they drew near again, and sucked the sweet juices from the body, first from one point and then another, until what had so recently been a creature vibrant with life became a shrunken, withered husk—to be flung from the web at nightfall. Most spiders are tidy housekeepers, destroying their snares daily to spin anew.

The bloated, evil creature moved meditatively about the shining sheet of silk it had cast over the man and the giant tarantula when they fell from the cliff above. Now only the tarantula moved feebly. Its body was outlined by a bulge in the concealing shroud, throbbing faintly as it still struggled with the spear in its vitals. The irregularly rounded protuberance offered a point of attack for the web spider. It moved quickly forward, and stung.

Galvanized into fresh torment by this new agony, the tarantula writhed in a very hell of pain. Its legs clustered about the spear still fastened into its body, struck out purposelessly, in horrible gestures of delirious suffering. Burl screamed as one of them touched him, and struggled himself.

His arms and head were free beneath the silken sheet because of the grease and oil that coated them. He clutched at the threads about him and strove to draw himself away from his deadly neighbor. The threads did not break, but they parted one from another, and a tiny opening appeared. One of the tarantula's attenuated limbs touched him again. With the strength of utter panic he hauled himself away, and the opening enlarged. Another struggle, and Burl's head emerged into the open air, and he stared down for twenty feet upon an open space almost carpeted with the chitinous remains of his present captor's former victims.

Burl's head was free, and his breast and arms. The fish slung over his shoulder had shed its oil upon him impartially. But the lower part of his body was held firm by the gummy snare of the web spider, a snare far more tenacious than any birdlime ever manufactured by man.

He hung in his tiny window for a moment, despairing.

Then he saw, at a little distance, the bulk of the monster spider, waiting patiently for its poison to take effect and the struggling of its prey to be stilled. The tarantula was no more than shuddering now. Soon it would be still, and the black-bellied creature waiting on the web would approach for its meal.

Burl withdrew his head and thrust desperately at the sticky stuff about his loins and legs. The oil upon his hands kept it from clinging to them, and it gave a little. In a flash of inspiration, Burl understood. He reached over his shoulder and grasped the greasy fish; tore it in a dozen places and smeared himself with the now rancid exudation, pushing the sticky threads from his limbs and oiling the surface from which he had thrust it away.

He felt the web tremble. To the spider, its poison seemed to have failed of effect. Another sting seemed to be necessary. This time it would not insert its fangs into the quiescent tarantula, but would sting where the disturbance was manifest—would send its deadly venom into Burl.

He gasped, and drew himself toward his window. It was as if he would have pulled his legs from his body. His head emerged, his shoulders—half his body was out of the hole.

The colossal spider surveyed him, and made ready to cast more of its silken sheet upon him. The spinnerets became active, and the sticky stuff about Burl's feet gave way! He shot out of the opening and fell sprawling, awkwardly and heavily, upon the earth below, crashing upon the shrunken shell of a flying beetle which had fallen into the snare and had not escaped.

Burl rolled over and over, and then sat up. An angry, foot-long ant stood before him, its mandibles extended threateningly, while its antennae waved wildly in the air. A shrill stridulation filled the air.

In ages past, when ants were tiny creatures of lengths to be measured in fractions of an inch, learned scientists debated gravely if their tribe possessed a cry. They believed that certain grooves upon the body of the insects, after the fashion of those upon the great legs of the cricket, might offer the means of uttering an infinitely high-pitched sound too shrill for man's ears to catch.

Burl knew that the stridulation was caused by the doubtful insect before him, though he had never wondered how it was produced. The cry was used to summon others of its city, to help it in its difficulty or good fortune.

Clickings sounded fifty or sixty feet away. Comrades were coming to aid the pioneer. Harmless save when interfered with—all save the army ant, that is—the whole ant tribe was formidable when aroused. Utterly fearless, they could pull down a man and slay him as so many infuriated fox terriers might have done thirty thousand years before.

Burl fled, without debate, and nearly collided with one of the anchoring cables of the web from which he had barely escaped a moment before. He heard the shrill sound behind him suddenly subside. The ant, short-sighted as all ants were, no longer felt itself threatened and went peacefully about the business Burl had interrupted, that of finding among the gruesome relics beneath the spider's web some edible carrion which might feed the inhabitants of its city.

Burl sped on for a few hundred yards, and stopped. It behooved him to move carefully. He was in strange territory, and as even the most familiar territory was full of sudden and implacable dangers, unknown lands were doubly or trebly perilous.

Burl too found difficulty in moving. The glutinous stuff from the spider's shroud of silk still stuck to his feet and picked up small objects as he went along. Old ant-gnawed fragments of insect armor pricked him even through his toughened soles.

He looked about cautiously and removed them, took a dozen steps and had to stop again. Burl's brain had been uncommonly stimulated of late. It had gotten him into at least one predicament—due to his invention of a spear—but had no less readily led to his escape from another. But for the reasoning that had led him to use the grease from the fish upon his shoulder in oiling his body when he struggled out of the spider's snare, he would now be furnishing a meal for that monster.

Cautiously, Burl looked all about him. He seemed to be safe. Then, quite deliberately, he sat down to think. It was the first time in his life that he had done such a thing. The people of his tribe were not given to meditation. But an idea had struck Burl with all the force of inspiration—an abstract idea.

When he was in difficulties, something within him seemed to suggest a way out. Would it suggest an inspiration now? He puzzled over the problem. Childlike—and savagelike—the instant the thought came to him, he proceeded to test it out. He fixed his gaze upon his foot. The sharp edges of pebbles, of the remains of insect-armor, of a dozen things, hurt his feet when he walked. They had done so ever since he had been born, but never had his feet been sticky so that the irritation continued with him for more than a single step.

Now he gazed upon his foot, and waited for the thought within him to develop. Meanwhile, he slowly removed the sharp-pointed fragments, one by one. Partly coated as they were with the half-liquid gum from his feet, they clung to his fingers as they had to his feet, except upon those portions where the oil was thick as before.

Burl's reasoning, before, we simple and of the primary order. Where oil covered him, the web did not. Therefore he would coat the rest of himself with oil. Had he been placed in the same predicament again, he would have used the same means of escape. But to apply a bit of knowledge gained in one predicament to another difficulty was something he had not yet done.

A dog may be taught that by pulling on the latchstring of a door he may open it, but the same dog coming to a high and close-barred gate with a latchstring attached will never think of pulling on this second latchstring. He associates a latchstring with the opening of the door. The opening of a gate is another matter entirely.

Burl had been stirred to one invention by imminent peril. That is not extraordinary. But to reason in cold blood, as he presently did, that oil on his feet would nullify the glue upon his feet and enable him again to walk in comfort—that was a triumph. The inventions of savages are essentially matters of life and death, of food and safety. Comfort and luxury are only produced by intelligence of a high order.

Burl, in safety, had added to his comfort. That was truly a more important thing in his development than almost any other thing he could have done. He oiled his feet.

It was an almost infinitesimal problem, but Burl's struggles with the mental process of reasoning were actual. Thirty thousand years before him, a wise man had pointed out that education is simply training in thought, in efficient and effective thinking. Burl's tribe had been too much preoccupied with food and mere existence to think, and now Burl, sitting at the base of a squat toadstool that all but concealed him, reexemplified Rodin's *Thinker* for the first time in many generations.

For Burl to reason that oil upon the soles of his feet would guard him against sharp stones was as much a triumph of intellect as any masterpiece of art in the ages before him. Burl was learning how to think.

He stood up, walked, and crowed in sheer delight, then paused a moment in awe of his own intelligence. Thirty-five miles from his tribe, naked, unarmed, utterly ignorant of fire, of wood, of any weapons save a spear he had experimented with the day before, abysmally uninformed concerning the very existence of any art or science, Burl stopped to assure himself that he was very wonderful.

Pride came to him. He wished to display himself to Saya, these things upon his feet, and his spear. But his spear was gone.

With touching faith in the efficacy of this new pastime, Burl sat promptly down again and knitted his brows. Just as a superstitious person, once convinced that by appeal to a favorite talisman he will be guided aright, will inevitably apply to that talisman on all occasions, so Burl plumped himself down to think.

These questions were easily answered. Burl was naked. He would search out garments for himself. He was weaponless.

He would find himself a spear. He was hungry—and would seek food, and he was far from his tribe, so he would go to them. Puerile reasoning, of course, but valuable, because it was consciously reasoning, consciously appealing to his mind for guidance in difficulty, deliberate progress from a mental desire to a mental resolution.

Even in the high civilization of ages before, few men had really used their brains. The great majority of people had depended upon machines and their leaders to think for them. Burl's tribefolk depended on their stomachs. Burl, however, was gradually developing the habit of thinking which makes for leadership and which would be invaluable to his little tribe.

He stood up again and faced upstream, moving slowly and cautiously, his eyes searching the ground before him keenly and his ears alert for the slightest sound of danger. Gigantic butterflies, riotous in coloring, fluttered overhead through the misty haze. Sometimes a grasshopper hurtled through the air like a projectile, its transparent wings beating the air frantically. Now and then a wasp sped by, intent upon its hunting, or a bee droned heavily along, anxious and worried, striving in a nearly flowerless world to gather the pollen that would feed the hive.

Here and there Burl saw flies of various sorts, some no larger than his thumb, but others the size of his whole hand. They fed upon the juices that dripped from the maggot-infested mushrooms, when filth more to their liking was not at hand.

Very far away a shrill roaring sounded faintly. It was like a multitude of clickings blended into a single sound, but was so far away that it did not impress itself upon Burl's attention. He had all the strictly localized vision of a child. What was near was important, and what was distant could be ignored. Only the imminent required attention, and Burl was preoccupied.

Had he listened, he would have realized that army ants were abroad in countless millions, spreading themselves out in a broad array and eating all they came upon far more destructively than so many locusts.

Locusts in past ages had eaten all green things. There were only giant cabbages and a few such tenacious rank growths in the world that Burl knew. The locusts had vanished with civilization and knowledge and the greater part of mankind, but the army ants remained as an invincible enemy to men and insects, and the most of the fungus growths that covered the earth.

Burl did not notice the sound, however. He moved forward, briskly though cautiously, searching with his eyes for garments, food, and weapons. He confidently expected to find all of them within a short distance.

Surely enough he found a thicket—if one might call it so—of edible fungi no more than half a mile beyond the spot where he had improvised his sandals to protect the soles of his feet.

Without especial elation, Burl tugged at the largest until he had broken off a food supply for several days. He went on, eating as he did so, past a broad plain a mile and more across, being broken into odd little hillocks by gradually ripening and suddenly developing mushrooms with which he was unfamiliar.

The earth seemed to be in process of being pushed aside by rounded protuberances of which only the tips showed. Blood-red hemispheres seemed to be forcing aside the earth so they might reach the outer air.

Burl looked at them curiously, and passed among them without touching them. They were strange, and to him most strange things meant danger. In any event, he was full of a new purpose now. He wished garments and weapons.

Above the plain a wasp hovered, a heavy object dangling beneath its black belly, ornamented by a single red band. It was a wasp—the hairy sand wasp—and it was bringing a paralyzed gray caterpillar to its burrow.

Burl watched it drop down with the speed and sureness of an arrow, pull aside a heavy, flat stone, and descend into the ground. It had a vertical shaft dug down for forty feet or more.

It descended, evidently inspected the interior, reappeared, and vanished into the hole again, dragging the gray worm after it. Burl, marching on over the broad plain that seemed stricken with some erupting disease from the number of red pimples making their appearance, did not know what passed below, but observed the wasp emerge again and busily scratch dirt and stones into the shaft until it was full.

The wasp had paralyzed a caterpillar, taken it to the already prepared burrow, laid an egg upon it, and filled up the entrance. In course of time the egg would hatch into a grub barely as long as Burl's forefinger, which would then feed upon the torpid caterpillar until it had waxed large and fat. Then it would weave itself a chrysalis and sleep a long sleep, only to wake as a wasp and dig its way to the open air.

Burl reached the farther side of the plain and found himself threading the aisles of one of the fungus forests in which the growths were hideous, misshapen travesties upon the trees they had supplanted. Bloated, yellow limbs branched off from rounded, swollen trunks. Here and there a pearshaped puffball, Burl's height and half as much again, waited craftily until a chance touch should cause it to shoot upward a curling puff of infinitely fine dust.

Burl went cautiously. There were dangers here, but he moved forward steadily, nonetheless. A great mass of edible mushroom was slung under one of his arms, and from time to time he broke off a fragment and ate of it, while his large eyes searched this way and that for threats of harm.

Behind him, a high, shrill roaring had grown slightly in volume and nearness, but was still too far away to impress Burl. The army ants were working havoc in the distance. By thousands and millions, myriads upon myriads, they were foraging the country, clambering upon every eminence, descending into every depression, their antennae waving restlessly and their mandibles forever threateningly extended. The ground was black with them, each was ten inches and more in length.

A single such creature would be formidable to an unarmed and naked man like Burl, whose wisest move would be flight, but in their thousands and millions they presented a menace from which no escape seemed possible. They were advancing steadily and rapidly, shrill stridulations and a multitude of clickings marking their movements.

The great helpless caterpillars upon the giant cabbages heard the sound of their coming, but were too stupid to flee. The black multitudes covered the rank vegetables, and tiny but voracious jaws began to tear at the flaccid masses of flesh.

Each creature had some futile means of struggling. The caterpillars strove to throw off their innumerable assailants by writhings and contortions, wholly ineffective. The bees fought their entrance to the gigantic hives with stings and wingbeats. The moths took to the air in helpless blindness when discovered by the relentless throngs of small black insects which reeked of formic acid and left the ground behind them denuded of every living thing.

Before the oncoming horde was a world of teeming life, where mushrooms and fungi fought with thinning numbers of giant cabbages for foothold. Behind the black multitude was—nothing. Mushrooms, cabbages, bees, wasps, crickets. Every creeping and crawling thing that did not get aloft before the black tide reached it was lost, torn to bits by tiny mandibles. Even the hunting spiders and tarantulas fell before the host of insects, having killed many in their final struggles, but overwhelmed by sheer numbers. And the wounded and dying army ants made food for their sound comrades.

There is no mercy among insects. Only the web spiders sat unmoved and immovable in their colossal snares, secure in the knowledge that their gummy webs would discourage attempts at invasion along the slender supporting cables.

Surging onward, flowing like a monstrous, murky tide over the yellow, steaming earth, the army ants advanced. Their vanguard reached the river, and recoiled. Burl was perhaps five miles distant when they changed their course, communicating the altered line of march to those behind them in some mysterious fashion of transmitting intelligence.

Thirty thousand years before, scientists had debated gravely over the means of communication among ants. They had observed that a single ant finding a bit of booty too large for him to handle alone would return to the ant city and return with others. From that one instance they deduced a language of gestures made with the antennae.

Burl had no wise theories. He merely knew facts, but he knew that the ants had some form of speech or transmission of ideas. Now, however, he was moving cautiously along toward the stamping grounds of his tribe, in complete ignorance of the black blanket of living creatures creeping over the ground toward him.

A million tragedies marked the progress of the insect army. There was a tiny colony of mining bees—Zebra bees—a single mother, some four feet long, had dug a huge gallery with some ten cells, in which she laid her eggs and fed her grubs with hard-gathered pollen. The grubs had waxed fat and large, became bees, and laid eggs in their turn, within the gallery their mother had dug out for them.

Ten such bulky insects now foraged busily for grubs within the ancestral home, while the founder of the colony had grown draggled and wingless with the passing of time. Unable to forage herself, the old bee became the guardian of the nest or hive, as is the custom among the mining bees. She closed the opening of the hive with her head, making a living barrier within the entrance, and withdrawing to give entrance and exit only to duly authenticated members of the the extensive colony.

The ancient and draggled concierge of the underground dwelling was at her post when the wave of army ants swept over her. Tiny, evil-smelling feet trampled upon her. She emerged to fight with mandible and sting for the sanctity of the hive. In a moment she was a shaggy mass of biting ants, rending and tearing at her chitinous armor. The old bee fought madly, viciously, sounding a buzzing alarm to the colonists yet within the hive. They emerged, fighting as they came, for the gallery leading down was a dark flood of small insects.

For a few moments a battle such as would make an epic was in progress. Ten huge bees, each four to five feet long, fighting with legs and jaw, wing and mandible, with all the ferocity of as many tigers. The tiny, vicious ants covered them, snapping at their multiple eyes, biting at the tender joints in their armor—sometimes releasing the larger prey to leap upon an injured comrade wounded by the huge creature they battled in common.

The fight, however, could have but one ending. Struggle as the bees might, herculean as their efforts might be, they were powerless against the incredible numbers of their assailants, who tore them into tiny fragments and devoured them. Before the last shred of the hive's defenders had vanished, the hive itself was gutted alike of the grubs it had contained and the food brought to the grubs by such weary effort of the mature bees.

The army ants went on. Only an empty gallery remained, that and a few fragments of tough armor, unappetizing even to the omnivorous ants.

Burl was meditatively inspecting the scene of a recent tragedy, where rent and scraped fragments of a great beetle's shiny casing lay upon the ground. A greater beetle had come upon the first and slain him. Burl was looking upon the remains of the meal.

Three or four minims, little ants barely six inches long, foraged industriously among the bits. A new ant city was to be formed and the queen ant lay hidden a half-mile away. These were the first hatchlings, who would feed the larger ants on whom would fall the great work of the ant city. Burl ignored them, searching with his eyes for a spear or weapon.

Behind him the clicking roar, the high-pitched stridulations of the horde of army ants, rose in volume. Burl turned disgustedly away. The best he could find in the way of a weapon was a fiercely toothed hind leg. He picked it up, and an angry whine rose from the ground.

One of the black minims was working busily to detach a fragment of flesh from the joint of the leg, and Burl had snatched the morsel from him. The little creature was hardly half a foot in length, but it advanced upon Burl, shrilling angrily. He struck it with the leg and crushed it. Two of the other minims appeared, attracted by the noise the first had made. Discovering the crushed body of their fellow, they unceremoniously dismembered it and bore it away in triumph.

Burl went on, swinging the toothed limb in his hand. It made a fair club, and Burl was accustomed to use stones to crush the juicy legs of such giant crickets as his tribe sometimes came upon. He formed a half-defined idea of a club. The sharp teeth of the thing in his hand made him realize that a sidewise blow was better than a spearlike thrust.

The sound behind him had become a distant whispering, high-pitched, and growing nearer. The army ants swept over a mushroom forest, and the yellow, umbrella-like growths swarmed with black creatures devouring the substance on which they found a foothold.

A great bluebottle fly, shining with a metallic luster, reposed in an ecstasy of feasting, sipping through its long proboscis the dark-colored liquid that dripped slowly from a mushroom. Maggots filled the mushroom, and exuded a solvent pepsin that liquefied the white firm "meat."

They fed upon this soup, this gruel, and a surplus dripped to the ground below, where the bluebottle drank eagerly. Burl drew near, and struck. The fly collapsed into a writhing heap. Burl stood over it for an instant, pondering.

The army ants came nearer, down into a tiny valley, swarming into and through a little brook over which Burl had leaped. Ants can remain underwater for a long time without drowning, so the small stream was but a minor obstacle, though the current of water swept many of them off their feet until they choked the brook bed, and their comrades passed over their struggling bodies dry-shod. They were no more than temporarily annoyed, however, and presently crawled out to resume their march.

About a quarter of a mile to the left of Burl's line of march, and perhaps a mile behind the spot where he stood over the dead bluebottle fly, there was a stretch of an acre or more where the giant, rank cabbages had so far resisted the encroachments of the ever-present mushrooms. The pale, cross-shaped flowers of the cabbages formed food for many bees, and the leaves fed numberless grubs and worms, and loud-voiced crickets which crouched about on the ground, munching busily at the succulent green stuff. The army ants swept into the green area, ceaselessly devouring all they came upon.

A terrific din arose. The crickets hurtled away in a rocketlike flight, in a dark cloud of wildly beating wings. They shot aimlessly in any direction, with the result that half, or more than half, fell in the midst of the black tide of devouring insects and were seized as they fell. They uttered terrible cries as they were being torn to bits. Horrible inhuman screams reached Burl's ears.

A single such cry of agony would not have attracted Burl's attention—he lived in the very atmosphere of tragedy—but the chorus of creatures in torment made him look up. This was no minor horror. Wholesale slaughter was going on. He peered anxiously in the direction of the sound.

A wild stretch of sickly yellow fungus, here and there interspersed with a squat toadstool or a splash of vivid color where one of the many "rusts" had found a foothold. To the left a group of awkward, misshapen fungoids clustered in silent mockery of a forest of trees. There a mass of faded green, where the giant cabbages stood.

With the true sun never shining upon them save through a blanket of thick haze or heavy clouds, they were pallid things, but they were the only green things Burl had seen. Their nodding white flowers with four petals in the form of a cross glowed against the yellowish-green leaves. But as Burl gazed toward them, the green became slowly black.

From where he stood, Burl could see two or three great grubs in lazy contentment, eating ceaselessly on the cabbages on which they rested. Suddenly first one and then the other began to jerk spasmodically. Burl saw that about each of them a tiny rim of black had clustered. Tiny black motes milled over the green surfaces of the cabbages. The grubs became black, the cabbages became black. Horrible contortions of the writhing grubs told of the agonies they were enduring. Then a black wave appeared at the further edge of the stretch of the sickly yellow fungus, a glistening, living wave, that moved forward rapidly with the roar of clickings and a persistent overtone of shrill stridulations.

The hair rose upon Burl's head. He knew what this was! He knew all too well the meaning of that tide of shining bodies. With a gasp of terror, all his intellectual preoccupations forgotten, he turned and fled in ultimate panic. And the tide came slowly on after him.

He flung away the great mass of edible mushroom, but clung to his sharp-toothed club desperately, and darted through the tangled aisles of the little mushroom forest with a heedless disregard of the dangers that might await him there. Flies buzzed about him loudly, huge creatures, glittering with a metallic luster. Once he was struck upon the shoulder by the body of one of them, and his skin was torn by the swiftly vibrating wings of the insect, as long as Burl's hand.

Burl thrust it away and sped on. The oil with which he was partly covered had turned rancid, now, and the odor attracted them, connoisseurs of the fetid. They buzzed over his head, keeping pace even with his headlong flight.

A heavy weight settled upon his head, and in a moment was doubled. Two of the creatures had dropped upon his oily hair, to sip the rancid oil through their disgusting proboscises. Burl shook them off with his hand and ran madly on. His ears were keenly attuned to the sound of the army ants behind him, and it grew but little farther away.

The clicking roar continued, but began to be overshadowed by the buzzing of the flies. In Burl's time the flies had no great heaps of putrid matter in which to lay their eggs. The ants—busy scavengers—carted away the debris of the multitudinous tragedies of the insect world long before it could acquire the gamy flavor beloved by the fly maggots. Only in isolated spots were the flies really numerous, but there they clustered in clouds that darkened the sky.

Such a buzzing, whirling cloud surrounded the madly running figure of Burl. It seemed as though a miniature whirlwind kept pace with the little pink-skinned man, a whirlwind composed of winged bodies and miltifaceted eyes. He twirled his club before him, and almost every stroke was interrupted by an impact against a thinly armored body which collapsed with a spurting of reddish liquid.

An agonizing pain as of a red-hot iron struck upon Burl's back. One of the stinging flies had thrust its sharp-tipped proboscis into Burl's flesh to suck the blood.

Burl uttered a cry—and ran full-tilt into the thick stalk of a blackened and draggled toadstool. There was a curious crackling as of wet punk or brittle rotten wood. The toadstool collapsed upon itself with a strange splashing sound. Many flies had laid their eggs in the fungoid, and it was a teeming mass of corruption and ill-smelling liquid.

With the crash of the toadstool's "head" upon the ground, it fell into a dozen pieces, and the earth for yards around was spattered with a stinking liquid in which tiny, headless maggots twitched convulsively.

The buzzing of the flies took on a note of satisfaction, and they settled by hundreds about the edges of the ill-smelling pools, becoming lost in the ecstasy of feasting while Burl staggered to his feet and darted off again. This time he was but a minor attraction to the flies, and but one or two came near him. From every direction they were hurrying to the toadstool feast, to the banquet of horrible, liquefied fungus that lay spread upon the ground.

Burl ran on. He passed beneath the wide-spreading leaves of a giant cabbage. A great grasshopper crouched upon the ground, its tremendous jaws crunching the rank vegetation voraciously. Half a dozen great worms ate steadily from their resting places among the leaves. One of them had slung itself beneath an overhanging leaf—which would have thatched a dozen homes for as many men—and was placidly anchoring itself in preparation for the spinning of a cocoon in which to sleep the sleep of metamorphosis.

A mile away, the great black tide of army ants was advancing relentlessly. The great cabbage, the huge grasshopper, and all the stupid caterpillars upon the wide leaves would soon be covered with the tiny biting insects. The cabbage would be reduced to a chewed and destroyed stump, the colossal, furry grubs would be torn into a myriad mouthfuls and devoured by the black army ants, and the grasshopper would strike out with terrific, unguided strength, crushing its assailants by blows of its powerful hind legs and bites of its great jaws. But it would die, making terrible sounds of torment as the vicious mandibles of the army ants found crevices in its armor.

The clicking roar of the ants' advance overshadowed all other sounds, now. Burl was running madly, breath coming in great gasps, his eyes wide with panic. Alone of all the world about him, he knew the danger behind. The insects he passed were going about their business with that terrifying efficiency found only in the insect world.

There is something strangely daunting in the actions of an insect. It moves so directly, with such uncanny precision, with such utter indifference to anything but the end in view. Cannibalism is a rule, almost without exception. The paralysis of prey, so it may remain alive and fresh—though in agony—for weeks on end, is a common practice. The eating piecemeal of still-living victims is a matter of course.

Absolute mercilessness, utter callousness, incredible inhumanity beyond anything known in the animal world is the natural and commonplace practice of the insects. And these vast cruelties are performed by armored, machinelike creatures with an abstraction and a routine air that suggests a horrible Nature behind them all.

Burl nearly stumbled upon a tragedy. He passed within a dozen yards of a space where a female dung beetle was devouring the mate whose honeymoon had begun that same day and ended in that gruesome fashion. Hidden behind a clump of mushrooms, a great yellow-banded spider was coyly threatening a smaller male of her own species. He was discreetly ardent, but if he won the favor of the gruesome creature he was wooing, he would furnish an appetizing meal for her sometime within twenty-four hours.

Burl's heart was pounding madly. The breath whistled in his nostrils—and behind him, the wave of army ants was drawing nearer. They came upon the feasting flies. Some took to the air and escaped, but others were too engrossed in their delicious meal. The twitching little maggots, stranded upon the earth by the scattering of their soupy broth, were torn in pieces. The flies who were seized vanished into tiny maws. The serried ranks of black insects went on.

The tiny clickings of their limbs, the perpetual challenges and cross-challenges of crossed antennae, the stridulations of the creatures, all combined to make a high-pitched but deafening din. Now and then another sound pierced the noises made by the ants themselves. A cricket, seized by a thousand tiny jaws, uttered cries of agony. The shrill note of the crickets had grown deeply bass with the increase in size of the organs that uttered it.

There was a strange contrast between the ground before the advancing horde and that immediately behind it. Before, a busy world, teeming with life. Butterflies floating overhead on lazy wings, grubs waxing fat and huge upon the giant cabbages, crickets eating, great spiders sitting quietly in their lairs waiting with invincible patience for prey to draw near their trapdoors or fall into their webs, colossal beetles lumbering heavily through the mushroom forests, seeking food, making love in monstrous, tragic fashion.

And behind the wide belt of army ants—chaos. The edible mushrooms gone. The giant cabbages left as mere stumps of unappetizing pulp, the busy life of the insect world completely wiped out save for the flying creatures that fluttered helplessly over an utterly changed landscape. Here and there little bands of stragglers moved busily over the denuded earth, searching for some fragment of food that might conceivably have been overlooked by the main body.

Burl was putting forth his last ounce of strength. His limbs trembled, his breathing was agony, sweat stood out upon his forehead. He ran, a little, naked man with the disjointed fragment of a huge insect's limb in his hand, running for his insignificant life, running as if his continued existence among the million tragedies of that single day were the purpose for which the whole of the universe had been created.

He sped across an open space a hundred yards across. A thicket of beautifully golden mushrooms (*Agaricus caesareus*) barred his way. Beyond the mushrooms a range of strangely colored hills began, purple and green and black and gold, melting into each other, branching off from each other, inextricably tangled.

They rose to a height of perhaps sixty or seventy feet, and above them a little grayish haze had gathered. There seemed to be a layer of tenuous vapor upon their surfaces, which slowly rose and coiled, and gathered into a tiny cloudlet above their tips.

The hills, themselves, were but masses of fungus, mushrooms and fungoids of every description, yeasts, "musts," and every form of fungus growth which had grown within itself and about itself until this great mass of strangely colored, spongy stuff had gathered in a mass that undulated unevenly across the level earth for miles.

Burl burst through the golden thicket and attacked the ascent. His feet sank into the spongy sides of the hillock. Panting, gasping, staggering from exhaustion, he made his way up the top. He plunged into a little valley on the farther side, up another slope. For perhaps ten minutes he forced himself on, then collapsed. He lay, unable to move further, in a little hollow, his sharp-toothed club still clasped in his hands. Above him, a bright yellow butterfly with a thirty-foot spread of wing, fluttered lightly.

He lay motionless, breathing in great gasps, his limbs stubbornly refusing to lift him.

The sound of the army ants continued to grow near. At last, above the crest of the last hillock he had surmounted, two tiny antennae appeared, then the black glistening head of an army ant, the foerunner of its horde. It moved deliberately forward, waving its antennae ceaselessly. It made its way toward Burl, tiny clickings coming from the movements of its limbs.

A little wisp of tenuous vapor swirled toward the ant, a wisp of the same vapor that had gathered above the whole range of hills as a thin, low cloud. It enveloped the insect—and the ant seemed to be attacked by a strange convulsion. Its legs moved aimlessly. It threw itself desperately about. If it had been an animal, Burl would have watched with wondering eyes while it coughed and gasped, but it was an insect breathing through air holes in its abdomen. It writhed upon the spongy fungus growth across which it had been moving.

Burl, lying in an exhausted, panting heap upon the purple mass of fungus, was conscious of a strange sensation. His body felt strangely warm. He knew nothing of fire or the heat of the sun, and the only sensation of warmth he had ever known was that caused when the members of his tribe had huddled together in their hiding place when the damp chill of the night had touched their soft-skinned bodies. Then the heat of their breaths and their bodies had kept out the chill.

This heat that Burl now felt was a hotter, fiercer heat. He moved his body with a tremendous effort, and for a moment the fungus was cool and soft beneath him. Then, slowly, the sensation of heat began again, and increased until Burl's skin was red and inflamed from the irritation.

The thin and tenuous vapor, too, made Burl's lungs smart and his eyes water. He was breathing in great, choking gasps, but the period of rest—short as it was—had enabled him to rise and stagger on. He crawled painfully to the top of the slope, and looked back.

The hillcrest on which he stood was higher than any of those he had passed in his painful run, and he could see clearly the whole of the purple range. Where he was, he was near the farther edge of the range, which was here perhaps half a mile wide.

It was a ceaseless, undulating mass of hills and hollows, ridges and spurs, all of them colored, purple and brown and golden-yellow, deepest black and dingy white. And from the tips of most of the pointed hills little wisps of vapor rose up.

A thin, dark cloud had gathered overhead. Burl could look to the right and left, and see the hills fading into the distance, growing fainter as the haze above them seemed to grow thicker. He saw, too, the advancing cohorts of the army ants, creeping over the tangled mass of fungus growth. They seemed to be feeding as they went, upon the fungus that had gathered into these incredible monstrosities.

The hills were living. They were not upheavals of the ground, they were festering heaps of insanely growing, festering mushrooms and fungus. Upon most of them a purple mold had spread itself so that they seemed a range of purple hills, but here and there patches of other vivid colors showed, and there was a large hill whose whole side was a brilliant golden hue. Another had tiny bright red spots of a strange and malignant mushroom whose properties Burl did not know, scattered all over the purple with which it was covered.

Burl leaned heavily upon his club and watched dully. He could run no more. The army ants were spreading everywhere over the mass of fungus. They would reach him soon.

Far to the right the vapor thickened. A column of smoke arose. What Burl did not know and would never know was that far down in the interior of that compressed mass of fungus, slow oxidization had been going on. The temperature of the interior had been raised. In the darkness and the dampness deep down in the hills, spontaneous combustion had begun.

Just as the vast piles of coal the railroad companies of thirty thousand years before had gathered together sometimes began to burn fiercely in their interiors, and just as the farmers' piles of damp straw suddenly burst into fierce flames from no cause, so these huge piles of tinderlike mushrooms had been burning slowly within themselves.

There had been no flames, because the surface remained intact and nearly airtight. But when the army ants began to tear at the edible surfaces despite the heat they encountered, fresh air found its way to the smoldering masses of fungus. The slow combustion became rapid combustion. The dull heat became fierce flames. The slow trickle of thin smoke became a huge column of thick, choking, acrid stuff that set the army ants that breathed it into spasms of convulsive writhing.

From a dozen points the flames burst out. A dozen or more columns of blinding smoke rose to the heavens. A pall of fume-laden smoke gathered above the range of purple hills, while Burl watched apathetically. And the serried ranks of army ants marched on to the widening furnaces that awaited them.

They had recoiled from the river, because their instinct had warned them. Thirty thousand years without danger from fire, however, had let their racial fear of fire die out. They marched into the blazing orifices they had opened in the hills, snapping with their mandibles at the leaping flames, springing at the glowing tinder.

The blazing area widened, as the purple surface was undermined and fell in. Burl watched the phenomenon without comprehension and even with thankfulness. He stood, panting more and more slowly, breathing more and more easily, until the glow from the approaching flames reddened his skin and the acrid smoke made tears flow from his eyes.

Then he retreated slowly, leaning on his club and looking back. The black wave of the army ants was sweeping into the fire, sweeping into the incredible heat of that carbonized material burning with an open flame. At last there were only the little bodies of stragglers from the great ant army, scurrying here and there over the ground their comrades had denuded of all living things. The bodies of the main army had vanished—burnt to crisp ashes in the furnace of the hills.

There had been agony in that flame, dreadful agony such as no man would like to dwell upon. The insane courage of the ants, attacking with their horny jaws the burning masses of fungus, rolling over and over with a flaming missile clutched in their mandibles, sounding their shrill war cry while cries of agony came from them—blinded, their antennae burnt off, their lidless eyes scorched by the licking flames, yet going madly forward on flaming feet to attack, ever attack this unknown and unknowable enemy.

Burl made his way slowly over the hills. Twice he saw small bodies of the army ants. They had passed between the widening surfaces their comrades had opened, and they were feeding voraciously upon the hills they trod on. Once Burl was spied, and a shrill war cry was sounded, but he moved on, and the ants were busily eating. A single ant rushed toward him. Burl brought down his club, and a writhing body remained to be eaten later by its comrades when they came upon it.

Again night fell. The skies grew red in the west, though the sun did not shine through the ever-present cloud bank.

Darkness spread across the sky. Utter blackness fell over the whole mad world, save where the luminous mushrooms shed their pale light upon the ground and fireflies the length of Burl's arm shed their fitful gleams upon an earth of fungus growths and monstrous insects.

Burl made his way across the range of mushroom hills, picking his path with his large blue eyes whose pupils expanded to great size. Slowly, from the sky, now a drop and then a drop, now a drop and then a drop, the nightly rain that would continue until daybreak began.

Burl found the ground hard beneath his feet. He listened keenly for sounds of danger. Something rustled heavily in a thicket of mushrooms a hundred yards away. There were sounds of preening, and of delicate feet placed lightly here and there upon the ground. Then the throbbing beat of huge wings began suddenly, and a body took to the air.

A fierce, down-coming current of air smote Burl, and he looked upward in time to catch the outline of a huge body—a moth—as it passed above him. He turned to watch the line of its flight, and saw a strange glow in the sky behind him. The mushroom hills were still burning.

He crouched beneath a squat toadstool and waited for the dawn, his club held tightly in his hands, and his ears alert for any sound of danger. The slow-dropping, sodden rain kept on. It fell with irregular, drumlike beats upon the tough top of the toadstool under which he had taken refuge.

Slowly, slowly, the sodden rainfall continued. Drop by drop, all the night long, the warm pellets of liquid came from the sky. They boomed upon the hollow heads of the toadstools, and splashed into the steaming pools that lay festering all over the fungus-covered earth.

And all the night long the great fires grew and spread in the mass of already half-carbonized mushroom. The flare at the horizon grew brighter and nearer. Burl, naked and hiding beneath a huge mushroom, watched it grow near him with wide eyes, wondering what this thing was. He had never seen a flame before.

The overhanging clouds were brightened by the flames. Over a stretch at least a dozen miles in length and from half a mile to three miles across, seething furnaces sent columns of dense smoke up to the roof of clouds, luminous from the glow below them, and spreading out and forming an intermediate layer below the cloudbanks.

It was like the glow of all the many lights of a vast city thrown against the sky—but the last great city had molded into fungus-covered rubbish thirty thousand years before. Like the flitting of airplanes above a populous city, too, was the flitting of fascinated creatures above the glow.

Moths and great flying beetles, gigantic gnats and midges grown huge with the passing of time, they fluttered and danced the dance of death above the flames. As the fire grew nearer to Burl, he could see them.

Colossal, delicately formed creatures swooped above the strange blaze. Moths with their riotously colored wings of thirty-foot spread beat the air with mighty strokes, and their huge eyes glowed like carbuncles as they stared with the frenzied gaze of intoxicated devotees into the glowing flames below them.

Burl saw a great peacock moth soaring above the burning mushroom hills. Its wings were all of forty feet across, and fluttered like gigantic sails as the moth gazed down at the flaming furnace below. The separate flames had united, now, and a single sheet of white-hot burning stuff spread across the country for miles, sending up its clouds of smoke, in which and through which the fascinated creatures flew.

Feathery antennae of the finest lace spread out before the head of the peacock moth, and its body was softest, richest velvet. A ring of snow-white down marked where its head began, and the red glow from below smote on the maroon of its body with a strange effect.

For one instant it was outlined clearly. Its eyes glowed more redly than any ruby's fire, and the great, delicate wings were poised in flight. Burl caught the flash of the flames upon two great iridescent spots upon the wide-spread wings. Shining purple and vivid red, the glow of opal and the sheen of pearl, all the glory of chalcedony and chrysoprase formed a single wonder in the red glare of burning fungus. White smoke compassed the great moth all about, dimming the radiance of its gorgeous dress.

Burl saw it dart straight into the thickest and brightest of the licking flames, flying madly, eagerly, into the searing, hellish heat as a willing, drunken sacrifice to the god of fire.

Monster flying beetles with their horny wing cases stiffly stretched blundered above the reeking, smoking pyre. In the red light from before them they shone like burnished metal, and their clumsy bodies with the spurred and fierce-toothed limbs darted like so many grotesque meteors through the luminous haze of ascending smoke.

Burl saw strange collisions and still stranger meetings. Male and female flying creatures circled and spun in the glare, dancing their dance of love and death in the wild radiance from the funeral pyre of the purple hills. They mounted higher than Burl could see, drunk with the ecstasy of living, then descended to plunge headlong to death in the roaring fires beneath them.

From every side the creatures came. Moths of brightest yellow with soft and furry bodies palpitant with life flew madly into the column of light that reached to the overhanging clouds, then moths of deepest black with gruesome symbols upon their wings came swiftly to dance, like motes in a bath of sunlight, above the glow.

And Burl sat crouched beneath an overshadowing toadstool and watched. The perpetual, slow, sodden raindrops fell. A continual faint hissing penetrated the sound of the fire—the raindrops being turned to steam. The air was alive with flying things. From far away, Burl heard a strange, deep bass muttering. He did not know the cause, but there was a vast swamp, of the existence of which he was ignorant, some ten or fifteen miles away, and the chorus of insect-eating giant frogs reached his ears even at that distance.

The night wore on, while the flying creatures above the fire danced and died, their numbers ever recruited by fresh arrivals. Burl sat tensely still, his wide eyes watching everything, his mind groping for an explanation of what he saw. At last the sky grew dimly gray, then brighter, and day came on. The flames of the burning hills grew faint as the fire died down, and after a long time Burl crept from his hiding place and stood erect.

A hundred yards from where he was, a straight wall of smoke rose from the still-smoldering fungus, and Burl could see it stretching for miles in either direction. He turned to continue on his way, and saw the remains of one of the tragedies of the night.

A huge moth had flown into the flames, been horribly scorched, and floundered out again. Had it been able to fly, it would have returned to its devouring deity, but now it lay immovable upon the ground, its antennae seared hopelessly, one beautiful, delicate wing burned in gaping holes, its eyes dimmed by flame and its exquisitely tapering limbs broken and crushed by the force with which it had struck the ground. It lay helpless upon the earth, only the stumps of its antennae moving restlessly, and its abdomen pulsating slowly as it drew pain-racked breaths.

Burl drew near and picked up a stone. He moved on presently, a velvet cloak cast over his shoulders, gleaming with all the colors of the rainbow. A gorgeous mass of soft, blue moth fur was about his middle, and he had bound upon his forehead two yard-long, golden fragments of the moth's magnificent antennae. He strode on, slowly, clad as no man had been clad in all the ages.

After a little he secured a spear and took up his journey to Saya, looking like a prince of Ind upon a bridal journey—though no mere prince ever wore such raiment in days of greatest glory.

For many long miles Burl threaded his way through a single forest of thin-stalked toadstools. They towered three man-heights high, and all about their bases were streaks and splashes of the rusts and molds that preyed upon them. Twice Burl came to open glades wherein open, bubbling pools of green slime festered in corruption, and once he hid himself fearfully as a monster scarabeus beetle lumbered within three yards of him, moving heavily onward with a clanking of limbs as of some mighty machine.

Burl saw the mighty armor and the inward-curving jaws of

the creature, and envied him his weapons. The time was not yet come, however, when Burl would smile at the great insect and hunt him for the juicy flesh contained in those armored limbs.

Burl was still a savage, still ignorant, still timid. His principal advance had been that whereas he had fled without reasoning, he now paused to see if he need flee. In his hands he bore a long, sharp-pointed chitinous spear. It had been the weapon of a huge, unnamed flying insect scorched to death in the burning of the purple hills, which had floundered out of the flames to die. Burl had worked for an hour before being able to detach the weapon he coveted. It was as long and longer than Burl himself.

He was a strange sight, moving slowly and cautiously through the shadowed lanes of the mushroom forest. A cloak of delicate velvet in which all the colors of the rainbow played in iridescent beauty hung from his shoulders. A mass of soft and beautiful moth fur was about his middle, and in the strip of sinew about his waist the fiercely toothed limb of a fighting beetle was thrust carelessly. He had bound to his forehead twin stalks of a great moth's feathery golden antennae.

Against the play of color that came from his borrowed plumage his pink skin showed in odd contrast. He looked like some proud knight walking slowly through the gardens of a goblin's castle. But he was still a fearful creature, no more than the monstrous creatures about him save in the possession of latent intelligence. He was weak—and therein lay his greatest promise. A hundred thousand years before him his ancestors had been forced by lack of claws and fangs to develop brains.

Burl was sunk as low as they had been, but he had to combat more horrifying enemies, more inexorable threatenings, and many times more crafty assailants. His ancestors had invented knives and spears and flying missiles. The creatures about Burl had knives and spears a thousand times more deadly than the weapons that had made his ancestors masters of the woods and forests.

Burl was in comparison vastly more weak than his forebears had been, and it was that weakness that in times to come would lead him and those who followed him to heights his ancestors had never known. But now—

He heard a discordant, deep bass bellow, coming from a spot not twenty yards away. In a flash of panic he darted behind a clump of mushrooms and hid himself, panting in sheer terror. He waited for an instant in frozen fear, motionless and tense. His wide, blue eyes were glassy.

The bellow came again, but this time with a querulous note. Burl heard a crashing and plunging as of some creature caught in a snare. A mushroom fell with a brittle snapping, and the spongy thud as it fell to the ground was followed by a tremendous commotion. Something was fighting desperately against something else, but Burl did not know what creature or creatures might be in combat.

He waited for a long time, and the noise gradually died away. Presently Burl's breath came more slowly, and his courage returned. He stole from his hiding place, and would have made away, but something held him back. Instead of creeping from the scene, he crept cautiously over toward the source of the noise.

He peered between two cream-colored toadstool stalks and saw the cause of the noise. A wide, funnel-shaped snare of silk was spread out before him, some twenty yards across and as many deep. The individual threads could be plainly seen, but in the mass it seemed a fabric of sheerest, finest texture. Held up by the tall mushrooms, it was anchored to the ground below, and drew away to a tiny point through which a hole gave on some yet unknown recess. And all the space of the wide snare was hung with threads, fine, twisted threads no more than half the thickness of Burl's finger.

This was the trap of a labyrinth spider. Not one of the interlacing threads was strong enough to hold the feeblest of prey, but the threads were there by thousands. A great cricket had become entangled in the maze of sticky lines. Its limbs thrashed out, smashing the snare lines at every stroke, but at every stroke meeting and becoming entangled with a dozen more. It thrashed about mightily, emitting at intervals the horrible, deep bass cry that the chirping voice of the cricket had become with its increase in size.

*　　*　　*

Burl breathed more easily, and watched with a fascinated curiosity. Mere death—even tragic death—as among insects held no great interest for him. It was a matter of such common and matter-of-fact occurrence that he was not greatly stirred. But a spider and his prey was another matter.

There were few insects that deliberately sought man. Most insects have their allotted victims, and will touch no others, but spiders have a terrifying impartiality. One great beetle devouring another was a matter of indifference to Burl. A spider devouring some luckless insect was but an example of what might happen to him. He watched alertly, his gaze traveling from the enmeshed cricket to the strange orifice at the rear of the funnel-shaped snare.

The opening darkened. Two shining, glistening eyes had been watching from the rear of the funnel. It drew itself into a tunnel there, in which the spider had been waiting. Now it swung out lightly and came toward the cricket. It was a gray spider *(Agelena labyrinthica)*, with twin black ribbons upon its thorax, next the head, and with two stripes of curiously speckled brown and white upon its abdomen. Burl saw, too, two curious appendages like a tail.

It came nimbly out of its tunnellike hiding place and approached the cricket. The cricket was struggling only feebly now, and the cries it uttered were but feeble, because of the confining threads that fettered its limbs. Burl saw the spider throw itself upon the cricket and saw the final, convulsive shudder of the insect as the spider's fangs pierced its tough armor. The sting lasted a long time, and finally Burl saw that the spider was really feeding. All the succulent juices of the now dead cricket were being sucked from its body by the spider. It had stung the cricket upon the haunch, and presently it went to the other leg and drained that, too, by means of its powerful internal suction pump. When the second haunch had been sucked dry, the spider pawed the lifeless creature for a few moments and left it.

Food was plentiful, and the spider could afford to be dainty in its feeding. The two choicest titbits had been consumed. The remainder could be discarded.

A sudden thought came to Burl and quite took his breath away. For a second his knees knocked together in self-induced panic. He watched the gray spider carefully with growing determination in his eyes. He, Burl, had killed a hunting spider upon the red-clay cliff. True, the killing had been an accident, and had nearly cost him his own life a few minutes later in the web spider's snare, but he had killed a spider, and of the most deadly kind.

Now, a great ambition was growing in Burl's heart. His tribe had always feared spiders too much to know much of their habits, but they knew one or two things. The most important was that the snare spiders never left their lairs to hunt—never! Burl was about to make a daring application of that knowledge.

He drew back from the white and shining snare and crept softly to the rear. The fabric gathered itself into a point and then continued for some twenty feet as a tunnel, in which the spider waited while dreaming of its last meal and waiting for the next victim to become entangled in the labyrinth in front. Burl made his way to a point where the tunnel was no more than ten feet away, and waited.

Presently, through the interstices of the silk, he saw the gray bulk of the spider. It had left the exhausted body of the cricket, and returned to its resting place. It settled itself carefully upon the soft walls of the tunnel, with its shining eyes fixed upon the tortuous threads of its trap. Burl's hair was standing straight up upon his head from sheer fright, but he was the slave of an idea.

He drew near and poised his spear, his new and sharp spear, taken from the body of an unknown flying creature killed by the burning purple hills. Burl raised the spear and aimed its sharp and deadly point at the thick gray bulk he could see dimly through the threads of the tunnel. He thrust it home with all his strength—and ran away at the top of his speed, glassy-eyed from terror.

A long time later he ventured near again, his heart in his mouth, ready to flee at the slightest sound. All was still. Burl had missed the horrible convulsions of the wounded spider, had not heard the frightful gnashings of its fangs as it tore at the piercing weapon, had not seen the silken threads of the tunnel ripped as the spider—hurt to death—had struggled with insane strength to free itself.

He came back beneath the overshadowing toadstools, stepping quietly and cautiously, to find a great rent in the silken tunnel, to find the great gray bulk lifeless and still, half-fallen through the opening the spear had first made. A little puddle of evil-smelling liquid lay upon the ground below the body, and from time to time a droplet fell from the spear into the puddle with a curious splash.

Burl looked at what he had done, saw the dead body of the creature he had slain, saw the ferocious mandibles, and the keen and deadly fangs. The dead eyes of the creature still stared at him malignantly, and the hairy legs were still braced as if further to enlarge the gaping hole through which it had partly fallen.

Exultation filled Burl's heart. His tribe had been but furtive vermin for thousands of years, fleeing from the mighty insects, hiding from them, and if overtaken but waiting helplessly for death, screaming shrilly in terror.

He, Burl, had turned the tables. He had slain one of the enemies of his tribe. His breast expanded. Always his tribesmen went quietly and fearfully, making no sound. But a sudden, exultant yell burst from Burl's lips—the first hunting cry from the lips of a man in three hundred centuries!

The next second his pulse nearly stopped in sheer panic at having made such a noise. He listened fearfully, but there was no sound. He drew near his prey and carefully withdrew his spear. The viscid liquid made it slimy and slippery, and he had to wipe it dry against a leathery toadstool. Then Burl had to conquer his illogical fear again before daring to touch the creature he had slain.

He moved off presently, with the belly of the spider upon his back and two of the hairy legs over his shoulders. The other limbs of the monster hung limp, and trailed upon the ground. Burl was now a still more curious sight as a gaily colored object with a cloak shining in iridescent colors, the golden antennae of a great moth rising from his forehead, and the hideous bulk of a gray spider for a burden.

He moved through the thin-stalked mushroom forest, and, because of the thing he carried, all creatures fled before him. They did not fear man—their instinct was slow-moving—but during all the millions of years that insects have existed, there have existed spiders to prey upon them. So Burl moved on in solemn state, a brightly clad man bent beneath the weight of a huge and horrible monster.

He came upon a valley full of torn and blackened mushrooms. There was not a single yellow top among them. Every one had been infested with tiny maggots which had liquefied the tough meat of the mushroom and caused it to drip to the ground below. And all the liquid had gathered in a golden pool in the center of the small depression. Burl heard a loud humming and buzzing before he topped the rise that opened the valley for his inspection. He stopped a moment and looked down.

A golden-red lake, its center reflecting the hazy sky overhead. All about, blackened mushrooms, seeming to have been charred and burned by a fierce flame. A slow-flowing golden brooklet trickled slowly over a rocky ledge, into the larger pool. And all about the edges of the golden lake, in ranks and rows, by hundreds, thousands, and by millions, were ranged the green-gold, shining bodies of great flies.

They were small as compared with the other insects. They had increased in size but a fraction of the amount that the bees, for example, had increased; but it was due to an imperative necessity of their race.

The flesh flies laid their eggs by hundreds in decaying carcasses. The others laid their eggs by hundreds in the mushrooms. To feed the maggots that would hatch, a relatively great quantity of food was needed, therefore the flies must remain comparatively small, or the body of a single grasshopper, say, would furnish food for but two or three grubs instead of the hundreds it must support.

Burl stared down at the golden pool. Bluebottles, greenbottles, and all the flies of metallic luster were gathered at the Lucullan feast of corruption. Their buzzing as they darted above the odorous pool of golden liquid made the sound Burl had heard. Their bodies flashed and glittered as they darted back and forth, seeking a place to alight and join in the orgy.

Those which clustered about the banks of the pool were still as if carved from metal. Their huge, red eyes glowed, and their bodies shone with an obscene fatness. Flies are the most disgusting of all insects. Burl watched them a moment, watched the interlacing streams of light as they buzzed eagerly above the pool, seeking a place at the festive board.

A drumming roar sounded in the air. A golden speck appeared in the sky, a slender, needlelike body with transparent, shining wings and two huge eyes. It grew nearer and became a dragonfly twenty feet and more in length, its body shimmering, purest gold. It poised itself above the pool and then darted down. Its jaws snapped viciously and repeatedly, and at each snapping the glittering body of a fly vanished.

A second dragonfly appeared, its body a vivid purple, and a third. They swooped and rushed above the golden pool, snapping in midair, turning their abrupt, angular turns, creatures of incredible ferocity and beauty. At the moment they were nothing more or less than slaughtering machines. They darted here and there, their many-faceted eyes burning with bloodlust. In that mass of buzzing flies even the most voracious appetite must be sated, but the dragonflies kept on. Beautiful, slender, graceful creatures, they dashed here and there above the pond like avenging fiends or the mythical dragons for which they had been named.

Only a few miles farther on Burl came upon a familiar landmark. He knew it well, but from a safe distance as always. A mass of rock had heaved itself up from the nearly level plain over which he was traveling, and formed an outjutting cliff. At one point the rock overhung a sheer drop, making an inverted ledge—a roof over nothingness—which had been preempted by a hairy creature and made into a fairylike dwelling. A white hemisphere clung tenaciously to the rock above, and long cables anchored it firmly.

Burl knew the place as one to be fearfully avoided. A Clotho spider *(Clotho Durandi, LATR)* had built itself a nest there, from which it emerged to hunt the unwary. Within that half-globe there was a monster, resting upon a cushion of softest silk. But if one went too near, one of the little inverted arches, seemingly firmly closed by a wall of silk, would open and a creature out of a dream of hell emerge, to run with fiendish agility toward its prey.

Surely, Burl knew the place. Hung upon the outer walls of the silken palace were stones and tiny boulders, discarded fragments of former meals, and the gutted armor from limbs of ancient prey. But what caused Burl to know the place most surely and most terribly was another decoration that dangled from the castle of this insect ogre. This was the shrunken, desiccated figure of a man, all its juices extracted and the life gone.

The death of that man had saved Burl's life two years before. They had been together, seeking a new source of edible mushrooms for food. The Clotho spider was a hunter, not a spinner of snares. It sprang suddenly from behind a great puffball, and the two men froze in terror. Then it came swiftly forward and deliberately chose its victim. Burl had escaped when the other man was seized. Now he looked meditatively at the hiding place of his ancient enemy. Someday—

But now he passed on. He went past the thicket in which the great moths hid during the day, and past the pool—a turgid thing of slime and yeast—in which a monster water snake lurked. He penetrated the little wood of the shining mushrooms that gave out light at night, and the shadowed place where the truffle-hunting beetles went chirping thunderously during the dark hours.

And then he saw Saya. He caught a flash of pink skin vanishing behind the thick stalk of a squat toadstool, and ran forward, calling her name. She appeared, and saw the figure with the horrible bulk of the spider upon its back. She cried out in horror, and Burl understood. He let his burden fall and then went swiftly toward her.

They met. Saya waited timidly until she saw who this man was, and then astonishment went over her face. Gorgeously attired, in an iridescent cloak from the whole wing of a great moth, with a strip of softest fur from a night-flying creature about his middle, with golden, feathery antennae bound upon his forehead, and a fierce spear in his hands—this was not the Burl she had known.

But then he moved slowly toward her, filled with a fierce delight at seeing her again, thrilling with joy at the slender gracefulness of her form and the dark richness of her tangled hair. He held out his hands and touched her shyly. Then, manlike, he began to babble excitedly of the things that had happened to him, and dragged her toward his great victim, the gray-bellied spider.

Saya trembled when she saw the furry bulk lying upon the ground, and would have fled when Burl advanced and took it upon his back. Then something of the pride that filled him came vicariously to her. She smiled a flashing smile, and Burl stopped short in his excited explanation. He was suddenly tongue-tied. His eyes became pleading and soft. He laid the huge spider at her feet and spread out his hands imploringly.

Thirty thousand years of savagery had not lessened the femininity in Saya. She became aware that Burl was her slave, that these wonderful things he wore and had done were as nothing if she did not approve. She drew away—saw the misery in Burl's face—and abruptly ran into his arms and clung to him, laughing happily. And quite suddenly Burl saw with extreme clarity that all these things he had done, even the slaying of a great spider, were of no importance whatever beside this most wonderful thing that had just happened, and told Saya so quite humbly, but holding her very close to him as he did so.

And so Burl came back to his tribe. He had left it nearly naked, with but a wisp of moth wing twisted about his middle, a timid, fearful, trembling creature. He returned in triumph, walking slowly and fearlessly down a broad lane of golden mushrooms toward the hiding place of his people.

Upon his shoulders was draped a great and many-colored cloak made from the whole of a moth's wing. Soft fur was about his middle. A spear was in his hand and a fierce club at his waist. He and Saya bore between them the dead body of a huge spider—aforetime the dread of the pink-skinned, naked men. But to Burl the most important thing of all was that Saya walked beside him openly, acknowledging him before all the tribe.

DREAMWORLD

by Isaac Asimov

Born in Petrovichi, U.S.S.R., Isaac Asimov (1920–   ) was brought to the United States in 1923 and became a naturalized citizen in 1928. After completing his Ph.D. in chemistry in 1948, he taught biochemistry at Boston University's School of Medicine, until becoming a full-time writer in 1958. Since then he has written more than 325 books.

As for the following story, all Marty and I can say is that it seems to be the only anticlimax yarn we've ever seen that works.

At thirteen, Edward Keller had been a science fiction devotee for four years. He bubbled with galactic enthusiasm.

His Aunt Clara, who had brought him up by rule and rod in pious memory of her deceased sister, wavered between toleration and exasperation. It appalled her to watch him grow so immersed in fantasy.

"Face reality, Eddie," she would say, angrily.

He would nod, but go on, "And I dreamed Martians were chasing me, see? I had a special death ray, but the atomic power unit was pretty low and—"

Every other breakfast consisted of eggs, toast, milk, and some such dream.

Aunt Clara said, severely, "Now, Eddie, one of these

nights you won't be able to wake up out of your dream. You'll be trapped! Then what?''

She lowered her angular face close to his and glared.

Eddie was strangely impressed by his aunt's warning. He lay in bed, staring into the darkness. He wouldn't like to be trapped in a dream. It was always nice to wake up before it was too late. Like the time the dinosaurs were after him—

Suddenly he was out of bed, out of the house, out on the lawn, and he knew it was another dream.

The thought was broken by a vague thunder and a shadow that blotted the sun. He looked upward in astonishment and he could make out the human face that touched the clouds.

It was his Aunt Clara! Monstrously tall, she bent toward him in admonition, mastlike forefinger upraised, voice too guttural to be made out.

Eddie turned and ran in panic. Another Aunt Clara monster loomed up before him, voice rumbling.

He turned and ran in panic. Another Aunt Clara monster loomed up before him, voice rumbling.

He turned again, stumbling, panting, heading outward, outward.

He reached the top of the hill and stopped in horror. Off in the distance a hundred towering Aunt Claras were marching by. As the column passed, each line of Aunt Claras turned their heads sharply toward him and the thunderous bass rumbling coalesced into words:

"Face reality, Eddie. Face reality, Eddie."

Eddie threw himself sobbing to the ground. Please wake up, he begged himself. Don't be caught in this dream.

For unless he woke up, the worst science-fictional doom of all would have overtaken him. He would be trapped, *trapped*, in a world of giant aunts.

THE THIRTY AND ONE

by David H. Keller

A psychiatrist, David H. Keller (1880–1966) was very much interested in abnormal behavior and mental breakdowns, themes that occur in a number of his classic works of fantasy and horror. In addition to his fiction, however, he also published a great number of professional articles and books.

Like many of his best stories, and probably as a result of training in psychoanalysis, the following heroic fantasy (in which a young woman faces a giant) can be given more than one interpretation.

Cecil, OverLord of Walling, in the Dark Forest, mused by the fire. The blind Singer of Songs had sung the sagas of ancient times, had waited long for praise and then, disquieted, had left the banquet hall guided by his dog. The Juggler had merrily tossed his golden balls into the air till they seemed a glistening cascade, but still the OverLord had mused, unseeing. The wise Homunculus had crouched at his feet uttering words of wisdom and telling tales of Gobi and the buried city of Ankor. But nothing could rouse the OverLord from his meditations.

At last, he stood up and struck the silver bell with a hammer of gold. Serving men answered the call.

"Send me the Lady Angelica and the Lord Gustro," he

commanded, and then once again sat down with chin in hand, waiting.

At last, the two came in answer to his summons. The Lady was his only daughter, as fair and as wise a Lady as there was in all Walling. Lord Gustro, someday, would be her husband, and help her rule in the Dark Forest. Meantime, he perfected himself in the use of the broadsword, lute, the hunting with the falcon, and the study of books. He was six feet tall, twenty years old, and had in him the makings of a man.

The three sat around the fire, two waiting to hear the one talk, the one waiting till he knew just how to say what had to be said. At last, Cecil began to talk:

"You no doubt know what is on my mind. For years I have tried to give happiness and peace and prosperity, to the simple folk of our land of Walling. We were well situated in a valley surrounded by lofty, impassable forests. Only one mountain pass connected us with the great, cruel, and almost unknown world around us. Into that world, we sent in springtime, summer, and fall our caravans of mules laden with grain, olives, wine, and uncut stones. From that world, we brought salt, weapons, bales of woolen and silken goods, for our needs. No one tried to molest us, for we had nothing much that they coveted. Perhaps safety made us grow soft, sleepy, and unprepared for danger.

"But it has come. We might have known there were things in that outer world we knew not of and therefore could not even dream of. But this spring, our first caravan winding over the mountains found, at the boundaries of the Dark Forest, a Castle blocking their way. Their mules were not birds and could not fly over; they were not moles and could not burrow under. And the lads with the mules were not warriors and could not break their way through. So they came back, unmolested, 'tis true, but with their goods unsold and unbartered.

"Now, I do not think that Castle was built by magic. I have personally looked at it, and it seems nothing but stone and mortar. And it is not held by an army of fighting men, for all we can hear is that one man holds it. But what a man! Half again as tall as our finest lad, and skilled in the use of weapons. I tried him out. One at a time, I sent to him John of the flying ax, and Herman who had no equal with the double-edged sword, and Rubin who could split a willow wand at two hundred paces with his steel-tipped arrow. These three men lie, worm food, in the ravine below the Castle. And meantime, our country is strangulated as far as trade is concerned. We have cattle in the meadow, and wood in the forest, and grain in the bin, but we have no salt, no clothes to cover us from the cold, no finery for our women, or weapons for our men. And we never will have these as long as this Castle and this man block our caravans.''

"We can capture the Castle and kill the Giant!" cried Lord Gustro, with the impetuosity of youth.

"How?" asked the OverLord. "Did I not tell you that the path is narrow? You know that. On one side, the mountains tower lofty as the flight of the bird and smooth as a woman's skin. On the other side is the Valley of the Dæmons, and no one has ever fallen into it and come back alive. The only path is just wide enough for one man or one man-led mule, and that path now leads through the castle. If we could send an army, 'twould be different. But only one man at a time can we send, and there is no man equal to successful combat with this Giant."

The Lady Angelica smiled as she whispered, "We may conquer him through chicanery. For example, I have seen this hall filled with fighting men and fair ladies almost put into an endless sleep by gazing at the golden balls flying through the air and back into the clever hands of the Juggler. And the Blind Singer of Songs can make anyone forget all except the music of his tales. And our Homunculus is very wise."

The OverLord shook his head. "Not thus will the question be answered. This madman wants one thing, and that one thing means everything in the lastward, as far as our land and people are concerned. Perhaps you have guessed. I will give you the demand ere you ask the question. Our Lady's hand in marriage, and thus, when I die, he becomes the OverLord of Walling."

Lady Angelica looked over at Lord Gustro. He looked at the OverLord's daughter. At last, he said:

"Better to eat our grain and eat our olives and drink our wine. Better that our men wear bearskins and our women cover themselves with the skins of deer. It would be best for them to wear shoes of wood than pantufles of unicorn skin brought from Araby. It were a sweeter fate for them to perfume their bodies with crushed violets and may-flowers from our forest than to smell sweet with perfumes from the trees of the unknown Island of the East. This price is too heavy. Let us live as our fathers and fathers' fathers lived, even climb trees like the monkey folk, than trust to such an OverLord. Besides, I love the Lady Angelica."

The Lady smiled her thanks. "I still am thinking of the use of intelligence overcoming brawn. Have we no wisdom left in Walling, besides the fair, faint dreams of weak woman?"

"I will send for the Homunculus," her father answered. "He may know the answer to that question."

The little man came in. He was a man not born of woman, but grown for seven years in a glass bottle, during all of which time he read books held before him by wise men, and was nourished with drops of wine and tiny balls of Asphodel paste. He listened to the problem gravely, though at times he seemed asleep. At last, he said one word.

"Synthesis."

Cecil reached over and, picking him up, placed him on one knee.

"Have pity on us, Wise Man. We are but simple folk and know but simple words. What is the meaning of this sage word?"

"I know not," was the peculiar answer. " 'Tis but a word that came to me out of the past. It has a sweet sound and methinks may have a meaning. Let me think. I recall now! It was when I was in the glass bottle that a wise man came and held before my eyes an illuminated parchment. On it was written, in words of gold, this word and its meaning.

"Synthesis. All things are one and one thing is all."

"Which makes it all the harder for me," sighed the Over-Lord of Walling.

The Lady Angelica left her seat and came over to her

father. She sank upon the bearskin at his feet and took the little hand of the dwarf in hers.

"Tell me, my dear Homunculus, what wise man 'twas who thus gave you the message on the illuminated parchment?"

"It was a very wise man and a very old man who lives by himself in a cave by the babbling brook, and yearly the simple folk take him bread and meat and wine, but for years no one has seen him. And perhaps he lives and perhaps he is dead, for all I know is that the food disappears. But perhaps the birds think that it is for them now that he lies sightless and thoughtless on his stone bed these many years."

"This is something we will find out for ourselves. Lord Gustro, order some horses, and the four of us will go to this man's cave. Three horses for us, my Lord, and an ambling pad for our little friend so naught of harm will befall him."

The four came to the cave, and the four entered it. A light burned at the far end, and there was the wise man, very old and with naught but his eyes telling of the intelligence that never ages. On the table before him in a tangled confusion were glasses and earthenware, and crucibles, and one each of astrolabe, alembic, and hourglass through which silver sands ran, and this was fixed with cunning machinery so that every day it tilted around and once more let the sand tell the passing of the twenty-and-four hours. There were books covered with mildewed leather and locked with iron padlocks and spider-webs. Hung from the wet ceiling was a representation of the sun with the planets revolving eternally around that fair orb, but the pitted moon alternated with light and shadows.

And the wise man read from a book written in letters made by those long dead, and now and then he ate a crust of bread or sipped wine from a ram's horn, but never did he stop reading. When they touched him on the shoulder to attract his attention, he shook them off, murmuring, "By the Seven Sacred Caterpillars! Let me finish this page, for what a pity were I to die without knowing what this man wrote some thousand years ago in Ankor."

But at last he finished the page and sat blinking at them with his wise eyes sunk deep into a mummy face while his body shook with the decrepitude of age. And Cecil asked him:

"What is the meaning of the word 'synthesis'?"

" 'Tis a dream of mine which only now I find the waking meaning of."

"Tell the dream," the OverLord commanded.

" 'Tis but a dream. Suppose there were thirty wise men learned in all wisdom obtained from the reading of ancient books on alchemy and magic and histories and philosophy. These men knew of animals and jewels such as margarites and chrysoberyls, and of all plants such as dittany which cures wounds, and mandragora which compelleth sleep (though why men should want to sleep, when there is so much to read and profit by the reading, I do not know). But these men are old and someday will die. So, I would take these thirty old men and one young man and have them drink a wine that I have distilled these many years, and by synthesis there would be only one body—that of the young man—but in that man's brain would be all the subtle and ancient wisdom of the thirty savants, and thus we would do century after century so no wisdom would be lost to the world."

The Lady Angelica leaned over his shoulder. "And have you made this wine?" she asked.

"Yes, and now I am working on its opposite, for why place thirty bodies into one unless you know the art of once again separating this one body into the original thirty. But that is hard. For any fool can pour the wine from thirty bottles into a single jar, but who is wise enough to separate them and restore them to their original bottles?"

"Have you tried this wine of synthetic magic?" asked the OverLord.

"Partly. I took a crow and a canary-bird and had them drink of it, and now, in yonder wicker cage, a yellow crow sits and nightly fills my cave with song as though it came from the lutes and citherns of faerie-land."

"Now, that is my thought," cried the Lady Angelica. "We will take the best and bravest fighters of our land, and the sweetest singer of songs, and the best juggler of golden balls, thirty of them, and I, myself, will drink of this wine of synthesis. Thus the thirty will pass into my body, and I will go and visit the Giant. In his hall, I will drink of the other wine, and there will be thirty to fight against the one. They will overcome him and slay him. Then I will drink again of the vital wine, and in my body I will carry the thirty conquerors back to Walling. Once there, I will again drink, and the thirty men will leave my body, being liberated by the wonder-wine. Some may be dead and others wounded, but I will be safe and our enemy killed. Have you enough of it—of both kinds?

The old man looked puzzled.

"I have a flagon of the wine of synthesis. Of the other, to change the synthesized back into their original bodies, only enough for one experiment, and mayhap a few drops more."

"Try those drops on that yellow bird," commanded Cecil.

The old man poured from a bottle of pure gold, graven with a worm that eternally renewed his youth by swallowing his tail, a few drops of a colorless liquid, and offered it to the yellow bird in the wicker cage. This the bird drank greedily, and of a sudden there were two birds, a black crow and a yellow canary, and ere the canary could pipe a song the crow pounced on it and killed it.

"It works," croaked the old man. "It works."

"Can you make more of the second elixir?" asked Lord Gustro.

"What I do once I can do twice," proudly said the ancient.

"Then start and make more, and while you are doing it, we will take the golden bottle and the flagon and see what can be done to save the simple folk of our dark forests, though this is an adventure that I think little of, for 'tis fraught with danger for a woman I love." Thus spake the OverLord.

And with the elixirs in a safe place, they rode away from the cave of the old man. But Lord Gustro took the OverLord aside and said:

"I ask a favor. Allow me to be one of these thirty men."

Cecil shook his head. "No. And once again and forever, NO! In the doing of this, I stand to lose the apple of my eye, and if she comes not back to me, I shall die of grief, and then you, and you alone, will be left to care for my simple folk. If a man has but two arrows and shoots one into the air, then he were wise to keep the other in his quiver against the day of need.''

The Lady Angelica laughed as she suspected the reason of their whispering.

''I will come back,'' she said laughingly, ''for the old man was very wise. Did you not see how the yellow bird divided into two, and the crow killed the canary?''

But the Homunculus, held in Lord Cecil's arms, started to cry.

''What wouldst thou?'' asked the kindly OverLord.

''I would be back in my bottle again,'' sobbed the little one. And he sobbed till he went to sleep, soothed by the rocking canter of the war horse.

Two evenings later, a concourse of brave men met in the banquet hall. There were great, silent, men, skilled in the use of mace, byrnies, and baldricks, who could slay with sword, sprear, and double-bitted battle-ax. The Juggler was there, and a Singer of Songs, and a Reader of Books, very young but very wise. And a man was there with sparkling eyes who could by his glance put men to death-sleep and waken them with a snap of the thumb and finger. And to these were added the OverLord and Lord Gustro and the trembling Homunculus, and on her throne sat the Lady Angelica, very beautiful and very happy because of the great adventure she had apart to play in. In her hand was a golden goblet, and in the hands of the thirty men, crystal glasses, and the thirty and one drinking vessels were filled with the wine of synthesis, for half of the flagon was poured out. But the flagon, half-filled, and the golden drug viand, the Lady Angelica hid beneath her shimmering robe. Outside, a lady's horse, decked with diamond-studded harness, neighed uneasy in the moonlight.

Lord Cecil explained the adventure, and all the thirty men sat very still and solemn, for never had they heard the like before, for they none feared a simple death, but this dissolution was a thing that made even the bravest wonder what the end would be. Yet, when the time came and the command was given, they one and all drained their vessels, and even as the Lady drank her wine, they drank to the last drop.

Then there was silence broken only by the shrill cry of a hoot owl, complaining to the moon concerning the doings of the night folk in the Dark Forest. The little Homunculus hid his face in the shoulder of the OverLord, but Cecil and Lord Gustro looked straight ahead of them over the banquet table to see what was to be seen.

The thirty men seemed to shiver and then grow smaller in a mist that covered them, and finally only empty places were left at the banquet table, and empty glasses. Only the two men and the Lady Angelica and the shivering Homunculus were left. The Lady laughed.

"It worked," she cried. "I look the same, but I feel different, for in me are the potential bodies of the thirty brave men who will overcome the Giant and bring peace to the land. And now I will give you the kiss of hail and farewell, and will venture forth on horse." Kissing her father on the mouth and her lover on the cheek and the little one on the top of his curly-haired head, she ran bravely out of the room. Through the stillness they could hear her horse's hooves, silver-shod, pounding on the stones of the courtyard.

"I am afraid," shivered the little one. "I have all wisdom, but I am afraid as to this adventure and its ending."

Lord Cecil comforted him. "You are afraid because you are so very wise. Lord Gustro and I would like to fear, but we are too foolish to do so. Can I do anything to comfort you, little friend of mine?"

"I wish I were back in my bottle," sobbed the Homunculus, "but that cannot be because the bottle was broken when I was taken from it, for the mouth of it was very narrow, and a bottle once broken cannot be made whole again."

All that night, Lord Cecil rocked him to sleep, singing to him lullabies, while Lord Gustro sat wakeful before the fire biting his finger nails, and wondering what the ending would be.

Late that night, the Lady Angelica arrived at the gate of the Giant's Castle, and blew her wreathed horn. The Giant dropped the iron-studded gate, and curiously peered at the lady on the horse.

"I am the Lady Angelica," said the Lady, "and I have come to be your bride if only you will give free passage to our caravans so we can commerce with the great world outside. When my father dies, you will be OverLord of the land, and perchance I will come to love you, for you are a fine figure of a man, and I have heard much of you."

The Giant towered over the head of her horse. He placed his hand around her waist and plucked her from the horse and carried her to his banquet hall and sat her down at one end of the table. Laughing in a somewhat silly manner, he walked around the room and lit pine torches and tall candles till at last the whole room was lighted. He poured a large glass of wine for the Lady and a much larger glass for himself. He seated himself at the other end of the table, and laughed again as he cried:

"It all is as I dreamed. But who would have thought that the noble Lord Cecil and the brave Lord Gustro would have been so craven! Let's drink to our wedding, and then to the bridal chamber."

And he drank his drink in one swallow. But the Lady Angelica took from under her gown a golden flask and raising it, she cried:

"I drink to you and your future, whatever it may be." And she drained the golden flask and sat very still. A mist filled the room and swirled widdershams in thirty pillars around the long oak table. When it cleared, there were thirty men between the Giant and the Lady.

The Juggler took his golden balls, and the man with the dazzling eyes looked hard on the Giant, and the Student took from his robe a Book and read the wise sayings of dead Gods backwards, while the Singer of Songs plucked his harp strings and sang of the brave deeds of brave men long dead. But the fighting men rushed forward, and on all sides started the battle. The Giant jumped back, picked a mace from the wall, and fought as never man fought before. He had two things in mind: to kill, and to reach the smiling Lady and strangle her with bare hands for the thing she had done to him. But ever between him and the Lady was a wall of men who, with steel and song and dazzling eyes, formed a living wall that could be bent and crushed but never broken.

For centuries after, in the halls of Walling, the blind singers of songs told of that fight while the simple folk sat silent and listened to the tale. No doubt as the tale passed from one singer, aged, to the next singer, young, it became ornamented and embroidered and fabricated into something somewhat different from what really happened that night. But even the bare truth-telling at first hand, as told in parts, at different times, by the Lady Angelica, was a great enough tale. For men fought and bled and died in that hall. Finally, the Giant, dying, broke through and almost reached the Lady, but then the Song Man tripped him with his harp, and the Wise Man threw his heavy tome in his face, and the Juggler shattered his three golden balls against the Giant's forehead, and, at the lastward, the glittering eyes of the Sleep-Maker fastened on the dying eyes of the Giant and sent him on his last sleep.

The Lady Angelica looked around the shattered hall and at the thirty men who had all done their part, and she said softly:

"These be brave men, and they have done what was necessary for the good of their country and for the honor of our land. I cannot forsake them or leave them hopeless."

She took the rest of the wine of synthesis and drank part, and to every man she gave a drink, even the dead men whose mouths she had to gently open to wipe the blood from the gritted teeth, ere she could pour the wine into their breathless mouths. And she went back to her seat, and sitting there, she waited.

The mist again filled the hall and covered the dead and dying and those who were not hurt badly but panted from the fury of the battle. When the mist cleared, only the Lady Angelica was left there, for all the thirty had returned to her body through the magic of the synthesizing wine.

And the Lady said to herself:

"I feel old and in many ways different, and my strength has gone from me. I am glad there is no mirror to show me my whitened hair and bloodless cheeks, for the men who have come back unto me were dead men, and those not dead were badly hurt. I must get back to my horse before I fall into a faint of death."

She tried to walk out, but, stumbling, fell. On hands and knees, she crawled to where her horse waited for her. She pulled herself up into the saddle, and with her girdle she tied herself there, and then told the horse to go home. But she lay across the saddle like a dead woman.

The horse brought her back. Ladies in waiting took her to bed, and washed her withered limbs, and gave her warm drinks, and covered her wasted body with coverlets of lamb's wool. The wise physicians mixed healing drinks for her, and finally she recovered sufficiently to tell her father and her lover the story of the battle of the thirty against the Giant, how he was dead and the land safe.

"Now go to the old man and get the other elixir," she whispered, "and when it works have the dead buried with honor and the wounded gently and wisely cared for. Then we will come to the end of the adventure, and it will be one that the Singers of Songs will tell of for many winter evenings to the simple folk of Walling."

"You stay with her, Lord Gustro," commanded the Over-Lord, "and I will take the wise Homunculus in my arms and gallop to the cave and secure the elixir. When I return we will have her drink it, and once again she will be whole and young again. Then I will have you two lovers marry, for I am not as young as I was, and I want to live to see the throne secure, and, the Gods willing, grandchildren running around the castle."

Lord Gustro sat down by his Lady's bed, and he took her wasted hand in his warm one. He placed a kiss on her white lips with his red warm ones, and he whispered: "No matter what happens and no matter what the end of the adventure, I will always love you, Heart-of-mine." And the Lady Angelica smiled on him, and went to sleep.

Through the Dark Forest galloped Cecil, OverLord of Walling, with the little wise man in his arms. He flung himself off his war horse, and ran quickly into the cave.

"Have you finished the elixir?" he cried.

The old man looked up, as though in doubt as to what the question was. He was breathing heavily now, and little drops of sweat rolled down his leathered face.

"Oh! Yes! I remember now. The elixir that would save the Lady, and take from her the bodies of the men we placed in her by virtue of our synthetic magic. I remember now! I have been working on it. In a few more minutes, it will be finished."

And dropping forward on the oak table, he died. In falling, a withered hand struck a golden flask and overturned it on the floor. Liquid amber ran over the dust of ages. A cockroach came and drank of it, and suddenly died.

"I am afraid," moaned the little Homunculus. "I wish I were back in my bottle."

But Cecil, OverLord of Walling, did not know how to comfort him.

THE LAW-TWISTER SHORTY

by Gordon R. Dickson

A native Canadian who emigrated to the United
States at the age of thirteen, Gordon R. Dickson
(1923–   ) has won both Hugo and Nebula awards.
He is perhaps best noted for romantic tales of adventure in which loyalty, honor, and duty are presented
as paramount concerns.

However, one of his other skills is humor—perhaps
best exemplified in the series of Hoka stories done
with Poul Anderson, but also featured in this de-
lightful tale of gigantic bearlike aliens.

"He's a pretty tough character, that Iron Bender—" said the
Hill Bluffer, conversationally. Malcolm O'Keefe clung to the
straps of the saddle he rode on the Hill Bluffer's back, as the
nearly ten-foot-tall Dilbian strode surefootedly along the narrow mountain trail, looking something like a slim Kodiak
bear on his hind legs. "But a Shorty like you, Law-Twister,
ought to be able to handle him, all right."

"Law-Twister . . ." echoed Mal, dizzily. The Right Hon-
orable Joshua Guy, Ambassador Plenipotentiary to Dilbia,
had said something about the Dilbians wasting no time in
pinning a name of their own invention on every Shorty (as
humans were called by them) they met. But Mal had not
expected to be named so soon. And what was that other name
the Dilbian postman carrying him had just mentioned?

"Who won't I have any trouble with, did you say?" Mal added.

"Iron Bender," said the Hill Bluffer, with a touch of impatience. "Clan Water Gap's harnessmaker. Didn't Little Bite back there at Humrog Town tell you anything about Iron Bender?"

"I . . . I think so," said Mal. Little Bite, as Ambassador Guy was known to the Dilbians, had in fact told Mal a great many things. But thinking back on their conversation now, it did not seem to Mal that the Ambassador had been very helpful in spite of all his words. "Iron Bender's the—er— protector of this Gentle . . . Gentle . . ."

"Gentle Maiden. Hor!" The Bluffer broke into an unexplained snort of laughter. "Well, anyway, that's who Iron Bender's protector of."

"And she's the one holding the three Shorties captive—"

"Captive? What're you talking about, Law-Twister?" demanded the Bluffer. "She's *adopted* them! Little Bite must have told you that."

"Well, he . . ." Mal let the words trail off. His head was still buzzing from the hypnotraining he had been given on his way to Dilbia, to teach him the language and the human-known facts about the outsize natives of this Earthlike world; and the briefing he had gotten from Ambassador Guy had only confused him further.

". . . Three tourists, evidently," Guy had said, puffing on a heavy-bowled pipe. He was a brisk little man in his sixties, with sharp blue eyes. "Thought they could slip down from the cruise by spaceliner they were taking and duck into a Dilbian village for a firsthand look at the locals. Probably had no idea what they were getting into."

"What—uh," asked Mal, "were they getting into, if I can ask?"

"Restricted territory! Treaty territory!" snapped Guy, knocking the dottle out of his pipe and beginning to refill it. Mal coughed discreetly as the fumes reached his nose. "In this sector of space we're in open competition with a race of aliens called Hemnoids, for every available, habitable world. Dilbia's a plum. But it's got this intelligent—if primitive—native race on it. Result, we've got a treaty with the Hemnoids restricting all but emergency contact with the Dilbians—by them or us— until the Dilbians themselves become civilized enough to choose either us or the Hemnoids for interstellar partners. Highly illegal, those three tourists just dropping in like that.''

"How about me?'' asked Mal.

"You? You're being sent in under special emergency orders to get them out before the Hemnoids find out they've been there,'' said Guy. "As long as they're gone when the Hemnoids hear about this, we can duck any treaty violation charge. But you've got to get them into their shuttle boat and back into space by midnight tonight—''

The dapper little ambassador pointed outside the window of the log building that served as the human embassy on Dilbia at the dawn sunlight on the cobblestoned Humrog Street.

"Luckily, we've got the local postman in town at the moment,'' Guy went on. "We can mail you to Clan Water Gap with him—''

"But,'' Mal broke in on the flow of words, "you still haven't explained—why me? I'm just a high school senior on a work-study visit to the Pleiades. Or at least, that's where I was headed when they told me my travel orders had been picked up, and I was drafted to come here instead, on emergency duty. There must be lots of people older than I am, who're experienced—''

"Not the point in this situation,'' said Guy, puffing clouds of smoke from his pipe toward the log rafters overhead. "Dilbia's a special case. Age and experience don't help here as much as a certain sort of—well—personality. The Dilbian psychological profile and culture is tricky. It needs to be matched by a human with just the proper profile and character, himself. Without those natural advantages the best of age, education, and experience doesn't help in dealing with the Dilbians.''

"But,'' said Mal, desperately, "there must be some advice you can give me—some instructions. Tell me what I ought to do, for example—''

"No, no. Just the opposite,'' said Guy. "We want you to

follow your instincts. Do what seems best as the situation arises. You'll make out all right. We've already had a couple of examples of people who did, when they had the same kind of personality pattern you have. The book anthropologists and psychologists are completly baffled by these Dilbians, as I say, but you just keep your head and follow your instincts. . . ."

He had continued to talk, to Mal's mind, making less and less sense as he went, until the arrival of the Hill Bluffer had cut the conversation short. Now, here Mal was—with no source of information left, but the Bluffer, himself.

"This, er, Iron Bender," he said to the Dilbian postman. "You were saying I ought to be able to handle him all right?"

"Well, if you're any kind of a Shorty at all," said the Bluffer, cheerfully. "There's still lots of people in these mountains, and even down in the lowlands, who don't figure a Shorty can take on a real man and win. But not me. After all, I've been tied up with you Shorties almost from the start. It was me delivered the Half-Pint Posted to the Streamside Terror. Hor! Everybody thought the Terror'd tear the Half-Pint apart. And you can guess who won, being a Shorty yourself."

"The Half-Pint Posted won?"

"Hardly worked up a sweat doing it, either," said the Hill Bluffer. "Just like the Pick-and-Shovel Shorty, a couple of years later. Pick-and-Shovel, he took on Bone Breaker, the lowland outlaw chief—of course, Bone Breaker being a lowlander, they two tangled with swords and shields and that sort of modern junk."

Mal clung to the straps supporting the saddle on which he rode below the Hill Bluffer's massive, swaying shoulders.

"Hey!" said the Hill Bluffer, after a long moment of silence. "You go to sleep up there, or something?"

"Asleep?" Mal laughed, a little hollowly. "No. Just thinking. Just wondering where a couple of fighters like this Half-Pint and Pick-and-Shovel could have come from back on our Shorty worlds."

"Never knew them, did you?" asked the Bluffer. "I've noticed that. Most of you Shorties don't seem to know much about each other."

"What did they look like?" Mal asked.

"Well . . . you know," said the Bluffer. "Like Shorties. All you Shorties look alike, anyway. Little, squeaky-voiced characters. Like you—only, maybe not quite so skinny."

"Skinny?" Mal had spent the last year of high school valiantly lifting weights and had finally built up his five-foot-eleven frame from a hundred and forty-eight to a hundred and seventy pounds. Not that this made him any mass of muscle—particularly compared to nearly a half-ton of Dilbian. Only, he had been rather proud of the fact that he had left skinniness behind him. Now, what he was hearing was incredible! What kind of supermen had the computer found on these two previous occasions—humans who could outwrestle a Dilbian or best one of the huge native aliens with sword and shield?

On second thought, it just wasn't possible there could be two such men, even if they had been supermen, by human standards. There had to have been some kind of a gimmick in each case that had let the humans win. Maybe, a concealed weapon of some kind—a tiny tranquilizer gun, or some such. . . .

But Ambassador Guy had been adamant about refusing to send Mal out with any such equipment.

"Absolutely against the treaty. Absolutely!" the little ambassador had said.

Mal snorted to himself. If anyone, Dilbian or human, was under the impression that *he* was going to get into any kind of physical fight with any Dilbian—even the oldest, weakest, most midget Dilbian on the planet—they had better think again. How he had come to be selected for this job, anyway. . .

"Well, here we are—Clan Water Gap Territory!" announced the Hill Bluffer cheerfully, slowing his pace.

Mal straightened up in the saddle and looked around him. They had finally left the narrow mountain trail that had kept his heart in his mouth most of the trip. Now they had emerged into a green, bowl-shaped valley, with a cluster of log huts at its lowest point and the silver thread of a narrow river spilling into it from the valley's far end, to wind down into a lake by the huts.

But he had little time to examine the further scene in detail.

Just before them, and obviously waiting in a little grassy hollow by an egg-shaped granite boulder, were four large Dilbians and one small one.

Correction—Mal squinted against the afternoon sun. Waiting by the stone were two large and one small male Dilbians, all with the graying fur of age, and one unusually tall and black-furred Dilbian female. The Hill Bluffer snorted appreciatively at the female as he carried Mal up to confront the four.

"Grown even a bit more yet, since I last saw you, Gentle Maiden," said the native postman, agreeably. "Done a pretty good job of it, too. Here, meet the Law-Twister Shorty."

"I don't want to meet him!" snapped Gentle Maiden. "And you can turn around and take him right back where you got him. He's not welcome in Clan Water Gap Territory; and I've got the Clan Grandfather here to tell him so!"

Mal's hopes suddenly took an upturn.

"Oh?" he said. "Not welcome? That's too bad. I guess there's nothing left but to go back. Bluffer—"

"Hold on, Law-Twister!" growled the Bluffer. "Don't let Gentle here fool you." He glared at the three male Dilbians. "What Grandfather? I see three grandpas—Grandpa Tricky, Grandpa Forty Winks and—" he fastened his gaze on the smallest of the elderly males, "old One Punch, here. But none of them are Grandfathers, last I heard."

"What of it?" demanded Gentle Maiden. "Next Clan meeting, the Clan's going to choose a Grandfather. One of these grandpas is going to be the one chosen. So with all three of them here, I've got the next official Grandfather of Clan Water Gap here, too—even if he doesn't know it himself, yet!"

"Hor!" The Bluffer exploded into snorts of laughter. "Pretty sneaky, Gentle, but it won't work! A Grandfather's no good until he's *named* a Grandfather. Why, if you could do things that way, we'd have little kids being put up to give Grandfather rulings. And if it came to that, where'd the point be in having a man live long enough to get wise and trusted enough to be named a Grandfather?"

He shook his head.

"No, no," he said. "You've got no real Grandfather here, and so there's nobody can tell an honest little Shorty like the Law-Twister to turn about and light out from Clan Territory."

"Told y'so, Gentle," said the shortest grandpa in a rusty voice. "Said it wouldn't work."

"You!" cried Gentle Maiden, wheeling on him. "A fine grandpa you are, One Punch—let alone the fact you're my own real, personal grandpa! You don't have to be a Grandfather! You could just tell this Shorty and this long-legged postman on your own—tell them to get out while they were still in one piece! You would have, once!"

"Well, once, maybe," said the short Dilbian, rustily and sadly. Now that Mal had a closer look at him, he saw that this particular oldster—the one the Hill Bluffer had called One Punch—bore more than a few signs of having led an active life. A number of old scars seamed his fur; one ear was only half there and the other was badly tattered. Also, his left leg was crooked as if it had been broken and badly set at one time.

"I don't see why you can't *still* do it—for your granddaughter's sake!" said Gentle Maiden sharply. Mal winced. Gentle Maiden might be good-looking by Dilbian standards— the Hill Bluffer's comments a moment ago seemed to indicate that—but whatever else she was, she was plainly not very gentle, at least, in any ordinary sense of the word.

"Why, Granddaughter," creaked One Punch mildly, "like I've told you and everyone else, now that I'm older I've seen the foolishness of all those little touches of temper I used to have when I was young. They never really proved anything— except how much wiser those big men were who used to kind of avoid tangling with me. That's what comes with age, Granddaughter. Wisdom. You never hear nowdays of One Man getting into hassles, now that he's put a few years on him—or of More Jam, down there in the lowlands, talking about defending his wrestling championship anymore."

"Hold on! Wait a minute, One Punch," rumbled the Hill Bluffer. "You know and I know that even if One Man and More Jam do go around *saying* they're old and feeble nowdays, no one in his right mind is going to take either one of them at their word and risk finding out if it is true.''

''Think so if you like, Postman,'' said One Punch, shaking his head mournfully. ''Believe that if you want to. But when you're my age, you'll know it's just wisdom, plain, pure wisdom, makes men like them and me so peaceful. Besides, Gentle,'' he went on, turning again to his granddaughter, ''you've got a fine young champion in Iron Bender—''

''Iron Bender!'' exploded Gentle Maiden. ''That lump! That obstinate, leatherheaded strap-cutter! That—''

''Come to think of it, Gentle,'' interrupted the Hill Bluffer, ''how come Iron Bender isn't here? I'd have thought you'd have brought him along instead of these imitation Grandfathers—''

''There, now,'' sighed One Punch, staring off at the mountains beyond the other side of the valley. ''That bit about imitations—that's just the sort of remark I might've taken a bit of offense at, back in the days before I developed wisdom. But does it trouble me nowdays?''

''No offense meant, One Punch,'' said the Bluffer. ''You know I didn't mean that.''

''None taken. You see, Granddaughter?'' said One Punch. ''The postman here never meant a bit of offense; and in the old days I wouldn't have seen it until it was too late.''

''Oh, you make me sick!'' blazed Gentle Maiden. ''You all make me sick. Iron Bender makes me sick, saying he won't have anything against this Law-Twister Shorty until the Law-Twister tries twisting the Clan law that says those three poor little orphans belong to me now!'' She glared at the Bluffer and Mal. ''Iron Bender said the Shorty can come find him, any time he really wanted to, down at the harness shop!''

''He'll be right down,'' promised the Bluffer.

''Hey—'' began Mal. But nobody was paying any attention to him.

''Now, Granddaughter,'' One Punch was saying, reprovingly. ''The Bender didn't exactly ask you to name him your protector, you know.''

''What difference does that make?'' snapped Gentle Maiden.

"I had to pick the toughest man in the Clan to protect me—that's just common sense; even if he *is* stubborn as an I-don't-know-what and thick-headed as a log wall! I know my rights. He's got to defend me; and there—" she wheeled and pointed to the large boulder lying on the grass—"there's the stone of Mighty Grappler, and here's all three of you, one of who's got to be a Grandfather by next Clan meeting—and you mean to tell me none of you'll even say a word to help me turn this postman and this Shorty around and get them out of here?"

The three elderly Dilbian males looked back at her without speaking.

"All right!" roared Gentle Maiden, stamping about to turn her back on all of them. "You'll be sorry! All of you!"

With that, she marched off down the slope of the valley toward the village of log houses.

"Well," said the individual whom the Hill Bluffer had called Grandpa Tricky, "guess that's that, until she thinks up something more. I might as well be ambling back down to the house, myself. How about you, Forty Winks?"

"Guess I might as well, too," said Forty Winks.

They went off after Gentle Maiden, leaving Mal—still on the Hill Bluffer's back—staring down at One Punch, from just behind the Bluffer's reddish-furred right ear.

"What," asked Mal, "has the stone of what's-his-name got to do with it?"

"The stone of Mighty Grappler?" asked One Punch. "You mean you don't know about that stone, over there?"

"Law-Twister here's just a Shorty," said the Bluffer, apologetically. "You know how Shorties are—tough, but pretty ignorant."

"Some *say* they're tough," said One Punch, squinting up at Mal, speculatively.

"Now, wait a minute, One Punch!" the Hill Bluffer's bass voice dropped ominously an additional half-octave. "Maybe there's something we ought to get straight right now! This isn't just any plain private citizen you're talking to, it's the official postman speaking. And *I* say Shorties're tough. *I* say I was there when the Half-Pint Posted took the Streamside

Terror; and also when Pick-and-Shovel wiped up Bone Breaker in a sword-and-shield duel. Now, no disrespect, but if you're questioning the official word of a government mail carrier—''

"Now, Bluffer," said One Punch, "I never doubted you personally for a minute. It's just everybody knows the Terror and Bone Breaker weren't either of them pushovers. But you know I'm not the biggest man around, by a long shot; and now and then during my time I can remember laying out some pretty good-sized scrappers, myself—when my temper got away from me, that is. So I know from personal experience not every man's as tough as the next—and why shouldn't that work for Shorties as well as real men? Maybe those two you carried before were tough; but how can anybody tell about this Shorty? No offense, up there, Law-Twister, by the way. Just using a bit of my wisdom and asking."

Mal opened his mouth and shut it again.

"Well?" growled the Bluffer underneath him. "Speak up, Law-Twister." Suddenly, there was a dangerous feeling of tension in the air. Mal swallowed. How, he thought, would a Dilbian answer a question like that?

Any way but with a straight answer, came back the reply from the hypnotrained section of his mind.

"Well—er," said Mal, "how can I tell you how tough I am? I mean, what's tough by the standards of you real men? As far as we Shorties go, it might be one thing. For you real men, it might be something else completely. It's too bad I didn't ever know this Half-Pint Posted, or Pick-and-Shovel, or else I could kind of measure myself by them for you. But I never heard of them until now."

"But you think they just *might* be tougher than you, though— the Half-Pint and Pick-and-Shovel?" demanded One Punch.

"Oh, sure," said Mal. "They could both be ten times as tough as I am. And then, again— Well, not for me to say."

There was a moment's silence from both the Dilbians, then the Bluffer broke it with a snort of admiration.

"Hor!" he chortled admiringly to One Punch. "I guess you can see now how the Law-Twister here got his name. Slippery? Slippery's not the word for this Shorty."

But One Punch shook his head.

"Slippery's one thing," he said. "But law-twisting's another. Here he says he doesn't even know about the stone of Mighty Grappler. How's he going to go about twisting laws if he doesn't know about the laws in the first place?"

"You could tell me about the stone," suggested Mal.

"Mighty Grappler put it there, Law-Twister," said the Bluffer. "Set it up to keep peace in Clan Water Gap."

"Better let me tell him, Postman," interrupted One Punch. "After all, he ought to get it straight from a born Water Gapper. Look at the stone there, Law-Twister. You see those two ends of iron sticking out of it?"

Mal looked. Sure enough, there were two lengths of rusty metal protruding from opposite sides of the boulder, which was about three feet in width in the middle.

"I see them," he answered.

"Mighty Gappler was just maybe the biggest and strongest real man who ever lived—"

The Hill Bluffer coughed.

"One Man, now . . ." he murmured.

"I'm not denying One Man's something like a couple of big men in one skin, Postman," said One Punch. "But the stories about Mighty Grappler are hard to beat. He was a stonemason, Law-Twister; and he founded Clan Water Gap, with himself, his relatives, and his descendants. Now, as long as he was alive, there was no trouble. He was Clan Water Gap's first Grandfather, and even when he was a hundred and ten nobody wanted to argue with him. But he worried about keeping things orderly after he was gone—"

"Fell off a cliff at a hundred and fourteen," put in the Bluffer. "Broke his neck. Otherwise, no telling how long he'd have lived."

"Excuse me, Postman," said One Punch. "But I'm telling this, not you. The point is, Law-Twister, he was worried like I say about keeping the Clan orderly. So he took a stone he was working on one day—that stone there, that no one but him could come near lifting—and hammered an iron rod through it to make a handhold on each side, like you see. Then he picked the stone up, carried it here, and set it down; and he made a law. The rules he'd made earlier for Clan

Water Gappers were to stand as laws, themselves—as long as that stone stayed where it was. But if anyone ever came along who could pick it up all by himself and carry it as much as ten steps, then that was a sign it was time the laws should change.''

Mal stared at the boulder. His hypnotraining had informed him that while Dilbians would go to any lengths to twist the truth to their own advantage, the one thing they would not stand for, in themselves or others, was an out-and-out lie. Accordingly, One Punch would probably be telling the truth about this Mighty Grappler ancestor of his. On the other hand, a chunk of granite that size must weigh at least a ton—maybe a ton and a half. Not even an outsize Dilbian could be imagined carrying something like that for ten paces. There were natural flesh-and-blood limits, even for these giant natives—or were there?

"Did anybody ever try lifting it, after that?" Mal asked.

"Hor!" snorted the Bluffer.

"Now, Law-Twister," said One Punch, almost reproachfully, "any Clan Water Gapper's got too much sense to make a fool of himself trying to do something only the Mighty Grappler had a chance of doing. That stone's never been touched from that day to this—and that's the way it should be."

"I suppose so," said Mal.

The Bluffer snorted again, in surprise. One Punch stared.

"You giving up—just like that, Law-Twister?" demanded the Bluffer.

"What? I don't understand," said Mal, confused. "We were just talking about the stone—"

"But you said you supposed that's the way it should be," said the Bluffer, outraged. "The stone there, and the laws just the way Mighty Grappler laid them down. What kind of a law-twister are you, anyway?"

"But . . ." Mal was still confused. "What's the Mighty Grappler and his stone got to do with my getting back these three Shorties that Gentle Maiden says she adopted?"

"Why, that's one of Mighty Grappler's laws—one of the ones he made and backed up with the stone!" said One

Punch. "It was Mighty Grappler said that any orphans running around loose could be adopted by any single woman of the Clan, who could then name herself a protector to take care of them and her! Now, that's Clan law."

"But—" began Mal again. He had not expected to have to start arguing his case this soon. But it seemed there was no choice. "It's Clan law if you say so; and I don't have any quarrel with it. But these people Gentle Maiden's adopted aren't orphans. They're Shorties. That's why she's going to have to let them go."

"So that's the way you twist it," said One Punch, almost in a tone of satisfaction. "Figured you'd come up with something like that. So, you say they're not orphans?"

"Of course, that's what I say!" said Mal.

"Figured as much. Naturally, Gentle says they are."

"Well, I'll just have to make her understand—"

"Not her," interrupted the Bluffer.

"Naturally not her," said One Punch. "If *she* says they're orphans, then it's her protector you've got to straighten things out with. Gentle says 'orphans,' so Iron Bender's going to be saying 'orphans,' too. You and Iron Bender got to get together."

"And none of that sissy lowland stuff with swords and shields," put in the Hill Bluffer. "Just honest, man-to-man teeth, claws, and muscle. You don't have to worry about Iron Bender going in for any of that modern stuff, Law-Twister."

"Oh?" said Mal, staring.

"Thought I'd tell you right now," said the Bluffer. "Ease your mind, in case you were wondering."

"I wasn't, actually," said Mal, numbly, still trying to make his mind believe what his ears seemed to be hearing.

"Well," said One Punch, "how about it, Postman? Law-Twister? Shall we get on down to the harness shop and you and Iron Bender can set up the details? Quite a few folks been dropping in the last few hours to see the two of you tangle. Don't think any of them ever saw a Shorty in action before. Know I never did myself. Should be real interesting."

He and the Hill Bluffer had already turned and begun to stroll down toward the village.

"Interesting's not the word for it," the Bluffer responded. "Seen it twice, myself, and I can tell you it's a sight to behold. . . ."

He continued along, chatting cheerfully while Mal rode along helplessly on Dilbian-back, his head spinning. The log buildings got closer and closer.

"Wait—" Mal said desperately, as they entered the street running down the center of the cluster of log structures. The Bluffer and One Punch both stopped. One Punch turned to gaze up at him.

"Wait?" One Punch said. "What for?"

"I—I can't," stammered Mal, frantically searching for an excuse, and going on talking meanwhile with the first words that came to his lips. "That is, I've got my own laws to think of. Shorty laws. Responsibilities. I can't just go representing these other Shorty orphans just like that. I have to be . . . uh, briefed."

"Briefed?" The Bluffer's tongue struggled with pronunciation of the human word Mal had used.

"Yes—uh, that means I have to be given authority—like Gentle Maiden had to choose Iron Bender as her protector," said Mal. "These Shorty orphans have to agree to choose me as their law-twister. It's one of the Shorty freedoms—freedom to not be defended by a law-twister without your consent. With so much at stake here—I mean, not just what might happen to me, or Iron Bender, but what might happen to Clan Water Gap laws or Shorty laws—I need to consult with my clients, I mean these other Shorties I'm working for, before I enter into any—er—discussion with Gentle Maiden's protector."

Mal stopped speaking and waited, his heart hammering away. There was a moment of deep silence from both the Bluffer and One Punch. Then One Punch spoke to the taller Dilbian.

"Have to admit you're right, Postman," One Punch said, admiringly. "He sure can twist. You understand all that he was talking about, there?"

"Why, of course," said the Bluffer. "After all, I've had a lot to do with these Shorties. He was saying that this isn't just any little old hole-and-corner tangle between him and Iron Bender—this is a high-class hassle to decide the law; and it's got to be done right. No offense, One Punch, but you, having been in the habit of getting right down to business on the spur of the moment all those years, might not have stopped to think just how important it is not to rush matters in an important case like this.''

"No offense taken, Postman," said One Punch, easily. "Though I must say maybe it's lucky you didn't know me in my younger, less full-of-wisdom days. Because it seems to me we were *both* maybe about to rush the Law-Twister a mite.''

"Well, now," said the Bluffer. "Leaving aside that business of my luck and all that about not knowing you when you were younger, I guess I have to admit perhaps I *was* a little on the rushing side, myself. Anyway, Law-Twister's straightened us both out. So, what's the next thing you want to do, Law-Twister?''

"Well . . ." said Mal. He was still thinking desperately. "This being a matter that concerns the laws governing the whole Water Gap Clan, as well as Shorty laws and the stone of Mighty Grappler, we probably ought to get everyone together. I mean we ought to talk it over. It might well turn out to be this is something that ought to be settled not by a fight but in—''

Mal had not expected the Dilbians to have a word for it; but he was wrong. His hypnotraining threw the proper Dilbian sounds up for his tongue to utter.

"—court," he wound up.

"Court? Can't have a court, Law-Twister," said One Punch. He and the Hill Bluffer had stopped in the middle of the village street when Mal started talking. Now a small crowd of the local Dilbians was gathering around them, listening to the conversation.

"Thought you knew that, Law-Twister," put in the Bluffer, reprovingly. "Can't have a Clan court without a Grandfather to decide things.''

"Too bad, in a way," said One Punch with a sigh. "We'd all like to see a real Law-Twister Shorty at work in a real court situation, twisting and slickering around from one argument to the next. But, just as the Bluffer says, Twister, we've got no Grandfather yet. Won't have until the next Clan meeting.''

"When's that?" asked Mal, hastily.

"Couple of weeks," said One Punch. "Be glad to wait around a couple of weeks far as all of us here're concerned; but those Shorty orphans of Gentle Maiden's are getting pretty hungry and even a mite thirsty. Seems they won't eat anything she gives them; and they even don't seem to like to drink the well water, much. Gentle figures they won't settle down until they get it straight that they're adopted and not going home again. So she wants you and Iron Bender to settle it right now—and, of course, since she's a member of the Clan, the Clan backs her up on that.''

"Won't eat or drink? Where are they?" asked Mal.

"At Gentle's house," said One Punch. "She's got them locked up there so they can't run back to that box they came down in and fly away back into the sky. Real motherly instincts in that girl, if I do say so myself who's her real grandpa. That, and looks, too. Can't understand why no young buck's snapped her up before this—"

"You understand, all right, One Punch," interrupted an incredibly deep bass voice; and there shouldered through the crowd a darkly brown-haired Dilbian, taller than any of the crowd around him. The speaker was shorter by half a head than the Hill Bluffer—the postman seemed to have the advantage in height on every other native Mal had seen—but this newcomer towered over everyone else and he was a walking mass of muscle, easily outweighing the Bluffer.

"You understand, all right," he repeated, stopping before the Bluffer and Mal. "Folks'd laugh their heads off at any man who'd offer to take a girl as tough-minded as Gentle, to wife—that is, unless he had to. Then, maybe he'd find it was worth it. But do it on his own? Pride's pride. . . . Hello there, Postman. This the Law-Twister Shorty?"

"It's him," said the Bluffer.

"Why he's no bigger'n those other little Shorties," said the deep-voiced Dilbian, peering over the Bluffer's shoulder at Mal.

"You go thinking size is all there is to a Shorty, you're going to be surprised," said the Bluffer. "Along with the Streamside Terror and Bone Breaker, as I recollect. Twister, this here's Gentle's protector and the Clan Water Gap harnessmaker, Iron Bender."

"Uh—pleased to meet you," said Mal.

"Pleased to meet you, Law-Twister," rumbled Iron Bender. "That is, I'm pleased now; and I hope I go on being pleased. I'm a plain, simple man, Law-Twister. A good day's work, a good night's sleep, four good meals a day, and I'm satisfied. You wouldn't find me mixed up in fancy doings like this by choice. I'd have nothing to do with this if Gentle hadn't named me her protector. But right's right. She did; and I am, like it or not."

"I know how you feel," said Mal, hastily. "I was actually going someplace else when the Shorties here had me come see about this situation. I hadn't planned on it at all."

"Well, well," said Iron Bender, deeply, "you, too, eh?" He sighed heavily.

"That's the way things go, nowdays, though," he said. "A plain simple man can't hardly do a day's work in peace without some maiden or someone coming to him for protection. So they got you, too, eh? Well, well-life's life, and a man can't do much about it. You're not a bad little Shorty at all. I'm going to be real sorry to tear your head off—which of course I'm going to do, since I figure I probably could have done the same to Bone Breaker or the Streamside Terror, if it'd ever happened to come to that. Not that I'm a boastful man; but true's true."

He sighed again.

"So," he said, flexing his huge arms, "if you'll just light down from your perch on the postman, there, I'll get to it. I've got a long day's work back at the harness shop, anyway; and daylight's daylight—"

"But fair's fair," broke in Mal, hastily. The Iron Bender lowered his massive, brown-furred hands, looking puzzled.

"Fair's fair?" he echoed.

"You heard him, harnessmaker!" snapped the Bluffer, bristling. "No offense, but there's more to something like this than punching holes in leather. Nothing I'd like to see more than for you to try—just try—to tear the head off a Shorty like Law-Twister here, since I've seen what a Shorty can do when he really gets his dander up. But like the Twister himself pointed out, this is not just a happy hassle—this is serious business involving Clan laws and Shorty laws and lots of other things. We were just discussing it when you came up. Law-Twister was saying maybe something like this should be held up until the next Clan meeting when you elect a Grandfather, so's it could be decided by a legal Clan Water Gap court in full session."

"Court—" Iron Bender was beginning when he was interrupted.

"We will *not* wait for any court to settle who gets my orphans!" cried a new voice, and the black-furred form of Gentle Maiden shoved through the crowd to join them. "When there's no Clan Grandfather to rule, the Clan goes by law and custom. Law and custom says my protector's got to take care of me, and I've got to take care of the little ones I adopted. And I'm not letting them suffer for two weeks before they realize they're settling down with me. The law says I don't have to and no man's going to make me try—"

"Now, hold on there just a minute, Gentle," rumbled Iron Bender. "Guess maybe I'm the one man in this Clan, or between here and Humrog Peak for that matter, who could make you try and do something whether you wanted it or not, if he wanted to. Not that I'm saying I'm going to, now. But you just remember that while I'm your named protector, it doesn't mean I'm going to let you order me around like you do other folk—any more than I ever did."

He turned back to the Bluffer, Mal, and One Punch.

"Right's right," he said. "Now, what's all this about a court?"

Neither the Bluffer nor One Punch answered immediately—and, abruptly, Mal realized it was up to him to do the explaining.

"Well, as I was pointing out to the postman and One Punch," he began, rapidly, "there's a lot at stake, here. I mean, we Shorties have laws, too; and one of them is that you don't have to be represented by a law-twister not your choice. I haven't talked to these Shorties you and Gentle claim are orphans, so I don't have their word on going ahead with anything on their behalf. I can't do anything important until I have that word of theirs. What if we—er—tangled, and it turned out they didn't mean to name me to do anything for them, after all? Here you, a regular named protector of a maiden according to your Clan laws, as laid down by Mighty Grappler, would have been hassling with someone who didn't have a shred of right to fight you. And here, too, I'd have been tangling without a shred of lawful reason for it, to back me up. What we need to do is study the situation. I need to talk to the Shorties you say are orphans—"

"No!" cried Gentle Maiden. "He's not to come *near* my little orphans and get them all upset, even more than they are now—"

"Hold on, now, Granddaughter," interposed One Punch. "We all can see how the Twister here's twisting and slipping around like the clever little Shorty he is, trying to get things his way. But he's got a point there when he talks about Clan Water Gap putting up a named protector, and then that protector turns out to have gotten into a hassle with someone with no authority at all. Why they'd be laughing at our Clan all up and down the mountains. Worse yet, what if that protector should lose—"

"*Lose?*" snorted Iron Bender, with all the geniality of a grizzly abruptly wakened from his long winter's nap.

"That's right, harnessmaker. *Lose!*" snarled the Hill Bluffer. "Guess there just might be a real man not too far away from you at this moment who's pretty sure you *would* lose—and handily!"

Suddenly, the two of them were standing nose to nose. Mal became abruptly aware that he was still seated in the saddle arrangement on the Bluffer's back and that, in case of trouble between the two big Dilbians, it would not be easy for him to get down in a hurry.

"I'll tell you what, Postman," Iron Bender was growling. "Why don't you and I just step out beyond the houses, here, where there's a little more open space—"

"Stop it!" snapped Gentle Maiden. "Stop it right now, Iron Bender! You've got no right to go fighting anybody for your own private pleasure when you're still my protector. What if something happened, and you weren't able to protect me and mine the way you should after that?"

"Maiden's right," said One Punch, sharply. "It's Clan honor and decency at stake here; not just your own feelings, Bender. Now, as I was saying, Law-Twister here's been doing some fine talking and twisting, and he's come up with a real point. It's as much a matter to us if he's a real Shorty-type protector to those orphans Maiden adopted, as it is to him and the other Shorties—"

His voice became mild. He turned to the crowd and spread his hands, modestly.

"Of course, I'm no real Grandfather," he said. "Some might think I wouldn't stand a chance to be the one you'll pick at that next Clan meeting. Of course, some might think I would, too—but it's hardly for me to say. Only, speaking as a man who *might* be named a Grandfather someday, I'd say Gentle Maiden really ought to let Law-Twister check with those three orphans to see if they want him to talk or hassle, for them."

A bass-voiced murmur of agreement rose from the surrounding crowd, which by this time had grown to a respectable size.

For the first time since he had said farewell to Ambassador Joshua Guy, Mal felt his spirits begin to rise. For the first time, he seemed to be getting some control over the events which had been hurrying him along like a chip swirling downstream in the current of a fast river. Maybe, if he had a little luck, now—

"Duty's duty, I guess," rumbled Iron Bender at just this moment. "All right then, Law-Twister—now, stop your arguing, Gentle, it's no use—you can see your fellow Shorties. They're at Gentle's place, last but one on the left-hand side of the street, here."

"Show you the way, myself, Postman," said One Punch.

The Clan elder led off, limping, and the crowd broke up as the Hill Bluffer followed him. Iron Bender went off in the opposite direction, but Gentle Maiden tagged along with the postman, Mal, and her grandfather, muttering to herself.

"Take things kind of hard, don't you, Gentle?" said the Hill Bluffer to her, affably. "Don't blame old Iron Bender. Man can't expect to win every time."

"Why not?" demanded Gentle. "I do! He's just so cautious, and slow, he makes me sick! Why can't he be like One Punch, here, when *he* was young? Hit first and think afterward—particularly when I ask him to? Then Bender could go around being slow and careful about his own business if he wanted; in fact, I'd be all for him being like that, on his own time. A girl needs a man she can respect; particularly when there's no other man around that's much more than half-size to him!"

"Tell him so," suggested the Bluffer, strolling along, his long legs making a single stride to each two of Gentle and One Punch.

"Certainly not! It'd look like I was giving in to him!" said Gentle. "It may be all right for any old ordinary girl to go chasing a man, but not me. Folks know me better than that. They'd laugh their heads off if I suddenly started going all soft on Bender. And besides—"

"Here we are, Postman—Law-Twister," interrupted One Punch, stopping by the heavy wooden door of a good-sized log building. "This is Gentle's place. The orphans are inside."

"Don't you go letting them out, now!" snapped Gentle, as Mal, relieved to be out of the saddle after this much time in it, began sliding down the Bluffer's broad back toward the ground.

"Don't worry, Granddaughter," said One Punch, as Mal's boots touched the earth. "Postman and I'll wait right outside the door here with you. If one of them tries to duck out, we'll catch him or her for you."

"They keep wanting to go back to their flying box," said Gentle. "And I know the minute one of them gets inside it, he'll be into the air and off like a flash. I haven't gone to all this trouble to lose any of them, now. So, don't you try anything while you're inside there, Law-Twister!"

Mal went up the three wooden steps to the rough plank

door and lifted a latch that was, from the standpoint of a human-sized individual, like a heavy bar locking the door shut. The door yawned open before him, and he stepped through into dimness. The door swung shut behind him, and he heard the latch being relocked.

"Holler when you want out, Law-Twister!" One Punch's voice boomed through the closed door. Mal looked around him.

He was in what was obviously a Dilbian home. A few pieces of heavy, oversize furniture supplemented a long plank table before an open fireplace, in which, however, no fire was now burning. Two more doors, also latched, were of rooms beyond this one.

He crossed the room and tried the right-hand door at random. It gave him a view of an empty, kitchenlike room with what looked like a side of beef hanging from a hook in a far corner. A chopping block and a wash trough of hollowed-out stone furnished the rest of the room.

Mal backed out, closed the door, and tried the one on his left. It opened easily, but the entrance to the room beyond was barred by a rough fence of planks some eight feet high, with sharp chips of stone hammered into the tops. Through the gap in the planks, Mal looked into what seemed a large Dilbian bed chamber, which had been converted into human living quarters by the simple expedient of ripping out three cabin sections from a shuttle boat and setting them up like so many large tin boxes on the floor under the lofty, log-beamed roof.

At the sound of the opening of the door, other doors opened in the transplanted cabin sections. As Mal watched, three middle-aged people—one woman and two men—emerged each from his own cabin and stopped short to stare through the gaps in the plank fence at him.

"Oh, no!" said one of the men, a skinny, balding character with a torn shirt collar. "A kid!"

"Kid?" echoed Mal, grimly. He had been prepared to feel sorry for the three captives of Gentle Maiden, but this kind of reception did not make it easy. "How adult do you have to be to wrestle a Dilbian?"

"Wrestle . . . !" It was the woman. She stared at him. "Oh, it surely won't come to that. Will it? You ought to be able to find a way around it. Didn't they pick you because you'd be able to understand these natives?"

Mal looked at her narrowly.

"How would you have any idea of how I was picked?" he asked.

"We just assumed they'd send someone to help us who understood these natives," she said.

Mal's conscience pricked him.

"I'm sorry—er—Mrs. . . ." he began.

"Ora Page," she answered. "This"—she indicated the thin man—"is Harvey Anok, and"—she nodded at the other—"Zora Rice." She had a soft, rather gentle face, in contrast to the sharp, almost suspicious face of Harvey Anok and the rather hard features of Zora Rice; but like both of the others, she had a tanned outdoors sort of look.

"Mrs. Page," Mal said. "I'm sorry, but the only thing I seem to be able to do for you is get myself killed by the local harnessmaker. But I do have an idea. Where's this shuttle boat you came down in?"

"Right behind this building we're in," said Harvey, "in a meadow about a hundred yards back. What about it?"

"Good," said Mal. "I'm going to try to make a break for it. Now, if you can just tell me how to take off in it, and land, I think I can fly it. I'll make some excuse to get inside it and get into the air. Then I'll fly back to the ambassador who sent me out here, and tell him I can't do anything. He'll have to send in force, if necessary, to get you out of this."

The three stared back at him without speaking.

"Well?" demanded Mal. "What about it? If I get killed by that harnessmaker it's not going to do you any good. Gentle Maiden may decide to take you away and hide you someplace in the mountains, and no rescue team will ever find you. What're you waiting for? Tell me how to fly that shuttle boat!"

The three of them looked at each other uncomfortably and then back at Mal. Harvey shook his head.

"No," he said. "I don't think we ought to do that. There's a treaty—"

"The Human-Hemnoid Treaty on this planet?" Mal asked. "But, I just told you, that Dilbian harnessmaker may kill me. You might be killed, too. Isn't it more important to save lives than worry about a treaty at a time like this?"

"You don't understand," said Harvey. "One of the things that treaty particularly rules out is anthropologists. If we're found here—"

"But I thought you were tourists?" Mal said.

"We are. All of us were on vacation on a spaceliner tour. It just happens we three are anthropologists, too—"

"That's why we were tempted to drop in here in the first place," put in Zora Rice.

"But that treaty's a lot more important than you think," Harvey said. "We can't risk damaging it."

"Why didn't you think of that before you came here?" Mal growled.

"You can find a way out for all of us without calling for armed force and getting us all in trouble. I know you can," said Ora Page. "We trust you. Won't you try?"

Mal stared back at them all, scowling. There was something funny about all this. Prisoners who hadn't worried about a Human-Hemnoid Treaty on their way to Dilbia, but who were willing to risk themselves to protect it now that they were here. A Dilbian female who wanted to adopt three full-grown humans. Why, in the name of all that was sensible? A village harnessmaker ready to tear him apart, and a human ambassador who had sent him blithely out to face that same harnessmaker with neither advice nor protection.

"All right," said Mal, grimly. "I'll talk to you again later—with luck."

He stepped back and swung closed the heavy door to the room in which they were fenced. Going to the entrance of the building, he shouted to One Punch, and the door before him was opened from the outside. Gentle Maiden shouldered suspiciously past him into the house as he emerged.

"Well, how about it, Law-Twister?" asked One Punch, as

the door closed behind Gentle Maiden. "Those other Shorties say it was all right for you to talk and hassle for them?"

"Well, yes . . ." said Mal. He gazed narrowly up into the large furry faces of One Punch and the Bluffer, trying to read their expressions. But outside of the fact that they both looked genial, he could discover nothing. The alien visages held their secrets well from human eyes.

"They agreed, all right," said Mal, slowly. "But what they had to say to me sort of got me thinking. Maybe you can tell me—just why is it Clan Water Gap can't hold its meeting right away instead of two weeks from now? Hold a meeting right now and the Clan could have an elected Grandfather before the afternoon's half over. Then there'd be time to hold a regular Clan court, for example, between the election and sunset; and this whole matter of the orphan Shorties could be handled more in regular fashion."

"Wondered that, did you, Law-Twister?" said One Punch. "It just crossed my mind earlier you might wonder about it. No real reason why the Clan meeting couldn't be held right away, I guess. Only, who's going to suggest it?"

"Suggest it?" Mal said.

"Why, sure," said One Punch. "Ordinarily, when a Clan has a Grandfather, it'd be up to the Grandfather to suggest it. But Clan Water Gap doesn't have a Grandfather right now, as you know."

"Isn't there anyone else to suggest things like that if a Grandfather isn't available?" asked Mal.

"Well, yes." One Punch gazed thoughtfully away from Mal, down the village street. "If there's no Grandfather around, it'd be pretty much up to one of the grandpas to suggest it. Only—of course I can't speak for old Forty Winks or anyone else—but I wouldn't want to be the one to do it, myself. Might sound like I thought I had a better chance of being elected Grandfather now, than I would two weeks from now."

"So," said Mal. "You won't suggest it, and if you won't I can see how the others wouldn't, for the same reason. Who else does that leave who might suggest it?"

"Why, I don't know, Law-Twister," said One Punch,

gazing back at him. "Guess any strong-minded member of the Clan could speak up and propose it. Someone like Gentle Maiden, herself, for example. But you know Gentle Maiden isn't about to suggest anything like that when what she wants is for Iron Bender to try and take you apart as soon as possible."

"How about Iron Bender?" Mal asked.

"Now, he just might want to suggest something like that," said One Punch, "being how as he likes to do everything just right. But it might look like he was trying to get out of tangling with you—after all this talk by the Bluffer, here, about how tough Shorties are. So I don't expect Bender'd be likely to say anything about changing the meeting time."

Mal looked at the tall Dilbian who had brought him here.

"Bluffer," he said, "I wonder if you—"

"Look here, Law-Twister," said the Hill Bluffer severely. "I'm the government postman—to all the Clans and towns and folks from Wildwood Valley to Humrog Peak. A government man like myself can't go sticking his nose into local affairs."

"But you were ready to tangle with Iron Bender yourself, a little while ago—"

"That was personal and private. This is public. I don't blame you for not seeing the difference right off, Law-Twister, you being a Shorty and all," said the Bluffer, "but a government man has to know, and keep the two things separate."

He fell silent, looking at Mal. For a moment neither the Bluffer nor One Punch said anything; but Mal was left with the curious feeling that the conversation had not so much been ended, as left hanging in the air for him to pick up. He was beginning to get an understanding of how Dilbian minds worked. Because of their taboo against any outright lying, they were experts at pretending to say one thing while actually saying another. There was a strong notion in Mal's mind now that somehow the other two were simply waiting for him to ask the right question—as if he had a handful of keys and only the right one would unlock an answer with the information he wanted.

"Certainly is different from the old days, Postman," said One Punch, idly, turning to the Bluffer. "Wonder what Mighty Grappler would have said, seeing Shorties like the Law-Twister among us. He'd have said something, all right. Had an answer for everything, Mighty Grappler did."

An idea exploded into life in Mal's mind. Of course! That was it!

"Isn't there something in Mighty Grappler's laws," he asked, "that could arrange for a Clan meeting without someone suggesting it?"

One Punch looked back at him.

"Why, what do you know?" the oldster said. "Bluffer, Law-Twister here is something to make up stories about, all right. Imagine a Shorty guessing that Mighty Grappler had thought of something like that, when I'd almost forgotten it myself."

"Shorties are sneaky little characters, as I've said before," replied the Bluffer, gazing down at Mal with obvious pride. "Quick on the uptake, too."

"Then there is a way?" Mal asked.

"It just now comes back to me," said One Punch. "Mighty Grappler set up all his laws to protect the Clan members against themselves and each other and against strangers. But he did make one law to protect strangers on Clan territory. As I remember, any stranger having a need to appeal to the whole Clan for justice was supposed to stand beside Grappler's stone—the one we showed you on the way in—and put his hand on it, and make that appeal."

"Then what?" asked Mal. "The Clan would grant his appeal?"

"Well, not exactly," said One Punch. "But they'd be obliged to talk the matter over and decide things."

"Oh," said Mal. This was less than he had hoped for, but still he had a strong feeling now that he was on the right track. "Well, let's go."

"Right," said the Bluffer. He and One Punch turned and strolled off up the street.

"Hey!" yelled Mal, trotting after them. The Bluffer turned around, picked him up, and stuffed him into the saddle on the postman's back.

"Sorry, Law-Twister. Forgot about those short legs of yours," the Bluffer said. Turning to stroll forward with One Punch again, he added to the oldster, "Makes you kind of wonder how they made out to start off with, before they had flying boxes and things like that."

"Probably didn't do much," offered One Punch in explanation, "just lay in the sun and dug little burrows and things like that."

Mal opened his mouth and then closed it again on the first retort that had come to his lips.

"Where you off to with the Law-Twister now, One Punch?" asked a graying-haired Dilbian they passed, who Mal was pretty sure was either Forty Winks or Grandpa Tricky.

"Law-Twister's going up to the stone of Mighty Grappler to make an appeal to the Clan," said One Punch.

"Well, now," said the other, "guess I'll mosey up there myself and have a look at that. Can't remember it ever happening before."

He fell in behind them, but halfway down the street fell out again to answer the questions of several other bystanders who wanted to know what was going on. So it was that when Mal alighted from the Bluffer's back at the stone of Mighty Grappler, there were just he and the Bluffer and One Punch there, although a few figures could be seen beginning to stream out of the village toward the stone.

"Go ahead, Law-Twister," said One Punch, nodding at the stone. "Make that appeal of yours."

"Hadn't I better wait until the rest of the Clan gets here?"

"I suppose you could do that," said One Punch. "I was thinking you might just want to say your appeal and have it over with and sort of let me tell people about it. But you're right. Wait until folks get here. Give you a chance to kind of look over Mighty Grappler's stone, too, and put yourself in the kind of spirit to make a good appeal. . . . Guess you'll want to be remembering this word for word, to pass on down the line to the other clans, won't you, Postman?"

"You could say I've almost a duty to do that, One Punch," responded the Bluffer. "Lots more to being a government postman than some people think. . . ."

The two went on chatting, turning a little away from Mal and the stone to gaze down the slope at the Clan members on their way up from the village. Mal turned to gaze at the stone, itself. It was still inconceivable to him that even a Dilbian could lift and carry such a weight ten paces.

Certainly, it did not look as if anyone had ever moved the stone since it had been placed here. The two ends of the iron rod sticking out from opposite sides of it were red with rust, and the grass had grown up thickly around its base. That is, it had grown up thickly everywhere but just behind it, where it looked like a handful of grass might have been pulled up, recently. Bending down to look closer at the grass-free part of the stone, Mal caught sight of something dark. The edge of some indentation, almost something like the edge of a large hole in the stone itself—

"Law-Twister!" The voice of One Punch brought Mal abruptly upright. He saw that the vanguard of the Dilbians coming out of the village was almost upon them.

"How'd you like me to sort of pass the word what this is all about?" asked One Punch. "Then you could just make your appeal without trying to explain it?"

"Oh—fine," said Mal. He glanced back at the stone. For a moment he felt a great temptation to take hold of the two rust-red iron handles and see if he actually could lift it. But there were too many eyes on him now.

The members of the Clan came up and sat down, with their backs straight and furry legs stuck out before them on the grass. The Bluffer, however, remained standing near Mal, as did One Punch. Among the last to arrive was Gentle Maiden, who hurried up to the very front of the crowd and snorted angrily at Mal before sitting down.

"Got them all upset!" she said, triumphantly. "Knew you would!"

Iron Bender had not put in an appearance.

"Members of Clan Water Gap," said One Punch, when they were all settled on the grass and quiet, "you all know what this Shorty, Law-Twister here, dropped in on us to do. He wants to take back with him the orphans Gentle Maiden adopted according to Clan law, laid down by Mighty Grappler. Naturally, Maiden doesn't want him to, and she's got her protector, Iron Bender—"

He broke off, peering out over the crowd.

"Where is Iron Bender?" the oldster demanded.

"He says work's work," a voice answered from the crowd. "Says to send somebody for him when you're all ready to have someone's head torn off. Otherwise, he'll be busy down in the harness shop."

Gentle Maiden snorted.

"Well, well. I guess we'll just have to go on without him," said One Punch. "As I was saying, here's Iron Bender all ready to do his duty; but as Law-Twister sees it, it's not all that simple."

There was a buzz of low-toned, admiring comments from the crowd. One Punch waited until the noise died before going on.

"One thing Law-Twister wants to do is make an appeal to the Clan, according to Mighty Grappler's law, before he gets down to tangling with Iron Bender," the oldster said. "So, without my bending your ears any further, here's the Law-Twister himself, with tongue all oiled up and ready to talk you upside down, and roundabout. Go ahead, Law-Twister!"

Mal put his hand on the stone of Mighty Grappler. In fact, he leaned on the stone and it seemed to him it rocked a little bit, under his weight. It did not seem to him that One Punch's introductory speech had struck quite the serious note Mal himself might have liked. But now, in any case, it was up to him.

"Uh-members of Clan Water Gap," he said. "I've been disturbed by a lot of what I've learned here. For example, here you have something very important at stake—the right of a Clan Water Gap maiden to adopt Shorties as orphans. But the whole matter has to be settled by what's really an emergency measure—that is, my tangling with Iron Bender—just because Clan Water Gap hasn't elected a new Grandfather lately, and the meeting to elect one is a couple of weeks away—"

"And while it's not for me to say," interrupted the basso voice of the Hill Bluffer, "not being a Clan Water Gapper myself, and besides being a government postman who's strictly not concerned in any local affairs—I'd guess that's what a lot of folks are going to be asking me as I ply my route between here and Humrog Peak in the next few weeks. 'How come they didn't hold a regular trial to settle the matter, down there in Clan Water Gap?' they'll be asking. 'Because they didn't have a Grandfather,' I'll have to say. 'How come those Water Gappers are running around without a Grandfather?' they'll ask—"

"All right, Postman!" interrupted One Punch, in his turn. "I guess we can all figure what people are going to say. The point is, Law-Twister is still making his appeal. Go ahead, Law-Twister."

"Well . . . I asked about the Clan holding their meeting to elect a Grandfather right away," put in Mal. A small breeze came wandering by, and he felt it surprisingly cool on his forehead. Evidently there was a little perspiration up there. "One Punch here said it could be done all right, but it was a question who'd want to *suggest* it to the Clan. Naturally, he and the other grandpas who are in the running for Grandfather wouldn't like to do it. Iron Bender would have his own reasons for refusing; and Gentle Maiden here wouldn't particularly want to hold a meeting right away—"

"And we certainly shouldn't!" said Gentle Maiden. "Why go to all that trouble when here we've got Iron Bender perfectly willing and ready to tear—"

"Why, indeed?" interrupted Mal in his turn. He was beginning to get a little weary of hearing of Iron Bender's readiness to remove heads. "Except that perhaps the whole Clan deserves to be in on this—not just Iron Bender and Maiden and myself. What the Clan really ought to do is sit down and decide whether it's a good idea for the Clan to have someone like Gentle Maiden keeping three Shorties around. Does the Clan really want those Shorties to stay here? And if not, what's the best way of getting rid of these Shorties? Not that I'm trying to suggest anything to the Clan, but if the Clan should just decide to elect a Grandfather now, and the Grandfather should decide that Shorties don't qualify as orphans—"

A roar of protest from Gentle Maiden drowned him out;

and a thunder of Dilbian voices arose among the seated Clan members as conversation—argument, rather, Mal told himself—became general. He waited for it to die down; but it did not. After a while, he walked over to One Punch, who was standing beside the Hill Bluffer, observing—as were two other elderly figures, obviously Grandpas Tricky and Forty Winks—but not taking part in the confusion of voices.

"One Punch," said Mal, and the oldster looked down at him cheerfully, "don't you think maybe you should quiet them down so they could hear the rest of my appeal?"

"Why, Law-Twister," said One Punch, "there's no point you going on appealing any longer, when everybody's already decided to grant what you want. They're already discussing it. Hear them?"

Since no one within a mile could have helped hearing them, there was little Mal could do but nod his head and wait. About ten minutes later, the volume of sound began to diminish as voice after voice fell silent. Finally, there was a dead silence. Members of the Clan began to reseat themselves on the grass, and from a gathering in the very center of the crowd, Gentle Maiden emerged and snorted at Mal before turning toward the village.

"I'm going to go get Bender!" she announced. "I'll get those little Shorties up here, too, so they can see Bender take care of this one and know they might just as well settle down."

She went off at a fast walk down the slope—the equivalent of about eight miles an hour in human terms.

Mal stared at One Punch, stunned.

"You mean," he asked him, "they decided not to do anything?"

A roar of explaining voices from the Clan members drowned him out and left him too deafened to understand them. When it was quiet once more, he was aware of One Punch looking severely down at him.

"Now, you shouldn't go around thinking Clan Water Gap'd talk something over and not come to some decision, Twister," he said. "Of course, they decided how it's all to go. We're going to elect a Grandfather today."

"Fine," said Mal, beginning to revive. Then a thought struck him. "Why did Gentle Maiden go after Iron Bender just now, then? I thought—"

"Wait until you hear," said One Punch. "Clan Water Gap's come up with a decision to warm that slippery little Shorty heart of yours. You see, everyone decided, since we were going to elect a Grandfather ahead of time, that it all ought to be done in reverse."

"In reverse?"

"Why, certainly," said One Punch. "Instead of having a trial, then having the Grandfather give a decision to let you and Iron Bender hassle it out to see whether the Shorties go with you or stay with Gentle Maiden, the Clan decided to work it exactly backward."

Mal shook his head dizzily.

"I still don't understand," he said.

"I'm surprised—a Shorty like you," said One Punch, reprovingly. "I'd think backward and upside down'd be second nature to a Law-Twister. Why, what's going to happen is you and Bender'll have it out *first*, then the best decision by a grandpa'll be picked, then the grandpa who's decision's been picked will be up for election, and the Clan will elect him Grandfather."

Mal blinked.

"Decision . . ." he began feebly.

"Now, my decision," said a voice behind him, and he turned around to see that the Clan's other two elderly members had come up, "is that Iron Bender ought to win. But if he doesn't, it'll be because of some Shorty trick."

"Playing it safe, eh, Forty Winks?" said the other grandpa who had just joined them. "Well, *my* decision is that with all his tricks, and tough as we've been hearing Shorties are, that the Law-Twister can't lose. He'll chew Iron Bender up."

The two of them turned and looked expectantly at One Punch.

"Hmm," said One Punch, closing one eye and squinting thoughtfully with the other at Mal. "My decision is that the Law-Twister's even more clever and sneaky than we think. My decision says Twister'll come up with something that'll fix things his way so that they never will tangle. In short, Twister's going to win the fight even before it starts.''

One Punch had turned toward the seated crowd as he said this, and there was another low mutter of appreciation from the seated Clan members.

"That One Punch," said Grandpa Tricky to Forty Winks, "never did lay back and play it safe. He just swings right in there twice as hard as anyone else, without winking."

"Well," said One Punch himself, turning to Mal, "there's Gentle Maiden and her orphans coming up from the village now with Iron Bender. You all set, Law-Twister?"

Mal was anything but set. It was good to hear that all three grandpas of Clan Water Gap expected him to come out on top; but he would have felt a lot better if it had been Iron Bender who had been expressing that opinion. He looked over the heads of the seated crowd to see Iron Bender coming, just as One Punch had said, with Gentle Maiden and three, small, human figures in tow.

His thoughts spun furiously. This whole business was crazy. It simply could not be that in a few minutes he would be expected to engage in a hand-to-hand battle with an individual more than one and a half times his height and five times his weight, any more than it could be that the wise men of the local Clan could be betting on him to win. One Punch's prediction, in particular, was so farfetched. . . .

Understanding suddenly exploded in him. At once, it all fitted together: the Dilbian habit of circumventing any outright lie by pretending to be after just the opposite of what an individual was really after; the odd reaction of the three captured humans who had not been concerned about the Human-Hemnoid Treaty of noninterference on Dilbia when they came *into* Clan Water Gap territory, but were willing to pass up a chance of escape by letting Mal summon armed human help to rescue them, now that they were here. Just suppose—Mal thought to himself feverishly—just suppose everything is just the opposite of what it seems . . .

There was only one missing part to this whole jigsaw puzzle, one bit to which he did not have the answer. He turned to One Punch.

"Tell me something," he said, in a low voice. "Suppose Gentle Maiden and Iron Bender *had* to marry each other. Do you think they'd be very upset?"

"Upset? Well, no," said One Punch, thoughtfully. "Come to think of it, now you mention it, Law-Twister—those two are just about made for each other. Particularly seeing there's no one else made big enough or tough enough for either one of them, if you look around. In fact, if it wasn't for how they go around saying they can't stand each other, you might think they really liked each other quite a bit. Why do you ask?"

"I was just wondering," said Mal, grimly. "Let me ask you another question. Do you think a Shorty like me could carry the stone of Mighty Grappler ten paces?"

One Punch gazed at him.

"Well, you know," he said, "when it comes right down to it, I wouldn't put anything past a Shorty like you."

"Thanks," said Mal. "I'll return the compliment. Believe me, from now on, I'll never put anything past a real person like you, or Gentle Maiden, or Iron Bender, or anyone else. And I'll tell the other Shorties that when I get back among them!"

"Why thank you, Law-Twister," said One Punch. "That's mighty kind of you—but, come to think of it, maybe you better turn around now. Because Iron Bender's here."

Mal turned—just in time to see the towering figure of the village harnessmaker striding toward him, accompanied by a rising murmur of excitement from the crowd.

"All right, let's get this over with!" boomed Iron Bender, opening and closing his massive hands hungrily. "Just take me a few minutes, and then—"

"*Stop!*" shouted Mal, holding up his hand.

Iron Bender stopped, still some twenty feet from Mal. The crowd fell silent, abruptly.

"I'm sorry!" said Mal, addressing them all. "I tried every way I could to keep it from coming to this. But I see now there's no other way to do it. Now, I'm nowhere near as sure as your three grandpas that I could handle Iron Bender, here, with one hand tied behind my back. Iron Bender might well handle *me*, with no trouble. I mean, he just might be the one real man who can tangle with a Shorty like me, and win. But, what if I'm wrong?''

Mal paused, both to see how they were reacting and to get his nerve up for his next statement. If I was trying something like this any place else, he thought, they'd cart me off to a psychiatrist. But the Dilbians in front of him were all quiet and attentive, listening. Even Iron Bender and Gentle Maiden were showing no indications of wanting to interrupt.

"As I say," went on Mal, a little hoarsely as a result of working to make his voice carry to the whole assemblage, "what if I'm wrong? What if this terrific hassling ability that all we Shorties have gets the best of me when I tangle with Iron Bender? Not that Iron Bender would want me to hold back any, I know that—"

Iron Bender snorted affirmatively and worked his massive hands in the air.

"—but," said Mal, "think what the results would be. Think of Clan Water Gap without a harnessmaker. Think of Gentle Maiden here without the one real man she can't push around. I've thought about those things, and it seems to me there's just one way out. The Clan laws have to be changed so that a Shorty like me doesn't have to tangle with a Clan Gapper over this problem."

He turned to the stone of Mighty Grappler.

"So—" he wound up, his voice cracking a little on the word in spite of himself, "I'm just going to have to carry this stone ten steps so the laws can be changed."

He stepped up to the stone. There was a dead silence all around him. He could feel the sweat popping out on his face. What if the conclusions he had come to were all wrong? But he could not afford to think that now. He had to go through with the business, now that he'd spoken.

He curled his hands around the two ends of the iron rod from underneath and squatted down with his knees on either side of the rock. This was going to be different from ordinary weight lifting, where the weight was distributed on the outer two ends of the lifting bar. Here, the weight was between his fists.

He took a deep breath and lifted. For a moment, it seemed

that the dead weight of the stone refused to move. Then it gave. It came up and into him until the near face of the rock thudded against his chest; the whole stone now held well off the ground.

So far, so good, for the first step. Now, for the second . . .

He willed strength into his leg muscles.

Up . . . he thought to himself . . . up. . . . He could hear his teeth gritting against each other in his head. Up . . .

Slowly, grimly, his legs straightened. His body lifted, bringing the stone with it, until he stood, swaying, the weight of it against his chest, and his arms just beginning to tremble with the strain.

Now, quickly—before arms and legs gave out—he had to take the ten steps.

He swayed forward, stuck out a leg quickly, and caught himself. For a second he hung poised, then he brought the other leg forward. The effort almost overbalanced him, but he stayed upright. Now, the right foot again . . . then the left . . . the right . . . the left . . .

In the fierceness of his effort, everything else was blotted out. He was alone with the stone he had to carry, wih the straining pull of his muscles, the brightness of the sun in his eyes, and the savage tearing of the rod ends on his fingers, that threatened to rip themselves out of his grip.

Eight steps . . . nine steps . . . and . . . ten!

He tried to let the stone down easily, but it thudded out of his grasp. As he stood half bent over, it struck upright in its new resting place in the grass, then half-rolled away from him, for a moment exposing its bottom surface completely, so that he could see clearly into the hole there. Then it rocked back upright and stood still.

Painfully, stiffly, Mal straightened his back.

"Well," he panted, to the silent, staring Dilbians of Clan Water Gap, "I guess that takes care of that. . . ."

Less than forty minutes later he was herding the three anthropologists back into their shuttle boat.

"But I don't understand," protested Harvey, hesitating in the entry port of the shuttle boat. "I want to know how you got us free without having to fight that big Dilbian—the one with the name that means Iron Bender.''

''I moved their law stone,'' said Mal, grimly. ''That meant I could change the rules of the Clan.''

''But they went on and elected One Punch as Clan Grandfather, anyway,'' said Harvey.

''Naturally,'' said Mal. ''He'd given the most accurate judgment in advance—he'd foretold I'd win without laying a hand on Iron Bender. And I had. Once I moved the stone, I simply added a law to the ones Mighty Grappler had set up. I said no Clan Water Gapper was allowed to adopt orphan Shorties. So, if that was against the law, Gentle Maiden couldn't keep you. She had to let you go and then there was no reason for Iron Bender to want to tangle with me.''

''But why did Iron Bender and Gentle decide to get married?''

''Why, she couldn't go back to being just a single maiden again, after naming someone her protector,'' Mal said. ''Dilbians are very strict about things like that. Public opinion *forced* them to get married—which they wanted to do anyhow, but neither of them had wanted to be the one to ask the other to marry.''

Harvey blinked.

''You mean,'' he said disbelievingly, ''it was all part of a plot by Gentle Maiden, Iron Bender, and One Punch to use us for their own advantage? To get One Punch elected Grandfather, and the other two forced to marry?''

''Now, you're beginning to understand,'' said Mal, grimly. He started to turn away.

''Wait,'' said Harvey. ''Look, there's information here that you ought to be sharing with us for the sake of science—''

''Science?'' Mal gave him a hard look. ''That's right, it was science, wasn't it? Just pure science, that made you and your friends decide on the spur of the moment to come down here. *Wasn't it?*''

Harvey's brows drew together.

''What's that question supposed to mean?'' he said.

''Just inquiring,'' said Mal. ''Didn't it ever occur to you that the Dilbians are just as bright as you are? And that they'd have a pretty clear idea why three Shorties would show up out of thin air and start asking questions?"

"Why should that seem suspicious to them?" Ora Page stuck her face out of the entry port over Harvey's shoulder.

"Because the Dilbians take everything with a grain of salt anyway—on principle," said Mal. "Because they're experts at figuring out what someone else is really up to, since that's just the way they operate, themselves. When a Dilbian wants to go after something, his first move is to pretend to head in the opposite direction."

"They told you that in your hypnotraining?" Ora asked.

Mal shook his head.

"No," he said. "I wasn't told anything." He looked harshly at the two of them and at the face of Rice, which now appeared behind Harvey's other shoulder. "Nobody told me a thing about the Dilbians except that there are a few rare humans who understand them instinctively and can work with them, only the book-psychiatrists and the book-anthropologists can't figure out why. Nobody suggested to me that our human authorities might deliberately be trying to arrange a situation where three book-anthropologists would be on hand to observe me—as one of these rare humans—learning how to think and work like a Dilbian, on my own. No, nobody told me anything like that. It's just a Dilbian sort of suspicion I've worked out on my own."

"Look here—" began Harvey.

"You look here!" said Mal, furiously. "I don't know of anything in the Outspace Regulations that lets someone be drafted into being some sort of experimental animal without his knowing what's going on—"

"Easy now. Easy . . ." said Harvey. "All right. This whole thing was set up so we could observe you. But we had absolute faith that someone with your personality profile would do fine with the Dilbians. And, of course, you realize you'll be compensated for all this. For one thing, I think you'll find there's a full six-year scholarship waiting for you now, once you qualify for college entrance. And a few other things, too. You'll be hearing more about them when you get back to the human ambassador at Humrog Town, who sent you here."

"Thanks," said Mal, still boiling inside. "But next time tell them to ask first whether I want to play games with the rest of you! Now, you better get moving if you want to catch that spaceliner!"

He turned away. But before he had covered half a dozen steps, he heard Harvey's voice calling after him.

"Wait! There's something vitally important you didn't tell us. How did you manage to pick up that rock and carry it the way you did?"

Mal looked sourly back over his shoulder.

"I do a lot of weight lifting," he said, and kept on going.

He did not look back again; and, a few minutes later, he heard the shuttle boat take off. He headed at an angle up the valley slope behind the houses in the village toward the stone of Mighty Grappler, where the Bluffer would be waiting to take him back to Humrog Town. The sun was close to setting, and with its level rays in his eyes, he could barely make out that there were four big Dilbian figures rather than one, waiting for him by the stone. A wariness awoke in him.

When he came up, however, he disocvered that the four figures were the Bluffer with One Punch, Gentle Maiden, and Iron Bender—and all four looked genial.

"There you are," said the Bluffer, as Mal stopped before him. "Better climb up into the saddle. It's not more than two hours to full dark, and even the way I travel we're going to have to move some to make it back to Humrog Town in that time."

Mal obeyed. From the altitude of the saddle, he looked over the Bluffer's right shoulder down at One Punch and Gentle Maiden and level into the face of Iron Bender.

"Well, good-bye," he said, not sure of how Dilbians reacted on parting. "It's been something, knowing you all."

"Been something for Clan Water Gap, too," replied One Punch. "I can say that now, officially, as the Clan Grandfather. Guess most of us will be telling the tale for years to come, how we got dropped in on here by the Mighty Law-Twister."

Mal goggled. He had thought he was past the point of surprise where Dilbians were concerned, but this was more than even he had imagined.

"*Mighty* Law-Twister?" he echoed.

"Why, of course," rumbled the Hill Bluffer, underneath him. "Somebody's name had to be changed, after you moved that stone."

"The postman's right," said One Punch. "Naturally, we wouldn't want to change the name of Mighty Grappler, seeing what all he means to the Clan. Besides, since he's dead, we can't very well go around changing his name and getting folks mixed up, so we just changed yours instead. Stands to reason if you could carry Mighty Grappler's stone ten paces, you had to be pretty mighty, yourself."

"But—well, now, wait a minute . . ." Mal protested. He was remembering what he had seen in the moment he had put the stone down and it had rocked enough to let him see clearly into the hole inside it, and his conscience was bothering him. "Uh—One Punch, I wonder if I could speak to you . . . privately . . . for just a second? If we could just step over here—"

"No need for that, Mighty," boomed Iron Bender. "I and the wife are just headed back down to the village, anyway. Aren't we, Gentle?"

"Well, *I'm* going. If you want to come too—"

"That's what I say," interrupted Iron Bender. "We're both just leaving. So long, Mighty. Sorry we never got a chance to tangle. If you ever get some spare time and a good reason, come back and I'll be glad to oblige you."

"Thanks . . ." said Mal. With mixed feelings, he watched the harnessmaker and his new wife turn and stride off down the slope toward the buildings below. Then he remembered his conscience and looked again down at One Punch.

"Guess you better climb down again," the Bluffer was saying, "and I'll mosey off a few steps myself so's not to intrude."

"Now, Postman," said One Punch. "No need for that. We're all friends here. I can guess that Mighty, here, could have a few little questions to ask or things to tell—but likely it's nothing you oughtn't to hear; and besides, being a government man, we can count on you keeping any secrets.''

"That's true," said the Bluffer. "Come to think of it, Mighty, it'd be kind of an insult to the government if you didn't trust me—"

"Oh, I trust you," said Mal, hastily. "It's just that . . . well . . ." He looked at One Punch. "What would you say if I told you that the stone there is hollow—that it'd been hollowed out inside?''

"Now, Mighty," said One Punch, "you mustn't make fun of an old man, now that he's become a respectable Grandfather. Anybody knows stones aren't hollow."

"But what would you say if I told you that that one is?" persisted Mal.

"Why, I don't suppose it'd make much difference you just *telling* me it was hollow," said One Punch. "I don't suppose I'd say anything. I wouldn't want folks to think you could twist me that easily, for one thing; and for another thing, maybe it might come in handy some time later, my having heard someone say that stone was hollow. Just like the Mighty Grappler said in some of his own words of wisdom—'It's always good to have things set up one way. But it's extra good to have them set up another way, too. Two ways are always better than one.' ''

"And very good wisdom that is," put in the Bluffer, admiringly. "Up near Humrog Peak there's a small bridge people been walking around for years. There *is* a kind of rumor floating around that it's washed out in the middle, but I've never heard anybody really say so. Never know when it might come in useful to have a bridge like that around for someone who'd never heard the rumor—that is, if there's any truth to the rumor, which I doubt.''

"I see," said Mal.

"Of course you do, Mighty," said One Punch. "You understand things real well for a Shorty. Now, luckily we don't have to worry about this joke of yours that the stone of Mighty Grappler is hollow, because we've got proof otherwise.''

"Proof?" Mal blinked.

"Why, certainly," said One Punch. "Now, it stands to reason, if that stone were hollow, it wouldn't be anywhere near as heavy as it looks. In fact, it'd be real light."

"That's right," said Mal, sharply. "And you saw me—a Shorty—pick it up and carry it."

"Exactly!" said One Punch. "The whole Clan was watching to see you pick that stone up and carry it. And we did."

"And that proves it isn't hollow?" Mal stared.

"Why sure," said One Punch. "We all saw you sweating and struggling and straining to move that stone just ten paces. Well, what more proof does a man need? If it'd been hollow like you say, a Shorty—let alone a mighty Shorty like you—would've been able to pick it up with one paw and just stroll off with it. But we were watching you closely, Mighty, and you didn't leave a shred of doubt in the mind of any one of us that it was just about all you could carry. So, that stone just *had* to be solid."

He stopped. The Bluffer snorted.

"You see there, Mighty?" the Bluffer said. "You may be a real good law-twister—nobody doubts it for a minute—but when you go up against the wisdom of a real elected Grandfather, you find you can't twist him like you can any ordinary real man."

"I . . . guess so," said Mal. "I suppose there's no point, then, in my suggesting you just take a look at the stone?"

"It'd be kind of beneath me to do that, Mighty," said One Punch, severely, "now that I'm a Grandfather and already pointed out how it couldn't be hollow, anyway. Well, so long."

Abruptly, as abruptly as Iron Bender and Gentle Maiden had gone, One Punch turned and strode off down the slope.

The Hill Bluffer turned on one heel, himself, and strode away in the opposite direction, into the mountains and the sunset.

"But the thing I don't understand," said Mal to the Bluffer, a few minutes later when they were back on the narrow trail, out of sight of Water Gap Territory, "is how . . . what would have happened if those three Shorties hadn't dropped in the way they did? And what if I hadn't been sent for? One Punch might have been elected Grandfather anyway, but how would Iron Bender and Gentle Maiden ever have gotten married?"

"Lot of luck to it all, I suppose you could say, Mighty," answered the Bluffer, sagely. "Just shows how things turn out. Pure chance—like my mentioning to Little Bite a couple of months ago it was a shame there hadn't been other Shorties around to watch just how the Half-Pint Posted and Pick-and-Shovel did things, back when they were here."

"You . . ." Mal stared, "mentioned . . ."

"Just offhand, one day," said the Bluffer. "Of course, as I told Little Bite, there weren't hardly any real champions around right now to interest a tough little Shorty—except over at Clan Water Gap, where my unmarried Cousin Gentle Maiden lived."

"Your *cousin*. . . ? I see," said Mal. There was a long, long pause. "Very interesting."

"Funny. That's how Little Bite put it, when I told him," answered the Bluffer, cat-footing confidently along the very edge of a precipice. "You Shorties sure have a habit of talking alike and saying the same things all the time. Comes of having such little heads with not much space inside for words, I suppose."

IN THE LOWER PASSAGE

by Harle Oren Cummins

The mystery man of our collection, Harle Oren Cummins is author of Welsh Rarebit Tales *(1902). In the introduction, Cummins claims the tales were actually written by fourteen different members of a Bostonian literary society. Probably this is just a literary convention, yet one story is copyrighted by E. B. Terhune. If anyone has any information, we'd certainly like to hear it.*

Though the following story is quite interesting, the author might be said to be largely aping Kipling.

We were sitting on the deck of the *Empress of India*, homeward bound for Southampton. I was returning on a six months' leave from hospital duty in Calcutta, and the Colonel was retiring from his post in the northern provinces, where he had served with credit for over fifteen years. He had resigned suddenly a month before. His resignation had been refused, whereupon he immediately gave up everything to his second in command, and took the next steamer home, for a year's stay, according to the belief of the home government, but with a private resolution never to return.

I knew that he had had some terrible experience in which his dearest friend, Lieutenant Arthur Stebbins, had been killed; but beyond that I was as ignorant as the home government which had refused to sanction his resignation. That night,

279

however, as we sat on deck, and felt the lingering tremor of the giant screw which was driving us back to home and civilization, something prompted the Colonel to confide in me.

"I was not acting in my official capacity when Arthur Stebbins and I went up into the Junga district," the Colonel said in answer to a chance remark of mine, "it was simply and solely to visit the haunted city of Mubapur. You have been in India for two years, and you may have heard some of the strange tales in regard to the place; but as nearly every little out-of-the-way province in India has its peculiar tale of hidden wealth or strange craft, you have probably paid no attention to the stories of Mubapur.

"I had heard the natives, when they thought no one was listening, speak of the lost tribe of Jadacks, which had once lived up among the Ora Mountains. It seems that they were not like other natives, but a white people almost giant in size, and their chief city was Mubapur. But years ago, some say ten, others fifty, and still others a hundred, for these natives have no idea of time, a great plague came upon the white tribe, and it was smitten from the land.

"They believed that the gods had in some way been offended, and that this people were annihilated in punishment. Anyway, we could not get one of our coolie boys within two miles of the place after nightfall; and they told strange stories of immense white creatures which flitted about the place, and of moanings and wailings which could be heard on still nights when the wind was from Mubapur.

"Stebbins and I were on a shooting expedition in the Junga district when he, remembering the wild tales he had heard, proposed that we turn aside, and make the two days' trip to the haunted city. As time was of no particular account just then, I agreed; and after leaving our coolie bearers two miles from the town, for they refused all bribes and ignored all threats to go farther, we entered the deserted and grass-grown streets of Mubapur. It was near dark when we arrived; and we decided to put up for the night in a little temple, the roof of which still defied the action of the wind and rain, and which offered us a comfortable retreat.

"As I was building a fire just outside the entrance preparatory to getting supper, I heard Stebbins call, and hurrying in, found him standing behind the chief altar of the place, and gazing down a steep stairway which apparently led into the bowels of the earth. He put up his hand as I entered, and whispered, 'Listen; do you hear anything?'

"I held my breath listening, and from somewhere down in the damp depths below I heard a strange sound floating upwards. It might have been a chant such as the hill men sing on the eve of battle; or it might have been only the wind soughing through underground passages, but anyway it was weird enough in its effect on both of us, so that we hurried out to the fire and busied ourselves getting supper. It is strange how differently the tales we had heard seemed in that ruined temple with night coming on, from what they had in the bright daylight in the market place at Calcutta.

"We slept very close together that night just inside the entrance to the temple, and all through the watches I fancied I heard that solemn dirge rising and falling in the stillness of the night. Once I awoke to find Stebbins talking softly, and I heard him mutter something about a great white beast; but when I looked at him his eyes were shut, and he was sleeping soundly.

"The next morning after breakfast I asked him the question for which I knew he was waiting—should we descend the narrow stairway into the passage? He was anxious to make the attempt; and after getting ready some torches and looking carefully to our guns, we started down the slippery stairway.

"The steps ended abruptly, and we found ourselves in a long, narrow passage. What struck me at once as peculiar as we proceeded were some little cavities in the floor at regular intervals, such as might have been made by a person walking continuously, as a prisoner walks in his cell. But the stride was nearly twice that of an ordinary man. After walking about fifty paces we came to another stairway leading to a still lower passage, and just as we were about to descend we heard a noise as of something running swiftly below us. I looked at Stebbins to see if he had seen anything, for he was nearer to the head of the stairway than I; but there was only a white, determined look on his face.

" 'Come on, Colonel,' he called, and led the way down the stairs. At the farther end of this passage we came to a square opening into a kind of vault, and we paused for a moment before it. Then, in that stillness of the tomb, sixty feet below the surface of the ground, and just on the other side of the little opening, we heard a low moaning, and I would have sworn it was a man who made the sounds.

"We held our rifles a little closer, and crawled through the aperture, pausing to look about us. We both nearly dropped our guns in our excitement; for, crouched in the farther corner, was a great white, hairy creature, watching us with red, flaming eyes. Then, even before we could recover ourselves, the thing gave a kind of guttural cry of anger, and started toward us. As it rose to its feet, I swear to you I turned sick as a woman. The beast was over eight feet tall, and was covered with a thick growth of hair which was snow white. Its arms were once and a half the length of those of a common man, and its head was set low on its shoulders like that of an ape or a monkey; but the skin beneath the hair was *as white as yours or mine.*

"I heard the Lieutenant's gun go off, but the Thing never stopped. I raised my four-bore and let drive with the left barrel; then, overcome with a nameless fear of that great white beast, I called wildly to Arthur to follow me, and plunged through the opening and ran with all my strength toward the upper passage. It was not until I felt the fresh air on my face that I stopped to take breath, and I was so weak I could scarcely stand. Then, if you can, imagine my horror to find that I was alone. The Lieutenant was nowhere in sight. I called down the passage, and I could hear my voice echoing down the dismal place, but there was no answer.

"Think what you may; but I tell you it took more courage for me to force myself down into that vault again than it would to have walked up the steps to the scaffold. I crept fearfully along the passage, calling weakly every few minutes, and dreading what I should find; but—there was nothing to find."

The Colonel paused, putting his hand over his eyes, and I could see by the moonlight that his face was white and drawn.

"And did you not find him in the lower passage?" I asked, when the silence had become oppressive.

"No, I did not find the Lieutenant," he answered; "but when I came to the little square opening before the vault, there were some bloody little pieces scattered about the floor, and the place was all slippery, but there was no Lieutenant. You know it takes four horses to pull a man apart, and you can judge of the strength of that white beast when I tell you that there was not left of Arthur Stebbins a piece as big as your two hands.

"As I looked at that floor with the ghastly things which covered it, a wild rage took possession of me. I knew that the creature was in the room beyond, for I could hear a crunching as a dog makes with a bone. I rushed through the opening, straight toward the corner where it was crouching. It saw me coming, and leaped to its feet. Again that sickening fear that I had felt before came over me; but I stood my ground and waited till it nearly reached me. Then, with the muzzle of my gun almost against it, I fired both barrels full into its breast.

"I must have fainted or gone off my head after that, for the next thing I knew I was lying in a native's hut on the Durbo road. Zur Khan, the man who owned the bungalow, said that he had found me four days before, wandering about on the plains, stark mad, and had taken me home."

"And the Thing in the passage?" I asked breathlessly. "Did you never go back?"

"Yes; when I had recovered a little, I went back to the Mubapur Temple," answered the Colonel; but he was silent for some minutes before he answered the first part of my question.

"In my report to the Government I said that Lieutenant Arthur Stebbins was torn to pieces in the lower passages of a Mubapur Temple by an immense white *ape*—but I lied," he added quietly.

CABIN BOY
by Damon Knight

Damon Knight (1922–   ) has been involved with science fiction and fantasy for over forty years as writer, critic, editor, organizer, and social historian. Works we particularly recommend include In Search of Wonder, *rev. ed. (1971),* The Best of Damon Knight *(1976), and* The Futurians *(1977).*

The following story of space-dwelling aliens is a whale of a tale. But its content swallows you so completely that you may forget to ask, "Where's the giant?" All we can say is, wait for the "hook" at the end.

I

The cabin boy's name was unspeakable, and even its meaning would be difficult to convey in any human tongue. For convenience, we may as well call him Tommy Loy.

Please bear in mind that all these terms are approximations. Tommy was not exactly a cabin boy, and even the spaceship he served was not exactly a spaceship, nor was the Captain exactly a captain. But if you think of Tommy as a freckled, scowling, red-haired, willful, prank-playing, thoroughly abhorrent brat, and of the Captain as a crusty, ponderous old man, you may be able to understand their relationship.

A word about Tommy will serve to explain why these

approximations have to be made, and just how much they mean. Tommy, to a human being, would have looked like a six-foot egg made of greenish gelatin. Suspended in this were certain dark or radiant shapes which were Tommy's nerve centers and digestive organs, and scattered about its surface were star-shaped and oval markings which were his sensory organs and gripping mechanisms—his "hands." At the lesser end was an orifice which expelled a stream of glowing vapor— Tommy's means of propulsion. It should be clear that if instead of saying "Tommy ate his lunch" or "Tommy said to the Captain . . ." we reported what really happened, some pretty complicated explanations would have to be made.

Similarly, the term "cabin boy" is used because it is the closest in human meaning. Some vocations, like seafaring, are so demanding and so complex that they simply cannot be taught in classrooms; they have to be lived. A cabin boy is one who is learning such a vocation and paying for his instruction by performing certain menial, degrading, and unimportant tasks.

That describes Tommy, with one more similarity—the cabin boy of the sailing vessel was traditionally occupied after each whipping with preparing the mischief, or the stupidity, that earned him the next one.

Tommy, at the moment, had a whipping coming to him and was fighting a delaying action. He knew he couldn't escape eventual punishment, but he planned to hold it off as long as he could.

Floating alertly in one of the innumerable corridors of the ship, he watched as a dark wave sprang into being upon the glowing corridor wall and sped toward him. Instantly, Tommy was moving away from it, and at the same rate of speed.

The wave rumbled: "Tommy! Tommy Loy! Where *is* that obscenity boy?"

The wave moved on, rumbling wordlessly, and Tommy moved with it. Ahead of him was another wave, and another beyond that, and it was the same throughout all the corridors of the ship. Abruptly the waves reversed their direction. So did Tommy, barely in time. The waves not only carried the Captain's orders but scanned every corridor and compartment of the ten-mile ship. But as long as Tommy kept between the waves, the Captain could not see him.

The trouble was that Tommy could not keep this up forever, and he was being searched for by other lowly members of the crew. It took a long time to traverse all of those winding, interlaced passages, but it was a mathematical certainty that he would be caught eventually.

Tommy shuddered, and at the same time he squirmed with delight. He had interrupted the Old Man's sleep by a stench of a particularly noisome variety, one of which he had only lately found himself capable. The effect had been beautiful. In human terms, since Tommy's race communicated by odors, it was equivalent to setting off a firecracker beside a sleeper's ear.

Judging by the jerkiness of the scanning waves' motion, the Old Man was still unnerved.

"Tommy!" the waves rumbled. "Come out, you little piece of filth, or I'll smash you into a thousand separate stinks! By Spore, when I get hold of you—"

The corridor intersected another at this point, and Tommy seized his chance to duck into the new one. He had been working his way outward ever since his crime, knowing that the search parties would do the same. When he reached the outermost level of the ship, there would be a slight possibility of slipping back past the hunters—not much of a chance, but better than none.

He kept close to the wall. He was the smallest member of the crew—smaller than any of the other cabin boys, and less than half the size of an Ordinary; it was always possible that when he sighted one of the search party, he could get away before the crewman saw him. He was in a short connecting corridor now, but the scanning waves cycled endlessly, always turning back before he could escape into the next corridor. Tommy followed their movement patiently, while he listened to the torrent of abuse that poured from them. He snickered to himself. When the Old Man was angry, everybody suffered. The ship would be stinking from stem to stern by now.

Eventually the Captain forgot himself and the waves flowed

on around the next intersection. Tommy moved on. He was getting close to his goal by now; he could see a faint gleam of starshine up at the end of the corridor.

The next turn took him into it—and what Tommy saw through the semitransparent skin of the ship nearly made him falter and be caught. Not merely the fiery pinpoints of stars shone there, but a great, furious glow which could only mean that they were passing through a star system. It was the first time this had happened in Tommy's life, but of course it was nothing to the Captain, or even to most of the Ordinaries. Trust them, Tommy thought resentfully, to say nothing to him about it!

Now he knew he was glad he'd tossed that surprise at the Captain. If he hadn't, he wouldn't be here, and if he weren't here . . .

A waste capsule was bumping automatically along the corridor, heading for one of the exit pores in the hull. Tommy let it catch up to him, then englobed it, but it stretched him so tight that he could barely hold it. That was all to the good; the Captain wouldn't be likely to notice that anything had happened.

The hull was sealed, not to keep atmosphere inside, for there was none except by accident, but to prevent loss of liquid by evaporation. Metals and other mineral elements were replaceable; liquids and their constituents, in ordinary circumstances, were not.

Tommy rode the capsule to the exit sphincter, squeezed through, and instantly released it. Being polarized away from the ship's core, it shot into space and was lost. Tommy hugged the outer surface of the hull and gazed at the astonishing panorama that surrounded him.

There was the enormous black half-globe of space—Tommy's sky, the only one he had ever known. It was sprinkled with the familiar yet always changing patterns of the stars. By themselves, these were marvels enough for a child whose normal universe was one of ninety-foot corridors and chambers measuring, at most, three times as much. But Tommy hardly noticed them. Down to his right, reflecting brilliantly from the long, gentle curve of the greenish hull, was a blazing yellow-white glory that he could hardly look at. A star, the first one he had ever seen close at hand. Off to the left was a tiny, milky-blue disk that could only be a planet.

Tommy let go a shout, for the sheer pleasure of its thin, hollow smell. He watched the thin mist of particles spread lazily away from his body, faintly luminous against the jet blackness. He shivered a little, thickening his skin as much as he could. He could not stay long, he knew; he was radiating heat faster than he could absorb it from the sun or the ship's hull.

But he didn't want to go back inside, and not only because it meant being caught and punished. He didn't want to leave that great, dazzling jewel in the sky. For an instant he thought vaguely of the future time when he would be grown, the master of his own vessel, and could see the stars whenever he chose; but the picture was too far away to have any reality. Great Spore, that wouldn't happen for twenty thousand years!

Fifty yards away, an enormous dark spot on the hull, one of the ship's vision devices, swelled and darkened. Tommy looked up with interest. He could see nothing in that direction, but evidently the Captain had spotted something. Tommy watched and waited, growing colder every second, and after a long time he saw a new pinpoint of light spring into being. It grew steadily larger, turned fuzzy at one side, then became two linked dots, one hard and bright, the other misty.

Tommy looked down with sudden understanding, and saw that another wide area of the ship's hull was swollen and protruding. This one showed a pale color under the green and had a dark ring around it: it was a polarizer. The object he had seen must contain metal, and the Captain was bringing it in for fuel. Tommy hoped it was a big one; they had been short of metal ever since he could remember.

When he glanced up again, the object was much larger. He could see now that the bright part was hard and smooth, reflecting the light of the nearby sun. The misty part was a puzzler. It looked like a crewman's voice, seen against space—or the ion trail of a ship in motion. But was it possible for metal to be alive?

II

Leo Roget stared into the rear-view scanner and wiped beads of sweat from his brown, half-bald scalp. Flaming gas from the jets washed up toward him along the hull; he couldn't see much. But the huge dark ovoid they were headed for was still there, and it was getting bigger. He glanced futilely at the control board. The throttle was on full. They were going to crash in a little more than two minutes, and there didn't seem to be a single thing he could do about it.

He looked at Frances McMenamin, strapped into the acceleration harness beside his own. She said, "Try cutting off the jets, why don't you?"

Roget was a short, muscular man with thinning straight black hair and sharp brown eyes. McMenamin was slender and ash-blond, half an inch taller than he was, with one of those pale, exquisitely shaped faces that seem to be distributed equally among the very stupid and the very bright. Roget had never been perfectly sure which she was, although they had been companions for more than three years. That, in a way, was part of the reason they had taken this wild trip: she had made Roget uneasy, and he wanted to break away, and at the same time he didn't. So he had fallen in with her idea of a trip to Mars—"to get off by ourselves and think"— and here, Roget thought, they were, not thinking particularly.

He said, "You want us to crash quicker?"

"How do you know we will?" she countered. "It's the only thing we haven't tried. Anyhow, we'd be able to see where we're going, and that's more than we can do now."

"All right," said Roget, "all *right*." She was perfectly capable of giving him six more reasons, each screwier than the last, and then turning out to be right. He pulled the throttle back to zero, and the half-heard, half-felt roar of the jets died.

The ship jerked backward suddenly, yanking them against the couch straps, and then slowed.

Roget looked into the scanner again. They were approaching the huge object, whatever it was, at about the same rate as before. Maybe, he admitted unwillingly, a little slower.

Damn the woman! How could she possibly have figured that one out in advance?

"And," McMenamin added reasonably, "we'll save fuel for the takeoff."

Roget scowled at her. "If there is a takeoff," he said. "Whatever is pulling us down there isn't doing it to show off. What do we do—tell them that was a very impressive trick and we enjoyed it, but we've got to be leaving now?"

"We'll find out what's doing it," said McMenamin, "and stop it if we can. If we can't, the fuel won't do us any good anyway."

That was, if not Frances' most exasperating trick, at least high on the list. She had a habit of introducing your own own argument as if it were not only a telling point on her side, but something you had been too dense to see. Arguing with her was like swinging at someone who abruptly disappeared and then sandbagged you from behind.

Roget was fuming, but he said nothing. The greenish surface below was approaching more and more slowly, and now he felt a slight but definite tightening of the couch straps that could only mean deceleration. They were being maneuvered in for a landing as carefully and efficiently as if they were going it themselves.

A few seconds later, a green horizon line appeared in the direct-view ports, and they touched. Roget's and McMenamin's couches swung on their gimbals as the ship tilted slowly, bounced and came to rest.

Frances reached inside the wide collar of her pressure suit to smooth a ruffle that had got crumpled between the volcanic swell of her bosom and the front of the transparent suit. Watching her, Roget felt a sudden irrational flow of affection and—as usually happened—a simultaneous notification that his body disagreed with his mind's opinion of her. This trip, it had been tacitly agreed, was to be a kind of final trial period. At the end of it, either they would split up or decide to make it permanent, and up to now, Roget had been silently determined that it was going to be a split. Now he was just as sure that, provided they ever got to Mars or back to Earth, he was going to nail her for good.

He glanced at her face. She knew, all right, just as she'd known when he'd felt the other way. It should have irritated him, but he felt oddly pleased and comforted. He unstrapped himself, fastened down his helmet, and moved toward the airlock.

He stood on a pale-green, almost featureless surface that curved gently away in every direction. Where he stood, it was brilliantly lighted by the sun, and his shadow was sharp and as black as space. About two thirds of the way to the horizon, looking across the short axis of the ship, the sunlight stopped with knife-edge sharpness, and he could make out the rest only as a ghostly reflection of starlight.

Their ship was lying on its side, with the pointed stern apparently sunk a few inches into the green surface of the alien ship. He took a cautious step in that direction, and nearly floated past it before he could catch himself. His boot magnets had failed to grip. The metal of this hull—if it *was* metal—must be something that contained no iron.

The green hull was shot through with other colors here, and it rose in a curious, almost rectangular mound. At the center, just at the tip of the earth vessel's jets, there was a pale area; around that was a dark ring which lapped up over the side of the ship. He bent to examine it. It was in shadow, and he used his helmet light.

The light shone through the mottled green substance; he could see the skin of his own ship. It was pitted, corroding. As he watched, another pinpoint of corruption appeared on the shiny surface, and slowly grew.

Roget straightened up with an exclamation. His helmet phones asked, "What is it, Leo?"

He said, "Acid or something eating the hull. Wait a minute." He looked again at the pale and dark mottlings under the green surface. The center area was not attacking the ship's metal; that might be the muzzle of whatever instrument had been used to pull them down out of their orbit and hold them there. But if it was turned off now . . . He had to get the ship away from the dark ring that was destroying it. He couldn't fire the jets otherwise, because they were half buried; he'd blow the tubes if he tried.

He said, "You still strapped in?"

"Yes."

"All right, hold on." He stepped back to the center of the little ship, braced his corrugated boot soles against the hard green surface, and shoved.

The ship rolled. But it rolled like a top, around the axis of its pointed end. The dark area gave way before it, as if it were jelly-soft. The jets still pointed to the middle of the pale area, and the dark ring still lapped over them. Roget moved farther down and tried again, with the same result. The ship would move freely in every direction but the right one. The attracting power, clearly enough, was still on.

He straightened dejectedly and looked around. A few hundred yards away, he saw something he had noticed before, without attaching any significance to it; a six-foot egg, of some lighter, more translucent substance than the one on which it lay. He leaped toward it. It moved sluggishly away, trailing a cloud of luminous gas. A few seconds later he had it between his gloved hands. It squirmed, then ejected a thin spurt of vapor from its forward end. It was alive.

McMenamin's head was silhouetted in one of the forward ports. He said, "See this?"

"Yes! What is it?"

"One of the crew, I think. I'm going to bring it in. You work the airlock—it won't hold both of us at once."

". . . All right."

The huge egg crowded the cabin uncomfortably. It was pressed up against the rear wall, where it had rolled as soon as Frances had pulled it into the ship. The two human beings stood at the other side of the room, against the control panel, and watched it.

"No features," said Roget, "unless you count those markings on the surface. This thing isn't from anywhere in the solar system, Frances—it isn't even any order of evolution we ever heard of."

"I know," she said abstractedly. "Leo, is he wearing any protection against space that you can see?"

"No," said Roget. "That's *him*, not a spacesuit. Look, you can see halfway into him. But—"

Frances turned to look at him. "That's it," she said. "It means this is his natural element—space!"

Roget looked thoughtfully at the egg. "It makes sense," he said. "He's adapted for it, anyhow—ovoid, for a high volume-to-surface ratio. Tough outer shell. Moves by jet propulsion. It's hard to believe, because we've never run into a creature like him before, but I don't see why not. On earth there are organisms, plants, that can live and reproduce in boiling water, and others that can stand near-zero temperatures."

"He's a plant, too, you know," Frances put in.

Roget stared at her, then back at the egg. "That color, you mean? Chlorophyll. It could be."

"Must be," she corrected firmly. "How else would he live in a vacuum?" And then, distressedly, "Oh, what a smell!"

They looked at each other. It *had* been something monumental in the way of smells, though it had only lasted a fraction of a second. There had been a series of separate odors, all unfamiliar and all overpoweringly strong. At least a dozen of them, Roget thought; they had gone past too quickly to count.

"He did it before, outside, and I saw the vapor." He closed his helmet abruptly and motioned McMenamin to do the same. She frowned and shook her head. He opened his helmet again. "It might be poisonous!"

"I don't think so," said McMenamin. "Anyway, we've got to try something." She walked toward the green egg. It rolled away from her, and she went past it into the bedroom.

In a minute she reappeared, carrying an armload of plastic boxes and bottles. She came back to Roget and knelt on the floor, lining up the containers with their nipples toward the egg.

"What's this for?" Roget demanded. "Listen, we've got to figure some way of getting out of here. The ship's being eaten up—"

"Wait," said McMenamin. She reached down and squeezed three of the nipples quickly, one after the other. There was a tiny spray of face powder, then one of cologne (*Nuit Jupitérienne*), followed by a jet of good Scotch.

Then she waited. Roget was about to open his mouth when another blast of unfamiliar odors came from the egg. This time there were only three: two sweet ones and one sharp.

McMenamin smiled. "I'm going to name him Stinky," she said. She pressed the nipples again, in a different order. Scotch, face powder, *Nuit Jupitérienne*. The egg replied: sharp, sweet, sweet.

She gave him the remaining combination, and he echoed it; then she put a record cylinder on the floor and squirted the face powder. She added another cylinder and squeezed the cologne. She went along the line that way, releasing a smell for each cylinder until there were ten. The egg had responded, recognizably in some cases, to each one. Then she took away seven of the cylinders and looked expectantly at the egg.

The egg released a sharp odor.

"If ever we tell anybody," said Roget in an awed tone, "that you taught a six-foot Easter egg to count to ten by selective flatulence—"

"Hush, fool," she said. "This is a tough one."

She lined up three cylinders, waited for the sharp odor, then added six more to make three rows of three. The egg obliged with a penetrating smell which was a good imitation of citron extract, Frances' number nine. He followed it immediately with another of his own rapid, complicated series of smells.

"He gets it," said McMenamin. "I think he just told us that three times three are nine." She stood up. "You go out first, Leo. I'll put him out after you and then follow. There's something more we've got to show him before we let him go."

Roget followed orders. When the egg came out and kept on going, he stepped in its path and held it back. Then he moved away, hoping the thing would get the idea that they weren't trying to force it but wanted it to stay. The egg wobbled indecisively for a moment and then stayed where it was. Frances came out the next minute, carrying one of the plastic boxes and a flashlight.

"My nicest powder," she said regretfully, "but it was the

only thing I could find enough of." She clapped her gloved hands together sharply, with the box between them. It burst, and a haze of particles spread around them, glowing faintly in the sunlight.

The egg was still waiting, somehow giving the impression that it was watching them alertly. McMenamin flicked on the flashlight and pointed it at Roget. It made a clear, narrow path in the haze of dispersed particles. Then she turned it on herself, on the ship, and finally upward, toward the tiny blue disk that was Earth. She did it twice more, then stepped back toward the airlock, and Roget followed her.

They stood watching as Tommy scurried off across the hull, squeezed himself into it and disappeared.

"That was impressive," Roget said. "But I wonder just how much good it's going to do us."

"He knows we're alive, intelligent, friendly, and that we come from Earth," said McMenamin thoughtfully. "Or, anyhow, we did our best to tell him. That's all we can do. Maybe he won't want to help us; maybe he can't. But it's up to him now."

III

The mental state of Tommy, as he dived through the hull of the ship and into the nearest radial corridor, would be difficult to describe fully to any human being. He was the equivalent of a very small boy—that approximation still holds good—and he had the obvious reactions to novelty and adventure. But there was a good deal more. He had seen living, intelligent beings of an unfamiliar shape and substance, who lived in metal and had some connection with one of those enormous, enigmatic ships called planets, which no captain of his own race dared approach.

And yet Tommy *knew*, with all the weight of knowledge accumulated, codified and transmitted over a span measured in billions of years, that there was no other intelligent race than his own in the entire universe, that metal, though life-giving, could not itself be alive, and that no living creature, having the ill luck to be spawned aboard a planet, could ever hope to escape so tremendous a gravitational field.

The final result of all this was that Tommy desperately wanted to go somewhere by himself and think. But he couldn't; he had to keep moving, in time with the scanning waves along the corridor, and he had to give all his mental energy to the problem of slipping past the search party.

The question was—how long had he been gone? If they had reached the hull while he was inside the metal thing, they might have looked for him outside and concluded that he had somehow slipped past them, back to the center of the ship. In that case, they would probably be working their way back, and he had only to follow them to the axis and hide in a chamber as soon as they left it. But if they were still working outward, his chances of escape were almost nil. And now it seemed more important to escape than it had before.

There was one possibility which Tommy, who, in most circumstances, would try anything, hated to think about. Fuel lines—tubes carrying the rushing, radiant ion vapor that powered the ship—adjoined many of these corridors, and it was certain that if he dared to enter one, he would be perfectly safe from detection as long as he remained in it. But, for one thing, these lines radiated from the ship's axis and none of them would take him where he wanted to go. For another, they were the most dangerous places aboard ship. Older crew members sometimes entered them to make emergency repairs, but they got out as quickly as they could. Tommy did not know how long he could survive there; he had an unpleasant conviction that it would not be long.

Only a few yards up the corridor was the sealed sphincter which gave entrance to such a tube. Tommy looked at it indecisively as the motion of the scanning waves brought him nearer. He had still not made up his mind when he caught a flicker reflected around the curve of the corridor behind him.

Tommy squeezed himself closer to the wall and watched the other end of the corridor approach with agonizing slowness. If he could only get around that corner . . .

The flicker of motion was repeated, and then he saw a thin rind of green poke into view. There was no more time to consider entering the fuel line, no time to let the scanning waves' movement carry him around the corner. Tommy put on full speed, cutting across the next wave and down the cross-corridor ahead.

Instantly the Captain's voice shouted from the wall, "Ah! Was that him, the dirty scut? After him, lads!"

Tommy glanced behind as he turned another corner, and his heart sank. It was no cabin boy who was behind him, or even an Ordinary, but a Third Mate—so huge that he filled nearly half the width of the corridor, and so powerful that Tommy, in comparison, was like a boy on a bicycle racing an express train.

He turned another corner, realizing in that instant that he was as good as caught: the new corridor ahead of him stretched straight and without a break for three hundred yards. As he flashed down it, the hulk of the Mate appeared around the bend behind.

The Mate was coming up with terrifying speed, and Tommy had time for only one last desperate spurt. Then the other body slammed with stunning force against his, and he was held fast.

As they coasted to a halt, the Captain's voice rumbled from the wall, "*That's* it, Mister. Hold him where I can see him!"

The scanning areas were stationary now. The Mate moved Tommy forward until he was squarely in range of the nearest.

Tommy squirmed futilely. The Captain said, "*There's* our little jokester. It's a pure pleasure to see you again, Tommy. What—no witty remarks? Your humor all dried up?"

Tommy gasped, "Hope you enjoyed your nap, Captain."

"Very good," said the Captain with heavy sarcasm. "Oh, *very* entertaining, Tommy. Now would you have anything more to say, before I put the whips to you?"

Tommy was silent.

The Captain said to the Mate, "Nice work, Mister. You'll get extra rations for this."

The Mate spoke for the first time, and Tommy recognized his high, affected voice. It was George Adkins, who had recently spored and was so proud of the new life inside his body that there was no living with him. George said prissily, "Thank you, sir, I'm sure. Of course, I really shouldn't have exerted myself the way I just did, in my state."

"Well, you'll be compensated for it," the Captain said testily. "Now take the humorist down to Assembly Five. We'll have a little ceremony there."

"Yes, sir," said the Mate distantly. He moved off, shoving Tommy ahead of him, and dived into the first turning that led downward.

They moved along in silence for the better part of a mile, crossing from one lesser passage to another until they reached a main artery that led directly to the center of the ship. The scanning waves were still stationary, and they were moving so swiftly that there was no danger of being overheard. Tommy said politely, "You won't let them be too hard on me, will you, sir?"

The Mate did not reply for a moment. He had been baited by Tommy's mock courtesy before, and he was as wary as his limited intelligence allowed. Finally he said, "You'll get no more than what's coming to you, young Tom."

"Yes, sir. I know that, sir. I'm sorry I made you exert yourself, sir, in your condition and all."

"You should be," said the Mate stiffly, but his voice betrayed his pleasure. It was seldom enough that even a cabin boy showed a decent interest in the Mate's prospective parenthood. "They're moving about, you know," he added, unbending a little.

"Are they, sir? Oh, you must be careful of yourself, sir. How many are there, please, sir?"

"Twenty-eight," said the Mate, as he had on every possible occasion for the past two weeks. "Strong and healthy—so far."

"That's remarkable, sir!" cried Tommy. "Twenty-eight! If I might be so bold, sir, you ought to be careful of what you eat. Is the Captain going to give you your extra rations out of that mass he just brought in topside, sir?"

"I'm sure *I* don't know."

"Gosh!" exclaimed Tommy. "I wish I could be sure . . ."

He let the pause grow. Finally the Mate said querulously, "What do you mean? Is there anything wrong with the metal?"

"I don't really know, sir, but it isn't like any we ever had before. That is," Tommy added, "since I was spored, sir."

"Naturally," said the Mate. "*I've* eaten all kinds myself, you know."

"Yes, sir. But doesn't it usually come in ragged shapes, sir, and darkish?"

"Of course it does. Everybody knows that. Metal is non-living, and only living things have regular shapes."

"Yes, sir. But I was topside, sir, while I was trying to get away, and I saw this metal. It's quite regular, except for some knobs at one end, sir, and it's as smooth as you are, sir, and shiny. If you'll forgive me, sir, it didn't look at all appetizing to me."

"Nonsense," said the Mate uncertainly. "Nonsense," he repeated, in a stronger tone. "You must have been mistaken. Metal can't be alive."

"That's just what I thought, sir," said Tommy excitedly. "But there are live things in this metal, sir. I saw them. And the metal wasn't just floating along the way it's supposed to, sir. I saw it when the Captain brought it down, and . . . But I'm afraid you'll think I'm lying, sir, if I tell you what it was doing."

"Well, what was it doing?"

"I swear I saw it, sir," Tommy went on. "The Captain will tell you the same thing, sir, if you ask him—he must have noticed."

"Sterilize it all, what *was* it doing?"

Tommy lowered his voice. "There was an ion trail shooting from it, sir. It was trying to get away!"

While the Mate was trying to absorb that, they reached the bottom of the corridor and entered the vast globular space of Assembly Five, lined with crewmen waiting to witness the punishment of Tommy Loy.

This was not going to be any fun at all, thought Tommy, but at least he had paid back the Third Mate in full measure. The Mate, for the moment, at any rate, was not taking any joy in his promised extra rations.

When it was over, Tommy huddled in a corner of the crew compartment where they had tossed him, bruised and smarting in every nerve, shaken by the beating he had undergone. The pain was still rolling through him in faint, uncontrollable waves, and he winced at each one, in spite of himself, as though it were the original blow.

In the back of his mind, the puzzle of the metal ship was still calling, but the other experience was too fresh, the remembered images too vivid.

The Captain had begun, as always, by reciting the Creed.

In the beginning was the Spore, and the Spore was alone.

(And the crew: *Praised be the Spore!*)

Next there was light, and the light was good. Yea, good for the Spore and the Spore's First Children.

(*Praised be they!*)

But the light grew evil in the days of the Spore's Second Children.

(*Woe unto them!*)

And the light cast them out. Yea, exiled were they, into the darkness and the Great Deep.

(*Pity for the outcasts in the Great Deep!*)

Tommy had mumbled his responses with the rest of them, thinking rebellious thoughts. There was nothing evil about light; they lived by it still. What must have happened—the Captain himself admitted as much when he taught history and natural science classes—was that the earliest ancestors of the race, spawned in the flaming heart of the Galaxy, had grown too efficient for their own good.

They had specialized, more and more, in extracting energy from starlight and the random metal and other elements they encountered in space; and at last they absorbed, willy-nilly, more than they could use. So they had moved, gradually and naturally, over many generations, out from that intensely radiating region into the "Great Deep"—the universe of thinly scattered stars. And the process had continued, inevitably; as the level of available energy fell, their absorption of it grew more and more efficient.

Now, not only could they never return to their birthplace, but they could not even approach a single sun as closely as some planets did. Therefore the planets, and the stars themselves, were objects of fear. That was natural and sensible. But why did they have to continue this silly ritual, invented by some half-evolved, superstitious ancestor, of "outcasts" and "evil"?

The Captain finished:

Save us from the Death that lies in the Great Deep . . .

(The creeping Death that lies in the Great Deep!)

And keep our minds pure . . .

(As pure as the light in the days of the Spore, blessed be He!)

And our course straight . . .

(As straight as the light, brothers!)

That we may meet our lost brothers again in the Day of Reuniting.

(Speed that day!)

Then the pause, the silence that grew until it was like the silence of space. At last the Captain spoke again, pronouncing judgment against Tommy, ending, "Let him be whipped!"

Tommy tensed himself, thickening his skin, drawing his body into the smallest possible compass. Two husky Ordinaries seized him and tossed him at a third. As Tommy floated across the room, the crewman pressed himself tightly against the wall, drawing power from it until he could contain no more. And as Tommy neared him, he discharged it in a crackling arc that filled Tommy's body with the pure essence of pain, and sent him hurtling across the chamber to the next shock, and the next, and the next.

Until the Captain had boomed, "Enough!" and they had carried him out and left him here alone.

He heard the voices of crewmen as they drew their rations. One of them was grumbling about the taste, and another, sounding happily bloated, was telling him to shut up and eat, that metal was metal.

That would be the new metal, however much of it had been absorbed by now, mingled with the old in the reservoir. Tommy wondered briefly how much of it there was, and whether the alien ship—if it *was* a ship—could repair even a little damage to itself. But that assumed life in the metal, and in spite of what he had seen, Tommy couldn't believe in it. It seemed beyond question, though, that there were living things inside the metal; and when the metal was gone, how would they live?

Tommy imagined himself set adrift from the ship, alone in space, radiating more heat than his tiny volume could absorb. He shuddered.

He thought again of the problem that had obsessed him ever since he had seen the alien, five-pointed creatures in the metal ship. Intelligent life was supposed to be sacred. That was part of the Creed, and it was stated in a sloppy, poetic way like the rest of it, but it made a certain kind of sense. No crewman or captain had the right to destroy another for his benefit, because the same heredity was in them all. They were all potentially the same, none better than another.

And you ate metal, because metal was nonliving and certainly not intelligent. But if that stopped being true . . .

Tommy felt he was missing something. Then he had it: In the alien ship, trying to talk to the creatures that lived in metal, he had been scared almost scentless—but underneath the fright and the excitement, he had felt wonderful. It had been, he realized suddenly, like the mystic completion that was supposed to come when all the straight lines met, in the "Day of Reuniting"—when all the far-flung ships, parted for all the billions of years of their flight, came together at last. It was talking to someone different from yourself.

He wanted to talk again to the aliens, teach them to form their uncouth sounds into words, learn from them. . . . Vague images swirled in his mind. They were products of an utterly different line of evolution. Who knew what they might be able to teach him?

And now the dilemma took shape. If his own ship absorbed the metal of theirs, they would die; therefore he would have to make the Captain let them go. But if he somehow managed to set them free, they would leave and he would never see them again.

A petty officer looked into the cubicle and said, "All right, Loy, out of it. You're on garbage detail. You eat after you work, if there's anything left. Lively, now!"

Tommy moved thoughtfully out into the corridor, his pain almost forgotten. The philosophical problems presented by the alien ship, too, having no apparent solution, were receding from his mind. A new thought was taking their place, one that made him glow inside with the pure rapture of the devoted practical jokester.

The whipping he was certainly going to get—and, so soon after the last offense, it would be a beauty—scarcely entered his mind.

IV

Roget climbed in, opening his helmet, and sat down warily in the acceleration couch. He didn't look at the woman.

McMenamin said quietly, "Bad?"

"Not good. The outer skin's gone all across that area, and it's eating into the lead sheathing. The tubes are holding up pretty well, but they'll be next."

"We've done as much as we can, by rolling the ship around?"

"Just about. I'll keep at it, but I don't see how it can be more than a few hours before the tubes go. Then we're cooked, whatever your fragrant little friend does."

He stood up abruptly and climbed over the slanting wall which was now their floor, to peer out the direct-view port. He swore, slowly and bitterly. "You try the radio again while I was out?" he asked.

"Yes." She did not bother to add that there had been no response. Here, almost halfway between the orbits of earth and Mars, they were hopelessly out of touch. A ship as small as theirs couldn't carry equipment enough to bridge the distance.

Roget turned around, said, "By God—" and then clenched his jaw and strode out of the room. McMenamin heard him walk through the bedroom and clatter around in the storage compartment behind.

In a few moments he was back with a welding torch in his hand. "Should have thought of this before," he said. "I don't know what'll happen if I cut into that hull—damn thing may explode, for all I know—but it's better than sitting doing nothing." He put his helmet down with a bang and his voice came tinnily in her helmet receiver. "Be back in a minute."

"Be careful," McMenamin said again.

Roget closed the outer lock door behind him and looked at the ravaged hull of the ship. The metal had been eaten away in a broad band all around the ship, just above the tail, as if a child had bitten around the small end of a pear. In places the clustered rocket tubes showed through. He felt a renewed surge of anger, with fear deep under it.

A hundred years ago, he reminded himself, the earliest space voyagers had encountered situations as bad as this one, maybe worse. But Roget was a city man, bred for city virtues. He didn't, he decided, know quite how to feel or act. What were you supposed to do when you were about to die, fifteen million miles from home? Try to calm McMenamin—who was dangerously calm already—or show your true nobility by making one of those deathbed speeches you read in the popular histories? What about suggesting a little suicide pact? There was nothing in the ship that would give them a cleaner death than the one ahead of them. About all he could do would be to stab Frances, then himself, with a screwdriver.

Her voice said in the earphones, "You all right?"

He said, "Sure. Just going to try it." He lowered himself to the green surface, careful not to let his knees touch the dark, corrosive area. The torch was a small, easily manageable tool. He pointed the snout at the dark area where it lapped up over the hull, turned the switch on and pressed the button. Flame leaped out, washing over the dark surface. Roget felt the heat through his suit. He turned off the torch to see what effect it had had.

There was a deep, charred pit in the dark stuff, and it seemed to him that it had pulled back a little from the area it was attacking. It was more than he had expected. Encouraged, he tried again.

There was a sudden tremor under him and he leaped nervously to his feet, just in time to avoid the corrosive wave as it rolled under him. For a moment he was only conscious of the thick metal of his boot soles and the thinness of the fabric that covered his knees; then, as he was about to step back out of the way, he realized that it was not only the dark ring that had expanded, that was still expanding.

He moved jerkily—too late—as the pale center area swept

toward and under him. Then he felt as if he had been struck by a mighty hammer.

His ears rang, and there was a mist in front of his eyes. He blinked, tried to raise an arm. It seemed to be stuck fast at the wrist and elbow. Panicked, he tried to push himself away, and couldn't. As his vision cleared, he saw that he was spread-eagled on the pale disk that had spread out under him. The metal collars of his wrist and elbow joints, all the metal parts of his suit, were held immovably. The torch lay a few inches away from his right hand.

For a few moments, incredulously, Roget still tried to move. Then he stopped and lay in the prison of his suit, looking at the greenish-cream surface under his helmet.

Frances' voice said abruptly, "Leo, is anything wrong?"

Roget felt an instant relief that left him shaken and weak. His forehead was cold. He said after a moment, "Pulled a damn fool trick, Frances. Come out and help me if you can."

He heard a click as her helmet went down. He added anxiously, "But don't come near the pale part, or you'll get caught too."

After a while she said, "Darling, I can't think of anything to do."

Roget was feeling calmer, somehow not much afraid anymore. He wondered how much oxygen was left in his suit. Not more than an hour, he thought. He said, "I know. I can't, either."

Later he called, "Frances?"

"Yes?"

"Roll the ship once in a while, will you? Might get through to the wiring or something, otherwise."

". . . All right."

After that, they didn't talk. There was a great deal to be said, but it was too late to say it.

V

Tommy was on garbage detail with nine other unfortunates. It was a messy, hard, unpleasant business, fit only for a cabin boy—collecting waste from the compartment and corridor receptacles and pressing it into standard capsule shapes, then hauling it to the nearest polarizer. But Tommy, under the suspicious eye of the petty officer in charge, worked with an apparent total absorption until they had cleaned out their section of the six inmost levels and were well into the seventh.

This was the best stragegic place for Tommy's departure, since it was about midway from axis to hull, and the field of operations of any pursuit was correspondingly broadened. Also, the volume in which they labored had expanded wedgewise as they climbed, and the petty officer, though still determined to watch Tommy, could no longer keep him constantly in view.

Tommy saw the officer disappear around the curve of the corridor, and kept on working busily. He was still at it, with every appearance of innocence and industry, when the officer abruptly popped into sight again about three seconds later.

The officer stared at him with baffled disapproval and said unreasonably, "Come on, come on, Loy. Don't slack."

"Right," said Tommy, and scurried faster.

A moment later Third Mate Adkins hove majestically into view. The petty officer turned respectfully to face him.

"Keeping young Tom well occupied, I see," said the Mate.

"Yes, sir," said the officer. "Appears to be a reformed character, now, sir. Must have learned a lesson, one way or another."

"Ha!" said the Mate. "Very good. Oh, Loy, you might be interested in this—the Captain himself has told me that the new metal is perfectly all right. Unusually rich, in fact. I've had my first ration already—very good it was, too—and I'm going to get my extras in half an hour or so. Well, good appetite, all." And, while the lesser crewmen clustered against the walls to give him room, he moved haughtily off down the corridor.

Tommy kept on working as fast as he could. He was draining energy he might need later, but it was necessary to quiet the petty officer's suspicions entirely, in order to give himself a decent start. In addition, his artist's soul demanded it. Tommy, in his own way, was a perfectionist.

Third Mate Adkins was due to get his extras in about half an hour, and if Tommy knew the Captain's habits, the Captain would be taking his first meal from the newly replenished reservoir at about the same time. That set the deadline. Before the half hour was up, Tommy would have to cut off the flow of the new metal, so that stomachs which had been gurgling in anticipation would remain desolately void until the next windfall.

The Mate, in spite of his hypochondria, was a glutton. With any luck, this would make him bitter for a month. And the Old Man—but it was better not to dwell on that.

The petty officer hung around irresolutely for another ten minutes, then dashed off down the corridor to attend to the rest of his detail. Without wasting a moment, Tommy dropped the capsule he had just collected and shot away in the other direction.

The rest of the cabin boys, as fearful of Tommy as they were of constituted authority, would not dare to raise an outcry until they spotted the officer coming back. The officer, because of the time he had wasted in watching Tommy, would have to administer a thorough lecture on slackness to the rest of the detail before he returned.

Tommy had calculated his probable margin to a nicety, and it was enough, barring accidents, to get him safely away. Nevertheless, he turned and twisted from one system of corridors to another, carefully confusing his trail, before he set himself to put as much vertical distance behind him as he could.

This part of the game had to be accomplished in a fury of action, for he was free to move in the corridors only until the Captain was informed that he was loose again. After that, he had to play hounds and hares with the moving strips through which the Captain could see him.

When the time he had estimated was three quarters gone, Tommy slowed and came to a halt. He inspected the corridor wall minutely, and found the almost imperceptible trace that showed where the scanning wave nearest him had stopped. He jockeyed his body clear of it, and then waited. He still had a good distance to cover before he dared play his trump, but it was not safe to move now; he had to wait for the Captain's move.

It came soon enough: the scanning waves erupted into simultaneous motion and anger. "Tommy!" they bellowed. "Tommy Loy! Come back, you unmentionable excrescence, or by Spore you'll regret it! Tommy!"

Moving between waves, Tommy waited patiently until their motion carried him from one corridor to another. The Captain's control over the waves was not complete: in some corridors they moved two steps upward for one down, in others the reverse. When he got into a downward corridor, Tommy scrambled out of it again as soon as he could and started over.

Gradually, with many false starts, he worked his way up to the thirteenth level, one level short of the hull.

Now came the hard part. This time he had to enter the fuel lines, not only for sure escape, but to gather the force he needed. And for the first time in his life, Tommy hesitated before something that he had set himself to do.

Death was a phenomenon that normally touched each member of Tommy's race only once—only captains died, and they died alone. For lesser members of the crew, there was almost no mortal danger; the ship protected them. But Tommy knew what death was, and as the sealed entrance to the fuel line swung into view, he knew that he faced it.

He made himself small, as he had under the lash. He broke the seal. Quickly, before the following wave could catch him, he thrust himself through the sphincter.

The blast of ions gripped him, flung him forward, hurting him like a hundred whips. Desperately he held himself together, thickening his insulating shell against that deadly flux of energy; but still his body absorbed it, till he felt a horrid fullness.

The walls of the tube fled past him, barely perceptible in the rush of glowing haze. Tommy held in that growing tautness with his last strength, meanwhile looking for an exit. He neither knew nor cared whether he had reached his goal; he had to get out or die.

He saw a dim oval on the wall ahead, hurled himself at it, clung, and forced his body through.

He was in a horizontal corridor, just under the hull. He drank the blessed coolness of it for an instant, before moving to the nearest sphincter. Then he was out, under the velvet-black sky and the diamond blaze of stars.

He looked around. The pain was fading now; he felt only an atrocious bloatedness that tightened his skin and made all his movements halting. Forward of him, up the long shallow curve of the hull, he could see the alien ship, and the two five-pointed creatures beside it. Carefully, keeping a few feet between himself and the hull, he headed toward it.

One of the creatures was sprawled flat on the polarizer that had brought its ship down. The other, standing beside it, turned as Tommy came near, and two of its upper three points moved in an insane fashion that made Tommy feel ill. He looked away quickly and moved past them, till he was directly over the center of the polarizer and only a few inches away.

Then, with a sob of relief, he released the energy his body had stored. In one thick, white bolt, it sparked to the polarizer's center.

Shaken and spent, Tommy floated upward and surveyed what he had done. The muzzle of the polarizer was contracting, puckering at the center, the dark corrosive ring following it in. So much energy, applied in one jolt, must have shorted and paralyzed it all the way back to the ship's nerve center. The Captain, Tommy thought wryly, would be jumping now!

And he wasn't done yet. Tommy took one last look at the aliens and their ship. The sprawled one was up now, and the two of them had their upper points twined around each other in a nauseating fashion. Then they parted suddenly, and, facing Tommy, wiggled their free points. Tommy moved purposefully off across the width of the ship, heading for the other two heavy-duty polarizers.

He had to go in again through that hell not once more, but twice. Though his nerves shrank from the necessity, there was no way of avoiding it. For the ship could not alter its course, except by allowing itself to be attracted by a sun or other large body—which was unthinkable—but it could rotate at the Captain's will. The aliens were free now, but the Captain had only to spin ship in order to snare them again.

Four miles away, Tommy found the second polarizer. He backed away a carefully calculated distance before he reentered the hull. At least he could know in advance how far he had to go—and he knew now, too, that the energy he had stored the first time had been adequate twice over. He rested a few moments; then, like a diver plunging into a torrent, he thrust himself into the fuel line.

. He came out again, shuddering with pain, and pushed himself through the exit. He felt as bloated as he had before. The charge of energy was not as great, but Tommy knew that he was weakening. This time, when he discharged over the polarizer and watched it contract into a tiny, puckered mass, he felt as if he could never move again, let alone expose himself once more to that tunnel of flame.

The stars, he realized dully, were moving in slow, ponderous arcs over his head. The Captain was spinning ship. Tommy sank to the hull and lay motionless, watching half attentively for a sight of the alien ship.

There it was, a bright dot haloed by the flame of its exhaust. It swung around slowly, gradually, with the rest of the firmament, growing smaller slowly.

"He'll get them before they're out of range," Tommy thought. He watched as the bright dot climbed overhead, began to fall on the other side.

The Captain had one polarizer left. It would be enough.

Wearily Tommy rose and followed the bright star. It was not a joke any longer. He would willingly have gone inside to the bright, warm, familiar corridors that led downward to safety and deserved punishment. But somehow he could not bear to think of those fascinating creatures—those wonderful playthings—going to fill the Captain's fat belly.

Tommy followed the ship until he could see the pale gleam of the functioning polarizer. Then he crawled through the hull once more, and again he found a sealed entrance to the fuel tube. He did not let himself think about it. His mind was numb already, and he pushed himself through uncaring.

This time it was worse than ever before; he had not dreamed that it could be so bad. His vision dimmed and he could barely see the exit, or feel its pressure, when he dragged himself out. Lurching drunkenly, he passed a scanning wave on his way to the hull sphincter, and heard the Captain's voice explode.

Outside, ragged black patches obscured his vision of the stars. The pressure inside him pressed painfully outward, again and again, and each time he held it back. Then he felt rather than saw that he was over the pale disk, and, as he let go the bolt, he lost consciousness.

When his vision cleared, the alien ship was still above him, alarmingly close. The Captain must have had it almost reeled in again, he thought, when he had let go that last charge.

Flaming, it receded into the Great Deep, and he watched it go until it disappeared.

He felt a great peace and a great weariness. The tiny blue disk that was a planet had moved its apparent position a little nearer its star. The aliens were going back there, to their unimaginable home, and Tommy's ship was forging onward into new depths of darkness—toward the edge of the Galaxy and the greatest Deep.

He moved to the nearest sphincter as the cold bit at him. His spirits lifted suddenly as he thought of those three stabs of energy, equally spaced around the twelve-mile perimeter of the ship. The Captain would be utterly speechless with rage, he thought, like an aged martinet who had had his hands painfully slapped by a small boy.

For, as we warned you, the Captain was not precisely a captain, nor the ship precisely a ship. Ship and captain were one and the same, hive and queen bee, castle and lord.

In effect, Tommy had circumnavigated the skipper.

THE COLOSSUS
OF YLOURGNE
by Clark Ashton Smith

*When we asked several fantasy experts for recom-
mendations of good giant stories we might have
missed, all mentioned the following eerie tale of
necromancy by Clark Ashton Smith (1893–1961).
It is indeed a vivid example of the strengths and
weaknesses of this neglected writer—if only some
Maxwell Perkins could have forced him to limit
his vocabulary to one obscure word per page,
how popular his imagination might have made
him.*

The Thrice-infamous Nathaire, alchemist, astrologer and necromancer, with his ten devil-given pupils, had departed very
suddenly and under circumstances of strict secrecy from the
town of Vyones. It was widely thought, among the people of
that vicinage, that his departure had been prompted by a
salutary fear of ecclesistical thumbscrews and fagots. Other
wizards, less notorious than he, had already gone to the stake
during a year of unusual inquisitory zeal; and it was well
known that Nathaire had incurred the reprobation of the
Church. Few, therefore, considered the reason of his going a
mystery; but the means of transit which he had employed, as
well as the destination of the sorcerer and his pupils, were
regarded as more than problematic.

A thousand dark and superstitious rumors were abroad;

and passers made the sign of the Cross when they neared the tall, gloomy house which Nathaire had built in blasphemous proximity to the great cathedral and had filled with a furniture of Satanic luxury and strangeness. Two daring thieves, who had entered the mansion when the fact of its desertion became well established, reported that much of this furniture as well as the books and other paraphernalia of Nathaire had seemingly departed with its owner, doubtless to the same fiery bourn. This served to augment the unholy mystery: for it was patently impossible that Nathaire and his ten apprentices, with several cartloads of household belongings, could have passed the ever-guarded city gates in any legitimate manner without the knowledge of the custodians.

It was said by the more devout and religious moiety that the Archfiend, with a legion of bat-winged assistants, had borne them away bodily at moonless midnight. There were clerics, and also reputable burghers, who professed to have seen the flight of dark, manlike shapes upon the blotted stars together with others that were not men, and to have heard the wailing cries of the hell-bound crew as they passed in an evil cloud over the roofs and city walls.

Others believed that the sorcerers had transported themselves from Vyones through their own diabolic arts, and had withdrawn to some unfrequented fastness where Nathaire, who had long been in feeble health, could hope to die in such peace and serenity as might be enjoyed by one who stood between the flames of the *auto-da-fé* and those of Abaddon. It was thought that he had lately cast his own horoscope, for the first time in his fifty-odd years, and had read therein an impending conjunction of disastrous planets, signifying early death.

Others still, among whom were certain rival astrologers and enchanters, said that Nathaire had retired from the public view merely that he might commune without interruption with various coadjutive demons; and thus might weave, unmolested, the black spells of a supreme and lycanthropic malice. These spells, they hinted, would in due time be visited upon Vyones and perhaps upon the entire region of Averoigne; and would no doubt take the form of a fearsome pestilence, or a wholesale invultuation, or a realm-wide incursion of succubi and incubi.

Amid the seething of strange rumors, many half-forgotten tales were recalled, and new legends were created overnight. Much was made of the obscure nativity of Nathaire and his dubitable wanderings before he had settled, six years previous, in Vyones. People said that he was fiend-begotten, like the fabled Merlin: his father being no less a personage than Alastor, demon of revenge; and his mother a deformed and dwarfish sorceress. From the former, he had taken his spitefulness and malignity; from the latter, his squat, puny physique.

He had traveled in Orient lands, and had learned from Egyptian or Saracenic masters the unhallowed art of necromancy, in whose practice he was unrivaled. There were black whispers anent the use he had made of long-dead bodies, of fleshless bones, and the service he had wrung from buried men that the angel of doom alone could lawfully raise up. He had never been popular, though many had sought his advice and assistance in the furthering of their own more or less dubious affairs. Once, in the third year after his coming to Vyones, he had been stoned in public because of his bruited necromancies, and had been permanently lamed by a well-directed cobble. This injury, it was thought, he had never forgiven; and he was said to return the antagonism of the clergy with the hellish hatred of an Antichrist.

Apart from the sorcerous evils and abuses of which he was commonly suspected, he had long been looked upon as a corrupter of youth. Despite his minikin stature, his deformity and ugliness, he possessed a remarkable power, a mesmeric persuasion; and his pupils, whom he was said to have plunged into bottomless and ghoulish iniquities, were young men of the most brilliant promise. On the whole, his vanishment was regarded as a quite providential riddance.

Among the people of the city there was one man who took no part in the somber gossip and lurid speculation. This man was Gaspard du Nord, himself a student of the proscribed sciences, who had been numbered for a year among the pupils of Nathaire but had chosen to withdraw quietly from the master's household after learning the enormities that would attend his further initiation. He had, however, taken with him much rare and peculiar knowledge, together with a certain insight into the baleful powers and night-dark motives of the necromancer.

Because of this knowledge and insight, Gaspard preferred to remain silent when he heard of Nathaire's departure. Also, he did not think it well to revive the memory of his own past pupilage. Alone with his books, in a sparsely furnished attic, he frowned above a small, oblong mirror, framed with an arabesque of golden vipers, that had once been the property of Nathaire.

It was not the reflection of his own comely and youthful though subtly lined face that caused him to frown. Indeed, the mirror was of another kind than that which reflects the features of the gazer. In its depths, for a few instants, he had beheld a strange and ominous-looking scene, whose participants were known to him but whose location he could not recognize or orientate. Before he could study it closely, the mirror clouded as if with the rising of alchemic fumes, and he had seen no more.

This clouding, he reflected, could mean only one thing: Nathaire had known himself watched and had put forth a counterspell that rendered the clairvoyant mirror useless. It was the realization of this fact, together with the brief, sinister glimpse of Nathaire's present activities, that troubled Gaspard and caused a chill horror to mount slowly in his mind: a horror that had not yet found a palpable form or a name.

2

The departure of Nathaire and his pupils occurred in the late spring of 1281, during the interlunar dark. Afterward a new moon waxed above the flowery fields and bright-leafed woods, and waned in ghostly silver. With its waning, people began to talk of other magicians and fresher mysteries.

Then, in the moon-deserted nights of early summer, there came a series of disappearances far more unnatural and inexplicable than that of the dwarfish, malignant sorcerer.

It was found one day, by gravediggers who had gone early to their toil in a cemetery outside the walls of Vyones, that no less than six newly occupied graves had been opened, and the bodies, which were those of reputable citizens, removed. On closer examination, it became all too evident that this removal had not been effected by robbers. The coffins, which lay asant or stood protruding upright from the mold, offered all the appearance of having been shattered from within as if by the use of extrahuman strength; and the fresh earth itself was upheaved, as if the dead men, in some awful, untimely resurrection, had actually *dug* their way to the surface.

The corpses had vanished utterly, as if hell had swallowed them; and, as far as could be learned, there were no eyewitnesses of their fate. In those devil-ridden times, only one explanation of the happening seemed credible: demons had entered the graves and had taken bodily possession of the dead, compelling them to arise and go forth.

To the dismay and horror of all Averoigne, the strange vanishment was followed with appalling promptness by many others of a like sort. It seemed as if an occult, resistless summons had been laid upon the dead. Nightly, for a period of two weeks, the cemeteries of Vyones and also those of other towns, of villages and hamlets, gave up a ghastly quota of their tenants. From brazen-bolted tombs, from common charnels, from shallow, unconsecrated trenches, from the marble-lidded vaults of churches and cathedrals, the weird exodus went on without cessation.

Worse than this, if possible, there were newly ceremented corpses that leapt from their biers or catafalques, and disregarding the horrified watchers, ran with great bounds of automatic frenzy into the night, never to be seen again by those who lamented them.

In every case, the missing bodies were those of young stalwart men who had died but recently and had met their death through violence or accident rather than wasting illness. Some were criminals who had paid the penalty of their misdeeds; others were men-at-arms or constables, slain in the execution of their duty. Knights who had died in tourney or personal combat were numbered among them; and many were the victims of the robber bands who infested Averoigne at that time. There were monks, merchants, nobles, yeomen, pages, priests; but none, in any case, who had passed the prime of life. The old and infirm, it seemed, were safe from the animating demons.

The situation was looked upon by the more superstitious as a veritable omening of the world's end. Satan was making war with his cohorts and was carrying the bodies of the holy dead into hellish captivity. The consternation increased a hundredfold when it became plain that even the most liberal sprinkling of holy water, the performance of the most awful and cogent exorcisms, failed utterly to give protection against this diabolic ravishment. The Church owned itself powerless to cope with the strange evil; and the forces of secular law could do nothing to arraign or punish the intangible agency.

Because of the universal fear that prevailed, no effort was made to follow the missing cadavers. Ghastly tales, however, were told by late wayfarers who had met certain of these liches, striding alone or in companies along the roads of Averoigne. They gave the appearance of being deaf, dumb, totally insensate, and of hurrying with horrible speed and sureness toward a remote, predestined goal. The general direction of their flight, it seemed, was eastward; but only with the cessation of the exodus, which had numbered several hundred people, did anyone begin to suspect the actual destination of the dead.

This destination, it somehow became rumored, was the ruinous castle of Ylourgne, beyond the werewolf-haunted forest, in the outlying, semimountainous hills of Averoigne.

Ylourgne, a great, craggy pile that had been built by a line of evil and marauding barons now extinct, was a place that even the goatherds preferred to shun. The wrathful specters of its bloody lords were said to move turbulently in its crumbling halls; and its chatelaines were the Undead. No one cared to dwell in the shadow of its cliff-founded walls; and the nearest abode of living men was a small Cistercian monastery, more than a mile away on the opposite slope of the valley.

The monks of this austere brotherhood held little commerce with the world beyond the hills; and few were the visitors who sought admission at their high-perched portals. But, during that dreadful summer, following the disappearances of the dead, a weird and disquieting tale went forth from the monastery throughout Averoigne.

Beginning with late spring, the Cistercian monks were compelled to take cognizance of sundry old phenomena in the old, long-deserted ruins of Ylourgne, which were visible from their windows. They had beheld flaring lights, where lights should not have been: flames of uncanny blue and crimson that shuddered behind the broken, weed-grown embrasures or rose starward above the jagged crenellations. Hideous noises had issued from the ruin by night together with the flames; and the monks had heard a clangor as of hellish anvils and hammers, a ringing of gigantic armor and maces, and had deemed that Ylourgne was become a mustering-ground of devils. Mephitic odors as of brimstone and burning flesh had floated across the valley; and even by day, when the noises were silent and the lights no longer flared, a thin haze of hell-blue vapor hung upon the battlements.

It was plain, the monks thought, that the place had been occupied from beneath by subterrestrial beings; for no one was seen to approach it by way of the bare, open slopes and crags. Observing these signs of the Archfoe's activity in their neighborhood, they crossed themselves with new fervor and frequency, and said their *Paters* and *Aves* more interminably than before. Their toils and austerities, also, they redoubled. Otherwise, since the old castle was a place abandoned by men, they took no heed of the supposed occupation, deeming it well to mind their own affairs unless in case of overt Satanic hostility.

They kept a careful watch; but for several weeks they saw no one who actually entered Ylourgne or emerged therefrom. Except for the nocturnal lights and noises, and the hovering vapor by day, there was no proof of tenantry either human or diabolic.

Then, one morning, in the valley below the terraced gardens of the monastery, two brothers, hoeing weeds in a carrot-patch, beheld the passing of a singular train of people who came from the direction of the great forest of Averoigne and went upward, climbing the steep, chasmy slope toward Ylourgne.

These people, the monks averred, were striding along in great haste, with stiff but flying steps; and all were strangely pale of feature and were habited in the garments of the grave. The shrouds of some were torn and ragged; and all were dusty with travel or grimed with the mold of interment. The people numbered a dozen or more; and after them, at intervals, there came several stragglers, attired like the rest. With marvelous agility and speed, they mounted the hill and disappeared at length amid the lowering walls of Ylourgne.

At this time, no rumor of the ravished graves and biers had reached the Cistercians. The tale was brought to them later, after they beheld, on many successive mornings, the passing of small or great companies of the dead toward the devil-taken castle. Hundreds of these liches, they swore, had filed by beneath the monastery; and doubtless many others had gone past unnoted in the dark. None, however, were seen to come forth from Ylourgne, which had swallowed them up like the undisgorging Pit.

Though direly frightened and sorely scandalized, the brothers still thought it well to refrain from action. Some, the hardiest, irked by all these flagrant signs of evil, had desired to visit the ruins with holy water and lifted crucifixes. But their abbot, in his wisdom, enjoined them to wait. In the meanwhile, the nocturnal flames grew brighter, the noises louder.

Also, in the course of this waiting, while incessant prayers went up from the little monastery, a frightful thing occurred. One of the brothers, a stout fellow named Theophile, in violation of the rigorous discipline, had made overfrequent visits to the wine-casks. No doubt he had tried to drown his pious horror at these untoward happenings. At any rate, after his potations, he had the ill luck to wander out among the precipices and break his neck.

Sorrowing for his death and dereliction, the brothers laid Theophile in the chapel and chanted their masses for his soul. These masses, in the dark hours before morning, were interrupted by the untimely resurrection of the dead monk, who, with his head lolling horribly on his broken neck, rushed as if fiend-ridden from the chapel and ran down the hill toward the demon flames and clamors of Ylourgne.

3

Following the above-related occurrence, two of the brothers who had previously desired to visit the haunted castle again applied to the abbot for this permission, saying that God would surely aid them in avenging the abduction of Theophile's body as well as the taking of many others from consecrated ground. Marveling at the hardihood of these lusty monks, who proposed to beard the Archenemy in his lair, the abbot permitted them to go forth, furnished with aspergilluses and flasks of holy water, and bearing great crosses of hornbeam, such as would have served for maces with which to brain an armored knight.

The monks, whose names were Bernard and Stephane, were boldly up at middle forenoon to assail the evil stronghold. It was an arduous climb, among overhanging boulders and along slippery scarps; but both were stout and agile, and, moreover, well accustomed to such climbing. Since the day was sultry and airless, their white robes were soon stained with sweat; but pausing only for brief prayer, they pressed on; and in good season they neared the castle, upon whose gray, time-eroded ramparts they could still descry no evidence of occupation or activity.

The deep moat that had once surrounded the place was now dry, and had been partly filled by crumbling earth and detritus from the walls. The drawbridge had rotted away; but the blocks of the barbican, collapsing into the moat, had made a sort of rough causey on which it was possible to cross. Not without trepidation, and lifting their crucifixes as warriors lift their weapons in the escalade of an armed fortress, the brothers climbed over the ruin of the barbican into the courtyard.

This too, like the battlements, was seemingly deserted. Overgrown nettles, rank grasses and sapling trees were rooted between its pavingstones. The high, massive donjon, the chapel, and that portion of the castellated structure containing the great hall had preserved their main outlines after centuries of dilapidation. To the left of the broad bailey, a doorway yawned like the mouth of a dark cavern in the cliffy mass of the hall-building; and from this doorway there issued a thin, bluish vapor, writhing in phantom coils toward the unclouded heavens.

Approaching the doorway, the brothers beheld a gleaming of red fires within, like the eyes of dragons blinking through infernal murk. They felt sure that the place was an outpost of Erebus, an antechamber of the Pit; but nevertheless, they entered bravely, chanting loud exorcisms and brandishing their mighty crosses of hornbeam.

Passing through the cavernous doorway, they could see but indistinctly in the gloom, being somewhat blinded by the summer sunlight they had left. Then, with the gradual clearing of their vision, a monstrous scene was limned before them, with ever-growing details of crowding horror and grotesquery. Some of these details were obscure and mysteriously terrifying; others, all too plain, were branded as if with sudden, ineffaceable hell-fire on the minds of the monks.

They stood on the threshold of a colossal chamber, which seemed to have been made by the tearing down of upper floors and inner partitions adjacent to the castle hall, itself a room of huge extent. The chamber seemed to recede through interminable shadow, shafted with sunlight falling through the rents of ruin: sunlight that was powerless to dissipate the infernal gloom and mystery.

The monks averred later that they saw many people moving about the place, together with sundry demons, some of who were shadowy and gigantic, and others barely to be distinguished from the men. These people, as well as their familiars, were occupied with the tending of reverberatory furnaces and immense pear-shaped and gourd-shaped vessels such as were used in alchemy. Some, also, were stooping above great fuming caldrons, like sorcerers busy with the brewing of terrible drugs. Against the opposite wall, there were two enormous vats, built of stone and mortar, whose circular sides rose higher than a man's head, so that Bernard and Stephane were unable to determine their contents. One of the vats gave forth a whitish glimmering; the other, a ruddy luminosity.

Near the vats, and somewhat between them, there stood a sort of low couch or litter, made of luxurious, weirdly figured fabrics such as the Saracens weave. On this the monks discerned a dwarfish being, pale and wizened, with eyes of chill flame that shone like evil beryls through the dusk. The dwarf, who had all the air of a feeble moribund, was supervising the toils of the men and their familiars.

The dazed eyes of the brothers began to comprehend other details. They saw that several corpses, among which they recognized that of Theophile, were lying on the middle floor, together with a heap of human bones that had been wrenched asunder at the joints, and great lumps of flesh piled like the carvings of butchers. One of the men was lifting the bones and dropping them into a caldron beneath which there glowed a ruby-colored fire; and another was flinging the lumps of flesh into a tub filled with some hueless liquid that gave forth an evil hissing as of a thousand serpents.

Others had stripped the graveclothes from one of the cadavers, and were starting to assail it with long knives. Others still were mounting rude flights of stone stairs along the walls of the immense vats, carrying vessels filled with semiliquescent matters which they emptied over the high rims.

Appalled at this vision of human and Satanic turpitude, and feeling a more than righteous indignation, the monks resumed their chanting of sonorous exorcisms and rushed forward. Their entrance, it appeared, was not perceived by the heinously occupied crew of sorcerers and devils.

Bernard and Stephane, filled with an ardor of godly wrath, were about to fling themselves upon the butchers who had started to assail the dead body. This corpse they recognized as being that of a notorious outlaw, named Jacques Le Loupgarou, who had been slain a few days previous in combat with the officers of the state. Le Loupgarou, noted for his brawn, his cunning and his ferocity, had long terrorized the woods and highways of Averoigne. His great body had been half eviscerated by the swords of the constabulary; and his beard was stiff and purple with the dried blood of a ghastly wound that had cloven his face from temple to mouth. He had died unshriven, but nevertheless, the monks were unwilling to see his helpless cadaver put to some unhallowed use beyond the surmise of Christians.

The pale, malignant-looking dwarf had now perceived the brothers. They heard him cry out in a shrill, imperatory tone that rose above the ominous hiss of the caldrons and the hoarse mutter of men and demons.

They knew not his words, which were those of some outlandish tongue and sounded like an incantation. Instantly, as if in response to an order, two of the men turned from their unholy chemistry, and lifting copper basins filled with an unknown, fetid liquor, hurled the contents of these vessels in the faces of Bernard and Stephane.

The brothers were blinded by the stinging fluid, which bit their flesh as with many serpents' teeth; and they were overcome by the noxious fumes, so that their great crosses dropped from their hands and they both fell unconscious on the castle floor.

Recovering anon their sight and their other senses, they found that their hands had been tied with heavy thongs of gut, so that they were now helpless and could no longer wield their crucifixes or the sprinklers of holy water which they carried.

In this ignominious condition, they heard the voice of the evil dwarf, commanding them to arise. They obeyed, though clumsily and with difficulty, being denied the assistance of their hands. Bernard, who was still sick with the poisonous vapor he had inhaled, fell twice before he succeeded in standing erect; and his discomfiture was greeted with a cachination of foul, obscene laughter from the assembled sorcerers.

Now, standing, the monks were taunted by the dwarf, who mocked and reviled them with appalling blasphemies such as could be uttered only by a bondservant of Satan. At last, according to their sworn testimony, he said to them:

"Return to your kennel, ye whelps of Ialdabaoth, and take

with you this message: *They that came here as many shall go forth as one.*"

Then, in obedience to a dreadful formula spoken by the dwarf, two of the familiars, who had the shape of enormous and shadowy beasts, approached the body of Le Loupgarou and that of Brother Theophile. One of the foul demons, like a vapor that sinks into a marsh, entered the bloody nostrils of Le Loupgarou, disappearing inch by inch, till its horned and bestial head was withdrawn from sight. The other, in like manner, went in through the nostrils of Brother Theophile, whose head lay wried athwart his shoulder on the broken neck.

Then, when the demons had completed their possession, the bodies, in a fashion horrible to behold, were raised up from the castle floor, the one with raveled entrails hanging from its wide wounds, the other with a head that drooped forward loosely on its bosom. Then, animated by their devils, the cadavers took up the crosses of hornbeam that had been dropped by Stephane and Bernard; and using the crosses for bludgeons, they drove the monks in ignominious flight from the castle, amid a loud, tempestuous howling of infernal laughter from the dwarf and his necromantic crew. And the nude corpse of Le Loupgarou and the robed cadaver of Theophile followed them far on the chasm-riven slopes below Ylourgne, striking great blows with the crosses, so that the backs of the two Cistercians were become a mass of bloody bruises.

After a defeat so signal and crushing, no more of the monks were emboldened to go up against Ylourgne. The whole monastery, thereafter, devoted itself to triple austerities, to quadrupled prayers; and awaiting the unknown will of God, and the equally obscure machinations of the Devil, maintained a pious faith that was somewhat tempered with trepidation.

In time, through goatherds who visited the monks, the tale of Stephane and Bernard went forth throughout Averoigne, adding to the grievous alarm that had been caused by the wholesale disappearance of the dead. No one knew what was really going on in the haunted castle or what disposition had been made of the hundreds of migratory corpses; for the light thrown on their fate by the monks story, though lurid and frightful, was all too inconclusive; and the message sent by the dwarf was somewhat cabalistic.

Everyone felt, however, that some gigantic menace, some black, infernal enchantment, was being brewed within the ruinous walls. The malign, moribund dwarf was all too readily identified with the missing sorcerer, Nathaire; and his underlings, it was plain, were Nathaire's pupils.

4

Alone in his attic chamber, Gaspard du Nord, student of alchemy and sorcery and quondam pupil of Nathaire, sought repeatedly, but always in vain, to consult the viper-circled mirror. The glass remained obscure and cloudy, as with the risen fumes of Satanical alembics or baleful necromantic braziers. Haggard and weary with long nights of watching, Gaspard knew that Nathaire was even more vigilant than he.

Reading with anxious care the general configuration of the stars, he found the foretokening of a great evil that was to come upon Averoigne. But the nature of the evil was not clearly shown.

In the meanwhile the hideous resurrection and migration of the dead was taking place. All Averoigne shuddered at the manifold enormity. Like the timeless night of a Memphian plague, terror settled everywhere; and people spoke of each new atrocity in bated whispers, without daring to voice the execrable tale aloud. To Gaspard, as to everyone, the whispers came; and likewise, after the horror had apparently ceased in early midsummer, there came the appalling story of the Cistercian monks.

Now, at last, the long-baffled watcher found an inkling of that which he sought. The hiding place of the fugitive necromancer and his apprentices, at least, had been uncovered; and the disappearing dead were clearly traced to their bourn. But still, even for the percipient Gaspard, there remained an undeclared enigma: the hell-dark sorcery that Nathaire was concocting in his remote den. Gaspard felt sure of one thing only: the dying, splenetic dwarf, knowing that his allotted time was short, and hating the people of Averoigne with a bottomless rancor, would prepare an enormous and maleficent magic without parallel.

Even with his knowledge of Nathaire's proclivities, and his awareness of the well-nigh inexhaustible arcanic science, the reserves of pit-deep wizardry possessed by the dwarf, he could form only vague, terrifical conjectures anent the incubated evil. But, as time went on, he felt an ever-deepening oppression, the adumbration of a monstrous menace crawling from the dark rim of the world. He could not shake off his disquietude; and finally he resolved, despite the obvious perils of such an excursion, to pay a secret visit to the neighborhood of Ylourgne.

Gaspard, though he came of a well-to-do family, was at that time in straitened circumstances; for his devotion to a somewhat doubtful science had been disapproved by his father. His sole income was a pittance, purveyed secretly to the youth by his mother and sister. This sufficed for his meager food, the rent of his room, and a few books and instruments and chemicals; but it would not permit the purchase of a horse or even a humble mule for the proposed journey of more than forty miles.

Undaunted, he set forth on foot, carrying only a dagger and a wallet of food. He timed his wanderings so that he would reach Ylourgne at nightfall in the rising of a full moon. Much of his journey lay through the great, lowering forest, which approached the very walls of Vyones on the eastern side and ran in a somber arc through Averoigne to the mouth of the rocky valley below Ylourgne. After a few miles, he emerged from the mighty wood of pines and oaks and larches; and thenceforward, for the first day, followed the river Isoile through an open, well-peopled plain. He spent the warm summer night beneath a beech tree, in the vicinity of a small village, not caring to sleep in the lonely woods where robbers and wolves—and creatures of a more baleful repute— were commonly supposed to dwell.

At evening of the second day, after passing through the

wildest and oldest portion of the immemorial wood, he came to the steep, stony valley that led to his destination. This valley was the fountainhead of the Isoile, which had dwindled to a mere rivulet. In the brown twilight, between sunset and moonrise, he saw the lights of the Cistercian monastery; and opposite, on the piled, forbidding scarps, the grim and rugged mass of the ruinous stronghold of Ylourgne, with wan and wizard fires flickering behind its high embrasures. Apart from these fires, there was no sign of occupation; and he did not hear at any time the dismal noises reported by the monks.

Graspard waited till the round moon, yellow as the eye of some immense nocturnal bird, had begun to peer above the darkling valley. Then, very cautiously, since the neighborhood was strange to him, he started to make his way toward the somber, brooding castle.

Even for one well used to such climbing, the escalade would have offered enough difficulty and danger by moonlight. Several times, finding himself at the bottom of a sheer cliff, he was compelled to retrace his hard-won progress; and often he was saved from falling only by stunted shrubs and briars that had taken root in the niggard soil. Breathless, with torn raiment, and scored and bleeding hands, he gained at length the shoulders of the craggy height, below the walls.

Here he paused to recover breath and recuperate his flagging strength. He could see from his vantage the pale reflection as of hidden flames, that beat upward on the inner wall of the high-built donjon. He heard a low hum of confused noises, whose distance and direction were alike baffling. Sometimes they seemed to float downward from the black battlements, sometimes to issue from subterranean depths far in the hill.

Apart from this remote, ambiguous hum, the night was locked in a mortal stillness. The very winds appeared to shun the vicinity of the dread castle. An unseen, clammy cloud of paralyzing evil hung removeless upon all things; and the pale, swollen moon, the patroness of witches and sorcerers, distilled her green poison above the crumbling towers in a silence older than time.

Gaspard felt the obscenely clinging weight of a more

burdenous thing than his own fatigue when he resumed his progress toward the barbican. Invisible webs of the waiting, ever-gathering evil seemed to impede him. The slow, noisome flapping of intangible wings was heavy in his face. He seemed to breathe a surging wind from unfathomable vaults and caverus of corruption. Inaudible howlings, derisive or minatory, thronged in his ears, and foul hands appeared to thrust him back. But, bowing his head as if against a blowing gale, he went on and climbed the mounded ruin of the barbican, into the weedy courtyard.

The place was deserted, to all seeming; and much of it was still deep in the shadows of the walls and turrets. Nearby, in the black, silver-crenellated pile, Gaspard saw the open, cavernous doorway described by the monks. It was lit from within by a lurid glare, wannish and eerie as marsh-fires. The humming noise, now audible as a muttering of voices, issued from the doorway; and Gaspard thought that he could see dark, sooty figures moving rapidly in the lit interior.

Keeping in the farther shadows, he stole along the courtyard, making a sort of circuit amid the ruins. He did not dare to approach the open entrance for fear of being seen; though, as far as he could tell, the place was unguarded.

He came to the donjon, on whose upper wall the wan light flickered obliquely through a sort of rift in the long building adjacent. This opening was at some distance from the ground; and Gaspard saw that it had been formerly the door to a stone balcony. A flight of broken steps led upward along the wall to the half-crumbled remnant of this balcony; and it occurred to the youth that he might climb the steps and peer unobserved into the interior of Ylourgne.

Some of the stairs were missing; and all were in heavy shadow. Gaspard found his way precariously to the balcony, pausing once in considerable alarm when a fragment of the worn stone, loosened by his footfall, dropped with a loud clattering on the courtyard flags below. Apparently it was unheard by the occupants of the castle; and after a little he resumed his climbing.

Cautiously he neared the large, ragged opening through which the light poured upward. Crouching on a narrow ledge, which was all that remained of the balcony, he peered in on a most astounding and terrific spectacle, whose details were so bewildering that he could barely comprehend their import till after many minutes.

It was plain that the story told by the monks—allowing for their religious bias—had been far from extravagant. Almost the whole interior of the half-ruined pile had been torn down and dismantled to afford room for the activities of Nathaire. The demolition in itself was a superhuman task for whose execution the sorcerer must have employed a legion of familiars as well as his ten pupils.

The vast chamber was fitfully illumed by the glare of athanors and braziers; and, above all, by the weird glimmering from the huge stone vats. Even from his high vantage, the watcher could not see the contents of these vats; but a white luminosity poured upward from the rim of one of them, and a flesh-tinted phosphorescence from the other.

Gaspard had seen certain of the experiments and evocations of Nathaire, and was all too familiar with the appurtenances of the dark arts. Within certain limits, he was not squeamish; nor was it likely that he would have been terrified overmuch by the shadowy, uncouth shapes of demons who toiled in the pit below him side by side with the black-clad pupils of the sorcerer. But a cold horror clutched his heart when he saw the incredible, enormous thing that occupied the central floor: the colossal human skeleton a hundred feet in length stretching for more than the extent of the old castle hall; the skeleton whose bony right foot the group of men and devils, to all appearance, were busily clothing with human flesh!

The prodigious and macabre framework, complete in every part, with ribs like the arches of some Satanic nave, shone as it it were still heated by the fires of an infernal welding. It seemed to shimmer and burn with unnatural life, to quiver with malign disquietude in the flickering glare and gloom. The great fingerbones, curving clawlike on the floor, appeared as if they were about to close upon some helpless prey. The tremendous teeth were set in an everlasting grin of sardonic cruelty and malice. The hollow eyesockets, deep as Tartarean wells, appeared to seethe with myriad, mocking lights, like the eyes of elementals swimming upward in obscene shadow.

Gaspard was stunned by the shocking and stupendous phantasmagoria that yawned before him like a peopled hell. Afterward he was never wholly sure of certain things, and could remember very little of the actual manner in which the work of the men and their assistants was being carried on. Dim, dubious, batlike creatures seemed to be flitting to and fro between one of the stone vats and the group that toiled like sculptors, clothing the bony foot with a reddish plasm which they applied and molded like so much clay. Gaspard thought, but was not certain later, that this plasm, which gleamed as if with mingled blood and fire, was being brought from the rosy-litten vat in vessels borne by the claws of the shadowy flying creatures. None of them, however, approached the other vat, whose wannish light was momently enfeebled, as if it were dying down.

He looked for the minikin figure of Nathaire, whom he could not distinguish in the crowded scene. The sick necromancer—if he had not already succumbed to the little-known disease that had long wasted him like an inward flame—was no doubt hidden from view by the colossal skeleton and was perhaps directing the labors of the men and demons from his couch.

Spellbound on that precarious ledge the watcher failed to hear the furtive, catlike feet that were climbing behind him on the ruinous stairs. Too late, he heard the clink of a loose fragment close upon his heels; and turning in startlement, he toppled into sheer oblivion beneath the impact of a cudgel-like blow, and did not even know that the beginning fall of his body toward the courtyard had been arrested by his assailant's arms.

5

Gaspard, returning from his dark plunge into Lethean emptiness, found himself gazing into the eyes of Nathaire: those eyes of liquid night and ebony, in which swam the chill, malignant fires of stars that had gone down to irremeable perdition. For some time, in the confusion of his senses, he could see nothing but the eyes, which seemed to have drawn him forth like baleful magnets from his swoon. Apparently disembodied, or set in a face too vast for human cognizance, they burned before him in chaotic murk. Then, by degrees, he saw the other features of the sorcerer, and the details of a lurid scene; and became aware of his own situation.

Trying to lift his hands to his aching head, he found that they were bound tightly together at the wrists. He was half lying, half leaning against an object with hard planes and edges that irked his back. This object he discovered to be a sort of alchemic furnace, or athanor, part of a litter of disused apparatus that stood or lay on the castle floor. Cupels, aludels, cucurbits, like enormous gourds and globes, were mingled in strange confusion with piled, iron-clasped books and the sooty cauldrons and braziers of a darker science.

Nathaire, propped among Saracenic cushions with arabesques of sullen gold and fulgurant scarlet, was peering upon him from a kind of improvised couch, made with bales of Orient rugs and arrases, to whose luxury the rude walls of the castle, stained with mold and mottled with dead fungi, offered a grotesque foil. Dim lights and evilly swooping shadows flickered across the scene; and Gaspard could hear a guttural hum of voices behind him. Twisting his head a little he saw one of the stone vats, whose rosy luminosity was blurred and blotted by vampire wings that went to and fro.

"Welcome," said Nathaire, after an interval in which the student began to perceive the fatal progress of illness in the pain-pinched features before him. "So Gaspard du Nord has come to see his former master!" The harsh, imperatory voice, with demoniac volume, issued appallingly from the wizened frame.

"I have come," said Gaspard, in laconic echo. "Tell me, what devil's work is this in which I find you engaged? And what have you done with the dead bodies that were stolen by your accursed familiars?"

The frail, dying body of Nathaire, as if possessed by some sardonic fiend, rocked to and fro on the luxurious couch in a long, violent gust of laughter, without other reply.

"If your looks bear creditable witness," said Gaspard, when the baleful laughter had ceased, "you are mortally ill, and the time is short in which you can hope to atone for your deeds of malefice and make your peace with God—if indeed it still be possible for you to make peace. What foul and monstrous brew are you preparing, to insure the ultimate perdition of your soul?"

The dwarf was again seized by a spasm of diabolic mirth.

"Nay, nay, my good Gaspard," he said finally. "I have made another bond than the one with which puling cowards try to purchase the goodwill and forgiveness of the heavenly Tyrant. Hell may take me in the end, if it will; but Hell has paid, and will still pay, an ample and goodly price. I must die soon, it is true, for my doom is written in the stars: but in death, by the grace of Satan, I shall live again, and shall go forth endowed with the mighty thews of the Anakim, to visit vengeance on the people of Averoigne, who have long hated me for my necromantic wisdom and have held me in derision for my dwarf stature."

"What madness is this whereof you dream?" asked the youth, appalled by the more than human frenzy and malignity that seemed to dilate the shrunken frame of Nathaire and stream in Tartarean luster from his eyes.

"It is no madness, but a veritable thing: a miracle, mayhap, as life itself is a miracle. . . . From the fresh bodies of the dead, which otherwise would have rotted away in charnel foulness, my pupils and familiars are making for me, beneath my instruction, the giant form whose skeleton you have beheld. My soul, at the death of its present body, will pass into this colossal tenement through the working of certain spells of transmigration in which my faithful assistants have also been carefully instructed.

"If you had remained with me, Gaspard, and had not drawn back in your petty, pious squeamishness from the marvels and profundities that I should have unveiled for you, it would now be your privilege to share in the creation of this prodigy. . . . And if you had come to Ylourgne a little sooner in your presumptuous prying, I might have made a certain use of your stout bones and muscles . . . the same use I have made of other young men, who died through accident or violence. But it is too late even for this, since the building of the bones has been completed, and it remains only to invest them with human flesh. My good Gaspard, there is nothing whatever to be done with you—except to put you safely out of the way. Providentially, for this purpose, there is an oubliette beneath the castle: a somewhat dismal lodging place, no doubt, but one that was made strong and deep by the grim lords of Ylourgne.''

Gaspard was unable to frame any reply to this sinister and extraordinary speech. Searching his horror-frozen brain for words, he felt himself seized from behind by the hands of unseen beings who had come, no doubt, in answer to some gesture of Nathaire: a gesture which the captive had not perceived. He was blindfolded with some heavy fabric, moldy and musty as a gravecloth, and was led stumbling through the litter of strange apparatus, and down a winding flight of ruinous, narrow stairs from which the noisome breath of stagnating water, mingled with the oily muskiness of serpents, arose to meet them.

He appeared to descend for a distance that would admit of no return. Slowly the stench grew stronger, more insupportable; the stairs ended; a door clanged sullenly on rusty hinges; and Gaspard was thrust forward on a damp, uneven floor that seemed to have been worn away by myriad feet.

He heard the grating of a ponderous slab of stone. His wrists were untied, the bandage was removed from his eyes, and he saw by the light of flickering torches a round hole that yawned in the oozing floor at his feet. Beside it was the lifted slab that had formed its lid. Before he could turn to see the faces of his captors, to learn if they were men or devils, he was seized rudely and thrust into the gaping hole. He fell through Erebus-like darkness, for what seemed an immense distance, before he struck bottom. Lying half stunned in a shallow, fetid pool, he heard the funereal thud of the heavy slab as it slid back into place far above him.

6

Gaspard was revived, after a while, by the chillness of the water in which he lay. His garments were half soaked; and the slimy, mephitic pool, as he discovered by his first movement, was within an inch of his mouth. He could hear a steady, monotonous dripping, somewhere in the rayless night of his dungeon. He staggered to his feet, finding that his bones were still intact, and began a cautious exploration. Foul drops fell upon his hair and lifted face as he moved; his feet slipped and splashed in the rotten water; there were angry, vehement hissings, and serpentine coils slithered coldly across his ankles.

He soon came to a rough wall of stone, and following the wall with his fingertips, he tried to determine the extent of the oubliette. The place was more or less circular, without corners, and he failed to form any just idea of its circuit. Somewhere in his wanderings, he found a shelving pile of rubble that rose above the water against the wall; and here, for the sake of comparative dryness and comfort, he ensconced himself, after dispossessing a number of outraged reptiles. The creatures, it seemed, were inoffensive, and probably belonged to some species of water snake; but he shivered at the touch of their clammy scales.

Sitting on the rubbleheap, Gaspard reviewed in his mind the various horrors of a situation that was infinitely dismal and desperate. He had learned the incredible, soul-shaking secret of Ylourgne, the unimaginably monstrous and blasphemous project of Nathaire; but now, immured in this noisome hole as in a subterranean tomb, in depths beneath the devil-haunted pile, he could not even warn the world of imminent menace.

The wallet of food, now more than half empty, with which he had started from Vyones was still hanging at his back; and he assured himself by investigation that his captors had not troubled to deprive him of his dagger. Gnawing a crust of stale bread in the darkness, and caressing with his hand the hilt of the precious weapon, he sought for some rift in the all-environing despair.

He had no means of measuring the black hours that went over him with the slowness of a slime-clogged river, crawling in blind silence to a subterrene sea. The ceaseless drip of water, probably from sunken hill-springs that had supplied the castle in former years, alone broke the stillness; but the sound became in time an equivocal monotone that suggested to his half-delirious mind the mirthless and perpetual chuckling of unseen imps. At last, from sheer bodily exhaustion, he fell into troubled, nightmare-ridden slumber.

He could not tell if it were night or noon in the world without when he awakened; for the same stagnant darkness, unrelieved by ray or glimmer, brimmed the oubliette. Shivering, he became aware of a steady draft that blew upon him: a dank, unwholesome air, like the breath of unsunned vaults that had wakened into cryptic life and activity during his sleep. He had not noticed the draft heretofore; and his numb brain was startled into sudden hope by the intimation which it conveyed. Obviously there was some underground rift or channel through which the air entered; and this rift might somehow prove to be a place of egress from the oubliette.

Getting to his feet, he groped uncertainly forward in the direction of the draft. He stumbled over something that crackled and broke beneath his heels, and narrowly checked himself from falling on his face in the slimy, serpent-haunted pool. Before he could investigate the obstruction or resume his blind groping, he heard a harsh, grating noise above, and a wavering shaft of yellow light came down through the oubliette's opened mouth. Dazzled, he looked up, and saw the round hole ten or twelve feet overhead, through which a dark hand had reached down with a flaring torch. A small basket, containing a loaf of coarse bread and a bottle of wine, was being lowered at the end of a cord.

Gaspard took the bread and wine, and the basket was drawn up. Before the withdrawal of the torch and the redepositing of the slab, he contrived to make a hasty survey of his dungeon.

The place was roughly circular, as he had surmised, and was perhaps fifteen feet in diameter. The thing over which he had stumbled was a human skeleton, lying half on the rubbleheap, half in the filthy water. It was brown and rotten with age, and its garments had long melted away in patches of liquid mold.

The walls were guttered and runneled by centuries of ooze, and their very stone, it seemed, was rotting slowly to decay. In the opposite side, at the bottom, he saw the opening he had suspected: a low mouth, not much bigger than a fox's hole, into which the sluggish water flowed. His heart sank at the sight; for, even if the water were deeper than it seemed, the hole was far too strait for the passage of a man's body. In a state of hopelessness that was like a veritable suffocation, he found his way back to the rubble pile when the light had been withdrawn.

The loaf of bread and the bottle of wine were still in his hands. Mechanically, with dull, sodden hunger, he munched and drank. Afterward he felt stronger; and the sour, common wine served to warm him and perhaps helped to inspire him with the idea which he presently conceived.

Finishing the bottle, he found his way across the dungeon to the low, burrowlike hole. The entering air current had strengthened, and this he took for a good omen. Drawing his dagger, he started to pick with the point at the half-rotten, decomposing wall, in an effort to enlarge the opening. He was forced to kneel in noisome silt; and the writhing coils of water snakes, hissing frightfully, crawled across his legs as he worked. Evidently the hole was their means of ingress and egress, to and from the oubliette.

The stone crumbled readily beneath his dagger, and Gaspard forgot the horror and ghastliness of his situation in the hope of escape. He had no means of knowing the thickness of the wall, or the nature and extent of the subterranes that lay beyond; but he felt sure that there was some channel of connection with the outer air.

For hours or days, it seemed, he toiled with his dagger, digging blindly at the soft wall and removing the debris that splashed in the water beside him. After a while, on his belly, he crept into the hole he had enlarged; and burrowing like some laborious mole, he made his way onward inch by inch.

At last, to his prodigious relief, the dagger point went through into empty space. He broke away with his hands the thin shell of obstructing stone that remained; then, crawling on in the darkness, he found that he could stand upright on a sort of shelving floor.

Straightening his cramped limbs, he moved on very cautiously. He was in narrow vault or tunnel, whose sides he could touch simultaneously with his outstretched fingertips. The floor was a downward incline; and the water deepened, rising to his knees and then to his waist. Probably the place had once been used as an underground exit from the castle; and the roof, falling in, had dammed the water.

More than a little dismayed, Gaspard began to wonder if he had exchanged the foul, skeleton-haunted oubliette for something even worse. The night around and before him was still untouched by any ray, and the air current, though strong, was laden with a dankness and moldiness as of interminable vaults.

Touching the tunnel sides at intervals as he plunged hesistantly into the deepening water, he found a sharp angle, giving upon free space at his right. The space proved to be the mouth of an intersecting passage, whose flooded bottom was at least level and went no deeper into the stagnant foulness. Exploring it, he stumbled over the beginning of a flight of upward steps. Mounting these through the shoaling water, he soon found himself on dry stone.

The stairs, narrow, broken, irregular, without landings, appeared to wind in some eternal spiral that was coiled lightlessly about the bowels of Ylourgne. They were close and stifling as a tomb, and plainly they were not the source of the air current which Gaspard had started to follow. Whither they would lead he knew not; nor could he tell if they were the same stairs by which he had been conducted to his dungeon. But he climbed steadily, pausing only at long intervals to regain his breath as best he could in the dead, mephitis-burdened air.

At length, in the solid darkness, far above, he began to hear a mysterious muffled sound: a dull but recurrent crash as of mighty blocks and masses of falling stone. The sound was unspeakably ominous and dismal, and it seemed to shake the unfathomable walls around Gaspard, and to thrill with a sinister vibration in the steps on which he trod.

He climbed now with redoubled caution and alertness, stopping ever and anon to listen. The recurrent crashing noise grew louder, more ominous, as if it were immediately above; and the listener crouched on the dark stairs for a time that might have been many minutes, without daring to go farther. At last, with disconcerting suddenness, the sound came to an end, leaving a strained and fearful stillness.

With many baleful conjectures, not knowing what fresh enormity he should find, Gaspard ventured to resume his climbing. Again, in the blank and solid stillness, he was met by a sound: the dim, reverberant chanting of voices, as in some Satanic mass or liturgy with dirgelike cadences that turned to intolerably soaring paeans of evil triumph. Long before he could recognize the words, he shivered at the strong, malefic throbbing of the measured rhythm, whose fall and rise appeared somehow to correspond to the heartbeats of some colossal demon.

The stairs turned, for the hundredth time in their tortuous spiral; and coming forth from that long midnight, Gaspard blinked in the wan glimmering that streamed toward him from above. The choral voices met him in a more sonorous burst of infernal sound, and he knew the words for those of a rare and potent incantation, used by sorcerers for a supremely foul, supremely maleficent purpose. Affrightedly, as he climbed the last steps, he knew the thing that was taking place amid the ruins of Ylourgne.

Lifting his head warily above the castle floor, he saw that the stairs ended in a far corner of the vast room in which he had beheld Nathaire's unthinkable creation. The whole extent of the internally dismantled building lay before him, filled with a weird glare in which the beams of the slightly gibbous moon were mingled with the ruddy flames of dying athanors and the coiling, multicolored tongues that rose from necromantic braziers.

Gaspard, for an instant, was puzzled by the flood of full moonlight amid the ruins. Then he saw that almost the whole inner wall of the castle, giving on the courtyard, had been removed. It was the tearing down of the prodigious blocks, no doubt through an extrahuman labor levied by sorcery, that he had heard during his ascent from the subterrene vaults. His blood curdled, he felt an actual horripilation, as he realized the purpose for which the wall had been demolished.

It was evident that a whole day and part of another night had gone by since his immurement; for the moon rode high in the pale sapphire welkin. Bathed in its chilly glare, the huge vats no longer emitted their eerie and electric phosphorescence. The couch of Saracen fabrics, on which Gaspard had beheld the dying dwarf, was now half hidden from view by the mounting fumes of braziers and thuribles, amid which the sorcerer's ten pupils, clad in sable and scarlet, were performing their hideous and repugnant rite, with its malefically measured litany.

Fearfully, as one who confronts an apparition reared up from nether hell, Gaspard beheld the colossus that lay inert as if in Cyclopean sleep on the castle flags. The thing was no longer a skeleton: the limbs were rounded into bossed, enormous thews, like the limbs of Biblical giants; the flanks were like an insuperable wall; the deltoids of the mighty chest were broad as platforms; the hands could have crushed the bodies of men like millstones . . . *But the face of the stupendous monster, seen in profile athwart the louring moon, was the face of the Satanic dwarf, Nathaire—remagnified a hundred times, but the same in its implacable madness and malevolence!*

The vast bosom seemed to rise and fall; and during a pause of the necromantic ritual, Gaspard heard the unmistakable sound of mighty respiration. The eye in the profile was closed; but its lid appeared to tremble like a giant curtain, as if the monster were about to wake; and the outflung hand, with fingers pale and bluish as a row of corpses, twitched unquietly on the castle flags.

An insupportable terror seized the watcher; but even this terror could not induce him to return to the noisome vaults he had left. With infinite hesitation and trepidation, he stole forth from the corner, keeping in a zone of ebon shadow that flanked the castle wall.

As he went, he saw for moment, through bellying folds of

vapor, the couch on which the shrunken form of Nathaire was lying pallid and motionless. It seemed that the dwarf was dead, or had fallen into a stupor preceding death. Then the choral voices, crying their dreadful incantation, rose higher in Satanic triumph; the vapors eddied like a hell-born cloud, coiling about the sorcerers in python-shaped volumes, and hiding again the Orient couch and its corpselike occupant.

A thralldom of measureless evil oppressed the air. Gaspard felt that the awful transmigration, evoked and implored with ever-swelling, liturgic blasphemies, was about to take place— had perhaps already occurred. He thought that the breathing giant stirred, like one who tosses in light slumber.

Soon the towering, massively recumbent bulk was interposed between Gaspard and the chanting necromancers. They had not seen him; and he now dared to run swiftly, and gained the courtyard unpursued and unchallenged. Thence, without looking back, he fled like a devil-hunted thing upon the steep and chasm-riven slopes below Ylourgne.

7

After the cessation of the exodus of liches, a universal terror still prevailed; a wide-flung shadow of apprehension, infernal and funereal, lay stagnantly on Averoigne. There were strange and disastrous portents in the aspect of the skies: flame-bearded meteors had been seen to fall beyond the eastern hills; a comet, far in the south, had swept the stars with its luminous bosom for a few nights, and had then faded, leaving among men the prophecy of bale and pestilence to come. By day the air was oppressed and sultry, and the blue heavens were heated as if by whitish fires. Clouds of thunder, darkling and withdrawn, shook their fulgurant lances on the far horizons, like some beleaguering Titan army. A murrain, such as would come from the working of wizard spells, was abroad among the cattle. All these signs and prodigies were an added heaviness on the burdened spirits of men, who went to and fro in daily fear of the hidden preparations and machinations of hell.

But, until the actual breaking-forth of the incubated menace, here was no one, save Gaspard du Nord, who had knowledge of its veritable form. And Gaspard, fleeing headlong beneath the gibbous moon toward Vyones, and fearing to hear the tread of a colossal pursuer at any moment, had thought it more than useless to give warning in such towns and villages as lay upon his line of flight. Where, indeed—even if warned—could men hope to hide themselves from the awful thing, begotten by Hell on the ravished charnel, that would walk forth like the Anakim to visit its roaring wrath on a trampled world?

So, all that night, and throughout the day that followed, Gaspard du Nord, with the dried slime of the oubliette on his briar-shredded raiment, plunged like a madman through the towering woods that were haunted by robbers and were-wolves. The westward-falling moon flickered in his eyes betwixt the gnarled, somber boles as he ran; and the dawn overtook him with the pale shafts of its searching arrows. The noon poured over him its white sultriness, like furnace-heated metal sublimed into light; and the clotted filth that clung to his tatters was again turned into slime by his own sweat. But still he pursued his nightmare-harried way, while a vague, seemingly hopeless plan took form in his mind.

In the interim, several monks of the Cistercian brotherhood, watching the gray walls of Ylourgne at early dawn with their habitual vigilance, were the first after Gaspard to behold the monstrous horror created by the necromancers. Their account may have been somewhat tinged by a pious exaggeration; but they swore that the giant rose abruptly, standing more than waist-high above the ruins of the barbican, amid a sudden leaping of long-tongued fires and a swirling of pitchy fumes erupted from Malebolge. The giant's head was level with the high top of the donjon, and his right arm, outthrust, lay like a bar of stormy cloud athwart the new-risen sun.

The monks fell groveling to their knees, thinking that the Archfoe himself had come forth, using Ylourgne for his gateway from the Pit. Then, across the mile-wide valley, they heard a thunderous peal of demoniac laughter; and the giant, climbing over the mounded barbican at a single step, began to descend the scarped and craggy hill.

When he drew nearer, bounding from slope to slope, his features were manifestly those of some great devil animated with ire and malice toward the sons of Adam. His hair, in matted locks, streamed behind him like a mass of black pythons; his naked skin was livid and pale and cadaverous, like the skin of the dead; but beneath it, the stupendous thews of a Titan swelled and rippled. The eyes, wide and glaring, flamed like lidless caldrons heated by the fires of the un-plumbed Pit.

The rumor of his coming passed like a gale of terror through the monastery. Many of the brothers, deeming dis-cretion the better part of religious fervor, hid themselves in the stone-hewn cellars and vaults. Others crouched in their cells, mumbling and shrieking incoherent pleas to all the saints. Still others, the most courageous, repaired in a body to the chapel and knelt in solemn prayer before the wooden Christ on the great crucifix.

Bernard and Stephane, now somewhat recovered from their grievous beating, alone dared to watch the advance of the giant. Their horror was inexpressibly increased when they began to recognize in the colossal features a magnified like-ness to the lineaments of the evil dwarf who had presided over the dark unhallowed activities of Ylourgne; and the laughter of the colossus, as he came down the valley, was like a tempest-borne echo of the damnable cachinnation that had followed their ignominious flight from the haunted strong-hold. To Bernard and Stephane, however, it seemed merely that the dwarf, who was no doubt an actual demon, had chosen to appear in his natural form.

Pausing in the valley bottom, the giant stood opposite the monastery with his flame-filled eyes on a level with the window from which Bernard and Stephane were peering. He laughed again—an awful laugh, like a subterranean rumbling—and then, stooping, he picked up a handful of boulders as if they had been pebbles, and proceeded to pelt the monastery. The boulders crashed against the walls, as if hurled from great catapults or mangonels of war; but the stout building held, though shaken grievously.

Then, with both hands, the colossus tore loose an immense rock that was deeply embedded in the hillside; and lifting this rock, he flung it at the stubborn walls. The tremendous mass broke in an entire side of the chapel; and those who had gathered therein were found later, crushed into bloody pulp amid the splinters of their carven Christ.

After that, as if disdaining to palter any further with a prey so insignificant, the colossus turned his back on the little monastery, and like some fiend-born Goliath, went roaring down the valley into Averoigne.

As he departed, Bernard and Stephane, still watching from their window, saw a thing they had not perceived heretofore: a huge basket made of planking, that hung suspended by ropes between the giant's shoulders. In the basket, ten men— the pupils and assistants of Nathaire—were being carried like so many dolls or puppets in a peddler's pack.

Of the subsequent wanderings and depradations of the colossus, a hundred legends were long current throughout Averoigne: tales of an unexampled ghastliness, a wanton diabolism without parallel in all the histories of that demon-pestered land.

The goatherds of the hills below Ylourgne saw him coming, and fled with their nimble-footed flocks to the highest ridges. To these he paid little heed, merely trampling them down like beetles when they could not escape from his path. Following the hill-stream that was the source of the river Isoile, he came to the verge of the great forest; and here, it is related, he tore up a towering ancient pine by the roots, and snapping off the mighty boughs with his hands, shaped it into a cudgel which he carried henceforward.

With this cudgel, heavier than a battering ram, he pounded into shapeless ruin a wayside shrine in the outer woods. A hamlet fell in his way, and he strode through it, beating in the roofs, toppling the walls, and crushing the inhabitants beneath his feet.

To and fro in a mad frenzy of destruction, like a death-drunken Cyclops, he wandered all that day. Even the fierce beasts of the woodland ran from him in fear. The wolves, in mid-hunt, abandoned their quarry and retired, howling dismally with terror, to their rocky dens. The black, savage hunting dogs of the forest barons would not face him, and hid whimpering in their kennels.

Men heard his mighty laughter, his stormy bellowing; they saw his approach from a distance of many leagues, and fled or concealed themselves as best they could. The lords of moated castles called in their men-at-arms, drew up their drawbridges and prepared as if for the siege of an army. The peasants hid themselves in caverns, in cellars, in old wells, and even beneath hay mounds, hoping that he would pass them by unnoticed. The churches were crammed with refugees who sought the protection of the cross, deeming that Satan himself, or one of his chief lieutenants, had risen to harry and lay waste the land.

In a voice like summer thunder, mad maledictions, unthinkable obscenities and blasphemies were uttered ceaselessly by the giant as he went to and fro. Men heard him address the litter of black-clad figures that he carried on his back, in tones of admonishment or demonstration such as a master would use to his pupils. People who had known Nathaire recognized the incredible likeness of the huge features, the similarity of the swollen voice, to his. A rumor went abroad that the dwarf sorcerer, through his loathly bond with the Adversary, had been permitted to transfer his hateful soul into this Titanic form; and, bearing his pupils with him, had returned to vent an insatiable ire, a bottomless rancor, on the world that had mocked him for his puny physique and reviled him for his sorcery. The charnel genesis of the monstrous avatar was also rumored; and, indeed, it was said that the colossus had openly proclaimed his identity.

It would be tedious to make explicit mention of all the enormities of the marauding giant. . . . There were people—mostly priests and women, it is told—whom he picked up as they fled, and pulled limb from limb as a child might quarter an insect . . . and there were worse things, not to be named in this record. . . .

Many eyewitnesses told how he hunted Pierre, the Lord of La Frenaie, who had gone forth with his dogs and men to chase a noble stag in the nearby forest. Overtaking horse and rider, he caught them with one hand, and bearing them aloft as he strode over the tree-tops, he hurled them later against the granite walls of the Chateau of La Frenaie in passing. Then, catching the red stag that Pierre had hunted, he flung it after them; and the huge bloody blotches made by the impact of the pashed bodies remained long on the castle stone, and were never wholly washed away by the autumn rains and the winter snows.

Countless tales were told, also, of the deeds of obscene sacrilege and profanation committed by the colossus: of the wooden Virgin that he flung into the Isoile above Ximes, lashed with human gut to the rotting, mail-clad body of an infamous outlaw; of the wormy corpses that he dug with his hands from unconsecrated graves and hurled into the courtyard of the Benedictine abbey of Perigon; of the Church of Ste. Zenobie, which he buried with its priests and congregation beneath a mountain of ordure made by the gathering of all the dungheaps from neighboring farms.

8

Back and forth, in an irregular, drunken, zigzag course, from end to end and side to side of the harried realm, the giant strode without pause, like an energumen possessed by some implacable fiend of mischief and murder, leaving behind him, as a reaper leaves his swath, an ever-lengthening zone of havoc, of rapine and carnage. And when the sun, blackened by the smoke of burning villages, had set luridly beyond the forest, men still saw him moving in the dusk, and heard still the portentous rumbling of his mad, stormy cachinnation.

Nearing the gates of Vyones at sunset, Gaspard du Nord saw behind him, through gaps in the ancient wood, the far-off head and shoulders of the terrible colossus, who moved along the Isoile, stooping from sight at intervals in some horrid deed.

Though numb with weariness and exhaustion, Gaspard quickened his flight. He did not believe, however, that the monster would try to invade Vyones, the especial object of Nathaire's hatred and malice, before the following day. The evil soul of the sorcerous dwarf, exulting in its almost infinite capacity for harm and destruction, would defer the crowning act of vengeance, and would continue to terrorize, during the night, the outlying villages and rural districts.

In spite of his rags and filth, which rendered him practically unrecognizable and gave him a most idsreputable air, Gaspard was admitted without question by the guards at the city gate. Vyones was already thronged with people who had fled to the sanctuary of its stout walls from the adjacent countryside; and no one, not even of the most dubious character, was denied admittance. The walls were lined with archers and pike bearers, gathered in readiness to dispute the entrance of the giant. Crossbowmen were stationed above the gates, and mangonels were mounted at short intervals along the entire circuit of the ramparts. The city seethed and hummed like an agitated hive.

Hysteria and pandemonium prevailed in the streets. Pale, panic-stricken faces milled everywhere in an aimless stream. Hurrying torches flared dolorously in the twilight that deepened as if with the shadow of impending wings arisen from Erebus. The gloom was clogged with intangible fear, with webs of stifling oppression. Through all this rout of wild disorder and frenzy, Gaspard, like a spent but indomitable swimmer breasting some tide of eternal, viscid nightmare, made his way slowly to his attic lodgings.

Afterward, he could scarcely remember eating and drinking. Overworn beyond the limit of bodily and spiritual endurance, he threw himself down on his pallet without removing his ooze-stiffened tatters, and slept soddenly till an hour halfway between midnight and dawn.

He awoke with the death-pale beams of the gibbous moon shining upon him through his window; and rising, spent the balance of the night in making certain occult preparations which, he felt, offered the only possibility of coping with the fiendish monster that had been created and animated by Nathaire.

Working feverishly by the light of the westering moon and a single taper, Gaspard assembled various ingredients of familiar alchemic use which he possessed, and compounded from these, through a long and somewhat cabalistic process, a dark-gray powder which he had seen employed by Nathaire on numerous occasions. He had reasoned that the colossus, being formed from the bones and flesh of dead men unlawfully raised up, and energized only by the soul of a dead sorcerer, would be subject to the influence of this powder, which Nathaire had used for the laying of resurrected liches. The powder, if cast in the nostrils of such cadavers, would cause them to return peacefully to their tombs, and lie down in a renewed slumber of death.

Gaspard made a considerable quantity of the mixture, arguing that no mere finger-pinch would suffice for the lulling of the gigantic charnel monstrosity. His guttering yellow candle was dimmed by the white dawn as he ended the Latin formula of fearsome verbal invocation from which the compound would derive much of its efficacy. The formula, which called for the cooperation of Alastor and other evil spirits, he used with unwillingness. But he knew that there was no alternative: sorcery could be fought only with sorcery.

Morning came with new terrors to Vyones. Gaspard had felt, through a sort of intuition, that the vengeful colossus, who was said to have wandered with unhuman tirelessness and diabolic energy all night through Averoigne, would approach the hated city early in the day. His intuition was confirmed; for scarcely had he finished his occult labors when he heard a mounting hubbub in the streets, and above the shrills, dismal clamor of frightened voices, the far-off roaring of the giant.

Gaspard knew that he must lose no time, if he were to post himself in a place of vantage from which he could throw his powder into the nostrils of the hundred-foot colossus. The city walls, and even most of the church spires, were not lofty enough for this purpose; and a brief reflection told him that the great cathedral, standing at the core of Vyones, was the one place from whose roof he could front the invader with success. He felt sure that the men-at-arms on the walls could do little to prevent the monster from entering and wreaking his malevolent will. No earthly weapon could injure a being of such bulk and nature; for even a cadaver of normal size, reared up in this fashion, could be shot full of arrows or transfixed by a dozen pikes without retarding its progress.

Hastily he filled a huge leathern pouch with the powder; and carrying the pouch at his belt, he joined the agitated press of people in the street. Many were fleeing toward the cathedral, to seek the shelter of its august sanctity; and he had only to let himself be borne along by the frenzy-driven stream.

The cathedral nave was packed with worshipers, and solemn masses were being said by priests whose voices faltered at times with inward panic. Unheeded by the wan, dispairing throng, Gaspard found a flight of coiling stairs that led tortuously to the gargoyle-warded roof of the high tower.

Here he posted himself, crouching behind the stone figure of a cat-headed griffin. From his vantage he could see, beyond the crowded spires and gables, the approaching giant, whose head and torso loomed above the city walls. A cloud of arrows, visible even at the distance, rose to meet the monster, who apparently did not even pause to pluck them from his hide. Great boulders hurled from mangonels were no more to him than a pelting of gravel; the heavy bolts of arbalests, embedded in his flesh, were mere slivers.

Nothing could stay his advance. The tiny figures of a company of pikesmen, who opposed him with outthrust weapons, were swept from the wall above the eastern gate by a single sidelong blow of the seventy-foot pine that he bore for a cudgel. Then, having cleared the wall, the colossus climbed over it into Vyones.

Roaring, chuckling, laughing like a maniacal Cyclops, he strode along the narrow streets between houses that rose only to his waist, trampling without mercy everyone who could not escape in time, and smashing in the roofs with stupendous blows of his bludgeon. With a push of his left hand he broke off the protruding gables, and overturned the church steeples with their bells clanging in dolorous alarm as they went down. A woeful shrieking and wailing of hysteria-laden voices accompanied his passing.

Straight toward the cathedral he came, as Gaspard had calculated, feeling that the high edifice would be made the special butt of his malevolence.

The streets were now emptied of people; but, as if to hunt them out and crush them in their hiding places, the giant thrust his cudgel like a battering ram through walls and windows and roofs as he went by. The ruin and havoc that he left was undescribable.

Soon he loomed opposite the cathedral tower on which Gaspard waited behind the gargoyle. His head was level with the tower, and his eyes flamed like wells of burning brimstone as he drew near. His lips were parted over stalactitic fangs in a hateful snarl; and he cried out in a voice like the rumbling of articulate thunder: "Ho! ye puling priests and devotees of a powerless God! Come forth and bow to Nathaire the master, before he sweeps you into limbo!"

It was then that Gaspard, with a hardihood beyond comparison, rose from his hiding place and stood in full view of the raging colossus. "Draw nearer, Nathaire, if indeed it be you, foul robber of tombs and charnels," he taunted. "Come close, for I would hold speech with you."

A monstrous look of astonishment dimmed the diabolic rage on the colossal features. Peering at Gaspard as if in doubt or incredulity, the giant lowered his lifted cudgel and stepped close to the tower, till his face was only a few feet from the intrepid student. Then, when he apparently convinced himself of Gaspard's identity, the look of maniacal wrath returned, flooding his eyes with Tartarean fire and twisting his lineaments into a mask of Apollyon-like malignity. His left arm came up in a prodigious arc, with twitching fingers that poised horribly above the head of the youth, casting upon him a vulture-black shadow in full-risen sun. Gaspard saw the white, startled faces of the necromancer's pupils, peering over his shoulder from their plank-built basket.

"Is it you, Gaspard, my recreant pupil?" the colossus roared stormily. "I thought you were rotting in the oubliette beneath Ylourgne—and now I find you perched atop of this accursed cathedral which I am about to demolish! . . . You had been far wiser to remain where I left you, my good Gaspard.''

His breath, as he spoke, blew like a channel-polluted gale on the student. His vast fingers, with blackened nails like shovel-blades, hovered in ogreish menace. Gaspard had furtively loosened his leathern pouch that hung at his belt, and had untied its mouth. Now, as the twitching fingers descended toward him, he emptied the contents of the pouch in the giant's face, and fine powder, mounting in a dark-gray cloud, obscured the snarling lips and palpitating nostrils from his view.

Anxiously he watched the effect, fearing that the powder might be useless after all, against the superior arts and Satanical resources of Nathaire. But miraculously, as it seemed, the evil lambence died in the pit-deep eyes, as the monster inhaled the flying cloud. His lifted hand, narrowly missing the crouching youth in its sweep, fell lifelessly at his side. The anger erased from the mighty, contorted mask, as if from the face of a dead man; the great cudgel fell with a crash to the empty street; and then, with drowsy, lurching steps and listless, hanging arms, the giant turned his back to the cathedral and retraced his way through the devastated city.

He muttered dreamily to himself as he went; and people who heard him swore that the voice was no longer the awful, thunder-swollen voice of Nathaire, but the tones and accents of a multitude of men, amid which the voices of certain of the ravished dead were recognizable. And the voice of Nathaire himself, no louder now than in life, was heard at intervals through the manifold mutterings, as if protesting angrily.

Climbing the eastern wall as it had come, the colossus went to and fro for many hours, no longer wreaking hellish wrath and rancor, but searching, as people thought, for various tombs and graves from which the hundreds of bodies that composed it had been so foully reft. From charnel to charnel, from cemetery to cemetery it went, through all the land; but there was no grave anywhere in which the dead colossus could lie down.

Then, toward evening men saw it from afar on the red rim of the sky, digging with its hands in the soft, loamy plain beside the river Isoile. There, in a monstrous and self-made grave, the colossus laid itself down, and did not rise again. The ten pupils of Nathaire, it was believed, unable to descend from their baskets, were crushed beneath the mighty body; for none of them was ever seen thereafter.

For many days no one dared to approach the place where the corpse lay uncovered in its dug grave. And so the thing rotted prodigiously beneath the summer sun, breeding a mighty stench that wrought pestilence in that portion of Averoigne. And they who ventured to go near in the following autumn, when the stench had lessened greatly, swore that the voice of Nathaire, still protesting angrily, was heard by them to issue from the enormous, rook-haunted bulk.

Of Gaspard du Nord, who had been the savior of the province, it is related that he lived in much honor to a ripe age, being the one sorcerer of that region who at no time incurred the disapprobation of the Church.

About the Editors

ISAAC ASIMOV has been called "one of America's treasures." Born in the Soviet Union, he was brought to the United States at the age of three (along with his family) by agents of the American government in a successful attempt to prevent him from working for the wrong side. He quickly established himself as one of this country's foremost science fiction writers and writes about everything, and although now approaching middle age, he is going stronger than ever. He long ago passed his age and weight in books, and with some 330 to his credit, threatens to close in on his I.Q. His novel *The Robots of Dawn* was one of the best-selling books of 1983 and 1984.

MARTIN H. GREENBERG has been called (in *The Science Fiction and Fantasy Book Review*) "the King of the Anthologists"; to which he replied, "It's good to be the King!" He has produced more than one hundred of them, usually in collaboration with a multitude of co-conspirators, most frequently the two who have given you *Giants*. A professor of regional analysis and political science at the University of Wisconsin—Green Bay, he is still trying to publish his weight.

CHARLES G. WAUGH is a professor of psychology and communications at the University of Maine at Augusta who is still trying to figure out how he got himself into all this. He has also worked with many collaborators, since he is basically a very friendly fellow. He has done some sixty-five anthologies and single-author collections, and especially enjoys locating unjustly ignored stories. He also claims that he met his wife via computer dating—her choice was an entire fraternity or him, and she has only minor regrets.